Praise for

DISCARD

Chaos Burning

"Dane has an extraordinary gift . . . While it's easy to fall in love with the hero, it's also easy to like the heroine."
—*RT Book Reviews*

"A super thriller . . . The lead couple is a solid paring of two alpha warriors while the evil enemy has been around seemingly forever." —*Genre Go Round Reviews*

"Compulsively readable . . . Interesting world-building, page-turning action and a truly satisfying romance."
—*Dear Author*

"[I] can't wait to see what Ms. Dane has in store for us next."
—*Under the Covers*

"Slow-building romance set in a well-developed world with characters you just can't help but love."
—*Dark Faerie Tales*

Heart of Darkness

"Fresh, fun, fast-paced paranormal romance. Spellbinding magic, a wry-humored, gutsy heroine and a sexy-as-sin hero put the charm on this witchy new series from multitalented, always fabulous Lauren Dane!"
—Lara Adrian, *New York Times* bestselling author

"Dane always delivers a steamy, exciting ride . . . She leaves me wanting more!"
—Larissa Ione, *New York Times* bestselling author

ed . . .

"Unputdownable . . . Great characters, wonderful world-building and, as always, a delicious romance. If you pick this book up, make sure you've cleared the afternoon."
—Ann Aguirre, national bestselling author

"The world Lauren Dane has created here is big and bold. "
—*Reading the Paranormal*

"I was riveted . . . Passion, magick and suspense . . . An instant favorite."
—*Joyfully Reviewed*

"The characters are compelling, the love scenes steamy hot and the world she has built sparks interest in the reader for more."
—*Fresh Fiction*

Further praise for Lauren Dane and her novels

"Pulse pounding . . . Dane delivers!"
—Jaci Burton, *New York Times* bestselling author

"Scintillating! . . .A roller coaster of emotion, intrigue and sensual delights . . . I was hooked."
—Vivi Anna, author of *The League of Illusion: Prophecy*

"Erotic . . . Sure to keep you reading late into the night."
—Anya Bast, *New York Times* bestselling author

"In a word . . . amazing."
—*RT Book Reviews*

continued

Wild Darkness

LAUREN DANE

B

BERKLEY SENSATION, NEW YORK

THE BERKLEY PUBLISHING GROUP
Published by the Penguin Group
Penguin Group (USA) LLC
375 Hudson Street, New York, New York 10014

USA • Canada • UK • Ireland • Australia • New Zealand • India • South Africa • China

penguin.com

A Penguin Random House Company

WILD DARKNESS

A Berkley Sensation Book / published by arrangement with the author

Berkley Sensation Books are published by The Berkley Publishing Group.
BERKLEY SENSATION ® is a registered trademark of Penguin Group (USA) LLC.
The "B" design is a trademark of Penguin Group (USA) LLC.

For information, address: The Berkley Publishing Group,
a division of Penguin Group (USA) LLC,
375 Hudson Street, New York, New York 10014.

ISBN: 978-0-425-26218-4

PUBLISHING HISTORY
Berkley Sensation mass-market edition / November 2013

PRINTED IN THE UNITED STATES OF AMERICA

10 9 8 7 6 5 4 3 2 1

Cover photo by Claudio Marinesco.
Cover design by Rita Frangie.
Interior text design by Laura K. Corless.

Chapter 1

HE tasted magick. Magick and blood rushed over his skin and through his system. His beast surged forward as he caught a human male by the back of the neck and threw him up against a nearby fence.

His beast raged within, aching to be let free. Ached to rip those who dared harm his protected to small pieces.

These humans had thrown firebombs into a community center that had been full of Others at the time. The parking lot had been full. Children had been playing on the field out back.

If it hadn't been for Clan Gennessee—who'd posted guards who'd noted the behavior of those humans who'd attacked them—they'd have been worse off. Fortunately, they'd acted immediately and evacuated.

His fist made contact with a man's face, satisfaction roaring through Faine as the human crumpled to the ground.

The air was filled with the stench of the fuel used in the firebombs. With sweat and fear. His beast loved the latter.

Most of the humans were down, but what caught his attention was *her*.

She strode through the melee like a Valkyrie. Her magick

sang with each step she took. Men fell all around her as she
managed to use her fists and her power to push them back.
Her face was a mask of fury and vengeance.

He blew out a breath as he took her in from head to toe.
Helena Jaansen was magnificent.

She was totally focused as they fought the humans for a
few minutes more before the threat they posed had been thoroughly dealt with. The police had not shown up yet, though
some ambulances had arrived and those who'd escaped the
building when it had been firebombed were being treated out
of the fray.

He watched her hungrily as things wound down, and when
it was over she put her fingers to her lips and whistled loudly.
Her men and women froze, turning their attention to her.

"I want a team working immediately to gather evidence.
Get the kits from the van. John and Evan, I want everything
on video. The police will arrive shortly. Do not impede them,
but do not cede ground either."

There was absolutely no doubt who was in charge and her
people responded quickly and efficiently.

"I'll keep an eye on these humans."

Helena looked to Faine. "Thank you. Feel free to break
something if they try to escape." She turned away, issuing
orders as she went.

The police rolled up seconds later, exiting their cars with
their weapons drawn.

Helena approached them, her hands up. "Nice timing. The
people responsible for trying to kill a community center full
of people are all there." She indicated where they'd taken
prisoners. "Subdued and bound until you arrived."

"On the ground!" one of the officers screamed.

Helena looked at them and then at the people they'd appre-
hended lined up at her feet. "My hands are up and my identification is in my back pocket. I am *not* going to get on the ground."

"We will shoot you if you don't comply."

One of her brows rose slowly. "You can try. Or you can do
your job and deal with this situation you avoided until you
figured it was over." *Like cowards* hung in the air, unspoken,

but not unheard. Magick crackled from her body as she spooled energy from the earth beneath her, from the air all around her.

She kept her hands up, but also her feet. "There's video of the attack. We've got a backup, just in case it gets *lost*. You're free to look at it. My people are guarding the room where the monitors are. It's in a relatively unscathed part of the building. Back door, up the stairs to your left. They know you're on the way, but they *will* continue to monitor as you watch. We'll wait right here with our hands up while you do."

"You don't give the orders here." The cop who stepped forward sneered. She was unmoved.

"Officer—" She leaned forward slightly, reading his name tag. "Officer Franklin. I'm Helena Jaansen, and as you're too late on the scene of an assault called in twenty minutes ago, let me catch you up to speed. I'm not giving orders. I'm letting you know how it is. You can either protect us all, as is your job, or you can refuse. In either case, *I* will protect my people. And you won't stop me from protecting children from these thugs. I have no desire to make this into an issue. But should you . . ." She shrugged. "I'm not a defenseless four-year-old just trying to jump rope. I can fight back."

The tension built up in the air all around her. And all around the witches who stood near her. They'd taken enough abuse and would endure no more. If the cop didn't figure that out, if he decided to ignore it and push his luck, Faine knew what would happen. And who'd still be walking when it was all over.

Another law enforcement guy came up through the crowd. "Stand down, officers," he called out.

Franklin looked back, clearly intending to countermand, but when he saw the blue windbreaker and the big, yellow FBI letters, he stopped. "This is out of your jurisdiction."

"You can put your hands down," the FBI guy told Helena. She did, but she kept her body at attention. "Firebombs are actually firmly in our jurisdiction. Especially when it's connected to a nationwide crime syndicate aimed at a certain group of citizens. That's right smack dab in our wheelhouse." He held out his identification to underline that.

One of Helena's brows rose again and Faine wanted to put his lips on it. So often she kept her features impassive, but she had a rogue eyebrow that said what she so rarely did out loud.

FBI guy looked back to Helena. "You were saying there was video of the event?"

"Marian?" One of Helena's people approached slowly, keeping her hands in plain sight. "Can you show Agent . . ."

"I'm Gil Anderson. Head of the new Cross Species Task Force."

"The what?" Officer Franklin and Helena said this in unison.

"We set up this week."

"Okay then. Marian, please show the agent up to the room with the monitors." Helena turned back to Anderson. "We have backups of the video, by the way. I was just telling Officer Franklin this."

"You don't trust us to be fair?" Anderson asked this after one of his agents went with Marian.

"Experience has taught us to be cautious about human motivations. I don't know you one way or the other. But I do know such evidence has been *lost* more than once since this mess started. And that makes me careful. Careful keeps people alive."

Anderson nodded. "Fair enough. Officer Franklin, please take the humans on the ground into custody. My people will conduct interviews at the station."

Thwarted, Officer Franklin put his hands on his hips. "You can't just jump in the middle of this!"

"I can. And I am. So, please get these men and women cuffed. Read them their rights and throw them in cells. Separately, please." Anderson turned back to Helena. "I'd like to interview you and your people as well."

"Fine."

Faine took up a spot next to her. She didn't seem to mind, but Anderson did. He looked Faine up and down, a frown on his face. Too bad.

Helena watched them begin to process the humans and

turned back to Anderson. "If any of these assholes gets *lost* on the way to the station, I'm going to be vexed, Agent."

"That would make two of us. Look, I'd prefer if we could start off on the right foot. I *am* here to help."

"You'll have to excuse my pessimism, Agent Anderson. Months of constant harassment, attacks, death and threats have left me less than trusting, even when someone claims they want to help."

Agent Anderson blew out a breath. "I understand that. I truly do. But this task force is in place to try and stop all that."

She nodded. "I'm Helena Jaansen. I work for Clan Gennessee."

Anderson looked up into Faine's face. "Faine Leviathan. I work for her."

Faine caught the ghost of a smile flitting over her lips. Just a brief flash before it was gone.

"You're a Were of some sort?"

"Of some sort." They'd all decided not to reveal the existence of anything beyond the Veil. For the time being, no humans needed to know a damned thing about Lycia or the packs of Lycians, part man, part giant wolf, who dominated it.

Helena decided to forge ahead. The FBI guy appeared to want to ask more about Faine and she didn't want that.

"At four p.m.—prime after-school time, by the way—the guards noticed a group of humans who seemed to be casing the building."

"How did they know to identify that behavior as casing?"

Helena just shot him a look. "Really, Agent Anderson?" There was no need to let on just how well trained and militarized Clan Gennessee was, or the level of training of those Others who made up their new unified defense force. Or hell, even the existence of such a defense force. However, they did need to understand the Others were not going to allow themselves to be victimized any more.

He sighed. "Fine. Go on. But don't think I'm not going to want to know just how well your people are trained."

He could want it until the sun burned out. She'd tell him what *she* wanted him to know and nothing more.

"They watched, notifying me and my people. One of the guards came out to get a closer look." Her mouth flattened briefly as he cast a look toward the body, covered by a sheet, that they'd moved out of the way of traffic. "He was attacked by two humans, shot in the head before he'd had a chance to react. The guards inside then began an evacuation of the Others inside the community center out the back as those humans threw what we later ascertained to be firebombs through the front windows of the community center.

"By this point, we'd arrived, having only been in La Habra. They have automatic weapons, but we also have our own mode of protection. One of the men you took away is Gentry Fenton, one of the lieutenants for PURITY."

"How many of them were there?"

"Fourteen at the first." Faine broke in with his rumbly voice. Despite the stress and grief of the situation, it still made all her parts tingly. "Then a van approached with six more."

Anderson interviewed her people, spoke to his own after they'd viewed the video and left two hours later.

PURITY had thrown twenty people with guns and bombs at a building full of kids and elderly people. It had been bad enough that some humans had gravitated toward the bigoted message of groups like PURITY and Humans First. But this sort of violence was on a whole different level.

And becoming rapidly more common. Her sister, along with one of the witches from Owen, Molly Ryan, had been injured multiple times, most recently in the bombing of a legislative hearing room.

The human separatists clearly had no problem killing and maiming, nor with harming humans who happened to be nearby. Things were escalating and they had to answer the threat with a defense of their own. She hated it. Hated that it was necessary.

Worse, she wasn't sure how much longer things could go on without erupting into full-blown civil war.

Chapter 2

THREE hours later, after she'd been interviewed many times over by law enforcement, after many calls from her own Clan leadership as well as leadership from several other Clans, Packs, Jamborees and other organizations, Helena blew out a breath and turned to face her people.

Despite their exhaustion, covered in soot, blood and no small amount of dirt, they waited for her to give them orders. Willing to do whatever she told them to, to protect their people.

Her gaze flitted over to the sheet and the two witches who'd been standing over it. She'd failed him. That Were who'd volunteered to be on her team. Who'd been doing his job and ended up dead for it. His pack members had shown up just a few minutes before, and as they were finally able to get past the police tape, were preparing to remove his body.

"I'll be expecting your detailed reports. Tomorrow morning. Alix, Sam and Marcus, I want you to be lead on this. Get all the pertinent info to me. I need to speak with The Gennessee, to brief her and the rest of the Governance Council

about this. She'll then relay that information to The Owen."
More calls, more conferences, more everything.

The Enforcer from the South Bay Pack approached.

"I'm sorry for your loss. He was a good soldier." Helena
carefully spoke, knowing grief was expected, but that wolves
felt it was an honor to die protecting Pack.

He inclined his head just slightly. The wolves in Southern
California had just undergone a huge leadership shake-up.
They'd been falling down on the job for years and recent
events had made it clear to National Pack that wolves who
understood what it meant to lead needed to be in charge.

The new alpha families had been much better in the
months since the Magister. But they had a lot of neglect to
undo. Sending people to help with the protection of all Others
was a great start.

"We appreciate the honor you paid him by having your
people watch over him. We'll be sending two replacements
tomorrow."

She wasn't going to argue. She needed every body she
could get. But it was hard, she knew firsthand, to put your
people in the line of fire.

"Thank you."

"As my Alpha has made clear, we're in this together. We
can't afford to let this break us."

She nodded. "No, we can't. But thank you anyway."

He turned, his wolves carrying the body away as they left
the scene.

She returned her attention to her people. "Let's go. Get
some rest. This all starts again in six hours."

Helena noted their emotional exhaustion, the shock on
their faces as it melded with rage and fear. She hated that she
couldn't fix it. Her life was jammed with so much stuff she
couldn't fix that it filled her with a sense of impotent rage all
her waking hours. She was a doer. That's how she was made.
And to not be able to attack a problem and fix it was slowly
wearing her down.

Faine walked ahead of her, opening the car door for her.
The passenger side. Hm. She allowed it because she was

beyond exhausted and driving in that state wasn't advisable. He pulled away from the curb and away from the scene. But it was still in her nose. In her head. The faces of all those Others who depended on her to protect them.

And the sheet covering the one she couldn't protect.

"I need to go back to the office." She pulled her phone from her pocket as she spoke to him. Eleven new messages.

She listened to them, returned a few, sent a dozen emails and texts, and when she looked up again to take a breather, she noted he was getting off the freeway far short of Pasadena.

"Why are you getting off here?"

"You're about to pass out. I'm taking you to my home."

"I have a couch in my office."

"You and your sister are very much alike." He grumbled this under his breath, but she heard it and it made her smile.

"She has blue hair and an atrocious sense of fashion."

"The outside doesn't matter. Your insides are the same. Stubborn. Do you think you'll be more effective if you work until you literally just fall over? Who will you be helping then?"

"You know how long I've been awake because you've been with me the whole time. I don't see you getting into your jammies."

"Jammies?"

"Pajamas. The clothes people sleep in."

"I don't sleep in any clothes."

Christ. As if her fascination with him wasn't bad enough, he had to put that image in her head?

But before she could really go there and imagine him, all nearly seven feet of hard muscle and ebony skin, naked and in her bed, he spoke again.

"And I'm four hundred years old, Helena. I am Lycian. I was bred to be up for days on end, fighting, marching, killing, all without sleep. You're a witch, and while you're powerful and fierce, you can't survive on two hours' sleep in two days."

"There were twenty humans in that group tonight. That means they're not flinching at sending their ranks to die. If I sleep, I'm not following up. How many people are going to die while I take a little nap?"

Failure wasn't something she liked at all. And in truth, she felt like she was drowning at least 60 percent of the time these days.

"You have people working three shifts. Trust them for six hours. Just six hours. You know you'll be far more alert and less inclined to make a mistake or miss something when you get some rest. Your magick will be stronger as well."

He was right. She knew he was. She'd used a lot of magick over the last few days. Her head hurt, her eyes felt like sandpaper and repeated adrenaline rushes followed by the crash afterward had left her muscles less and less responsive.

"Fine, but I'll sleep on my couch at the office."

"No need." He pulled down a street with a huge gate at the end. High fences surrounded the neighborhood just beyond. One of the first fortified enclaves in Southern California. Designed by Others for Others ultimate safety. Round the clock security.

He pulled up to a gate that slid open after the guard recognized him. He paused, handed over a card that was scanned and approved before it was returned.

"My place is right here. You can have my bed and I'll take the guest room. It's a big bed. It'll be another forty-five minutes to get out to Pasadena. That's forty-five minutes you could be sleeping instead. It's really all about economy, right?"

He was very, very bossy. But once she'd allowed herself to agree to sleep, her will to argue was gone.

He drove down the main street of the mini subdivision before taking a left. Guard towers dotted the several-square-block area. Barriers much like those that had been put into place outside public buildings in the wake of the 9/11 attacks surrounded those high fences to ward off any attempts at car bombs.

The outer walls were all warded by the most powerful Full Council witches Gennessee had. As were all the houses. Guards, nearly all of them shifters, prowled the streets day and night. A bustling new industry of witches who hired out to ward homes and businesses had sprung up.

Many in the area now lived this way and other such enclaves were being prepared or were already being moved into all across the country. It made her sad, but at least it kept them safer.

He pulled into his garage and she realized she'd never even been to his house before. She trudged to the connecting door as he turned off the alarm. "Wait here."

He went in first. She wanted to make a crack about how they'd just gone through eight different security checkpoints and two different alarms to get this far. But she'd seen so much happen in the last months after the Magister had come and turned everything upside down. So much death and destruction.

She kept her mouth shut and waited patiently until he came back to her. "Come in."

It was a surprise, how nice the place was inside. He worked so much and traveled as often as she did that she didn't have any idea when he would have had the time to get the furniture and housewares inside.

"My sister."

She shook herself out of her thoughts. "What?"

"You were wondering how this place got decorated. My sister came from Lycia and she took care of everything. I'm not here that often, but when I am, it's nice to have a comfortable home to return to. A safe one."

"Oh. That's nice." And it was. She wondered if he was homesick at all but didn't have the energy to engage. She'd ask him another time.

He pushed a door open and she saw the massive bed and may have sighed wistfully.

"I can take the guest room, you know. Or the couch. I'm just going to pass out anyway." She was sure she didn't begin to sound convincing.

He sighed and shook his head. "Silly female. This is the best bed in the house. As your host, it's my job to give it to you. Also, it's the quietest room. Use it and make me happy."

"I need a shower first. I'm covered in soot."

Another door pushed open to reveal a bathroom. "I'll get you something to sleep in. Towels are in that cabinet there."

And then she was alone to get rid of her filthy clothes, leaving them in a pile in the corner. She'd deal with the towel after she was clean, not wanting to get the ones in the cabinet dirty.

Hot water rained down on her skin as she made her way into the stall. She simply stood there, letting it wash over her for long minutes.

There had been far too many showers like this one. Where she'd stood and hoped all the death would wash off. But it was bone deep and she wondered when, if ever, she'd be able to let go of the things she'd seen . . . and done . . . over the last months.

People relied on her to make good choices. And she'd failed. More than once. And the price for that failure had been injury. It had been death.

She had no answers. Just Band-Aid fixes to stumble from one thing to the next and hope she didn't mess up so badly more people ended up dead.

Never in her life, not even in the time after her engagement had broken, had she felt more alone. More totally overwhelmed by everything. And there was no time for it. No space to let herself relax even a little. Because the hits just kept coming.

Never in her life had she been so afraid.

Her sobs tore from her diaphragm, rusty and sharp and full of everything she tried to shove far away from her mind all day long. Tearing that open and bringing it back made her nauseated.

She let the tears come as she scrubbed her hair. As she saw the soot and blood head down the drain. She would let herself have these minutes and then she'd pull herself back together again because there wasn't any more margin for error. She didn't have any more room to wallow or worry. She had to keep on keeping on.

Because there was no one else to do the job.

She reined it all back. Made herself stop crying as she turned her face up to the water. Letting it heat her through to cut her shivers.

When she stepped out her legs were a great deal more steady. The warm air in the bathroom was welcome and she was grateful that he'd turned the heat up. Lycians, like shifters, had high body temps, so quite often their homes tended to be cool.

But like his brother, Simon, her sister Lark's boyfriend—mate, whatever he was—he seemed to thrive on taking care of people he considered his to protect. Helena knew she'd become one of them.

She liked it. Even as it chafed sometimes. It was nice to have someone taking care of her when it felt like pretty much every moment of her existence now was about taking care of everyone else.

Also? He was hot and criminally sexy. When he turned all that on her it made her a little fluttery inside.

They'd been sort of dancing around each other for months but she was way too busy to enter into anything with anyone, much less a big, bossy Lycian prince who clearly had issues with the word *no*.

When she wiped the steam from the mirror she noticed that he'd left a huge shirt on top of a towel. She hadn't even heard him come into the room, and then hoped he hadn't heard her crying.

She had a reputation as an ice bitch. Crying ruined that image. Though he'd never say a word, he'd know all the same.

After a cursory towel dry of her hair, she braided it quickly, put on the T-shirt that came to her knees—which was good since she had no clean underpants—and shuffled into the bedroom where he'd left a pitcher of water, some snacks and had even turned the blankets back.

That care nearly brought her tears back, so instead she shoved some crackers into her face, gulped down three glasses of water and lay back.

Once she did that, even as she felt herself falling toward sleep, she couldn't help recounting the last several days. One skirmish after another. Like a horror movie.

An assault by four kids at a high school in Fountain Valley. The shifter they'd attacked had handled it himself but they'd

had to stop a near riot when the human parents of the bullies
had shown up at the kid's house, demanding blood.

Vandalism in Garden Grove. A restaurant had had its windows broken out; anti-Other graffiti had been spray painted
on the walls. The interior had been totally destroyed and the
food ruined.

A car set on fire in La Habra, which was where they'd been
when they got the call about the community center in Whittier
and had rushed over, only to have to engage in an actual, no
shit, pitch battle on the street with crazy people who thought
it was totally okay to kill kids and old people.

She hated this world. Hated that people wanted to kill her
simply because she was different. Hated that her friend Molly
had been attacked and was now in two casts because of the
rising threat of the human separatist groups.

These were her former neighbors. The kids she and her
sister, Lark, had gone to school with. People she used to think
were her friends. The dividing lines had been drawn and the
gulf between them got deeper by the day.

And now that Molly had given an ultimatum to the humans
to leave the Others alone and stop trying to harm them or
strip them of their rights as Americans, those lines kept getting drawn.

They were in a brief limbo period as Molly recovered, but
soon they'd be on the road again and Helena would most likely
again be on the security detail for those Others who were
traveling all across the country addressing crowds of humans,
Others and legislators of all types. Trying to educate. Trying
to mediate. Trying to stop an all-out war before it broke out.

But the edges of the world were torn and frayed. Helena
wasn't sure how much longer things would hold before
snapping.

Chapter 3

HER ringing phone woke her up just a little more than four hours after she'd finally fallen asleep. Still heavy with exhaustion, Helena managed to grab it and answer.

"Jaansen."

It was Lark, Helena's little sister and the Hunter of Clan Owen. "I'm so sorry to wake you. I know you probably just got to sleep after all that insanity last night."

For years she and Lark had run Gennessee's hunter team together, but over the last months things had changed. Lark had left, moved to Seattle to run Owen's team. She'd also nearly been killed during the battle to defeat the Magister. But the best part of the last months was that she and Lark had finally gotten past the things that had been keeping them apart and were once more as close as they'd been.

Another high point was that Lark had found love in an unlikely place, Faine's older brother, Simon. It made Helena feel a lot better that Lark had someone so tough at her back. But she missed her sister fiercely, especially during such dark times.

Helena sighed, managing to sit, stacking pillows at her back. "It's fine. Hazard of the job. What's up?"

"We need to get together. A videoconference call. Can you be at Gennessee in thirty minutes?"

Helena noted it was nine in the morning. "I'm not at my apartment. I slept at Faine's last night. I can probably do an hour, or an hour and a half depending on traffic." But it wouldn't be pretty. All her clothes and stuff were at her place, though she had some in her office, so that would work too.

"Really now? I figured it would be Tosh."

Sato? "You what? Never mind. Your brain works in mysterious and twisted ways. As for Faine? Don't get excited. He gave me his bed and slept in the guest room."

"Bummer. You should give Lycians a try. Just sayin'. Big and braw. Totally know their way around a lady. Centuries of being hot dudes serve a gal well. Though they are bossy. Especially royal ones. That's a drawback."

"I have enough people trying to manage me on a daily basis, I don't need to go adding more. Also, a little busy saving the world right now."

Lark snorted. "There's always time for nookie. That's Simon's motto, though he says it in a more smooth and genteel way than me. I'll link you into the call in two hours. Bring Faine, he's needed too. And Dad."

Helena blew out a breath. "I take it the road show is about to start again?"

Helena and Lark referred to the group of Others who'd been traveling all around the country and addressing humans and Others about legislative and civil rights issues the Others Road Show.

"Yes. Some changes. So be ready."

"Changes? Lovely. All right. See you in two."

She got out of bed, realizing she had no change of clothes but her dirty ones from the night before. At least the shirt Faine had given her came to her knees.

As quietly as she could manage, she went into the bathroom to clean up. She kept some disposable toothbrushes and a makeup kit in her bag. Too many nights like last night in the past few months had taught her to be prepared.

But once she'd gotten into the bathroom she noted her

clothes from the day before had been laundered and folded, left on the counter with a new toothbrush.

She smiled. He was a good host and a nice man. Lycian. Whatever. He was welcoming and took care of her when she needed it. It was blessedly appreciated.

She managed to clean up into some semblance of humanity with some mascara and lip gloss, rebrushing and braiding her hair before she went out into the main room. She had split ends and was in dire need of a cut. Helena avoided even looking at the wreck of her nails. She usually spent time at her stylist *and* time at the range. No time for her stylist at all, though sadly, a lot of real-life experience with fight preparedness of late.

As much as she hated it, she'd have to wake Faine up, as he was expected at the meeting. She had the car he'd driven, which was from the Gennessee fleet, but they might as well drive in together since they both needed to be there.

And. Well, she could admit she liked being around him. He smelled good. He was huge and battle hardened so it was nice to have him at her back.

But he was already awake. Standing in his kitchen with a mug of coffee in his hand and a smile on his face.

He looked good. Like so good her libido stood up and saluted him. Stupid libido. Didn't it know she had shit to take care of and jumping on Faine Leviathan was not on her to-do list? This was Lark's fault for putting the idea in her head.

"Thanks for washing my clothes. I appreciate it." She waved at herself, hoping he couldn't tell how awkward she suddenly felt.

"Not a problem. Mine needed washing too. Nicer to have clean ones than to trudge around covered in soot and blood."

"Or a T-shirt so big it could have been a dress."

He looked her up and down slowly and she couldn't have moved if she had to.

"You'd have made it look like a designer outfit. You have that way. I heard your phone." His tone changed back to business. "I figured you'd need some breakfast before you have to rush off to work. Coffee is done and I'm nearly finished with all the ingredients for a breakfast burrito."

She got herself a cup of coffee and freshened his as well. Now that she could smell breakfast she was aware of how ridiculously hungry she was. "I was trying to be quiet, though I was going to have to disturb you anyway, I'm sorry to say."

"Sit." He indicated the table. "I only need about three hours' sleep a night. I've been up about half an hour. Let's eat and you can tell me about what I'm needed for."

"Wow. I wish I only needed three hours. I could get so much more done."

He pulled a chair out and waited until she sat. He befuddled her sometimes.

"You run yourself ragged. You and your sister both. Molly too. None of you are superhuman. You need rest or you'll just fall apart. I know you need to charge your magick and you can't if you constantly rush from one emergency to the next."

He placed a number of platters heaping with food on the table before he sat to join her. He began to fill his plate and she followed suit, feeling better after she'd taken a few bites.

"It's not like I plan it that way. It seems that my whole life has been reduced to running from one emergency to the next. Ugh, I'm whining. Sorry." She sighed and ate some more.

"Anyway, thank you. For everything." She started speaking once she'd filled up a little. They needed to get moving soon and she might as well tell him what was up. "I'm afraid I'm going to have to ask you for more help."

Faine put his mug down but continued to eat. "You're not whining, so stop apologizing. I'm here to help. Tell me what you need."

"It was Lark on the phone. I need to be at a videoconference at Gennessee in two hours. Well, an hour and forty-five minutes now. They want you to be there too."

"Like you, this is the job I signed on for. I'm pleased to do it, especially if it aids you."

She blew out a breath. "I don't want you to regret that."

He snorted, finishing his plate of food rapidly. "I was bred to do this. Much like you." He stood. "Finish up. There's aluminum foil in the pantry if you want to make an extra burrito or two to take with us. I'm going to change and we can get moving. The traffic should be a little better by this point."

She watched his retreat and totally ogled his butt. *Magnificent ass.*

HE'D wanted to talk with her on the drive out, but she'd taken one call after the next, working on her laptop as she did. Helena was rarely still. Most of him approved of this. She was a woman who knew her mind, who understood the severity of the situation and put all her attention on solving it. There was an intensity about her that he responded to. That her people responded to and seemed to be calmed and focused by.

But on the other hand, she'd taken one hit after the next and he wanted her to have just a brief respite from all this damned tragedy. Intensity like hers tended to take a great deal of energy and focus. Never having a break from it was hard on body and mind. He knew it was taking a toll on her. Knew the stress beat at her, splintering and drowning her. He wanted to protect her when he could. Knew on some level that the way she made him feel was different than he'd felt about anyone before. And he accepted it.

He could also admit he wanted her attention. He liked it when she focused on him. All that bright intelligence homed in on whatever he was saying.

"Why Pasadena?" he managed to ask once they'd gotten off the freeway and were headed to the Gennessee headquarters.

She looked up from her work with a smile and he was glad he asked. "Magick is good here. It's clean, runs in strong ley lines from the mountains out to the ocean. When they first settled here—Owen witches I mean—they had their headquarters down in what's now Long Beach. Near the port. But about fifteen years later, we settled out here. We sort of, I don't know, dug in. The Gennessees have had houses out this way for the last three generations. My family are just over there in those hills." She pointed. "Of course, we've got satellite offices all over the state. The territory is too big to manage otherwise."

"I like the mountains. It's nice to be able to go run."

"It's not as heavily forested as close to the city as Seattle is. But it's good. The wildness of it all, city and nature, feeds my magick."

Helena's magick was vibrant. Golden yellows and blues. Lark's was electric in a different way. But Helena's had a taste his beast could identify with its eyes closed.

Driving that thought from his mind wasn't too hard as he headed through the streets to the office. More police presence of late. And now, he noted, they were far more militarized.

He wasn't alone. "Automatic weapons. Christ." She blew out a breath as she noted the cop on a nearby corner.

"At least here they have some decent relations with Gennessee."

"Decent." She shrugged. "Getting worse though. It's factionalizing more by the day. Out here it's not too bad. We've worked with them since the Magister. But their relationship with the shifters is more tenuous."

"The packs down here have some problems. Lazy to have let things get so bad."

He disapproved quite deeply of how poorly and disorganized the werewolves ran themselves in Southern California. They had big problems with rogue wolves, so big they allowed the witches to cull their numbers. Lycians handled their own problems. In Faine's opinion, to have allowed not just outsiders but another race to deal with an issue of their own making rendered them weak.

"They could take lessons from the Wardens. Undisciplined down here. Someone needs to take over and whip them into shape."

She laughed and he turned, not very used to hearing the sound from her. He liked it. His beast liked it too. "What?"

"You and Simon are so judgy when it comes to the wolves here. It's cute."

"Cute?" He snorted, not sure if he should be offended or not. "I'm not cute."

"You totally are. They *are* undisciplined down here. For too long they just let things happen and didn't really care to enforce their own rules. But they're trying now. If they don't

rise to the occasion, they're screwed. I guess if facing oblitera-
tion can't up your game, you're beyond help."

He grumbled, not entirely satisfied. "To have witches cull-
ing their rogue wolves is a disgrace. Lex Warden should take
over. They'd be better off with real leadership."

"Lex has enough on his hands right now. I think they're
scared. Which is good. They switched out their leadership.
If they can use this to tighten their pack up and be better, they
deserve the chance. It's not that I enjoyed having to do their
enforcement. I didn't. I have enough to do without being their
boogeyman. But these are dark times. Their new Alpha is
stepping up since they pushed the old one out. We can't all
be as awesome as Lycians."

He hmphed.

"I'm not joking. You and your brother are trained in ways
I could only dream of getting my people up to. But for them
it's been a huge cultural shift. They've done their own thing
for so long and it's hard to get used to the new reality. I don't
like it much either, but you adapt or you die. If they don't get
their act together, it's Cade Warden they need to worry over,
not Lex."

Cade Warden was the Supreme Alpha of the National
Pack. In charge of all the Packs in the United States. Though
Faine had only met him in person once or twice, he'd been
impressed by Cade's power and commitment to protect his
wolves. It was an Alpha's job after all, but one that was difficult, especially now.

"I should thank the wolves down here anyway." Helena
spoke as he turned down the street where the Gennessee
offices were.

"Why is that?"

"Tracking wolves is serious business. Because I had to do
it so often for so long, I'm good at it. It's made me a better
hunter." She turned and then laughed at his expression.
"What? I'm trying to have a glass-half-full moment."

"I've yet to see you track, but I've seen you in several other
guises as a warrior. You're quite good. If you'd like, I'm
always happy to help with training of any kind."

"Really?"

He turned to her, smiling at the excitement in her tone as they waited in line for security to come and examine the car.

"Yes, of course." He liked that she'd responded in such an enthusiastic manner. He also liked the possibility of working closely together with her in that way.

Witches at the security points checked for magick as well as bombs and guns. No car was allowed to park in their lot without a pass and a check.

The witch who'd come nodded at Helena, taking the pass and running it through her handheld. Helena was adamant that everyone, including her, have their documentation reviewed each and every time. All visitors were logged. All employees were monitored as well. Owen had adopted this policy recently, as had several other Clans and Packs.

Helena had told him it impressed the gravity of their situation in ways her saying so never could. Every day they were confronted with the severity of what was happening. Each time they had to run a security protocol, or be the subject of one, it underlined it. Made them safer because of it on multiple levels.

She was right.

Once they'd gone through the car check, it would be an armed camp inside. Even before the Magister they'd prepared and trained their hunter team. That level of preparedness was an adaptation to the far more dangerous environment they lived in and was now an international model for the other Clans and covens dealing with the new threat post-Magister.

Once they'd been waved through and he'd taken a spot in the garage, she got out, bending to grab her things. He wanted to take her bags but knew she wouldn't allow it or anything anyone could ever perceive as weakness. She moved like a predator, her gaze flitting from place to place as they moved. Evaluating. Always measuring threat.

It was so sexy he had to look away, pushing his beast firmly beneath the skin.

From there they passed through more checkpoints, including a fingerprint and retina scan, and finally they were on their way to the restricted floor where the hunters and Full Council's offices were.

"I'll see you in the conference room in ten minutes." She stopped at the end of the hallway, touching his arm briefly. "Thanks again for the ride." She handed him a bundle. "I made you two more burritos."

He paused, filled with warmth and something else he didn't examine too closely right then. *She'd taken care of him.*

She blushed, which charmed him more. "I mean, you made all the food and I was wrapping up an extra for myself. You have to keep your strength up if you're going to drag me all over the place."

He took the bundle, briefly placing his hands over hers. "Thank you. I'll see you in a few minutes."

Trying not to be flustered by the way he'd put his hands over hers, the warmth still on her skin, Helena headed to her office. Once she'd closed her door, she changed into one of her more professional outfits and did a better job with her makeup while going through her messages.

Grateful for her assistant and her top people who she'd hand all this stuff off to, she headed into the conference room. It was already filling up. Though he'd gone into a sort of retirement after an injury years before, her father waited at the table. He taught her everything she knew and had run the hunter crew long before she and Lark had been born.

He stood to give her a hug. "Good morning, sweetheart. Call your mother today, all right? She worries."

Helena smiled at him. He worried too, she knew, though both her parents seemed to be doing better since she and Lark had finally worked through some long-standing but stupid personal stuff and were once again as close as they had been before.

United Jaansen sisters made a scary threat. It was fun to be that once more instead of mourning the distance between herself and her sister.

"Will do. I have to stock up on her tea anyway."

"That'll make her happy. She's not in a position to do much for you or your sister. But her teas and tinctures are something

tangible. Does all three of you good, and when all my girls
are happy, it does me good too." He said it quietly, making
sure no one else heard, knowing she'd be embarrassed. But
it warmed her. She needed that.

Swallowing back the emotion, she nodded to the head of
the table where Rebecca Gennessee sat as leader of the Clan,
several of the Full Council to her right and left.

As a woman, Rebecca was someone Helena had grown up
thinking of as an aunt. But when she embodied The Gennessee, she was every inch a leader. Slightly aloof, her magick
rolled off her in waves. It was awe-inspiring as well as
comforting.

"Thank you for the detailed report on yesterday's situations. Do we have any new information regarding the fire-
bombing?" Rebecca nodded in Helena's direction.

"I've checked in with the local police this morning. They
told me nothing. The FBI has a new task force. I touched on
that in my update to you. I'll get you more information when
I get it. As of now I have a call in to the agent who was on the
scene in Whittier last night. I'll update you when I hear back."

Before anything else could be discussed, the videoconference started with Lark's face on the screen, which widened
back a little to show Meriel Owen at the head of the table in
Seattle.

Meriel spoke, clearing her throat. "I appreciate everyone
coming together for this. I know things are busy right now
but I figured if we could do it all at once with all the involved
parties, it would be the best use of our time. Molly is going
to start us off. Just quickly, before we do that though, I wanted
to say Lex Warden, who is the liaison between the werewolves
and the COO, is here. We've also got Grace Warden, the
female Supreme Alpha; Max de La Vega, the Alpha of the de
La Vega Jamboree and the liaison with the COO for the cat
shifters; along with his brother, Gibson, who is their Bringer.
Lark will liaise with the Vampires when we're done here."

The Vampires had been pushed past their patience when
a car carrying their protected was attacked and the Vampires
and humans inside were killed. They'd pulled back and were

a breath away from open war with the humans. For the time being, Molly was keeping this from happening with her mixture of charisma, common sense and breathtaking ability to cajole just about anyone about anything.

Breathtaking or not, that would only last so long. Everyone was pushed to their limit and a lot rode on what happened over the next little while.

Meriel introduced everyone else and, finally, Molly took over.

The video equipment didn't hide the healing wounds on her forehead and right cheek, though the bruises were mostly faded. Or the brace on her wrist. She'd been attacked in a federal hearing room just two weeks before. It was a lucky thing she was alive. Now she was not only alive, but Helena noted the light of ferocity in her gaze as well.

"We're going to need to get moving again. Our road show has to get back to work if we want to take advantage of this window we've got. I've been in contact with senators Sato and Sperry, along with Representative Carroll. This new FBI task force is Senator Sato's idea and he was able to convince the justice department to give it some actual teeth. It's staffed with Others as well as humans, and will operate out of three major cities at this point, each taking a third of the country. How was it, Helena?"

"The locals waited far too long to respond to the scene and when they did arrive, they were hostile. I regret to say this is not unusual. However, once the FBI came on scene, things changed. They listened to me and followed up. My people reported that their agents were respectful and thorough. I don't know what that means other than our brief exposure last night, I'm still waiting on a call today, but at least we've got that much."

"Good." Molly made a quick note before looking back to the screen. "Helena, I'd like you to take the point on this team. I've spoken with The Gennessee and she's given her support."

Helena blinked, surprised by Molly's request.

"As most of you are aware, Helena runs the hunter team for Gennessee. It's her efforts and innovation that've kept the

West Coast witches safe. And through them, other witches as they are trained by members of her crew." Molly spoke and Helena saw herself through the other woman's eyes. It was flattering and sort of overwhelming.

"With major help from Lark." Helena didn't want anyone thinking she was taking all the credit for what she'd done with her sister.

Lark broke in. "Helena's leadership is exactly what the team needs."

"There's no one I trust more to head this team than Helena." Rebecca spoke from her place at the head of the table and Helena realized she was one of the last to know about this. The full council of Owen and Gennessee both had discussed it to let it get this far, and Lark had known that morning when she'd called too.

Part of her job was understanding that other people made the decisions she carried out. She accepted it. But part of Helena, the part she walled off and kept to herself and let no one else rule, was pissed that no one, including her sister, had bothered to bring this up with her first. She could have told Helena on the phone earlier, at least to allow her to be prepared.

Resentment was useless, no matter how valid. So she shoved it away and focused on her job.

Rebecca spoke again. "The witches are leading this charge with the human government. It makes sense that we are in charge of any security team to protect our people. It's no secret we're the most human looking of the Others and there's no sense in not using that to our tactical advantage." She paused to let that settle in. "We've got a prominent place on the Council of Others as well, and Helena, I'll expect you to sit on their defense task force."

Over the phone lines Helena heard the rumble of shifter agreement to that.

Okay then. She started making mental notes to hit the ground running once the meeting ended.

"Owen is in total agreement. Lark will be here working on continuing our nationwide training for Others but she will continue to liaise with Molly and Helena and the other members of the Council of Others regarding our internal and external security." Meriel nodded. "Faine, if we could continue to rely on your help and the support of Lycia, I'd consider it a favor if you could serve as Helena's lieutenant on this security team. She'll need to be protected while she's protecting everyone else."

"Of course, Ms. Owen. I would be honored. You have Leviathan support for as long as you require it." Faine rumbled this from his space next to Helena and the echo of it seemed to brush her skin.

"We start tomorrow afternoon in Sacramento with a two p.m. meeting. Helena, if you could get with Sato's people as soon as possible, I'd appreciate it," Molly added. "We're arriving late tonight. I'm going to forward you the details."

"We'll have you met at the airport and escorted in. I'll leave for Sacramento as soon as I can to ready things. I assume Gage will be part of your detail?"

Originally, Faine had been Molly's bodyguard, but when things had gotten very serious between Molly and Gage and she'd been injured, Owen had sent Faine to Los Angeles to help Helena while Molly had been confined to her bed for a while.

From the look on Gage's face, Helena wagered no one, not even a nearly seven-foot-tall Lycian, would be good enough to take care of Molly. He'd want to do it himself and she understood that.

"Yes." Gage spoke, looking sort of feral. Though still smoking hot. Aside from the attempts to kill her, Molly was a lucky woman. "I'll touch base with you in an hour or so with more information."

Helena nodded.

The call ended and Helena turned to her father, a man who'd run the hunter corps before she and Lark had taken over when they were in their early twenties. "You have to take over for me here until I'm back."

He sighed and Rebecca mirrored that sound.

She shrugged. "I can't do it all if I'm going to be traveling so much. There's too much here that should be covered. You know the job already. People respect you. You've worked with most everyone on the team and they need to rely on a leader. Our people need to be safe."

Her father nodded. "I'll step in, but not as your replacement. I'll be your other lieutenant here. It's the best way. You lead this crew and you do it better than anyone else could."

She didn't say it, but it hung between them unspoken anyway. *Anyone but Lark.*

She swallowed but didn't argue. "Fine. Work with Marian and Evan. They're in charge while I'm gone. I'm briefing everyone." She glanced at her watch. "In twenty minutes in our common room. I need to be out of here by noon."

Her father nodded. "On it."

They dispersed and Faine waited for her. "I'll drive. We can take my car to Sacramento."

"You can fly up if you like. It's a long drive. No use both of us having to drive. I just want to get started and it'll take a while to arrange flights. And I like to take all my weapons."

He just raised one brow at her, daring her to keep arguing. She wanted to, just on principle and just because she wasn't one to turn down a dare. But she needed to get moving.

And every time they got into an argument, she only ended up more attracted to him.

"Fine. Thank you. If you drive I can work."

"*Or* you can sleep."

"No time for that." She needed to contact the hunters in the San Francisco office to have them meet her in Sacramento. She'd leave the majority of her people in place, but she'd used the witches from the San Francisco office several times before so they knew the routine and would work perfectly.

He frowned at her and she had to swallow back her demand to know how it was he could do that and still look so good.

"See you in just a few minutes at the briefing." She turned and left, taking a thick file folder from her assistant, who walked at her side as they headed to the hunter's conference room.

"All the information is here. I printed out everything Molly and Lark sent. The hotel has a floor set aside for you in Sacramento. The usual. Get me your schedule and I'll take care of all the reservations for the team as well. Your special ammo is in the lockbox. I'll have it loaded when you're ready."

Just the balance of their world all in her hands.

No pressure.

Chapter 4

HELENA stood at the head of the room, pacing just slightly as she addressed her crew. Her father, David, sat off to the side, letting her hold the reins, which Faine respected. His own father tended to be like that. He was the symbolic head of Leviathan, but Pere, Faine's oldest brother, ran things.

"I don't know how long this is going to take. As head of this new team, I expect to be gone at least seventy percent of the time, so in my absence from this office, David will take the lead, along with Marian and Evan. Things need to continue as they've been. I want three shifts of patrols, and keep on those police bands. I'll still check in via video for the daily briefings when I can, and you know you can contact me if you need to. We'll continue our position here. We will not back down when locals demand it when our people are in danger. This is the new normal, folks. No one seems interested in protecting our witches, but it's our job. We will do it. They want to tell us what our power is. But no one knows better than we do. We don't need to be given our power, it's already ours."

Heads nodded throughout the room and Faine noted the pride on David Jaansen's face. This was a man who'd raised

his children from birth—if the stories he'd heard were true—
to be hunters. Considering the performance of both Jaansen
sisters, he'd done an exemplary job.

These hunters believed in her. Followed her orders without
hesitation. That was rare. And important. He wondered if she
even saw it.

"I need to get on the road now so I can get into Sacramento.
John, you're with me. Caspar and Bridget will be coming over
from San Francisco to staff the Road Show team. I'll be rotat-
ing staff through, so if you're interested, let Sasha know. She's
keeping a list. The rotations will be in two-week increments."
Helena paused. "Any questions?"

A few hands went up.

"You're guarding the human? Why not have his own take
care of him?"

Helena tapped the back of her hand with her pen for a
moment. "He's risking everything to back us. We're guarding
the whole group, including the other legislators who are Others. It's the right thing to do. He does have staff to guard him.
But we're better than they are."

Her smile was cocky, but she told the truth. Despite the
danger, it had been the Other guards who'd kept everyone
alive, even in the midst of bombings.

A few more procedural questions and she was stalking to
the car, her arms full of files.

Faine carried a big lockbox of ammunition that had been
specially created to deal with the mages. The Others knew
some of the mages still allied themselves with the human hate
groups, and they worked on regular humans too. She used
guns, knives and magick on her job.

A lot of Others hesitated in using human weapons on their
law enforcement teams, though that was changing. In large
part due to Helena and Lark.

Faine remembered the look on her face when she'd slapped
a magazine of the special ammo in place. She told him she
wasn't about to waste a tool if she could use it to protect her
people. He liked her ruthless streak.

A lot.

"I need to stop at my house to grab some clothes," she said as she got in the car.

He drove the fifteen minutes to her apartment, noting that the warding was still in place and holding. The building was owned by a Clan family and was guarded, not quite as openly as the enclave he lived in, but it was a magickal fortress so he approved.

"I shouldn't be too long." The wards recognized her, flaring to life as they admitted her and Faine, re-knitting in their wake. "Sorry about the mess."

He laughed at that; unless she described a glass on the counter as a mess, he had no idea what she meant. The place was ruthlessly neat and orderly otherwise. "I've seen how your sister is. This is positively orderly."

She shrugged. "She's a slob. Sort of an anomaly as most witches are orderly. But Simon is a neat freak so I'm sure she works to keep it in check. Mostly." There was affectionate amusement in her tone but he knew things between the two hadn't always been so easy.

He wanted her to share that story with him. Of how she and her sister had ended up falling away from each other for the last few years. He knew the details from Lark's perspective, but he wondered how the story went from Helena's point of view.

"Make yourself at home. I'll be out in a few."

She grabbed a suitcase from the hall closet and disappeared into her bedroom. He contented himself with wandering the living room, looking at her books and the pictures on her shelves.

The woman won a lot of stuff. There were blue ribbons tucked here and there. Not really on display, but in and amongst her things. Statues and plaques. Pictures of her on graduation day, with her arm around Lark, her parents standing with them.

She'd been a swimmer. A runner too. Certainly a prolific reader if her shelves were any indicator. Books were everywhere, and of all types and genres. All in ruthless order by subject and even in like spine colors.

But there was nothing on her walls. They were all the same

basic white as most apartments. No pictures hung. No open books sat on the arms of the chair or couch. She lived there, but the space didn't feel like a home.

Helena came out shortly with a suitcase, a weapons case and another smaller bag; given the scent, probably her toiletries.

"Your weapons case is larger than the suitcase holding your clothes."

She laughed and the sound of it tightened things low in his belly.

"A girl needs priorities. Also, I have clothes in Sacramento. I've got a room there, at the Gennessee building I mean. Weapons? Well, those I keep with me because I have favorites. I can buy four of the same shirt in two colors, but my guns? Well, they're a lot more expensive and I'm partial to how they fit my hand."

He sucked in a breath and the moment between them stretched. "There's a lot to be said for a woman who appreciates a weapon the way you do."

"Yeah?"

He nodded but refrained from saying anything else. They needed to stop at his place and to get on the road. And he sensed the immensity of anticipation between them. Something was going to happen but it wasn't the time, no matter how much he wanted it to be.

He cleared his throat. "Have everything you need?"

She swallowed hard and he tasted her thundering pulse in the air between them. "Yeah. If I forget something I can always pick up a replacement."

He led the way out after she let him grab one of her bags.

SHE wasn't surprised that Faine drove ridiculously fast. Or that he had the reflexes to handle the road at eighty without batting an eye.

At his place he exchanged her company car for his. A sleek and sexy BMW. The engine purred even as it roared down the freeway.

Settling back into the embrace of the seat, she pulled out

her pad, a pen and her phone. She needed to call Agent Anderson because he'd left her a message while she was in her meeting back at Gennessee.

"Agent Anderson, it's Helena Jaansen retuning your call."

"Hello there. I just wanted to check in with you after last night's events. I wanted you to hear this from me, but Gentry Fenton is out on bail."

"What?" She wanted to turn the car around and go hunt him down so she could snap his neck. And then she wanted to find this FBI agent to do the same.

"This was over our objections. We argued that he be held without bail. But his attorneys were able to show a lack of an arrest record, no history of violence, he's got a business in Signal Hill and roots in the community. They argued that he wasn't a flight risk."

"This is bullshit. Utter and total bullshit. One of my people *died* last night. Children were targeted! Or don't they count because they're shifters? No one gives a shit because only human children deserve to be able to play without being bombed by terrorists?"

"I understand. I'm pissed off too, Helena. I promise you this was not what we wanted. My people will keep an eye on him and the others to be sure they don't leave the jurisdiction. Hell, maybe they'll lead us to something useful."

"The other ones were released too?"

He blew out a breath and she knew the magick threatened to boil over from her belly.

"The ones that weren't in the hospital. I'm sorry."

"What judge would allow that?"

He paused so long she understood it. That was the problem. The judge was a pro PURITY person and had acted accordingly.

"We were able to get an order for all of them to stay at least five hundred feet away from any known Other community centers or other organizations. Believe me when I say if they step one foot in that five hundred feet we will pull them in."

"Where a judge will just let them go." When she hung up,

she needed to get one of her team post photographs of the men arrested the night before out on the website and to all the community centers they knew of.

"I'm sure you're aware that we will consider it self-defense if any of these men get anywhere near our property." And who knew if there'd be enough left of the perpetrators to call the cops over when it was all said and done?

"Helena, I know this is atrocious. Please understand this task force is on your side. We want to stop all these hate crimes. We're doing the best we can, and we can do more if you help us."

"And what does that mean?"

"I'm not saying you don't have the right to defend your-selves. But a less confrontational manner . . ."

"You'll need to give Rebecca Gennessee a call on that one. Good luck to you with that. I can tell you it is the policy—a policy we made very clear to Humans First two weeks ago—that we would no longer be turning the other cheek. If you firebomb our children, we will be confronting the hell out of any garbage washing up on our shores trying to do it again."

She hung up, so pissed that she knew if she kept talking to him she'd say something worse.

"I used to be so much more diplomatic," she snarled. "Lark, she was the hothead. I was the calm one. Look at me now, hanging up on FBI agents."

"I heard. The conversation I mean. I think you showed amazing restraint, as it happens."

"I like having you around. You're a bad influence. And I mean that in the best way." She grinned at him, some of her anger ebbing. "I need to make calls about all this stuff."

"Go on. I'm not going anywhere."

Helena handled calls for two hours more, including one to Rebecca Gennessee, who let forth a curse-laden invective the likes of which Helena rarely heard. She actually felt sorry for Agent Anderson, who she did believe meant well.

She instructed her staff to deal with the alerts to all com-munity centers, covens, clans, et cetera, with the pictures of the PURITY people who'd been released. They'd have their own team watching the men, and if they got anywhere near anything that could harm an Other, they'd know what a mistake they'd made.

Eventually Faine pulled off the freeway and into a place for some food. It was a little diner she'd stopped at often enough on her way to San Francisco. Nothing fancy, but a lot of food for reasonable prices and their iced tea was good. But their milkshakes were heaven.

It was also run by shifters, which made her feel safer.

She dug into her cheeseburger and watched him drain a milkshake and order another as he demolished a French dip and shifted to his next plate.

"I envy your metabolism."

He smiled her way. "You seem to do okay."

"I have a physical job. But if I ate like you, I'd be unable to move."

"There are benefits to being Lycian."

Being in a diner run by shifters, being surrounded by Others of all types, meant it was easier to speak about their world without fear. It was nice.

So nice she wanted to keep the topic away from current events. And know more about him, too.

"Tell me about it. What's Lycia like?"

His surprised smile made her glad she'd asked. "It's beautiful. Forests and lakes mainly."

"Industrial? Or? I'm sorry. I know my ignorance is shameful. I guess you're my brother-in-law and I don't know much of anything about where you come from."

"We've never taken much effort to educate Others here on what we're like." He lifted a shoulder. "Not industrial. We do have machines and production, but it's nowhere near the scale you have here. Life is slower."

"Easier I suppose when you live so long."

He nodded. "Yes. There's no rush-rush-rush attitude there. Life is savored. There's much time spent with family and Pack. Our young are kept home for far longer than yours. We tend to live in familial groups. Leviathan land is very large, spread out over hundreds of miles. We live in clusters, usually with our immediate family. I'll take you. When we get some breathing room that is."

She smiled. "To Lycia? Really?"

"You'd like that?"

"Are you kidding? I'd love that. I've been dying to go since Lark first told me about it. A world of warriors? I'm thrilled."

His smile, which was normally laid-back and slightly dirty, widened into something else. "It would be an honor to take you."

"If we survive Thunderdome, that is."

"Thunderdome?"

"How long have you been here? On this side of the Veil, I mean."

"Mainly I've lived in Lycia. My father has a private security force; I have been a lieutenant there. I came here and lived for thirty years or so in the eighteen hundreds. That was an interesting time. Then for about a decade in your nineteen twenties. I've only been here for short periods of time since."

"Thunderdome is from a movie. Dick of a leading man, but it's a fun movie. Plus, Tina Turner is in it, big win. Essentially it's an arena, two men enter, one man leaves." She bet they had stuff like that in Lycia for real.

"Ah, I understand. You and your sister like cultural references."

"I can see I need to expose you to more movies. You know, update your knowledge. There's plenty of downtime stuck in hotels on this damned roadshow. I'll take your education on." She winked. "Also, I can't quite believe you're old enough to have been here in the eighteen hundreds."

They paid the bill and headed back to the car after a stop at the mini mart when they gassed up. You never knew when you were going to need Red Vines or peanut M&Ms after all.

Soon he was back on the freeway, which had been mainly empty once they'd cleared the Grapevine and had descended into Central California. They hit pockets of traffic here and there, but nothing too heavy.

He started to speak again, taking up the conversation from

back at the diner. "The world here was different then. In eighteen forty. I lived in London."

"Really? Did you go to balls and dress up and all that stuff?"

"I had a wife."

She paused. "A *human* wife?"

"All our lives we're taught to avoid humans. Short life-span, you see, means that should you love one, you'll see them grow old and die. Thirty years is nothing to me. But to her, my Lydia, it was from the bloom of her youth until she passed, devastated by tuberculosis. She was fifty-five. Which for then was a ripe old age."

Helena hadn't even thought of him being married. She tried to wrap her head about it.

"I'm sorry."

"It was over two hundred and fifty years ago."

"Well, seems to me that to you, that's not so long ago. And some things aren't so easy to get over."

He breathed out. His eyes were hidden behind some snazzy sunglasses so it was hard to know what he was feeling just then.

"Was it difficult? The fact that they'd have seen you as black?"

He was nearly unbearably handsome. Tall and broad. Dark skin, luscious lips, deep brown eyes. Like Simon, he tended to dress up in suits. He often looked like he'd stepped out of a magazine ad for designer menswear. But in eighteen forty, people would have been less accepting of his skin color.

"I had a lot of money. That tends to ease the way. There were plenty who did not speak to me and who avoided my presence. But more who sought ways to ease me into their company because of the wealth I possessed. The rumor was that I was an African prince of some sort."

"Well, you are a prince, so that part was true."

He snorted. "Yes. I haven't thought of Lydia in some time. Thank you."

"What was she like?"

She had no idea why she asked. It wasn't really her thing

to poke around about a man's old girlfriends or exes. But his Lydia had been dead over two hundred and fifty years. It wasn't like there was a threat. Nor should she even be thinking about it that way because, hello, she was his friend and colleague.

"Kind. Beautiful. They'd needed the income and no one had offered for her. It made her sad. She knew horses really well. That's how I got to know her. She wasn't helpless like many women of her time were bred to be. She was smart and well read. I loved her." He shrugged. "We got on. We married and she moved into my home and we had a life together for a time. She died and I went back to Lycia."

"Did she know? What you were, I mean?"

"No. It wasn't something she could have accepted."

Helena reached out, squeezing his hand. She couldn't imagine having to hide such a big part of yourself that way. She wondered if he felt like half a person.

"You have a good heart, Helena."

She laughed. "Don't tell anyone."

"Do you think it's a secret?"

"I understand how people see me. Lark is the touchy-feely one. She's wisecracks and wild-colored hair. I'm the cold, logical one."

He harrumphed. "She's certainly touchy-feely, as you say. But she's got her share of cold logic and you have your share of warmth and compassion. I see how you are with your people. You risk your life for them daily. Others see it as well."

She shrugged, uncomfortable. He changed the subject.

"What do you think of Lark and Simon?"

"As a couple?"

"Yes."

"I like Simon. He seems to adore my sister. She doesn't let him run her life. He's strong and able to protect her, but he lets her do her own thing. She needs someone like that. She's happy and so I'm happy."

"It's good that you are so close."

"We've had our rough spots, trust me. But I love my sister and would do anything for her. It keeps me going. I hate that she's in Seattle. It's been a good move for her, though."

"She's been hugely integral to strengthening the Owen hunter team. She credits you often with things she teaches to her people."

"We ran this squad for years. Were raised in it. She's good at what she does. The best, really."

"Hm. She says the same about you, and from what I've seen, she's right."

"I've made mistakes." Her tone was laced with regret. He knew there were things unsaid. He had a level of intuition he knew he got from his mother, who was a high-ranked demoness. As much as he wanted to poke at her to get her to reveal her hurt spots, he realized it was wiser with Helena to let her come to it in her own way.

"You were engaged once. It didn't work out. Tell me about it."

"'Didn't work out' is a pretty way to put it, I suppose." Her phone rang and she answered quickly.

"Jaansen."

She thought she could avoid the subject. Faine wisely kept his snort mental as he continued to drive. She was silly to think so. He could wait. He was good at it. Trained to wait for the perfect opportunity to pounce and disarm his prey.

He'd grown to know her over the months they'd traveled around, guarding Molly and the others. He was four hundred years old and he knew when a female interested him on more than just a friendly level.

She looked at his mouth longer than was necessary. Her pupils got larger when she stared at him. Her pulse sped and her skin warmed. The aroma was enough to bring his beast to the skin every time. She wasn't the only one interested.

He wanted to know Helena better. A lot better.

And so he'd wait.

ONE of her San Francisco hunters waited for her as they entered the Sacramento offices of Clan Gennessee. She nodded once and the hunter relaxed. Slightly.

"Caspar, good to see you. You know Faine."

They'd made the nearly six-and-a-half-hour drive in five and some change, even after stopping for lunch. He loved driving. Didn't do it much in Lycia, but here he had a sleek, powerful machine. The straight shot from Los Angeles to Sacramento gave him an excellent opportunity to drive hard and fast. It was nearly as good as sex.

Nearly. Faine kept his focus on Caspar and tried not to think about sex. With Helena.

Caspar nodded seriously at Faine and turned his attention back to Helena.

"We need to get up to speed here. I'm going to get changed and then head over to Senator Sato's home. We're meeting there instead of his office. He's concerned about leaks and security issues at the capital offices."

"Yes, ma'am. I'll be working on the schedule then. Just come by when you're ready and I'll drive you over."

Faine would wait to disagree with that until they were alone.

Again that nod before she headed upstairs, he followed in her wake. The office building was three stories and held work-spaces along with several apartments and a central kitchen. It was where they'd be staying in Sacramento. The last time they were in town, they'd stayed at a hotel, but Helena had decided to keep them at the Gennessee building. All in one place. All locked down like a fortress.

Faine approved. Especially after they'd gone through several checkpoints and he'd noted snipers on rooftops.

"Faine, you can take a few hours' downtime if you like. I'll take Caspar with me."

He simply looked at her. "Let me unpack my things and get the other stuff from the trunk inside. Then we can *all* head over together."

"You're very stubborn." She unlocked a room and he decided to take the one across the hall. "I'm going to shower and get ready. Meet you out here in forty-five."

He paused, touching her arm. "If I'm stubborn I could take lessons from you. You're the one who needs downtime. At least eat."

Her smile was pale, but there. "Tosh says there'll be dinner served at the meeting. Shifters will be in attendance so you know it'll be a huge spread. You really don't need to come. I'm capable of protecting myself."

"You most certainly are. But I'll be there. Protecting you while you protect everyone else. That's how it works." He kissed her forehead and stepped back. "See you in forty-five."

Chapter 5

HE'D kissed her forehead. It was . . . startlingly tender. Not patronizing, though she nearly wished it had been. She could have easily resisted patronizing.

The phantom of his touch remained on her skin as she got out of the car at the airfield where the plane carrying Molly and her team had just landed.

She greeted Molly as they got off the plane.

"Just a gentle hug." Helena smiled. "The bruises are fading. Too bad, you looked like a hard-ass with them."

Molly grinned. "I did?"

"Totally."

"You can sign my cast with prison graffiti then. You know, for effect."

Helena chuckled. "Gotcha. Though I'll have to look some up on Google. Wouldn't want to do something that looked tough but really meant, *I'm a fluffy bunny, pet me and give me a cookie.*"

"I've missed you. You look tired though." Molly's smile faded into a concerned frown.

"Let's get you in the car. You can keep lecturing me once we're behind bulletproof glass." Helena led them the few feet from the plane to where the cars waited. Faine stood at the door, bowing slightly when he saw Molly. Her friend smiled back, tiptoeing up to kiss his cheek.

Gage shook Faine's hand and clasped his forearm before sliding into the car next to Molly. "Faine will ride with you. I'll be in the car just ahead." She closed the door and moved to the car in front, leading them all from the airfield and back to the Gennessee building.

She knew Faine frowned, but he was too disciplined to question his orders in front of anyone. She had her reasons.

It was after one in the morning so the traffic was light. They'd driven by a few protests earlier on their way over to Sato's place, but now things were quiet. She was glad to see, though, that despite the lateness of the hour, her staff at the garage they used to park their vehicles in was on the ball, using all the checks she'd put into place.

Once inside she showed Molly and Gage their room, got the rest of the group settled and told Molly she'd meet with her in fifteen minutes to brief her on the day's events.

As she figured, Faine caught up with her in the hall outside her room. "I'm *your* guard. I can't do that from another car."

"I can't do my job effectively if all my best weapons aren't spread around. If my car had been attacked, you'd have been able to deal with it immediately. You wouldn't have been in the car that was hit. If your car had been, I could have dealt with it and you'd have been there to aid Molly and Gage."

He paused, thinking, and finally nodded. "I understand your reasoning. But I do not like being separated from you when there are dangerous situations."

She knew what he meant, of course. But the possessive edge in his words sent a thrill through her.

Dangerous.

Dangerous and stupid to let herself get any measure of woo-woo over this male. He was too much, like all alpha males were. Too much to handle. Too intense. Too everything.

But she tingled nonetheless.

"Okay then. I'm going downstairs to talk with Molly and Gage. Are you coming?"

"Yes. That would be good."

He followed, the heat of him at her back.

"I'll listen to your update but only if you have a cup of tea with me and maybe some toast or something. Helena, you look beat." Molly came into the common room looking moderately relaxed.

"Sit. I'll get the water on." Gage gave them both a look that dared them to argue, so Helena nodded her thanks and sat across from Molly.

"Says the woman with two casts."

"Gage scowls at me until I rest. Aside from re-knitting broken bones, I'm doing all right. I even got eight hours' sleep for three nights in a row this week. And don't tell anyone, but I napped twice."

"Because she was nearly asleep on her feet," Gage called out from where he set the kettle on the stove.

She winked at Molly, who rolled her eyes, but looked back to Gage with affection all over her features.

"So fill me in."

"Went to Sato's place earlier." Helena tucked her feet beneath herself as she leaned back into the couch cushions. "We've got a basic schedule for tomorrow and the day after. You've got a series of hearings and meetings. The wolves sent their people over to sniff the rooms and they'll be in place tomorrow as well."

Gage looked to Faine, who shrugged. "These have been trained by National. Bomb sniffers, that sort of thing. I trust them."

Helena barely resisted the urge to snap her fingers. She got it, they were all experts and Faine had worked with Gage more than Gage had worked with her. But.

"In the future, I'd appreciate it if you spent even a minute amount of time pretending you take my word for things. Or do me the respect of being more aboveboard in asking someone else's opinion. This is either my team or you can run it yourself."

Gage started as everyone grew very quiet. Then he blushed.

"You're right. I meant no disrespect, but I can see how it came off that way."

Molly smoothly intervened. "I think the water is about to boil."

Faine stood. "I'll get it. Rain—that's Helena's mother— sent a dozen kinds of tea for us."

"Oh, your mother's tea is delicious." Molly's pleasure was genuine. "She sent some up care of Lark for me while I was healing."

"She likes to take care of people. I'll let her know your reaction; it'll totally make her day. And it'll give me another reason to call and check in. My dad, well, he's the hunter. She's the nurturer. She just hangs on and claps when we win things and tries to get us to hug it out instead of punching each other when we have conflict."

Gage laughed. "I think our mothers would get along great."

"When this mess dies down, they want to have a big party for Simon and Lark, you'll meet them then. Having met your mother a time or two, Gage, I'm sure they'll hit it off."

Faine came back with tea and he simply stared at her until she took a sip.

"I had the schedule sent to Rita." Rita was Molly's assistant. Molly was a control freak, like they all were to some extent. She liked to know things in advance and any changes to her schedule were to be made with her knowledge or she got pissed. Helena totally understood that and tried to work within those guidelines.

"First thing you've got is a meet with Sato, Carroll and Sperry. It's at nine thirty. Then a closed-door meeting where they want to talk with us about this new FBI task force they've created recently."

Molly snorted. "The one you said you hung up on earlier today?"

Helena blew out a breath. "Yes. It was stupid. I shouldn't have."

"No, you totally should have." Gage sipped his tea. "From what you said, it's lucky you didn't tell him off first."

"I understand. Totally. You're frustrated. We're all frustrated, and letting Fenton go was offensive beyond bearing. They need to understand that we're not going to take this stuff quietly. I'm not mad. It was just by way of reference." Molly reached over and patted Helena's arm.

"I don't even know how you stay so calm."

"I think your mom puts drugs in the tea."

Helena barked a laugh. "I wouldn't put it past her. So anyway, I've got clearance for all the members of our team and their guard. Because I'm on Sato, I'll be able to use some of their back hallways and that sort of thing."

"I'm worried about Tosh." Molly's brow furrowed. "He's human. He's got no natural defenses."

"He's no slouch, Moll. He was in the navy. He's a JAG. He knows how to defend himself. I went through his home and his office—back before the bombing, I mean—and gave him a list of improvements I thought he could make, and when I was at his house earlier tonight, he'd made them. All of them. And his personal guard includes a former Ranger and former marine."

"Well, it's his own people trying to harm him." Gage lifted a shoulder.

Helena got it. Tosh liked Molly. Respected her and felt protective of her. A man like Gage would be jealous of that. Sato was spectacularly handsome and charismatic too. That would rankle.

"Look, Tosh is a good man. He's risking himself not for points or votes, but because this is the right thing to do. And it's made him a target. I'm happy to be on his team. I met some of Sperry's team tonight too." One of them couldn't tear her eyes away from Faine and an unreasonable desire to jab her pen in the female shifter's eyes had washed through Helena. "They're all highly trained. They did listen to me about having bomb-sniffing dogs used before all your public hearings here in Sacramento and also in DC."

Molly nodded, making notes with her good hand. "When is the next hearing on 877?" House Bill 877 was a far-reaching anti-Other bill that would, among other things, chip all non-humans with GPS trackers, put them in relocation camps and divest them of property and their jobs. There was a Senate companion bill that wasn't quite as bad, but still gouged a hole in their civil liberties and essentially made them non-citizens without any basic rights.

"Thursday. I'll have Evan get with Mia's people on getting you all flown out." Mia was the pilot, a shifter, who'd been helping out. "I tried to convince Sato to fly with us, but he's insisting on commercial air travel so I'll accompany him back to DC Wednesday evening."

"As will I."

Faine hadn't insisted. He'd simply not taken any other idea seriously. He would be at her side. It was his job and that was that. It had been . . . reassuring. Just knowing she had someone at her back had made the situation slightly less unbearable.

"I don't like it. You're not safe." Gage brushed a thumb through his beard.

"No. I'm not. But that's the point of a guard, Gage. You know it. He's even less safe. I was able to convince him to go first class at least. We'll take up the whole section, which I like."

"You can't take a weapon through security."

"As I'm a senator's guard, I can. But it's not worth all the hassle, and you know there *will* be hassle because I'm a witch. But I've got Faine. He's a weapon. And my magick." The funny thing about magick was that it was a hell of a lot stronger when a witch flew. Something about the atmosphere being thinner. She didn't know all the whys of it, just that while she was on that plane she didn't need a handgun. She'd be stronger than anyone else on board.

"I'll speak with him about flying on one of our planes from now on when I see him." Molly looked at her notes a moment.

"He's not going to agree. It will look bad, like he's in our pay or something. He's got enough to deal with."

"You seem to know him pretty well." Gage lifted a brow.

"He likes her." Faine lifted his own in Gage's direction and the two shared a look.

"He's a man with principles. It's logical. Also, it's sort of my job to know people."

Molly snorted. "It seems that many men are not entirely reasonable when it comes to Toshio Sato."

"Why? Because he's hot, intelligent and powerful?" Helena laughed and Molly joined in.

"Come on. Our tea has been consumed. Helena, you need to rest. I know Molly does too. Let's get to bed. Tomorrow is a long day." Gage clearly wanted to be done with the subject.

And bed sounded really good, so she allowed it.

They all headed back to where the rooms were, Gage and Molly disappearing into theirs. Faine continued to walk her to her door. He knew she didn't need it, heaven knew she was utterly capable of protecting herself.

And yet.

He liked being around her. Liked watching over her, even if to just remove a tiny bit of the weight she always seemed to carry for everyone else.

She opened her door and he leaned against the jamb. Startled, she looked up at him, smiling nervously. "Thanks for your help today. I got a lot of work done because you did all the driving."

"It's my job. But it was also my pleasure. Do you plan to work out tomorrow morning?"

She nodded. "I'll get up at six or so. There's a workout space here. I'll run a few miles on the treadmill and then hit the shooting range." She lifted one shoulder.

"If you don't mind, come get me. I need to work out as well."

"Sure. And we can leave from there. If you like, I mean. Since you're on my personal detail. It'll be good to have you with me. Just the sight of you will keep the violence-on-a-whim people back." Her smile was genuine and maybe even a touch flirtatious.

He'd shifted closer and she hadn't moved back. The tension between them heated, simmering as the scent of her blush reached his senses. She licked her lips and the scent of loam and fur rose.

Her eyes widened and she faltered a moment, and Faine knew his control had slipped. But she'd talked weapons, praised his size and then licked those damnable lips. A Lycian could only take so much.

"My beast." He pondered whether he should continue. If

he should explain to her how much the warrior she was called to him. She was so very strong, and yet, frayed at the edges. Fragile at times. Which was even more irresistible.

"Oh." She blinked several times. "Should I be worried?"

He bent, brushing his lips over hers, savoring the heat of her before he stood again, taking a step back. "Not for your safety. Good night, Helena. I'll see you in the morning."

He left her there, but not before he caught sight of the way she pressed her fingertips to her lips.

SHE woke up without an alarm, at six. Pretty much the same way she had most every morning of her adult life. She lay in bed awhile and thought about her day. It was her way of meditating, of getting herself organized for the hours—and the challenges—she faced.

The meetings would be stressful because the state capital was so crowded. Mainly it was state business handled there. Sato had a senatorial office near the capitol building where he met with his constituents and held meetings. But due to the insanity of the security concerns, his people worked with the state folks and they'd let them use their conference spaces, even for federal issues. Of course the hearings they were going to dealt with State of California business, so Sato would only be there if they needed him to speak on federal issues.

It was mind-blowing, all the different local, county, state and federal issues they drowned in. So many different egos to soothe, everyone had their own turf, their own rules to adhere to, their own processes. At least all Helena needed to do was be sure no one got hurt. All the politics were Molly's problem.

She pushed out of bed. A hard workout would help cut through some of the stress burning through her muscles. She'd run and lift weights and shoot at things and then she'd shower. By the time they needed to head over to Sato's office to pick him up, she'd be in a better mental space for all the things she'd need to do that day.

She got dressed quickly, dealing with her hair, securing it in a ponytail after she'd washed her face and brushed her teeth. Her sneakers were on and she headed across the hall to knock on Faine's door.

Faine.

He'd kissed her. Had gotten up in her face and kissed her. Her mouth still felt the touch, the brush of his lips against hers. The dirty truth was that she'd been hot for Faine Leviathan from the first moment she'd seen him. He was everything she'd never known she found alluring in a man.

She'd been standing with Lark talking about the hows and whys of a speaking event with Molly and he'd come around a corner with Simon. The two were clearly brothers, both dressed quite nattily in suits. But Faine was eleven thousand kinds of delicious. He moved in a long lope, and yet there was a predator's grace in him. People got out of his way, probably without even realizing it. He'd smiled as Simon had spoken, and then his gaze, which had been taking in the surroundings, had landed on Helena's and it shocked her to her toes.

It had only deepened the longer she knew him.

Cocky. Self-assured. He knew what he wanted and he simply considered it his due when he got it. He was a badass with his fists. She'd never seen him shift, but she had the feeling he was a big ol' beast then too. He was gorgeous and his voice was a low, gravelly rumble she felt in her gut every time he spoke.

He watched her, she'd noticed, like a predator watches prey. Not the same way the human separatists watched her. It wasn't that he thought less of her in any way. But like she fascinated him and he was taking down everything she did for when he decided to run her to ground.

She bet he was the type to bite a girl's neck to hold her in place when he got her into bed.

A flash of heat raced over her skin at the idea.

So of course, that's when he opened his door. "Well, good morning to you, Helena." One of his brows went up like he knew she'd just been imagining him naked and sexing her up until she passed out.

She blew out a breath. "Morning. Ready to run?"

"Yes, I am."

Chapter 6

"THESE things are not allowed in the hearing room." A burly human male—obviously a private guard of some type—blocked her way.

They'd spent the day before in one meeting after the next all over the capitol complex. That day they ventured into a town-hall-type space near Sato's Federal Building office.

So this joker, with his prison white-power ink and his permanent scowl that said more about his lack of intelligence than his toughness, had no business at all stopping her entry to any public space.

Tosh was right behind her, Sperry on his other side. Fanned out in the hallway was the rest of the group with their various guards. It was monumentally stupid for this guy to think he had any chance at all of stopping them.

Helena ignored him, moving to go around him. And he made the mistake of touching her. "I said—"

She grabbed his wrist, twisting and bending it, levering his arm, forcing him to his knees. She leaned down, getting close enough to say in a low tone, laced with magick, "I don't give a fuck what you said other than, *Please let me get the door for you, ma'am*."

He began to grab for a weapon and she bent his wrist harder. Just a bit more and she'd break something.

"I wouldn't recommend that."

"Get off me, bitch."

Helena kept his wrist, though other security had begun to gather around. Harsh, whispered orders were being given all around her but she put all her focus on this asshole at her feet.

One thing she noticed more than anything else was the presence of a handgun at his back. She'd had to go through a full-body pat-down and a metal detector. So how was it this asshole had a gun?

"Why does this man have a weapon?" Straightening, still keeping her tight hold on him, she managed to ask this calmly, feeling anything but.

"You need to let him go. Now." A police officer approached.

She remained exactly where she was, keeping her body between the approaching cop and Senator Sato. "My name is Helena Jaansen and I am part of Senator Sato's security detail. This man accosted me as I attempted to enter the hearing room. I'm going to need one of you to come and take his weapon before I let him go. For the safety of myself and the people I'm guarding."

"You don't give the orders here, witch." The cop's lip curled and she narrowed her gaze at him for a moment.

Helena centered herself, connecting with her magick, spooling more up from the earth beneath her feet. "This isn't going to end well, Officer. Now. You can do your job, or I will break this man's wrist, and even if you shoot me, my people will take out every last one of you in this hallway. And for what? I'm not letting this man go. He's got a weapon and I'm protecting a United States senator. Once you have taken his weapon, I will happily let him go."

She caught Gage's attention and he had the same readiness about him.

It was Tosh who spoke next. Pulling all his authority

around himself, but keeping himself behind her, which was very smart.

"Officer, you're going to need to help Ms. Jaansen immediately. Remove the weapon from the gentleman on the ground, pat him down and then you may take him into custody."

The cop sighed, but moved to obey, removing the gun. Helena let go of the wrist of the guy on the ground and he tried to lunge at her. But she was prepared and far more than a prison thug in the pay of asshole bigots.

Feet solidly planted, her balance braced for trouble, she cocked her fist and gave him a solid right to his mouth, sending him sprawling as she neatly stepped back.

"I'll give you another if you move even a tiny bit." She didn't take her attention from the guy on the ground but she addressed the cop as more streamed into the hallway. "If I were your boss, you'd be sitting out the next few weeks on administrative leave as you went through the process of getting fired. You're sloppy. Sloppy gets people killed."

"I don't need any advice from you."

"Please." She rolled her eyes as the cop got the other guy in cuffs and hauled him to his feet. "Of the two of us, only one is good at their job. And it's not you. I hope you think your stupidity can protect you, because your piss-poor training sure won't."

She glanced back at her people and then headed into the room where it was already standing-room only.

THE following day, Tosh smiled at the sight of Helena coming back into the room. "Thank you for all your help this trip. I hope DC will be calmer."

Delilah laughed. "I doubt that. But, Helena, I believe you scared a few years' life from that one cop in the hallway earlier. Nicely done."

The sound of that laugh did things to him. He'd been working closely with Delilah Sperry for months now. Even before he knew she was a werewolf he'd been attracted to her. She was long and lean with keen eyes that missed absolutely nothing. Her hair was a tawny gold and she often had it back from a face that managed to be delicate and bold all at once.

They'd danced around each other for a few months now. Tosh had been so busy at what felt like every single moment of his waking day, he'd told himself it wasn't the time.

But the heightened danger had only sharpened his hunger for the delightfully sexy, canny and powerful Senator Delilah Sperry.

"He should have been scared. If he'd have been one of my people I'd have busted him back to cleaning toilets. We did meet with his boss later while you two were in another meeting with Molly. He apologized for the past two days' worth of unpleasantness from his officers." Helena took the glass of water his assistant handed her. "They're short-staffed like everyone else. But he was a good man and I accepted his apology. They've got their own problems in the ranks, I suppose."

Helena was distracted. And exhausted. Tosh saw it around her edges and hoped the way Faine stared at her meant the wolf—whatever he was—would see to it she got some rest.

"I appreciate you handling that. Ben was just singing your praises earlier today." Delilah spoke of Ben Stoner of the Great Lakes Pack and her own Alpha, as she hailed from Chicago. "We appreciate all the effort the witches are putting into this. You're smart and strong and we're proud to be protected by you all."

Helena tipped her chin slightly and Toshio knew it was a sign of thanks and respect. "That's a nice thing to hear. His and Tegan's Enforcer team is something I admire a great deal. We should get moving to the airport now. I've received several reports that Others can get hassled quite a bit going through security so we should build in the extra time. I'm spoiled in that I've been flying privately of late, so I've been able to avoid most of that nonsense."

Delilah's mouth hardened. "The last time I flew I was chosen for an enhanced pat-down. They held me up for an entire hour. Everything was fine until they ran my ticket through. I've asked about whether or not there's some sort of TSA tracking system for Others, but I can't get any answers. Which only says there is one."

Helena nodded. "Oh yes, you know there's a list."

That turned Tosh's stomach. Lists of Others got very close to what had happened over and over throughout history. Keeping track of people because they were different—and not in a way that protects society like lists of sex offenders or violent felons—wasn't the America he believed in.

"I'm sorry." He sighed.

Helena shrugged. "You're trying to stop it. That's what counts. In the meantime, we can't make a huge deal of it or we get picked on even worse. They've got so much power these days that even raising this treatment as an issue while it's occurring is cause for them to not let someone fly. So for now, we plan ahead and document everything."

"Doesn't mean we have to like it." Delilah stood, brushing the front of her skirt down. "But she's right. Let's get moving. I'd like to sleep in my own bed tonight and we all need the rest before we deal with Marlon tomorrow."

Tosh nearly snarled at his fellow senator's name. Marlon Hayes had become a legislative mouthpiece for the PURITY movement and it turned his stomach every time he had to deal with the man. There'd be a hearing first thing in the morning on the companion bill to House Bill 877, the Domestic Security Act. A fine-sounding name for a bill that would strip Others of their civil and human rights along with their property and citizenship.

At least they got to move through security in a shorter line, but Helena was pulled aside for an enhanced check, which took an extra half hour. She was far more patient than he was, and it wasn't until he started making calls and taking down names that things moved more quickly. They still checked her, but the overt slowing down of the process stopped and they got on with it.

The unfairness of it deeply bothered him. No one should be treated this way and yet it was happening. It happened every day to many people. And it wasn't right.

He was relieved when they finally boarded and got settled in. The flight attendants were friendly and helpful and he was seated next to Delilah. It did wonders for his mood.

The entire flight Tosh considered ways to ask Delilah over for a drink when they arrived back in DC. But things kept coming up. He got interrupted by his aide many times over. The times he spoke to Delilah they were in a group and it wasn't the right place to ask.

And by the time they landed he was so tired his eyes burned and all he could think about was a hot shower and a good night's sleep. Still, he'd made a decision to move forward and, that done, he rarely lost sight of something he'd set his mind to do. Within the next two days he would ask Delilah over for a drink. He could do this. It was long past time.

THE plane touched down and Helena managed to get everyone into a car and safely delivered to their Washington, DC, homes, where they all had personal security, and she and Faine joined the rest of the Others at a huge house owned by the National Pack.

"You should go to sleep." Faine shouldered her bag once they'd entered the front gates and she let him. Too tired to refuse.

"I'm surprised there aren't any protesters."

"I suppose they may not know this location is Other-owned yet. Are you even listening? You're dead on your feet. As usual. You should rest."

She grinned at the agitation in his voice, for some reason cheered by needling him. Stupid, really, to poke at a giant beast wearing a man's skin. But she liked to live dangerously. "No. Come on. I'm hungry."

He frowned at her, but followed her into the house where the magick of all the Others inside greeted his senses, easing his tension.

"It's so nice to be in a friendly space." He watched as the frown lines around her eyes eased back and that made him feel better.

"I was just thinking that."

Molly got up as they entered the main living room. "Hello, you two. Glad you got in all right. Come on upstairs. I'll show you your rooms and you can put your bags down."

They followed her up the stairs and down a long hallway to the end. Molly turned to Helena. "I put you facing the courtyard. The plants out there make me feel better. I figured you'd think so as well."

The room was nice sized and had an en suite bathroom.

"Faine is on the other side."

He nodded. "Thank you, Molly." He turned to Helena. "I'll be back in a moment and then you and I are eating some dinner."

"There's a huge kitchen here. Cade Warden sent a chef down so there's a lot of food as well. Are you all right?"

"It's been a challenging day," Faine said as he came back into Helena's bedroom. "We were chosen for an enhanced search at the airport. There was a fight between three security people, one of whom was an asshole but the other two, also human, were not. Sato had to intervene and make calls to get it moved along. The plane trip was long, but thankfully, as we took up the entire first-class cabin, we didn't have to deal with much animosity."

Molly looked to Helena. "But you felt it."

Helena nodded, pressing her fingers to her temples.

"You can feel it?" He pushed his anger that she hadn't said so down as far as he could. She wasn't a natural sharer, this one, but he wanted her to lighten her damned load with him sometimes just the same.

It was Molly who spoke to explain. "A lot of negative energy, especially when it's aimed at you and you're in a confined space, is toxic. Planes tend to amplify our magick as well, so it's a one-two punch." Molly took Helena's hands. "Why don't you go out into the courtyard for a recharge? I'll let the chef know you'll be eating in a few minutes. But clear out all that bad energy, you'll feel better and the food will go down easier too."

Faine wanted to scoop her up and cosset her. He had no idea all the dirty looks and nasty comments people made under their breath would affect her like that.

"Is it all right if I come along?"

Helena shrugged. "Sure."

Molly took them down a back staircase—slowly and carefully in her walking cast—and showed them through large French doors into an enclosed courtyard, full of life. Container gardens spilled with plants and flowers.

"Gage and I are in the living room watching movies when you're ready." Molly hugged Helena and then Faine and went back inside.

Faine settled on a bench and watched as Helena took her shoes and socks off, along with her sweater, leaving her in a T-shirt that showed the whipcord strength of her upper body. She freed her hair from the bun she'd been wearing, running her fingers through it as she did.

Then she wandered through the path, letting her outstretched fingertips brush over the plants, against the bark of the trees, through the rushing water of the water feature. She stepped up and then down into the bed of a large garden space.

He saw it then, the light of her aura as she drew all the magick around her. It settled against her skin like snowflakes and then seemed to melt into her. She breathed slow and deep as she walked. Occasionally she'd pause, burying her face in a bunch of leaves or flowers.

This side of her was soft. Lush and so achingly intimate it was as if he'd been spying on her. But she'd allowed it. Moved around knowing he was there watching.

A gift of her inner life and the weight of that settled. Not crushing. *Anchoring.*

She'd been sort of tattered when they'd arrived. Her spine hunched, the tension rolling from her in waves. But when she came back to him, settling next to him on the bench, that was gone. Her ragged spaces seemed to have filled in. Her aura was brilliant, sunny yellow, the blue of the sky at summer.

She stretched. "This garden is fantastic. Whoever tends it does so with love. Every leaf seems to vibrate with it."

"You can feel things like that?"

"Not always. But living things most especially. My mother says we get it through her. Lark is much the same, though she's got this crazy affinity with birds. We've always loved being outdoors. There's so much ambient magick in a garden.

If it's tended by someone who truly loves the work, the magick seems to leap to you when you call for it. The energy, the life force of the plant life fills in all your empty spots. I don't know how to explain it."

"Seems to me you're doing just fine."

"I have a lot of plants in my apartment, but at the house I used to share with Lark, we had an inner courtyard like this and it was full of plants. After crazy shifts we'd often just sit out there and have a glass of wine, letting all the bad business wisp away. My mother is a big gardener. She loves it. All the stuff from her teas comes from her gardens at their house. I guess we do get it from her, though I'm not that gifted with green things. She's special that way."

He smiled. "Thank you."

"For what?" She clearly had no idea.

"For letting me share in this with you. This private side of yourself."

"Oh. Well. I figured you'd find something restorative out here too. Shifters have that connection with nature as well. Different, but it's there."

He snorted. "I'm *not* a shifter."

She turned, a mischievous grin on her lips, and his heart lightened.

"You're human and you shift into a wolf."

"You enjoy poking at me, don't you?"

She raised a brow, but said nothing else and he chuckled.

"I'm Lycian. I am a beast who wears a man's skin sometimes. And other times I wear fur. But I am always who I am, no matter the skin I wear. I do not need the moon or the tides. If I bit you, you'd bleed, but you wouldn't be infected."

"Did I insult you?" Her levity was gone, her question genuine.

He snorted a laugh and took her hand, squeezing it a moment. "No. We're related in a distant manner, to shifters. But we are not the same."

"Thank you for educating me. There's so much I don't know about everything out there in the universe. I thought I did until the Magister. Not knowing things makes me nervous."

"There's so much out there. Miraculous things."

"I envy you that knowledge."

"I can share it with you. If you like. I already said we'd go to Lycia when there's a lull of a few days. There are other places. Beyond the Veil, I mean. I can part it, we can travel so you can see it all."

"I'd really like that."

And so he'd make it happen.

Her stomach growled. "Shall we go in and eat?"

He leaned in close. "After."

"After?"

He reached out, cupping the back of her neck as he brushed his lips over hers. He'd intended a brief kiss, but she opened, sighing into him. Once that breath entered his system there was nothing brief about it.

He sank into her mouth, sliding his tongue over her juicy bottom lip and then inside, tasting the sweetness of her, the spice of her magick as it rose against him, twining around his.

Loam and fur, sun-dappled leaves and the lap of a lake against the shore filled him. Her magick, snowflakes and pomegranate slid around it. They were opposites and yet complementary.

Something clicked in him. An utter surety that he'd felt rarely enough that he trusted it to his toes.

He took her hand, squeezing it as he pulled away.

She nipped his bottom lip and he was back for more, deepening, his tongue dancing with hers. The sounds of the night all around them began to filter through the heat of their kiss. Of traffic on the street, voices just inside the house, the merrily running water just a few feet away.

When he broke the kiss, it was only because he knew there would be more.

Laughter sounded from inside and she smiled. "Let's go in."

He stood and she took his outstretched hand, letting him pull her up.

Chapter 7

"**SO,** you want to talk about anything?" Molly tried to hide her smile when she sidled up to Helena as they both filled their plates at breakfast.

"You scare me. It's so early and you're so perky. I do, however, covet that blouse."

Molly preened a little. "It's so nice to be around someone else who loves clothes as much as I do. Also? Fifty percent off. Sale rack. It was missing a button, but I can sew enough for that."

"Nice score. The color is good on you." It was true, Molly's coloring worked well with the deep blue of the silk.

"Thanks. One of these days I'm going to take you shopping with me so you can show me all the places I can find clothes with enough pockets to hide weapons."

Helena laughed. "You have Gage. You don't need to hide weapons."

"He does come in handy." Molly blushed. "I have no idea how you manage to look like you've walked out of an ad for designer clothes when I know you've got guns and knives on your person, and you'll still be able to run and kick people in the face."

They moved to the table and sipped coffee.

"It's a gift." Helena winked. "It is hard to find pants cut right for ease of face-kicking though. The thing is, magick is easier to use, I don't need special clothes for it and it's free. Unfortunately, when I'm doing four things at once, a nice face kick clears the decks for me to do other things and not run my power down. Plus? It's really satisfying to kick a jack-wagon in the face."

"What's going on between you and Faine? I'm sorry for my bluntness." Molly's laugh told Helena she was no such thing. "He's going to be lumbering down here with Gage any minute and I want to hear all the details."

Helena hoped she wasn't blushing. "Nothing really. I mean." She looked toward the door and, finding the hallway empty, she leaned closer to Molly and kept her voice down. "He kissed me. A few times now. I like him. He's ridiculously easy to look at, he's got fists the size of giant hams, his butt is spectacular and he doesn't try to do my job or treat me like a fragile flower. But, it's just a kiss or three. We don't have a lot of time to make it anything else, and that's okay because he kisses pretty damned well."

"I figured Tosh would make a move."

"You're the second person who's said that to me lately. He is a lovely man, handsome, powerful, he knows how to wear a suit and I bet he knows his way around a lady's business. But it's not me he's into. It's Delilah. He gets a dreamy look on his face when he's looking at her and thinks no one notices. Hello. My *job* to notice things." Tosh really was cute, the way he crushed on Delilah.

"He's always looking at your boobs. I just figured . . ."

Helena barked a laugh. "He's a dude, Molly. Plus, if I do say so myself, I have great boobs. But when Delilah talks he watches her mouth. He likes to touch her a lot and he finds any excuse he can to seek her opinion and to sit next to her. Boobs are one thing—he looks at yours too, though he's at least pretty wily and I figured no one noticed. But when a dude can't stop looking at a woman's mouth that's a whole different level of interest."

Molly's eyes widened and she nodded. "Oh my goddess, you're totally right! I've noted that he seems to listen to her well and now that you mention it, he does look at her mouth. Ha! I'm going to rub Gage's face in this so much!"

Helena laughed as she ate her bacon. "He used to get that line between his brows every time you and Tosh would talk. And then he'd be all, 'Oh, we're just casual, it's not a big deal' about you."

Molly rolled her eyes. "Lucky for him he's gotten past that point now."

"He is lucky. You're a good catch. You smooth him out when he gets ragged."

"Thank you. He's . . . well, I never expected him."

Helena figured that's how it always worked. "It's always the ones you *do* expect who fuck you over. You have your list—and I know you did, because we're alike that way—so you get the guy who is 9 of 10 on that list and you feel so accomplished. And he turns out to be wrong for you in every way."

"You lucked out. I mean, I don't know the whole story. But the broken engagement."

Helena liked Molly a great deal. They were alike in temperament, which helped just then when she decided to share.

"He hit on my sister. He was a fool and so was I for never seeing it. He was so perfect on the outside. He had a great job. He drove a great car. He was handsome, but not too handsome. His family was a great family. He stood up when my mother came into a room. My judgment is flawed, clearly, because I didn't see past any of it to who he really was."

Molly waved that away. "You were what? Twenty?"

"Twenty-three. I'd known him for years." He'd made her feel pretty.

"We all make mistakes. I'm sure Lark made him sorry he hit on her, and you did the right thing by breaking up right away."

"I'm assuming you heard the whole story."

"No, I mean, I knew he hit on Lark and she told you and

you broke things off and things were tense between you two for a while. But that's really it."

"Things weren't tense because I blamed her. I would never, ever have believed she'd betray me like that. He was mistaken in any attempt to claim that. I should thank him though because once he tried that it made it even easier to cart him to the curb and leave him there. He was a dick. *Is* a dick. I doubt he's changed." She chewed her bottom lip.

"You don't have to say more. But if you want to, I'm here. I like you, Helena. I consider you a friend and I'd like you to confide in me, but I understand it's hard."

"My judgment is bad. That's really it. Later, once he was gone and I looked back, I could see it all so clearly. All the stuff he did that was crappy. But I missed it during the relationship. Or maybe I ignored it. Either way?" Helena shrugged. "It was pretty obvious. I didn't care that he looked at other women. He's a dude, they all do. Most of them just do it well enough that we don't notice too much."

"That's respect."

"Exactly. I look too, for heaven's sake. But my sister. My. Sister. Lark never in a million years would do that to me. No matter what. I never doubted that. It just, it sucked that he'd try to betray me in any sense, but with the person I was closest to in the world. Hell, maybe I was jealous that he preferred her to me."

Molly sniffed. "He did it to hurt you. He chose her because it would hurt you if you found out. Yes, Lark is lovely and I quite enjoy her. But he didn't hit on her because he preferred her; he hit on her because he could, because he liked the thrill of the potential to get caught. And, I'd wager, he figured that even if she turned him down she'd never tell because Lark didn't want to hurt you."

Helena paused, thinking that over. "I guess I hadn't thought of it that way." She smiled, buttering her toast. "He seriously misjudged her if that was the case. She gave him a black eye and then she dragged him, by the ear mind you, to me and told me what he'd done. She was so outraged."

"He's clearly lucky to be walking without a permanent limp."

She smiled at Molly. "He is."

"Things are better now. Well, not like in the big picture, which seems to be full of bombings and shootings and that sort of thing. But Lark and I are close again. I've missed that. She's in Seattle though. But maybe . . . maybe it's better that way." Maybe Lark needed to be in a place where she could make her own decisions, which were clearly better than Helena's choices anyway.

"She misses you a great deal. And I know what you mean about things being better, some things anyway."

"Gage."

Molly nodded. "Yes. We had some rocky moments. But in the end, he comes to me. He accepts his feelings and he's at my side. I'm glad to have that. Especially now when things seem so dark. But back to Faine. Things are moving in a good direction. I like that because he's a sweetheart and you deserve someone like him."

"Well, don't go registering us at department stores or any- thing. Just a kiss. Things are way too busy for anything else, and to be totally honest with you, I don't know if I'm cut out for a relationship."

Molly thought this was hilarious. "Not a kiss. *Kisses.* Which is different. Also, he's not some twenty-four-year-old human. Lycians, like all alpha males"—she snorted—"they don't play around like that. He's four hundred. He and Simon, males like them, they know what they want and they will stop at nothing until it happens. He's not smitten with you. Not only smitten anyway. He wants you. He watches you work and it's clear he approves. I say ride that train because you need it."

Helena guffawed. "You're sort of dirty."

Molly winked. "Don't tell anyone."

"Ha. It'll be our secret."

Shortly after that they heard footsteps down the back stairs.

"Thanks for listening."

Molly shrugged. "I can say the same. It's what friends do.

Also? Can't wait to see the looks on their faces as they realize we've been talking and they don't know about what."

"My respect for you grows every time I see you." Helena winked and went back to her breakfast as Faine and Gage entered the room.

TOSH didn't see much more than Helena's back and Faine to her right. Big dude, and *so* not like any shifter he'd ever seen. Then again, it wasn't like he had a huge amount of experience with shifters.

Speaking of . . .

He looked to his left and caught Delilah's profile. "You all right?"

The crowd all around them surged, but he trusted his people and Helena's magick to hold it all back. When things were tense like this, he could sense Delilah's otherness. The wildness in her eyes, just beneath her skin. It made him a little sweaty. In a good way.

But just then she was angry.

"I don't spend ninety hours a week working for my constituents to have people call me names. Oh sure, we're supposed to have thick skins, but how much deeper can these assholes dig, huh?"

He wanted to brush the hair away from her forehead, wanted to ease her stress. God knew there was enough to go around just then. Raised voices buffeted them from all sides, though he was pleased to note it wasn't all negative. But Marlon knew how to pack a hearing room, he'd been doing it for years, and stupid, fearful people were easily manipulated.

Helena held a hand up, bringing them all to a stop. So serious, his friend. All business as she spoke to the capitol police officer who was at the side door where they'd entered the room. He nodded and Faine went first, two other guards followed and then Helena waved them forward.

"Remember the days when the worst thing about a hearing with Marlon Hayes was having to listen to his asshattery for an hour?"

Delilah giggled a moment and touched his shoulder. "Thanks for that. I needed the laugh."

They moved to their seats at the dais and Helena settled a few rows higher with several other aides and guards. She'd gone into some sort of watchfulness, still, seemingly calm and relaxed, but he knew better.

"Funny how *he* doesn't need bodyguards." Tosh lifted his chin in Senator Hayes' direction as the smarmy bastard glad-handed his way over. He shot a glare toward Molly, who was, this time, sitting on the panel with the rest of the experts.

"If he keeps pushing this agenda, he will. I've spoken with a lot of my people back home. Things are getting worse. If he pushes, he's going to get way more than he bargained for. They keep underestimating people they themselves refer to as monsters. Which is a tactical error of epic proportions." Delilah moved to her seat, just a row behind, and pulled her notes out.

It was and he knew it. The Others were done waiting around to be protected by their government and law enforcement. They were done being patient, and people like Marlon Hayes were too caught up in the power politics of appealing to the hateful fringe that they lost sight of what was really going on.

Toshio feared for everyone. For humans most of all, because they were afraid and he understood that fear. Understood, too, that witches like Molly Ryan were attempting to keep communication open between humans and Others to alleviate the fear.

Sadly, he also understood that it was humans like Hayes who were too eager to label that attempt at openness as some sort of manipulation. In the end, if humans didn't reject the hateful assurances of Marlon Hayes and PURITY that they only had to corral the Others and detain them, treat them like animals and the problem would disappear—if they didn't see it for the lie it was, it would be to their detriment.

There was no way. The humans could pass all the laws they wanted, but if they tried to enact them . . . well, there'd be open civil war with an enemy they could have easily kept as an ally. An enemy far more powerful than even hysteria pushers like Hayes could understand.

He blew out a breath and paid attention as the hearing was called to order.

HELENA kept an eye on the room as she listened to the hearing start up.

"This bill isn't about harming the nonhumans, as they've preached to you. This bill is about *protecting* natural-born Americans. Real Americans who are human. You saw what they did with their little speech threatening us all. This bill doesn't call to kill anyone. It will assure us all that these abominations are no longer allowed to live among us and hide their real agenda."

Real agenda? Goddess, Helena rarely lost her shit, but she found herself having to hold it together instead of walking over and popping this fool in the face. She'd been trying for months now to get the Others to remember not all humans were this way. But people like Hayes and PURITY's Carlo Powers were gaining traction, and that made it a lot harder to remember that.

It went on this way for some time longer until he finally shut up and it was Tosh's turn.

"Two generations ago, my grandfather served this country in World War Two. He did so while his family was being held in a camp. He did so despite the fact that his pregnant wife had been removed from their home and his business had been taken from him. My father was born in a relocation camp and my grandmother nearly died because of the lack of real medical facilities and care. All because his last name was Sato. Even after the war was over and my grandfather, who'd been decorated twice, returned home, he had to spend the next several years getting his family's life back on track because the government refused to return his business and he'd lost his home."

Hayes interrupted. "You see? His family listened and did what the government told them to. Even served in the military like his kind should have to prove their loyalty. What makes any of you think you're better than that?"

Sato interrupted, his face hard. "Senator Hayes misses the point, so let me be clearer. My kind, my family's kind, is American. *What happened to my family was wrong.* It was a miscarriage of justice. It was not what this country should be. My grandfather was better than the people who harmed his family, yes, but the harm was done. People died. People lost everything and it did not make us safer. It did not make us better people. The Domestic Safety Act does not make us better Americans. It does not make us safer. It takes Americans and strips them of their rights. It depersonalizes them and puts them in camps. Some of the provisions in this bill bear a horrifying similarity to things done to the Jews during World War Two in Germany. Tracking chips. Camps. Restricted movements. Removal of property and redistribution to the government. How long before we put them on trains and steal their gold watches? This bill is wrong."

Helena wanted to stand up and cheer.

But he wasn't done. "Two weeks ago a so-called expert panel was here at the capitol to testify about this bill. Not a single Other was on that panel. Worse, when an Other—Molly Ryan—was given time by members of this body, the room was hit with three bombs and Ms. Ryan was severely injured. Today we have an expert panel with actual experts on it and I'd like them to each introduce themselves. Once we've got that out of the way we can get to questions and answers."

The introductions went fine and then the questions from the senators started.

Lynn Reed, Carlo Powers' second-in-command nationwide, was on the panel, just a few seats down from Molly. Helena caught the shift in her energy, the darkness inside her gut as she spoke. There was a great deal of hate, but more than that, a sheer greed for power. If it wasn't Others, this woman would be screeching about something else. She liked scaring people, liked using fear as her cudgel to whip folks into a frenzy.

"The proof is that these monsters lived next door to us for generations and never once revealed themselves until they brought down some sort of retribution on their heads. This thing that killed so many of them was divine punishment for their evil. Whatever pact they made to keep the remaining ones safe is what we need to know. Why haven't they told us about this pact?"

Molly sighed heavily. "We haven't told you because there is no pact. No divine retribution for existing. What happened to us—to us and not you—was an ancient power. It was not about punishment. It fed on our magickal energy and we were able to defeat it, but not without a heavy cost. It has nothing to do with humans at all. And nothing to do with this bill, so if we could get back to the subject at hand, that would be a better use of our time."

"You don't get to decide what we talk about." Marlon Hayes sneered at Molly.

Sato interrupted. "The hearing is regarding the Domestic Safety Act. As a matter of fact, it's the topic and it's quite helpful if we stick to that. We were all sent here to do a job. The people's business. To get sidetracked by all this other stuff is not helpful. Nor is it the people's business. So if we can get back to the topic at hand, please."

Hayes turned, red faced. "You're insulting Ms. Reed when she's answering a question."

"That's enough, Marlon. The question was asked, we got a bunch of nonsense. Her time is up and so is yours. Moving on." Delilah Sperry narrowed her gaze, daring Hayes to continue.

Lynn Reed spoke from the table. "You're going to spend eternity in hell, Delilah Sperry. I don't have to listen to you."

Delilah waved a hand, appearing bored. "That's Senator Sperry to you." But Helena saw her energy, knew she choked back rage. Her wolf pressed against the woman's skin, but she held it together.

"My constituents voted for me knowing I was a werewolf. As for eternity, mind your own and get your nose out of mine. Now, back to the question. Ms. Ryan, can you please address the issue of registration and how it would impact the witches in your Clan?"

Molly nodded once and smoothly dove in. Any time Reed tried to interrupt her she simply continued to speak and Helena thought a few times she might have even used her magick to hold the floor. But if she had, Molly was too damned good to get caught, so good Reed had no idea. Which was a positive thing because heaven knew if she thought she was being hexed to shut the hell up, she'd flip out.

"The issue is," Reed spoke again at the end of the hearing, "we don't know that they haven't been manipulating us all along. What if they decide to use their magic to harm us? Make us do something wrong? Maybe they've done that since the beginning. We have no proof they haven't."

Molly's mouth tightened, but she didn't interrupt and Helena wanted to laugh, knowing her friend was annoyed.

"I can only refer you back to reality. The reality where we're sitting here in a room where some of you want to put us in concentration camps. If we had the ability to make you all our puppets, why would we allow people to bomb our schools and homes? Why would we sit here and listen to this hateful drivel when we could just use our power and make you do whatever we wish?"

"You can't prove you don't."

What was this, third grade?

"You can't prove a negative. It's impossible and it makes me wonder what you're getting out of scaring people and stirring all this violence." This from Delilah.

"I don't have to answer to you and your people."

"My people? United States senators?"

The time was up. Many of the senators, including Sato, needed to be in other hearings, so it broke quickly, if not without some verbal sparring.

Since it was no longer Other business and since Sato had a really busy schedule, his security people took over and Helena headed down to where Molly stood speaking with Cade Warden and Faine.

Lynn Reed hung at the outer edges of the group, watching through narrowed eyes as she waited on Hayes to approach her.

Interesting dynamic there.

"Nicely done, Ms. Ryan." Helena bowed slightly. "Ready? You have a few hours free and then it's to the interview." She didn't say more than that. Although she'd used some magick to keep what she said quiet, she didn't want to risk Molly's safety. The more exposure she had to PURITY and the people at the top, the more she was convinced they were behind the major attacks. Not just the low-ranked idiots who got gung ho, but the very top.

Molly looked back over her shoulder at Reed, who emanated so much negative energy it was palpable, even at a distance.

"Yes, I'm done here."

"Brace yourselves. We need to go out that way and the hallway looks packed." Gage came back from the doors where he'd peeked out.

"Absurd that we can't be safe in the halls of Congress, for heaven's sake." Molly sent a glare Hayes' way, but he was too busy slavering all over Reed to notice.

Helena moved forward. "Faine and I will take point. Gage, you're on Molly." They began to move, the rest of her crew taking on their own places to guard the rest of the group.

The hall outside was always loud, Helena figured. Daily work in Congress would be full of contentious issues as well as mundane stuff. Staffers moved through the crowds, some on phones, some heatedly talking amongst themselves. There were protesters for every cause imaginable on their way to hearing rooms.

Normally she'd have found it fascinating. Now she just found it distracting and worrisome. A lot of people to keep an eye on. A lot of energy to try to wade through to get past the normal frustration and anger at issues not related to them in any way.

She put out a low heat energy field around herself and Faine. He cut his gaze to her quickly and then was back on the job once he'd ascertained there wasn't a problem. She'd experimented with something similar a few days before and it seemed to keep humans back. She didn't need to hurt anyone; she just wanted to keep a space bubble around their group.

Molly moved slow because she was still on crutches and Helena didn't want her jostled.

When they got to the main doors leading outside it was a whole new level of challenge. Several hundred people had gathered on the steps. Some holding signs with the usual and lame "God hates werewolves/witches/Others" along with the gamut of abomination, warnings of danger and violence, that sort of thing.

A counter-protest was just steps away, meeting at the edges. In some places there seemed to be earnest discussion and debate, but in others there was jostling, angry, raised voices and the chance for far worse than words and shoving.

So much potential for things to go bad in so many ways. She spoke to Faine, knowing that even with the din all around he'd hear her.

"Faine, I'm going to need you to pick Molly up so we can move quickly. Gage, you're on them. I'm going to clear a path."

Several of the Weres who'd accompanied Cade Warden showed up, ready to follow her lead. She explained what she needed and even Molly simply sighed and let Faine pick her up. Gage started to argue, but Helena lifted a brow.

"I'm not arguing with your orders. I wanted to tell you something bad is coming. I can feel it."

She knew his gift was a sort of intuitive foresight of intention. If he felt something, it was out there and it was her job to deal with it.

She nodded. "Keep tight. Keep alert."

Helena adjusted her spell, speaking under her breath to make the field around them a little larger and a little hotter. She added an aversion spell to overlay it. Nothing that would create an emotional aversion, but enough of a hint to back up and let them pass.

Since the Magister it had seemed a lot easier to bend her magick to her will. One positive from all that negative, she supposed.

She scanned the crowd as they went, her hands free should she need to repel anyone or use her weapons.

Which was good because the moment the crowd recognized them, the angry voices raised and the crowd turned to face them. Helena cut toward the side, making a hole for the group. Her spell held and she only needed to push people back twice, more due to crowd surge than anything else.

Helena was glad she'd called ahead for the cars to be brought for them. Having to wait at the curb for their ride would have only exposed them to danger for longer.

They idled nearby. Safe harbor. She hustled the group in that direction, scanning the crowd for weapons, people's faces for signs of violence, the air all around for any signs of impending negative action.

Later, she figured she was so busy doing that, she'd missed the sick feeling emanating from the vehicle in front of her until a split second before the air sucked from all around them and then blew outward in a hot wave.

Time slowed as Helena moved to respond, trusting Faine to deal with Molly as she called her magick fast and hard, yanking it from the air around her and the ground at her feet. It filled her instantly in a painful slice as she managed it. As she used her magick to push back against the explosion, to repel the flaming metal and burning tires.

Dimly she realized the car behind it had also blown and she managed her magick to repel it as well.

It filled her, raw power. Bright and searing hot. Her filters were down so she could take in as much as she could as fast as possible. It roared through her, responding to her will, but she knew enough to understand that could change.

So much magick she knew she'd have trouble regulating it, keeping it from going wild and burning her to the bone. But she needed all she could get to keep her people, and the crowd behind her, safe from all the flying wreckage.

She held it even as she tasted blood and her nose began to drip. Her skin burned and as the energy around her from the bomb died down, she shoved it all away, back to the twisted metal, which groaned as she hit the pavement on her knees, the blood from her nose and mouth staining the front of her shirt.

Damn it. That much blood would never come out and she really loved that blouse.

Her vision grayed at the edges as she swayed, fighting consciousness and beginning to lose.

She heard Faine roar and then snarl. "Shit. Shit! Helena?"

Faine had been watching the crowd, taking care not to hold Molly too tightly, not to bump her casts or injure her. And then he turned, noting Helena's body language had stiffened, her focus shifted to the curb where the vehicles were.

Helena was right in front of the vehicle and she shouted for them to get down and he felt the air suck away and then the taste of her magick as she pulled it from all around. He'd covered Molly with his body, expecting the blow of the flaming wreckage, but instead he'd watched as Helena had shouted in a language he rarely heard, her hands drawing runes as she wove the spell. He knew channeling that much power was dangerous for anyone, a fact underlined when her nose started to bleed.

He heard Gage shouting at people to get back, heard the panic behind him as humans scattered. All he could do was watch, helpless as she took all that power and shoved it at the explosion.

Molly spoke to him quietly. "She'll be all right. She's strong." But her words were nearly a question. Not quite, but close enough that it only scared him more.

He'd only held himself in place because he knew that if he'd disturbed Helena she could have lost control of her magick. And his job was Molly right then. He'd promised Helena and he couldn't break that promise.

But when Helena dropped to her knees and pitched forward, blood all over her face, he made sure Gage was there with Molly before he exploded up, running to her. He scooped Helena into his arms as the sounds of sirens began to break through the wall of power she'd kept between the car and the crowd.

He shook so fucking hard it was a challenge to stand, but he did, holding her close, breathing her in until he was sure she was alive and would be all right. Her blood was everywhere, freaking him out.

"Damn it, Helena Jaansen, you will open those eyes right this moment. You're scaring me." He gave her his best officer-issuing-orders voice and hoped the fear wasn't showing.

Her eyes fluttered open, unfocused at first, but then she seemed to grasp consciousness with a gasp. "Is everyone all right?"

He growled. "Everyone but you, brown eyes. What the fuck do you think you're doing?"

She sighed, turning her face into his chest. "Not failing."

Chapter 8

"**WE** need to get her help." He turned to Gage, still holding Helena.

Gage held his hands up, approaching slowly, understanding exactly what it meant to be wild with the need to protect the woman you loved. "When the ambulance arrives, we'll send her first. You go with her."

Helena stirred, trying to get down and he held her tighter.

"Stop that."

"So imperious." She blinked. So slowly he found his panic fighting to return. "Stop growling. I'm all right. The police are going to want to question us all. And I'm not leaving the scene."

"I'm taking over the team." Gage sighed. "Temporarily. Helena, you're covered in blood. You've burned yourself out handling that much power at once. I don't even know what the hell you just did, but it had to have fried your circuits." He said the last very quietly and Faine realized he wasn't the only one who'd been amazed at what Helena had done.

"In case you haven't noticed, a riot is brewing. We need to get Molly out of here, along with the rest of the group. We need to be sure Tosh, Delilah and Parrish Carroll are all okay, along with all the Others who work here at the capitol."

"Caspar has already gotten on making sure Sato and everyone else is all right. *You* are not all right."

"I've called to have a car sent over immediately." Before Helena could argue with Gage any further, Cade Warden stepped forward. "Ms. Jaansen, I'm in your debt for what you just did. I can see the physical toll as well. How about we get you back to the house where you can rest? Then you can have your needs tended by Others instead of humans."

"That's probably best." Gage nodded.

Faine held her tighter. "Unless she needs a hospital, in which case, your need for privacy can be hanged. You're not going to sacrifice her for that. I won't allow it."

Things got very still for long moments. Even Helena stopped trying to move. Cade's brow rose, but a smile fought at the corner of his mouth. Yes, yes, Faine knew he'd made a declaration on several levels, but he didn't care. There was no way he'd allow Helena's needs to be shunted to the side.

"I'd never allow that either." Gage put an arm around Molly's shoulders. "She's my friend and my boss. But she'll be more comfortable in private, and treated by our own people. If it turns out she needs more care, we'll get it for her. I swear to you."

Agent Anderson came jogging over along with several other FBI agents and cops. The rest fanned out, immediately getting to work. "Jesus. Is everyone all right?"

Helena coughed on the poisonous black smoke from the wreckage and Faine stepped away so she could breathe easier, Anderson following as he did.

"Put me down," Helena ordered. But he heard the pain in her words and ignored her.

"Agent Anderson, as you can see, Ms. Jaansen was injured while she protected the crowd from the explosion. She needs to be back at the home we're staying in so she can rest. We need to get all our people out of here." Faine's jaw was clenched so tight he was sure it creaked when he spoke.

Anderson nodded, paling as he took Helena in. "Come on.

We'll talk to you all while we drive you over. Do we need to stop at the hospital?"

"I don't need a doctor."

Faine didn't know if he agreed with that point, but for the time being he let it go because he wanted her out of there and that was happening.

"Molly and Gage first." Helena gave him a look that dared him to argue. "Be sure she doesn't need to go to the hospital. She's still healing from the last time."

"*She's* fine and she will be very cross with you if you don't get your butt into that car right now." Molly gave Helena a stern look and Helena snorted.

"It's my job to protect you."

"And you did." Emotion bled into Molly's voice. "You did. Please. For me?"

That seemed to do the trick and she allowed herself to be loaded into one of the SUVs Cade Warden had brought to the curb.

Anderson spoke to one of the officers on the scene and he loaded in with them, one of his cars following the group.

"You can wait until she's resting before you question her."

Anderson sent him a look but Faine just ignored it. He'd done all the order taking he was going to for the time being. Helena was fragile in his arms, bloody, trembling, the glass shimmering in her hair, and he had to clamp down the urge to let his beast take over and rampage through that crowd back there to find who did this.

Helena started speaking. "I don't know much. We came out from the hearing. I'd called about ten minutes before to have the cars brought around." Her face changed. "Goddess, the drivers. Someone needs to check to see if they're—"

Anderson interrupted. "My people are on the scene now. I'll let you know what we find. But you can't do anything about it. Just relax and keep talking."

"The protesters were yelling, shoving. I was focused on that. I missed the signs until I was too close. Until we were all too close."

Faine saw that she took it personally. As if it were her fault.

"Christ, Helena. You're one person. You were dealing with the most emergent threat, all those people shoving around." Gage held Molly's hand like he planned to never let her go.

"I should have seen it. It's my job." Helena's words were lost in a flurry of hacking coughs. Anderson handed her a moistened handkerchief. She continued coughing until Faine's ribs hurt just listening to it.

"The smoke is toxic. It's better out than inside you." Anderson shrugged at Faine's look. "I've worked more than my fair share of bomb scenes."

She took a drink from a bottle of cold water. "I saw something off. Felt it. But then the air sort of sucked away. I think the bomb was under the passenger side, front. That's where the blast seemed to come from."

"You should have died, being that close. Your, um, powers protected you?"

Gage interrupted. "Her powers protected *everyone* all around us. She . . . Witches have reservoirs of power, she pulled hers up too fast, she did it to shove as much as she could back at the blast to protect everyone. Not just our people, but the humans on those steps. That sort of thing is harmful. She's bleeding because she burst capillaries with the exertion. She needs to rest. To restore her magick and let her body heal itself."

Faine wanted to kiss Gage for that defense of Helena.

"Thank you. For what you did. You may not hear it from humans, though it's clear you were a hero today. But you'll hear it from me." Anderson leaned forward to touch Helena's knee and before he knew it, Faine found himself cutting off a possessive growl at the human male.

Helena raised a brow even in her exhausted state. He'd have to talk with her. Later, when she wasn't on the verge of collapse.

ONCE Anderson had gone, Molly tutted and fussed while Gage looked on, amused. "You need to get cleaned up. I've laid out a robe in the bathroom. Are you sure you don't want to go to the hospital? They have Others on staff. I know this from the last time we were bombed here." Molly handed her the glass of juice Helena had already half drained. She obediently finished it.

She returned in less than a minute with more juice and pushed it Helena's way.

"Molly, you know I adore you, but girl, back up or I am going to lose my mind." Helena waved her away.

"Fine. But I'm calling your mother to see who we can speak to around here who will help you get yourself recharged." Molly sniffed and before Helena could argue, she left the room.

"What did you do?" Gage hefted himself up onto the bathroom counter as Helena attempted to clean her face.

Faine sighed and took the cloth from her, washing the soot away and getting it wet again. He gently pushed her hands back. "Hush and let me work. I've been dressing field wounds longer than witches have been in the New World."

She rolled her eyes, but held still as he dabbed at her skin.

"What do you mean? I protected you all, that's my job."

Gage blew out a breath. "I have never seen a spell like that, Helena. Ever."

"Oh. That. Well, all right, I suppose you've experienced your magick building, growing, since the Magister, right?"

Gage nodded.

"Since I was young, a big part of my power has been sort of intuitive. I haven't had to learn spells the same way others do. I just sort of knew what I needed and then I did it. Since the Magister, my magick has . . . leapt to me in a wholly new way. It's easier to call it no matter the place. But there are less filters so it comes hard and fast unless I regulate it. I knew I needed a lot to hold that energy from the blast back. There's no Font here like there is in Gennessee or Owen territory and I was worried about siphoning from any witches around me. So I yanked it hard from the air and the earth. It was so much."

Faine grimaced. "Are you going to be all right? Did you do permanent damage?"

"No, I'll be fine. I'm crispy and if I had to do any major magick just now I'd be fucked. But rest will restore me."

"More than that, how did you do it? Sure, you can call more power, but that spell was awe-inspiring. You . . . what?"

"I just . . . I knew I needed to block the blast somehow. I didn't have a physical shield or a wall to hide behind. It occurred to me that it was physics, that's all magick is anyway. I just used energy to push back at the energy of the blast. The opposite of the wave from the explosion so it repelled. I don't know if I could do it again in the same way, only that if I had to do something similar in the future, I could."

"Can you teach me? Do you think it could stop a bullet?"

"I don't know about a bullet. But I think I can help you visualize a wall of energy. I don't know your gifts that well and like I said, it's not spellwork, not completely. I knitted something together on the fly but that was to focus my power in one spot and keep it from feeding back and harming me."

"You mean like bleeding from the nose and mouth?" Faine wanted to shake her and order her to never, ever do such a thing again. But he knew she would. And that she could was apparently a big deal. She was a warrior like he was. Just a few days ago he accepted it, but now the stakes were higher, and his feelings? Well, they'd adjusted and deepened, which made it far more difficult to accept that she'd put herself in danger.

"When I was young I got nosebleeds all the time. My dad says it's because I have a poor sense of moderation." Her smile was wry and he sighed, charmed.

"I think I can teach you to spool the power better. Still quickly, but with more control." Gage nodded. "As for my gifts? They've been growing, as yours seem to have. I can sense intent. I knew there was danger in that crowd. Mortal danger. But I couldn't see it as the cars."

"You both chose the obvious dangers and focused, which is the way it should be. There are so many things to constantly be aware of, you can only examine so many at once." Faine shrugged. It was true. Yes, they'd missed the cars being a possible threat, but in their place he'd have done the same. He *had* done the same.

"I need to check in with the people at the garage here. I instituted a policy and it's been in place for months now. All vehicles are monitored in the garage and they're examined on entry and exit for physical issues as well as spellwork that isn't mine or anyone else's from my team."

Faine sighed; the female was flat-out insane. "Why don't you take a shower first? Then you can eat out in the garden and sleep. You can call and bark orders at people and have them brought here while you eat." She started to argue and he held a hand up. "I'm saying you're the leader of this team. You will be needed again, as will your magick. You're depleted right now, you said so yourself. So get back to 100 percent first and then get back out there. You can deal with the car and your people while you handle getting yourself taken care of."

Gage nodded. "He's right. Don't make me go over your head and have The Gennessee overrule you."

"Molly has to stay in for the rest of the day then. And I need you to call Tosh's office to be sure he's all right, as well as any Others who work at the capitol."

Gage nodded. "We can do that." He hopped down and headed for the door. "You amazed me today. I've seen some amazing magick—after all, I was there watching Meriel and her mother stop the Magister. What you did today ranks up there."

Helena blushed as he left the room.

"Do you need help showering?" Faine asked.

One of her brows went up. "You offering?"

"Don't poke at me right now. I'm not all right. My beast is more agitated than the man."

She paused, he could tell, trying to figure out what to say. "I'm fine, thank you for offering. I can stand long enough to take a shower. But if you would ask the chef to make me something high in protein and green vegetables, I'd appreciate that."

He sucked in a breath but didn't stop himself from pressing a kiss to her forehead. When she asked for his help it always did things to his system. "I'll be listening for you. Just yell if you need help. I mean it."

She nodded and he left before he could say or do anything else.

Chapter 9

SHE knew Lark would call. The only surprise was how long it took. She'd showered, spoken with her team about the car, mourned two who'd been killed, eaten, been fussed over by Faine and Molly and escaped finally by going to sit out in the middle of the raised beds in the garden to recharge.

She'd scowled everyone away and finally had returned inside, finding a small sitting room and settling on a couch with a blanket, reading her mail and taking calls.

Helena answered her sister's call with, "I'm all right."

"The only reason I am not on a plane to you right now is because of that. Gage has been keeping me updated but I figured you'd had long enough and I needed to hear your voice."

Helena smiled, touched at that.

"Christ, Hellie, what the hell? Car bombs? Do you think we should pull the plug and bring people home?"

"I'm going to take the next few hours to think on that. I ate some lunch and sat in the garden for an hour. My nose isn't bleeding anymore and my teeth haven't fallen out, so I'm counting that as a win."

"Don't joke. This is serious. You could have died." Lark's voice was stern, but the fear bled through.

"Yeah, like when you got shot. Twice. Saving the world."

"Goddamn, we're fucking awesome, huh?" Tension broken, Lark soldiered on. "What's the situation with the cars? I know there is simply no way you didn't have a process in place to check the undercarriage of any and all vehicles you use."

"I do." Though it was nice that her sister knew that of her. "There were two SUVs. Both were checked thoroughly before they left here. Both were in a secure garage. I went through the security footage for the last twenty-four hours and there's nothing. No one approached either vehicle until this morning when we left and then when they came back they were checked and checked again when they left to retrieve us. There's a checkpoint at the gates at the capitol too and the cars were clear."

"What the fuck?"

"Somewhere between those gates and the drive near the building where we were at the hearing our drivers were stopped, shot in the head, left in a Dumpster and the attackers took over. There are cameras *everywhere* but, conveniently, several were out of commission for a few hours today." The anger rushed through her again at the thought.

"Are you kidding me?"

"They don't care. I wanted to hold out as long as I could, you know? A lot of humans are good people like Tosh. But this other stuff? Bombings and attacks and bills to put us in camps? That's not right, damn it. Cameras being turned off so my drivers could be murdered? It's like a movie plot, for god's sake!"

Lark sighed heavily. "We receive death threats on a daily basis now. It's . . . I've forgotten what it was like before."

Helena understood. She nearly had too.

"Both those men, humans according to Anderson, were killed in the blast. The second car was also bombed, but half the vest he wore malfunctioned so the blast wasn't as large. They'd moved to the passenger seat to get closer to us when we came down to load everyone in. I suppose we should be thankful they detonated before I reached the door."

"I hate this. *Hate it*. Gage told me you pulled some mighty magick out of your tool bag today. He said he'd never seen anything like it and that you nearly fried yourself doing it."

"Honestly? I don't know where it came from. Only that it happened. I'm glad for it and a headache is a price I'm willing to pay for that result."

"Yeah? And if you'd died?"

"It's my job to protect people. If that means I die doing it, well, I signed on for that. You know you'd do better at this than me, but there's no one else so I'm doing the best I can."

"What the hell are you talking about? Do you really think that? That I'd believe anyone was better suited for this job than you? You're the *only* one I trust to oversee it all."

Helena swallowed hard. "Lark, that's not the best idea."

Her sister cursed beneath her breath. "Oh shut up. If you're going to bring up the haven thing, just stop."

"You can pretend it doesn't matter, but it was my decision to send the witches to the havens. And that got them killed. All those lives in my hands and they're dead."

"It wasn't the choice that killed them, Helena. What happened was so much beyond what any of us could combat. We're all of us fucking treading water here."

When the Magister's attacks got worse, and more and more Others were turning up missing and dead, The Gennessee called together the Full Council and they decided to send the most vulnerable witches in the Clan to the havens. Havens were safe spots, well away from the city, guarded. Helena had been the deciding vote to send the witches—supposedly—out of harm's way. Until one of the smaller havens in Indio had been discovered and all twenty-two witches there, including five children, had disappeared.

One glaring fact remained. "But *you* didn't make that choice."

Lark sucked in a breath. "I could have, though. *It was a perfectly reasonable choice to make.* It could have easily been me. You didn't make the wrong choice. Hell, how many Others died when the Magister manifested? Huh? I didn't stop it in time. We lost a lot of people, Helena. We did the best we could. You and me, we had the weight of all those lives on our shoulders and we did all we could with what we had."

And it hadn't been enough. Helena had to live with that knowledge every day.

Lark broke into her thoughts. "I know we haven't had enough time to talk about all this stuff. We need to. But I want to be face-to-face when we do. I want to be able to knock out a few bottles of wine and hash everything out. That's not happening anytime soon, but it will. Just know that. In the meantime, you have to stop blaming yourself for what happened at the haven. You are the person I trust more than anyone else to do this. I mean that."

Tears came, surprising her. All the hard-won walls she'd built against the well of emotion and fear crumbled at the edges. *Oh goddess, not now.* She just couldn't. Didn't want to talk about the haven thing anymore. There was nothing to be done about it. It was over and the shame of her failure would hopefully make her a better hunter. "I'll call you when I learn more. Rebecca is having a phone conference with Meriel and some of the other witches about whether or not continuing this road show is viable. I'm sure you'll hear when I do, but I'll check in when I know anything."

Lark paused and Helena knew she wanted to say more. But thankfully, she didn't. "All right. I love you. Please be safe."

"I love you too." She hung up and with a groan, heaved herself up from the couch. She had work to do.

Faine seemed to appear out of nowhere, scowling at her and blocking her exit from the room. "Sit back down. What can I get for you?"

"I need to work."

"You need to rest."

"You're not the boss of me."

"Thank heavens. I can't imagine what a shitty job that would be. You're disobedient and reckless and you take on far more than you're responsible for."

She didn't know how it happened, but suddenly she found herself gasping on a sob and a flood of tears.

He softened, a sad smile marking his lips. "Come on." He

took her hand and led her to her room, pulling her blankets back. "In."

"Please go away." She tried to pull the covers up over her head, but he lay down next to her, pinning her in place with the bed coverings, the heat of him soothing as well as discomfiting.

"I'm not going anywhere. Just let it go. Get it all out." He settled in, pulling her into his arms. The power of it, of letting go and being taken care of, soothed, was nearly overwhelming. And then his magick rose, teasing hers just when she wasn't sure she was capable of even the most basic of spells.

She didn't have the energy to hold him back and hold herself together at the same time. His power was warm and wild, it seemed to rush through her veins, teasing her senses, enticing, seducing.

She opened her eyes to peek at him and found him staring at her, a look of wonder stamped on his features.

"I never expected you."

"What?" She wiped her face with the edge of her sleeve. No doubt she was red and puffy and her hair was a mess because she had jammed it into a ponytail after her shower.

"You're more than I ever imagined you'd be." He snorted, leaning close to kiss each eyelid. "So tender. You take so much on and you do it with such power and ability that no one would know how fragile you are just underneath."

"Great. On top of everything else, I'm fragile."

"*No*. Helena, you're magnificent. You're the finest female I have ever beheld in my entire existence. And believe me, I've seen a lot in many worlds. You are strong. Righteous. Courageous. Today, you nearly killed me when you pulled that spell together. But you did it and you did it because that's what you do. You protected your people and even those humans who'd just been insulting you because you're that person."

She closed her eyes, willing the newly sprung tears to go away.

"It is all right to cry sometimes. You don't need to hide in the shower, or pretend to be above it. It doesn't make you less of a warrior."

Her eyes snapped open.

"Yes, I heard you that night at my house. And it broke my heart because you are so strong and yet, you don't think you can lean on anyone else. Just for a little while." He tipped her chin so she was looking into his eyes. "You can lean on me. You can cry and know I respect you. You can cry and know I've fallen apart a little after a battle like the one you've been waging for months. Everyone has to break a little or they'll break all the way."

"Why?"

He thumbed her tears away and she was instantly sorry she'd asked because she wasn't sure she could handle the answer.

"I think you know. But that's all right, I'll give you the words because I need to say them out loud. Make my declaration."

Declaration?

He laughed at her reaction. "Scared?"

"You're sort of scary."

His grin made her less afraid of what he'd say and more interested in what he'd look like naked.

"I'm very scary. But not to you. I want you to lean on me because *I want you*. I want all of you, Helena Jaansen. Since the first time I met you I knew you were special. And everything I've seen since has only confirmed that. I thought it was a passing fancy at first. You're beautiful and powerful. A male like me finds those qualities fairly irresistible." He grinned again and she groaned.

He stole a kiss and with it her breath.

"I was in Seattle and with Molly while you had your own job to do, but then our paths kept crossing. And I got to know you. I saw through your prickly demeanor and the quite frankly bizarre way you keep all your clothes and shoes color coordinated and arranged according to length, height, whatever. You're trying to control things in a world utterly out of control. And you are doing it with all your might and that, Helena, is why I cannot get you out of my head. You are singular. You are the female I was meant to find and love."

"*Love?* Listen here, buster, I have a horrible track record with love. Also I've only known you a few months."

"That witch you were engaged to was a fool. It doesn't mean you have a horrible track record. It means you hadn't found the right male until now. As far as being too soon to love you? Pah."

She laughed, unable to resist being delighted. "Pah?"

"Pah." He nodded his head once. "You're a thing of light and magick. You are not human. Don't cling to what they can't see because they refuse to look with something other than their eyes. I'm not human. I'm not young or inexperienced either. I've loved before. And that love wasn't anything compared to what you make me feel every time I think about you. Months I've watched you fight. I've watched you give orders. I've watched you make passionate arguments about things you believed in. I've watched you protect and defend and I've watched you break apart when you couldn't save people. It's so intimate, that glimpse I get every once in a while when your defenses are down and you let me in. I know what I feel. I know what I want. I want you. And I know you want me. I know how you watch me. I tasted your desire when you kissed me. Each time you've kissed me. There's no reason to pretend otherwise. It's a waste of time."

She struggled to keep up. Struggled to make sense of how she felt. Of the truth in his words and her bone-deep fear that if she trusted them she'd end up hurt far worse than anything she'd ever felt before.

Fear that she'd fail at this like she'd failed those witches at the haven.

He *was* different. On every level. She knew from Lark that Lycian males put the alpha in alpha male. That was a lot to manage, even if it came in a package that looked as good as the one looming over her, blanketing her in all those feel-good hormones that were designed to part a girl from her underpants.

"You can't run scared from me, you know. First, you're too dominant for that. Second, you're too honest for it. Third, I'm a predator and that only makes you hotter to me." A flash of his grin and though she was going to groan she only managed a breathy sound. "Last, you're a highly sensual being and you know just exactly how it will be between us physically."

Her heart stuttered as he traced a fingertip down her chest, between her breasts, down to her belly button, circling it slowly.

"And because you feel it too. This magnetic thing between us. This thread that pulls us together each time we're near each other."

She opened her mouth to deny it but couldn't. She was drawn to him on so many levels.

His smile changed and tightened things low in her belly. "I locked the door. And I think I know something else that will help you get your energy back up."

She gulped.

"I know this momentary reprieve from your bossiness is just that—temporary. So I figure it's best to divest you of your clothing before you start arguing."

Chapter 10

HE waited to see if she was on board and she didn't argue, thank the heavens.

She was hurt and he wanted to go slow, reined himself in the best he could as he got to his knees and started to pull his shirt off.

But he should have known Helena would have her own ideas. Quicker than he'd expected, she grabbed his wrist, moving to get to her knees facing him. "No. I want to."

She leaned in close, breathing him in at his neck, sending gooseflesh skittering over his skin. After he'd laid himself bare before her, after he'd seen those walls of hers break and the tears come, he needed this more than he could articulate. Needed to connect with her on a whole new level.

"Have at it." Even to his own ears, his words were breathy and a little shaky. She rendered him into a nervous, needy mass. Even with Lydia it hadn't been like this.

She pulled his shirt up and off, tossing it to the side, skimming her palms over his chest. "I love these." She pressed kisses over his marks. "Four hundred years of your life, all over your skin."

With each major achievement in a Lycian's life, he or she received ink from the family elders, turning each Lycian into a walking record of their honor and service. He and his siblings were the most marked in Lycia other than their father. He wore his skin with a great deal of pride. That she found it beautiful only made him want to preen for her gaze.

That she *understood* just how much it meant made him rejoice that he'd found this female.

She traced over the trails of ink. Over dates and words, over animals and maps, kissing here and there as she did. It was difficult not to push her back and feast on her skin, but he managed to hold still, his beast taking over and standing proudly for her to examine him.

"Your body is ridiculous." She looked up into his gaze, a smile marking her lips.

He didn't resist the urge to dip and take a taste of her mouth, his fingers sliding through her hair, taking it down from the ponytail. He breathed her in, the scent of her hair, of her skin, of everything that made her. His beast stirred, satisfied, but demanding more.

"Ridiculous bad or ridiculous good?"

She laughed, her head tipping back, and he feasted on the line of her neck, warm and supple skin, heavy with her scent and the tang of her magick.

"So, even four-hundred-year-old males who look like you do fish for compliments?"

"Only from the most beautiful women in the world."

He unbuttoned her blouse and eased it away from her body, pausing to take in the sight of the pale silk camisole she wore underneath. "You have marks too?" He figured she would. He knew her sister had them; he'd seen them when she'd come to Lycia for the binding ceremony and had worn a backless gown.

She hummed her delight as he kissed her shoulders and over to her neck. "Yes. Lark and I wanted to honor all the big moments. It sort of became a competition to see who got what tattoo first."

"You and your sister are very competitive." He brushed his fingertips over a scar on her side and another on her upper arm.

"Rogue wolf," she gasped as he licked over the inside of her arm, at the elbow.

"And where is that wolf today?"

"Nowhere."

He smiled against her skin. So fierce. "You should probably know up front just how sexy I find it when you say such things."

He pulled the right strap down, kissing to her elbow, then followed up with the left. But he leaned back, speechless after he'd pulled the camisole free of her body and she knelt there, her upper body in nothing but her bra. And the beginnings of a wash of bruises. He'd be angry about that later.

"We've competed at everything I can remember since we were little kids. Never in a mean-spirited way. I've always felt that we push each other to be our best. Sometimes we manage to do it right."

"You and I are going to have to discuss this guilt you seem to carry over things you can't possibly really be guilty for. After."

His annoyance at her self-blame dissolved like smoke as he took her in. Long and lean, fit. Layers of muscle defined her upper arms. Her tits were freaking magnificent in a barely there wisp of a pale blue bra.

"I don't say a lot, but fifty thousand pages of poetry could be written about you."

The harsher edges of need on her features eased into a flattered smile. And a blush.

"Do you know I can smell you when you blush?" He slid his thumbs over her nipples through the bra and she arched into his touch.

"Huh?"

He popped the hooks at the back and removed the bra, exposing all that glorious tawny skin to his gaze. "Am I distracting you?" He gently laid her back on the bed, pulling the soft pants from her long-as-sin legs. Her panties were in the boy-short style, accentuating her belly and thighs and most likely her ass.

But she'd have to stand up for him to see and he didn't want that. Not right then. He pulled her underpants from her, leaving her totally naked.

"When you blush it heats your skin and your scent rises. I've never smelled anything like you before. Your magick smells like snowflakes and pomegranate. And sex. Heaven help me, when you heat up my beast wants to drop to his knees and worship you."

"Wow, you're lethal with your mouth."

He laughed, loving the way her gaze never left his hands at his waistband as he unbuttoned and unzipped his jeans and shimmied from them and his shorts.

"I haven't even begun to show you just how talented I am with my mouth."

She sucked in a breath. "I can't wait."

Helena knew, somewhere in the back of her mind, the place she was actively ignoring, that having sex with Faine was a monumentally bad idea.

But he was too much. Big and tall, broad shouldered. Covered in ink and muscles and tight skin. She sighed happily as she took him in. He smiled, knowing she was objectifying him. Totally digging it, and who was she to judge? The way his gaze ate up every bit of her body thrilled her to her toes.

He kissed her slow and deep, his lips were sure and gentle. At first. But once he lay against her, skin to skin, he hissed as she arched. His skin was hot, nearly scalding hers, and yet she couldn't get more. Her magick seemed to wake and radiate outward in a way that left her dizzy.

And that gentle, sure kiss deepened. He'd teased her mouth open but now he took. Demanded more as his tongue slid into her mouth, sliding against hers. She held on, her nails digging into the skin of his back, urging him closer.

He growled. Like, really growled. His beast making itself known, and she hadn't had any idea how much she'd like it.

But she really, *really* liked it. There was something dangerous about what lurked just beneath the smooth, debonair surface of this male. That she had no fear at all he'd ever use it to harm her was . . . *interesting* to say the least.

He'd made the comment that she knew they'd have awesome sexytimes and he'd been right. She'd had the feeling it would be combustible. But this was something else. The way not only her body reacted, but her magick rose to meld with his, wasn't something she'd experienced before.

His mouth left hers, cruising down her jaw, pausing at the hollow of her throat, licking over the skin there until she made a sound she had no idea she could make.

More kisses. Down over each breast, down her belly, those big hands pressed her thighs wide open and he took a long lick. And then another. Over and over and he did, indeed, show her just how talented he was with his mouth.

Twice.

She was still shaking with her second climax when he slid the head of his cock through her and then barely inside.

Her lethargy was replaced by renewed need.

"More." She rolled her hips, taking a bit more of him.

"I'm *trying* to take it slow, but you're making it hard."

She laughed, opening her eyes so she could look up at him.

"What are you laughing at?"

"I'm supposed to make it hard. That's the point."

He got it, laughing, bending to kiss her quickly. "Funny."

"You can tell if I'm, um, fertile and stuff, right? Lark said you guys have some sort of Spidey-sense about that."

"Spidey-sense? Like the comic book?" He shook his head. "You're very fertile. So fertile it's a struggle not to sniff you all the time. But you're not in a time of your cycle when you can get pregnant."

"This is a weird conversation. Fuck me instead."

He grinned and pressed all the way inside until she gave him a low moan. "Your wish is mine to make a reality."

He really was good with words.

But even better with his body.

She wrapped her thighs around his waist and grabbed two

handfuls of his rock-hard ass and held on as he kept his thrusts
deep and slow. She tried to speed him up, but he simply gave
her a raised brow and did exactly what he wanted.

She'd probably never admit it out loud, but it was hot when
he was that way.

Time seemed to stretch until there was nothing but the feel
of him inside her, his weight against her, the scent of his skin,
of clean sweat and sex. There was only Faine and Helena, and
she liked that more than she wanted to really think on deeply.

"I think I'm ready," he murmured as he began to speed up.
He changed his angle and suddenly each thrust brushed the
length of his cock over her clit and built her up again until she
came once more, so hard her teeth tingled. He snarled and followed, capturing her mouth as he climaxed with a long groan.

Wow seemed totally redundant, but she found herself sighing it as he pulled her close, burying his face in her hair. She
felt the curve of his lips against her neck as he smiled.

"Indeed."

MOLLY tapped on her door a few minutes later and Helena
was glad she'd had the time to get dressed again. Though
Faine still lounged in her bed and seemed to have no intention
of moving.

Not that she had any complaints about all that gorgeous
and naked. Damn.

Helena opened the door, smiling when she saw Molly.

She moved into the hall, closing the door in her wake, but
Molly's facial expression told her she'd seen Faine in bed.

"*Well now.* How are you feeling?"

Helena couldn't help it, she laughed. "Um, better. What's up?"

"I'm just letting you know I've done a call in to a national
news show. It'll air during their breaking news spots and later
this evening on the evening news cycle. They've asked me in
for a face-to-face interview but Gage said no."

Helena nodded. "Smart man you've got there. Molly,
they're trying to kill you. Let's not give them any chances.
At least not any more today."

"I know. Would it be all right if they sent a camera crew here? I feel like we need to respond to this and if we don't, the vacuum is filled by others like PURITY."

"Are those assholes claiming responsibility?"

"No. They're saying we did it to harm the human protesters."

"What?"

"Come on. Let me get you up to date on everything that's happened in the last two hours."

Helena pulled her hair up into a ponytail as she followed. She *did* feel better, like the time with Faine had filled her reserves in a way nothing else could have. Sex as a restorative? All righty then.

"Tosh has called, everyone there is okay. They've got extra guards on him, Delilah and Parrish. There are Others who still haven't come out. They may not at this point given the threats and the holes in capitol security. He appeared on television about half an hour ago and hailed you as a hero for saving all those bystanders."

"Me?"

Molly turned, taking Helena's hand. "You. Helena, you risked your life to save hundreds of people. All in full view. This will change a lot of people's minds about us. You did the right thing even though they'd just been calling out insults and threatening to shoot you in the head. That changes people's perceptions."

"Glad my near death can help PR."

Molly frowned. "I didn't mean it that way. But the fact is, it did."

"I know you didn't. I'm sorry for snapping at you. You should know I'm going to recommend to The Gennessee and Meriel that we end this traveling road show. The security risks are too great and in the end, we endanger even more people. I know you believe in this, but I can't stand behind it after today."

Molly nodded. "I understand." They went into the living room, which had been transformed into a makeshift media room. Laptops sat on multiple surfaces. Caspar stood when she came in and began to clap. People looked up, smiling when they saw her and got up, clapping as well.

Warmth rushed through her. Humility chasing it.

She put a hand up to stop them. "Thank you, all. I appreciate it. But the fact remains that a hole in security created that situation today. And we lost two good people because of that. Each of you did your job and that saved lives. If anyone deserves applause, it's you all."

Molly grinned and they sat, Molly continuing to fill her in.

The president had made a statement condemning the bombings. She'd also stated her belief that Others were citizens and had the same rights everyone else had, including the right to address their grievances to their government without being bombed. She called for calm and a cease in the escalation in violence.

"How about she signs an Executive Order saying so?" Helena appreciated the nice statement, but for goodness' sake, it was time to back that up with the power of the presidency.

"I know. My sources say she's trying to let this all work out through states and up to her before she does anything like that. She wants to help, but she's got a big job."

"Fuck that. If she wanted to help, she'd help. All this talk is getting us killed. We need her to be a leader now."

Molly nodded. "I agree."

Tosh had also done a news conference with Parrish Carroll and Delilah Sperry at his side. In it they hailed Helena as a hero who'd selflessly risked her life to save all the people on the steps, including the ones protesting her very existence. The FBI, headed by Anderson's task force, had issued a brief statement as well, saying preliminary evidence indicated the attack was domestic terrorism *a la* suicide vests.

PURITY had their own press conference where they accused the Others of the bombings for publicity and to make them look bad. Humans First had been very quiet and it made Helena wonder why.

"You know it has to be one of their people." Gage came in with Faine—who gave her a smile that made her tingle a little, and handed her a mug before sitting at her side.

"Drink that. Your mother has called twice and forbade us to disturb you, but she said when you were ready you needed to drink as many cups of this tea as you can."

Oh, he disturbed her all right. But it was too late to run.

Helena just gulped it down, knowing it would taste horrible, but that if her mother said to drink it, she'd better just obey or face Rain's wrath.

She grimaced and then shuddered. "Not one of her better-tasting mixes, but as she'll totally make you tell her and she's quite hard to fib to, you can now give her the truth." She put the mug down. "I do believe it was Humans First and PURITY behind this. The more I think about the way Lynn Reed was acting in that hearing, the more I'm convinced she knew something was up. In any case, I've got to call in to speak with Gennessee. I was just telling Molly that I'm recommending we end this tour. She can do her testimony via video if necessary. And let's be honest, everyone has said what needs saying. I'm concerned about what's going on with our own people."

"Cade left to go deal with the wolves. He said to let you know we had the use of their plane if we needed it." Gage sat back. Even in the house his gaze was never still, always roving, looking for possible trouble.

"We do. All this moving around exposes us to a threat I simply can't protect adequately from. Not anymore."

She'd take Molly back to Seattle and then get down to Los Angeles. She'd probably have to go to a meeting of the Council of Others. She had three messages from them already, but she wanted to check on her people as well.

Chapter 11

THEY got off the plane in Seattle and she smiled at the sight of her sister on the tarmac.

Lark gave her a hug, kissing her cheek. "Hey you."

"Hey yourself. Thanks for the escort. I'm going to stick around here and catch a ride down south."

"You're not."

Lark and Helena both turned, surprised by Faine's rumble of disagreement. Simon just burst out laughing.

"I'm not?" Helena gave him a look that would have sent any other person running. But not this giant. No, he just looked back.

"You're not. You're going to my house and you're going to rest for a day and then we will go wherever we're needed next."

"You have a house here too?"

"I have multiple houses. It's a smart thing to have places you can retreat to when necessary." He shrugged, looking every bit like a prince as he did so.

"You've been appointed my guardian?"

"I believe we've already discussed this issue. You need a keeper sometimes because without one you will run yourself into the ground. In case you've forgotten, and let me hasten to add that *I* have not, you nearly died today. You stopped an explosion, and in doing so you bled from the nose and mouth. You need to sleep. Not nap, like you did earlier. You need to eat a real meal and then you need to have a hot bath and then you need to sleep for an uninterrupted eight hours. Then you'll be well enough to go about saving the world and risking your life again."

Lark gave Helena a wide-eyed look. "So when did this happen?"

Helena threw her hands up in the air. "It's like I'm not even here."

"I'm taking Molly home. Everyone else is going home or to the hotel. I'll talk with you later. Just let me know where you end up." Gage gave her a one-armed hug before disappearing with Molly, who gave her two thumbs up and a wink.

"We should get out of the open." Simon held a hand out to Lark, who looked back and forth between Helena and Faine.

Lark pulled her aside. "They're going to hear everything we say, but let's pretend they can't, okay? You can stay with us. There's plenty of room. Or you can go back to Los Angeles. I do think he's got a point. If you go back home, Mom is going to show up at your place with a basket full of goop, tea and tinctures and she will make you consume them all while covered in sticky stuff that will make you itch out the poison or whatever. And then she'll make you tempeh loaf. Or you can stay here, have steak, some good scotch and cheesecake. While you tell me when you and Faine hooked up."

"Is this supposed to be a choice? Mom's tempeh loaf or letting that giant wolf over there tell me what to do?"

Lark laughed. "You fucked a Lycian and, from the looks of it, he's not just interested in a few days between the sheets. They latch on and then you're done."

"I boned him, I didn't marry him."

"I'm not a wolf," Faine called out, amusement clear in his tone.

"Beast, Lycian. Whatever. Bossy, and the sex wasn't so good I've lost my mind."

Lark cocked her head and dared her to keep lying.

She sighed. "Okay so it was. But . . ."

"There are no buts. He's right. You need to rest. Also? They come with one setting. Bossy. Domineering. They're used to being in charge. But they're worth it. At least the Leviathan brothers are." Lark smirked. "Come on." Lark took her hands. "I don't see you enough and you've had a rough day. Let me take care of you. Let's catch up a little. Please? Before he and Simon can start making plans for world domination?"

"Just Lark domination, pixie." Simon smiled at Lark, who waved it away as they walked toward the brothers.

"Faine's place happens to be our place. He's just poking at you. Come on back. I'll grill some steaks and we can relax. I'd like to spend time with you and my brother for a change." Simon gave her a little bow and she knew she was giving in before she did it.

"**SO** while Lark has Helena cornered off in your room, interrogating her, let me do a little interrogation of my own. What's going on?"

Faine stood on his brother's deck, looking out over all the wildness just beyond. He breathed deep of the trees and earth. "It's good here."

Simon grunted. "There's plenty of acreage just up the road for you to build your own house. But I figure you'll be settling in Los Angeles at this point. How long has this been going on between you and Helena?"

Faine blew out a breath. He'd been holding all this inside for some time and it felt good to finally be able to talk about it with someone who'd understand. "I've been attracted to her for some time. Months now. Probably since the first time I laid eyes on her. Until today it was just kisses." He pushed away from the rail he'd been leaning against, pacing. "She could have died. It just hit me and then I saw her in an exposed moment. Emotionally, I mean. It was . . . I couldn't resist any longer and I realized it was stupid to have resisted as long as I have. I don't know, at first I felt like perhaps I should have waited, talked it all over with her before we had sex."

Grabbing his glass, he turned to face Simon, letting the smoke of the scotch dance over his senses.

The scent of the meat rose as Simon put the steaks on the grill. "She's a big girl, as Lark is so fond of saying. She knows what we are. Her sister is my *Ne'est*, after all. Helena knows what she wants. If she hadn't been interested and hadn't wanted you, she would have punched you in the head and kicked you out of her room."

Faine guffawed. "They're a lot alike, I imagine. You appear to be unharmed so you must be doing something right."

Simon growled. "Infuriating, these Jaansen females. They've got a penchant for placing themselves between danger and their people. Drives me nuts."

"And you wouldn't have it any other way." Faine understood it because he felt the same. The danger of what Helena did made him crazy, but he respected her path a great deal.

Simon snorted. "No. It's an integral part of who she is. One of the reasons I love Lark so much. She's a warrior. As Helena is a warrior."

"As *we* are. But you and I are nearly seven-foot-tall males who share existence with a beast bearing razor sharp teeth and claws. We've been bred for what we are in ways they can't be. They're far more physically fragile."

Simon gave one of his infuriatingly calm shoulder shrugs. "That's all true. The fact that they're warriors like we are makes it easier—rationally—to accept the danger they put themselves in. But the fact that I love Lark so deeply is always a challenge to ration. But I do and it's who she is. There's no way around that, and if I don't accept it, we can't be together. Let's not avoid the fact that you're not only Lycian."

Faine blew out a breath. "Yes. She knows my mother is a demoness so it's not as if it's a secret. But when is it I'm supposed to bring up that the two halves of my being unite to make me cleave to the right female for life? Especially when she knows I was married at one time and I wasn't bonded to Lydia?"

"You loved Lydia, yes. But she was human. And you and I both know there's love and there's *forever* love. You didn't make it up. It simply is. Given that one of your siblings is bonded to her sister, I suppose it means our genetics seem to click with theirs. It's not a surprise that you'd fall for her. She's beautiful. Willful. Passionate and fiery about things. And she's got a most excellent left hook."

Faine snorted a laugh. "She does. And some other stuff she does, Krav Maga, that stuns me when she does it. She's so fragile though, just beneath that tough exterior. It calls to me."

Simon nodded. "And you want to protect her. You know by now that you can only do so much. The Jaansen women are not going to be managed. You have to be sneaky about it. And really? You have to accept the whole package. That means they come home bloody at least once a month. Though lately it's more. I'm hoping it slows down at some point."

Faine scrubbed hands over his face. "I want to take her to Lycia. Things are so busy just now it hasn't been possible. But soon. I want to take her and explain everything."

"She's your *Ne'est* then?"

Lycians weren't like werewolves in the sense that they didn't have the same sort of fated mate bond with their partner. Most Lycians had plural marriages. Faine was born when his and Simon's father had two other wives. Many married or had long-term partnerships. But they had long life spans and they loved and embraced that love. Sometimes it was short term. Sometimes it was longer term, sometimes it meant more than one spouse.

But for some, usually in ruling families, there were special bonds. A voluntary bond that united a couple together for their entire lives. Tila, Faine's mother, and Cross, his and Simon's father, had chosen to perform the binding after Simon's mother had died. Lark was his brother's *Ne'est*. His key. Their union was forever and highly respected by their people.

Faine felt that for Helena. And more than that, he was half demon, and demons tended to imprint on mates in the way of cat shifters. Intense attraction and then a voluntary binding. The two parts of Faine's being had united in their hunger for Helena. He wanted her and he wanted her forever.

It all came down to just how Helena felt about it all.

"She is my *Ne'est*." Faine blew out a breath. "Now I just need to convince her of that."

Simon laughed as he turned the steaks. "Unsolicited advice?"

Faine shrugged. "Always appreciated."

"They've grown up in the human world. Concepts of love are different for them. It took a while for Lark to come around when I first told her she was my key. Even though they're witches they live in a world of what they can see more than what they can feel when it comes to romance."

This had occurred to him. It had been a positive when he'd interacted with human women. He kept it light and that was fine. Back home he'd had more than enough company when he desired it, but Lycians were on the same page. They knew what he was, what he wanted, and those females who wanted more looked elsewhere.

He had thirty years with Lydia and it had been wonderful. But every time he went to his parents' house, he saw their connection, saw what their bond was and he yearned for that. Had waited hundreds of years for it.

He hadn't expected Helena. When he'd told her that, it was the total truth. Yes, sure, she was desirable on many levels. That hadn't been the surprise part. It was that sweetness he glimpsed, as well as the ferocity in battle—that combination had been his undoing.

"We broached the subject earlier today and she blew it off. But she didn't get out of bed either." Faine raised a shoulder and grinned. His shoulder had ached for an hour after they'd been together. The nails she'd raked over his skin had left a mark that should have healed faster.

That they hadn't was just another sign she was meant to be his. A mate's marks faded slower because they were meant to be shown off.

Simon's laugh was knowing. Faine knew his brother and his mate had an intense connection. "Keep a first-aid kit handy and watch your blood pressure. She's as wild and hard to manage as her little sister, I'll wager."

"Yes. They share a tendency to work until they fall over."

"You'll need to provide incentive to get her into bed. It doesn't get easier. Lark works herself to exhaustion. I'm glad Helena is here, maybe they'll both rest a little. At least relax."

"The next step is war. You know that." Unlike Lark and Helena, Faine and his brothers had been through war. More than once. He wished it wasn't heading in that direction. War sucked for everyone involved. But the humans, the ones who kept provoking the Others with acts of violence, weren't going to listen until they were taught a hard lesson.

And sometimes hard lessons were bloody.

Simon sighed. "Yes. They have fought against it. But you can't not react to what happened. We've tried diplomacy and it's not working."

"**HOW** do you handle it? Being around such a big person all the time?" Helena asked as she pulled on some thick socks. Lark hadn't bothered with any pretense; she'd led Helena to Faine's room and Helena hadn't argued. What would the point of that have been?

"The doorways around here are big." Lark winked. "You mean his presence?" Lark sat on the floor, leaning back against the chair. "If I sit on the bed, my scent will be there and he'll get agitated. Lycians are particular and Faine's going to want your smells all over the place."

"See, that's part of what I mean." Helena pulled a pillow into her lap to lean on. "It's so sudden. Yesterday he was one of my guards. Today he sexed me into a puddle of goo. I've never . . . *shew*, suffice it to say he's got some moves."

Lark laughed, pushing her hair from her face. "A body lives a few centuries and they seem to pick up some stuff. If he's anything like Simon, well, you'll be well satisfied. No worries there. As for handling him? If you tell anyone this I will deny it." Lark sent her a prim look and she laughed.

"Cross my heart."

"I sort of like it. He's so big and bossy and he pushes into my space like he was meant to be there. It's comforting. No one has ever taken care of me the way he does. But at the same time, he respects my job. Oh, he gets pissy when I come home bloody or when I don't get enough sleep, and he comes along with me a lot when I'm out in the field. But he's seven hundred years old and built like a tank, it's not like I can't use him. If I include him when I can he's more mellow about things."

"Faine seems to be all right with the physical stuff I do. He helps kick ass when I need it. But today he was so mad at me. I bled all over him and he never batted an eye. I bet the shirt I ruined cost more than I make in a month. He gets personally offended when I'm run-down and I think he and Mom might be uniting to keep me drinking all her potions and stuff."

"Mom loves Simon. As for sudden." Lark took a deep breath. "Look, I was freaked out when Simon first started all this love stuff. He took me to Lycia and all this *Ne'est* talk came up. I denied it for a while, and to be honest, I needed the time to process. But in my gut, I knew he was it. He told me that I wasn't human and that I lived in a world of magick and what I believed even though I couldn't see it, and why not believe I could love him? He was right. I've never been so convinced of anything in my life than how I feel about him. And since the bond? I don't need a man to be complete and neither do you. But he makes me whole in a way I never could have imagined before he came along. He's everything." Lark shrugged. "Plus, sudden? Come on. I know he kissed you before."

"Well, yes, he did. They were fabulous kisses. But what we did today? Well, that's a whole different level."

"You're scared."

Helena looked out over the hills beyond, at the sway of the treetops in the breeze. The stars were out and she wondered if the sky looked different in Lycia.

"I have so many people depending on me right now. I can't afford to make any more mistakes."

"You don't have to bond with him tomorrow. Though, if I know Faine and he's enough like his brother, he'll want that eventually. As for mistakes . . ."

"I can't. I cannot talk about it anymore. I've had a challenging day. I'm barely holding it together and if you make me talk about the haven, I'll lose it."

"You can cut yourself a damned break for once in your life."

"No, not now." She pushed from the bed and Lark moved to her, pulling her into a hug.

"You could have died today. Please don't do that. I don't know what I'd do without you."

Helena returned her sister's hug. Holding on to what she'd always counted on.

They went out to the deck where both men waited. The scent of food made Helena's stomach growl.

"Come on then, let's get you fed." Faine moved to her, putting an arm around her shoulder, and she didn't mind one bit, which seemed odd, but whatever.

They settled at the table. The air was cool and she was glad she'd taken Lark up on the offer of the sweatshirt that currently shielded her from the breeze.

Food got passed around and all was quiet for several minutes as everyone filled up.

"Are you patrolling tonight?" Helena sipped her tea as she spoke to her sister.

"Not tonight. I took it off when I knew you'd be here. I figured you'd want to go out with me and then I'd have to be the bad cop and make you stay in and I really wanted to hang out with you instead and make you rest."

"I endorse that." Faine leaned back, his body radiating heat.

"Me as well." Simon gave his brother a nod of solidarity.

Helena rolled her eyes. "I'm fine."

Lark waved a hand. "No, you aren't. I saw you change clothes. You have bruises on your torso from the concussion of the blast."

"But that's all I have. I'll take bruises over being blown to bits in a car bomb."

Lark's mouth hardened. "We can't let this go unanswered."

Helena blew out a breath. "Rebecca is so angry. I've never seen her like this. I sat in on a meeting she had with the Full Council. They're done with diplomacy. I've been officially pulled from Sato. She has a meeting in an hour or so with the other leaders. She said she'd call me when it shook out."

Helena was silent for a while. "I recommended the creation of a defense force."

Lark nodded. "That would be my recommendation as well."

"We need a presence out there. We need the humans to get a physical idea that we are here and we will defend ourselves. Patrols. That sort of thing."

"I think the wolves would be up for that. I don't know about the Vampires. They've already declared war on the humans. It's just been in a holding pattern while we tried out this road show." Lark's gaze locked to her sister's. "The road show was a good idea."

Helena forked up some steak. "Sure. But we can't do it all on our own. Yes, there are humans like Tosh and maybe more of them than those like Carlo Powers. But the fact is, we've been targeted with violence time and time again. We've tried diplomacy. Molly delivered her speech and warned them, and now it's time to follow up the talk with action."

"How about a run first? Simon and Faine can shift and you and I can do a nice hard jog to get rid of all the day's tension. You'll sleep like a rock tonight. We can do it and be back here by the time Rebecca is finished with her meeting. We can even use the hot tub afterward."

"Oooh, you've got a deal."

They finished eating and headed back to their rooms to change. Or rather, Helena needed to change but Simon and Faine wouldn't need clothes to shift. Not that that would stop him from coming along to watch her change like a big ol' perv.

She hadn't seen him in his other form yet and she was looking forward to it.

His gaze narrowed as she winced when she pulled her running bra on.

"It makes me want to rip someone's throat out to see you in pain."

He stepped to her, gently sliding his fingertips over her skin.

"I'm all right. But if you mean to stick around, you need to know this isn't the last time you're going to see me bruised up."

"I'm not going anywhere." He kissed her long and slow. "But I still want to rip someone's throat out for harming you."

He took her hand and she followed him out to the deck where Lark and Simon waited.

Both males had on shorts, which they discarded once they reached the treeline.

Helena used her magick to amp up her night vision and let the trees, the dirt and leaves, all the plants speak to her. All that magick seemed to flow around them like the tide.

Faine bent and the air seemed to shimmer and then he was gone. Or the human was gone and there stood a massive wolf-like beast. His shoulders nearly reached hers.

"Wow. You're huge."

He rumbled, pressing against her as she ran her hand through his fur, which was surprisingly soft. He looked back at her, still Faine, still shining with intelligence.

"Should we run?"

He tore out ahead, Simon following, nipping his brother's heels, pulling ahead.

"They're going to do that awhile. Let's go." Lark started, her steps sure and fast on the trail.

"No fair! This is home field advantage."

In the distance, Lark flipped her the bird and kept running. Helena got her ass moving, hurrying to catch up.

Faine felt trouble before he saw it. There was joy. Clan and pack togetherness. Running with his brother, his *Ne'est* near enough to scent on the wind.

It was good.

And then the jarring change. Steel. Man-made things in a wild space. Gun oil. Black powder but something else. He growled and slowed. Simon was adjusting, slowing and moving back, Faine knew, to be sure Lark and Helena were covered.

There were No Hunting signs all around the property and it was May, the only hunting allowed around the area was turkey. He doubted it was a law-breaking turkey hunter who'd sent the hackles on his neck rising.

To his right.

Faine slowed and got low, moving with more stealth than anyone watching ever could have imagined possible from an animal so large.

His beast sensed a threat to his mate. An incursion onto protected land. Neither could be borne.

The thread Helena was at the other end of hummed. She was close, but concentrating. His beast was not worried. She was exemplary. A fine mate, canny and vicious.

They'd hunt this interloper together.

Simon moved off to the left, flanking the intruder.

A burst of sound as the human realized he was surrounded by two huge beasts with sharp teeth and claws. A scream and then running, night birds breaking into flight, a beacon to where the human was.

Helena and Lark streaked off, clearly as comfortable hunting with each other as Faine and Simon were.

He growled and snarled, taking off, Simon bounding ahead and east.

It was another several minutes until they reached a trail.

Helena bent, her hand on a tire track. Her magick flowed through the space.

Faine edged next to her, pressing against her as he bent to scent the area. The other thing he'd smelled back near the house had been silver.

He pushed her, getting her attention.

"What?" Her voice was low, her gaze moving around, vigilant.

He jerked his head back in the direction of the house.

"No. We should track this vehicle out to the main road."

"We can't catch him. Not at this point," Lark said as she came back to them. "Simon is running ahead to see, but chances are, once they hit the pavement they took off and won't look back. Seems they pissed their pants at the sight of a big giant—"

Her voice was drowned out by the sound of a huge explosion. The ground shook beneath Faine's paws and he knocked both women down, keeping them beneath his body.

Simon came tearing back up the trail, teeth bared. He skidded to a stop, sniffing and poking at Lark until she grunted, sitting up. Faine moved back.

"Something blew up. Let's go see what it was."

But Faine had a feeling he knew exactly what it was.

* * *

HELENA let him lead. It wasn't like she could keep up with him anyway. At full speed she'd never seen anything faster. Not in person. And Simon? When he'd come back after the explosion? He was a blur of movement, of shining, sharp bared teeth and bunched muscle that had made the span of his shoulders so wide it had sent a ribbon of fear though her.

Helena had faced rogue werewolves and had been fucked up a time or two. But if she'd ever bumped into a Lycian who meant her harm, she'd have been long in the grave.

Still, it didn't help the sense of dread as the glow in the sky grew. The scent of burning wood choked the beauty of the pine needles she'd been breathing in only minutes before, and when they got to the top of the rise, Faine waited, the shorts he'd pulled off before he'd shifted were on again.

"I'm sorry."

Lark started forward and Helena grabbed her hand, moving with her.

Just ahead was their beautiful home, engulfed in a raging fire, the front of it blown off.

"Oh my god." Lark clapped her free hand over her mouth and Helena put an arm around her as they watched. Simon had been taking up the rear, guarding them, but he'd shifted back and pulled Lark into his arms.

"You're okay. I'm okay. Helena and Faine are okay. It's just stuff. It can be rebuilt. You can't be replaced, Pixie. A house can be."

Lark cried, burying her face in Simon's chest, and Faine stood behind Helena, pulling her back against his body, wrapping his arms around her.

"We need to call the fire department. And Meriel."

"The cars were in the garage. All our stuff was in the house, including the cell phones." Lark's voice was numb.

Helena would do what she could to make things better. "I'll go to the house down the hill to call. It's only half a mile or so. I'll be back as soon as I can."

"You're not going anywhere." Faine kept his hold on her.

"You don't have any clothes on. You're nearly seven feet tall. No one is going to want to answer the door if you come with me. I'll be back. You can trail me from the treeline if you like."

He turned her slowly. "You'd let me do that?"

Surprised, she cocked her head. "Lark and Simon's house just got blown up. I'm sure you're concerned the people at the house down the road might be in danger, or the perpetrators who did this could be hiding between here and there. I'll need the backup. I don't have any weapons on me, or a phone, and my magick is depleted." She shrugged. "It makes sense."

"Faine, keep an eye on her. Kill anyone who looks at her the wrong way. You got me?"

Helena had never heard Simon's voice that way. His beast must have been very close to the surface. His magick seemed to spark against his skin, hot and full of rage.

She took Lark's hand. "I'll be back as soon as I can."

Faine shifted again and they ran to the road and then he watched from the trees as she kept to the road.

The neighbors were agitated at first to have been woken up, but once she explained that she needed them to call 911, that their house was on fire and everything was inside, including her phone, they invited her inside where she made the call and also notified Meriel, who said she'd send someone over immediately and urged them to stay safe.

They invited her to stay until the fire trucks arrived, but she explained her sister and brother-in-law were waiting. The neighbors kindly sent her back with a thermos of hot tea and sweaters.

And a reminder that not all humans were like the ones who'd blown her sister's home up.

Chapter 12

HELENA moved through the office with singular purpose. She'd flown back to Los Angeles and would be heading back to Seattle in only a few hours to meet with the full Council of Others. This time she'd be addressing the new military arm of the COO.

The FBI was still at Lark's. Still sifting through the smoking rubble looking for clues. Anderson had come out to oversee everything himself. Lark had spent the night across the hall from Faine and Helena at the hotel where the Clan put up out-of-town visitors.

Lark had left first thing upon waking to head back to the house. Simon had gone as well, which at least made Helena feel better knowing her sister would have some backup if she needed it.

But it was Rain Jaansen who stepped out of the warren-like maze of cubbies, offices and conference rooms that held the Gennessee Hunter Corps.

Her mother caught sight of her and, with a happy cry, pulled Helena into her arms, hugging her tight as she murmured endearments. Then she pushed back with surprising strength, shaking her daughter once, hard. "Oh my goddess! You could have been killed! You and your sister are going to be the death of me yet. How could you do that? How could you throw yourself and your magick in front of a bomb? A bomb, Helena Marie?" By that point Rain was weeping and Helena just pulled her mother back into her arms.

"I'm all right. See? I even drank gallons of your tea. I swear. There were even witnesses."

Her mother kept on, the words tumbling from her mouth like a hard rain. "And your sister's house was blown up? How much do you expect me and Dad to take? Why can't you two do something safe for a living? Nice and safe with no bombs and no guns and no one wanting to kill you? Be a travel agent or a high school gym teacher."

"That's not her path, Rain." Her father joined them in the hallway, pausing to kiss Helena's temple. "Your daughters are meant for great things. They're protectors and we just have to believe in their skill and their training."

He hugged Helena and whispered. "You scared the hell out of me, girl. You and your sister cool it on the nearly getting killed stuff, why don't you?"

She was so glad she'd come back. There was nothing like a hug from your mother and father.

"Trying."

"Try harder." He let her go. "Everyone is waiting." His gaze flicked to her left and then up and up some more. "Hey, Faine."

"Mr. Jaansen." Faine bowed slightly and then gave Rain a smile that told Helena the two of them were thick as thieves while planning to make Helena drink nasty-tasting tea. "Ms. Jaansen."

Rain smiled back prettily and her dad sent Helena a raised brow.

Helena shrugged. "I don't know. Simon's the same way. It's got nothing to do with me."

Faine rumbled a laugh. "Not so. It's got everything to do with you."

"I can see we need to talk." Her dad gave Faine the once-over.

"Ugh. What we need is to go to the meeting of the Full Council. Then it's right back to the airport."

"Can I go to your place and pack you a bag?"

Helena turned to her mom again. "Yes, please. That would be so appreciated. And can you please pack some of those spell volumes? The ones I've been working through are on the dresser in my bedroom. Take Evan with you."

No one would be traveling without a guard anymore. The world had just changed and if they didn't change with it, more people would end up dead, and it sure wasn't going to be her mother, if Helena had any say.

"Don't worry, I've gotten used to it." Rain rolled her eyes, but squeezed Helena's hand. "I'll run over and be back as soon as I can."

When she entered the room, The Gennessee, because that's most definitely who Rebecca Gennessee was right then, stood up and began clapping.

Blushing furiously, Helena looked to the side and then behind herself.

"Oh for goodness' sake. Helena Jaansen, you're a hero. Stop looking around," her father said in her ear as they moved to sit.

She waved at them to stop. "Thank you. Very much. But I didn't do anything special."

Rebecca gave her a very imperious look. "You stopped an explosion. How is that not anything special? I can't stop a bomb and I'm a Full Council witch."

"To be honest? I think many of us can do far more than we could before the Magister. So if I can deflect the energy of an explosion, imagine what a Full Council witch can do?"

Rebecca nodded, sitting down. "You make a good point. Then again, my point still stands. What you did was an act of service and heroism. You saved lives and you, my darling hunter, did it on television."

"On television?"

Rebecca laughed, clearly delighted to relay the news.

"Someone in the crowd was filming with a cell phone. When the pigs at PURITY began to accuse us of setting it up to make ourselves look better, the camera video began to flow in. Some from people who counted us as enemies until the moment you would have died to protect them."

Helena blew out a breath. This was double edged. Good that they were seen to have saved lives. But now that the humans knew they had this sort of power, who was to say that they wouldn't want to try to harness that power for military use or worse?

She said as much, only more diplomatically.

Rebecca sat back, her fingers steepled in front of her mouth. "You've done a lot of growing up since you took this job. The Helena who came on to the squad with her sister wouldn't have seen that nuance. You're right, of course. Which is one of my reservations about getting too close with some of these humans in government like Agent Anderson. A nice man, yes, but he doesn't serve two masters. He's a government man and I don't doubt that he'd throw you in the back of a truck and take you away where you'd never see the light of day if he thought it would serve his government."

There it was. The baldest of truths out there. And some words when spoken couldn't be taken back.

It was no longer *their* government. It was *his* government. The gulf had grown far deeper than they could manage to bridge with talking and debate.

"I agree. And it is my recommendation that we create a military arm of the Council of Others. We need to protect ourselves and send out patrols. We can no longer rely on the human authorities to protect us. They want to put us in camps and put GPS chips in our bodies."

Rebecca nodded. "I will address all of Clan Gennessee, along with the Owen, who will address the Owen's members. In that address, we will urge our witches to move into one of the armed enclaves popping up all over the West Coast. We will help as we can with expenses, but we can't protect everyone in their own neighborhoods. We're fortunate that a great many witches already tend to live in clusters. I'd like for you and your people to give me a concrete idea of who can be protected in the current population situation. And then how we can get those who are too far out or all alone in a part of town protected."

"The group who runs the enclave Faine lives in down in Huntington Beach has two witches on their board. I'll liaise with them about setting up other groups, as well as touch base with the hunter arms of different Other groups in our territory. There's strength in numbers and shared resources will lessen the financial burden as well."

"I wish we didn't have to do this. But we do and I am fortunate to have such a fine staff to make it happen. Helena, I know you and Faine have to get back to Seattle for the big meeting. I'll be joining you via video."

"I'll get you the information as soon as I can. I'll start the calls now." She nodded, standing.

"Your sister is well?"

"Yes. Shaken up. Simon had just finished construction on the house less than a year ago. Most of the furnishings and things inside were destroyed. But we weren't. We'd been out on a run. But there was someone on the trail with a gun and silver ammo. They think they know what Simon and Faine are."

"And they're willing to kill. We knew this before. With Molly. With the countless Others who've been assaulted and killed since this mess started. And we need to be willing to defend ourselves with that same zeal. If it's us or them, Helena, it will damn well be us."

Helena agreed.

AFTER the meeting Faine held her up at the airfield. "I need to leave you for a few hours. I'll see you in Seattle when you land."

Helena narrowed her gaze his way. "What are you up to?"

He took her shoulders. "Twice. Twice in one day these humans have tried to kill what is mine to protect. This cannot go unanswered."

Part of her thrilled at the possessive note in his tone and

the other part, the one not near any erogenous zones, tightened up. "Yours?"

"Hush. You know it's true and things are too dire to deny it any longer. I'm not playing silly games. You are mine to protect. I can accept that you need time to fully embrace what is between us. But I won't accept that you don't understand what is there. And what my nature is. I'm not a human male. I have more patience on most everything, but not this."

"I don't know what to say."

His severity washed away on a smile. He kissed her quickly. "A first."

"Ha. What are you going to do?"

"I'm going home for a bit. Simon is meeting me there. I'll let you know the outcome when I see you when you get off this plane. You'll be safe while you're in the air."

Safe as she could be anyway. Nowhere was totally safe. Not anymore.

"I'm absolutely sure this is going to mean trouble for me."

His grin was back. A brief flash of teeth. "I'll see you soon."

She got on the plane and he got into a car and sped away.

He met Simon in the wide field just on the other side of the Veil. They clasped forearms and headed to the main house.

"What did you tell Lark?"

"I told her I was coming here. She's . . ." Simon's mouth flattened in a hard line. "She's shaken in a way I haven't seen. This was her home. The one place she felt safe, and now she doesn't have that. She's damned lucky I don't just toss her ass through the Veil and move us both here permanently."

Faine blew out a breath.

"I told her I had had enough and I was speaking to my father. I didn't say what about exactly. I got the feeling she just assumed it was to inform Father of the bombing, and given the amount of things she has to manage today, I didn't give her any more detail. Helena?"

"I told her twice in one day what was mine to protect was

threatened and it couldn't be borne any longer, and that I was coming here. I'm guessing her assumptions were the same as Lark's."

Pere's soldiers came out to greet them as they moved to the house where their oldest brother and their father awaited them.

Cross Leviathan gave both his sons a raised brow as they entered his office and went to one knee. He touched the backs of their heads. "Get up and tell me what brings you here. Not that I'm unhappy to see you. I'm pleased, but I can see this isn't a social call."

Simon got straight to it. "My home was bombed yesterday. Set ablaze. A near total loss."

Cross's eyes widened as he turned his attention to Faine.

"Yesterday, before that, a car Helena and I would have been riding in was bombed. She repelled the force of the explosion with her magick and passed out, bleeding from the nose and mouth from the exertion. We were also with Simon and his *Ne'est* when his home was attacked."

"Helena, hmm? This is our little pixie's sister? You've been a busy male, Faine."

"She is mine."

The simple words were enough for Cross. And for Pere, who smiled from his place at their father's right.

"The violence by the humans against Others continues to escalate. We have tried diplomacy. Molly Ryan has delivered an articulate message about our limits being reached." Simon shrugged.

Lark was shot twice when they'd sent the Magister from the human realm. But Simon had killed the shooter. It had been enough to hold back on a declaration of war by Lycia. But this was different.

"When you were here with Lark before, we called a council of war. You have all the beasts of Lycia at your beck and call." Pere spoke this time. Cross was the elder, but it was Pere who really ran things. "Simon, you are my voice on that side of the Veil. Faine, we wish to meet your Helena when you are able to bring her."

"What is she to you? Will you take her in marriage?" His father asked this with hooded eyes.

"She is . . . she is everything. My key."

He nodded. "As you know, I had love before I bonded with Tila. I cared for Simon's mother with everything I am. But the difference now? What I have with my *Ne'est* and anyone who came before is immense. I am glad that you cleave to this witch. I know how much our little bird cares for and respects her sister. We will welcome her to our Pack when she is ready to come here to perform the binding."

"I'm working on it."

"Your mother says you've never failed to convince a female to give you what you wanted. I doubt you will this time either."

Simon snorted. "The Jaansen sisters are a world apart. But Helena is worthy."

Faine was proud to have the words from his brother.

They thanked their father and brother and headed back, both males loath to leave their protected alone for too long in a world full of people who wished for nothing less than their annihilation.

Chapter 13

TOSH felt it was his turn to face some danger. He looked to his left at Delilah, who was his escort to this Council of Others meeting.

He hadn't been surprised that Helena had recommended the Others cease their PR travel. After all, how much could they be expected to endure? How many more of their people had to die just to be heard?

But he knew it was more than a simple cease of travel. The bomb at the capitol building, the *second* such incident in less than a month, had only underlined the tenuous nature of the situation. And then the attack and subsequent destruction of Simon and Lark's home and the evidence of an armed male with silver ammunition on a trail on Simon's land.

Spiraling out of control and heading to war. Which is why he needed to address the Council to try his best to alleviate the mounting tensions that he worried would explode into a war neither side would really win. And it would definitely end with far too much damage to recover from.

Encroaching on a werewolf's land the way those who'd bombed Simon Leviathan's house had done had broken so many rules Toshio knew it would be an uphill battle to get the Others to ease back. More than that, Simon's woman and Helena—Faine's woman, Tosh suspected—had been there. The mate of a shifter being endangered would push both males into hyper-protective mode.

He knew Simon and Faine were more than normal werewolves. Werewolves were large, but the Leviathan brothers were beyond large, they were massive. The werewolves treated them with respect and a bit of awe, but it was clear they were apart somehow.

"Simon and Faine aren't werewolves, so what are they?" Tosh asked Delilah, who accompanied him on the trip.

"It's not safe for anyone to know more than they already do. Not for any of us. And this is a public place."

Her words were severe and she must have noted that because she relaxed and took his hand, squeezing it and then, as if she were surprised by her action, letting go quickly.

"After this, will you have a drink with me?" He blurted it before he changed his mind.

Clearly surprised—again—Delilah started, and then she smiled. "A *drink* drink? Like you like me as a female? Or a collegial drink?"

He got caught up in the shape of her mouth as she smiled. "Huh?"

She rolled her eyes. "Are you asking because you're interested in me romantically or is this just a drink like you'd have with anyone else who served in the senate?"

He blushed, he knew it. "I don't feel the same way about Senator Harley that I do about you. I've been meaning to ask you to dinner for some time, but things have been . . . crazy. I realized if I didn't move now I might lose my chance."

"It's about time, Toshio. I was beginning to wonder, you know, if I was imagining things between us."

"Not imagining it. So yes to the drink?"

"You can buy me a drink and dinner when all this is finished."

"I'll even spring for chocolate cake." He knew she had a fondness for it.

She leaned in and her scent wrapped around him, holding on tight. "I might just let you kiss me."

He laughed, taking her hand and kissing her knuckles before turning all business again. "Two slices then. So I think with the Council, you should take the lead. Your voice is important. They've heard mine."

"Just take my cues. Molly will be there, along with Helena, so there will be friendly faces. But this isn't human communication any more. There are things shifters do . . . I'll need to show my obeisance to my Alpha. I'm here to address them not only as an elected official, but as a wolf as well."

He nodded. "I understand. We're on your turf. I'll defer to your expertise."

She laughed. "Well, one step at a time. The Vampires were our biggest worry. But now that there've been two bombs in less than twenty four hours, both attacking Others, one in the den of a very powerful male? It's going to be very bad. The wolves and cats are going to follow the lead of Simon, who's older than everyone else and far better trained."

She was giving him information, what she could anyway, about Simon and Faine. That trust was important to him.

"If we lose the wolves and cats as well as the Vampires, I'm not sure we can stop a declaration of war by the COO. There's only so much we're going to take and we're going into scary territory."

"I know, believe me, I know. I'm hoping you can sway them."

"I'm not sure I should, to be totally honest with you. We've been turning the other cheek and we're bleeding. Our children are being killed. We're not safe in our homes. Talk isn't protecting us anymore. It is not our nature to allow harm to our people to go unchallenged. Cade has been holding things together but he's out of patience."

Tosh knew he had a seemingly insurmountable task ahead of him. The Others he'd met and knew were good people. They deserved to be safe in their own damned country. "I understand. But if we can get them to hold back until I can convince the president to issue an executive order to declare all Others to have the same citizenship they had before, things might calm down."

"Maybe. But again, that's words. I don't know if words are enough."

She shrugged and he hoped they were enough to get them through before even more people got killed.

THEY'D been taken to an outbuilding on Cascadia land. They'd been sniffed and searched and one of Helena's witches was there to examine them as well.

"They're making sure we haven't been spelled on any level." Delilah had softened in some ways. Tosh wasn't sure if it was him or the fact that she now had dual loyalties. But in other ways, her humanness had muted and that Otherness she had moved to the forefront.

She moved differently and, heaven help him, Tosh thought it was the sexiest thing he'd ever seen. Other wolves cast their eyes down when she walked past, and occasionally, she was the one who did the casting of her eyes away.

Dominance politics were nothing new to Toshio. This was just a different type, but he understood it and felt more relaxed for it.

"I wonder where Molly and Helena are?"

Delilah looked around the huge space. "I don't know, but there's something up. It might just be that Simon and Lark's home was attacked and things are very bad. But it could be something else."

"Great. Something else. Because we didn't have enough stuff."

A woman he recognized as Nina Warden came out, all business. She clapped her hands to get everyone's attention. "Please take your seats. There are cards so do sit where your card is."

"Hierarchy dominance," Delilah murmured, explaining.

"Not so different from how we sit on the dais in committee meetings."

She gave him a lopsided smile. "True."

Luckily he was seated next to Delilah so he'd be nearby someone who could save him from making a horrible etiquette faux pas.

Helena and Lark came out with several other witches. Helena gave a loud, piercing whistle to shut people up. "If everyone could be quiet for a bit, we're going to cloak this space and dampen the sound so we can't be listened in on."

There was an uproar as people shouted out the question on Tosh's mind.

Finally, Nina frowned them all into total silence. "We will explain once the process is finished. Now kindly do be quiet as you've been asked."

Tosh kept his questions to himself as he watched the sisters work. Hands moving in concert, speaking under their breath as they traced the outline of the room.

Finally, they stepped back and it was like when a plane reached cruising altitude. His ears felt the pressure and then it eased.

Helena nodded to Nina and the sisters moved to their places at the table.

"Meriel Owen is going to address the committee about some new developments."

Meriel stood. "Just half an hour ago I received some information that changes everything. What I'm going to say is not known by many people. But it's necessary now. When we defeated the Magister, several weeks later we received visitors from the other side of the Veil. They had new information for us about how the Magister works.

"We didn't *destroy* the Magister. From what we understand, it's nearly indestructible. It may as well be as no one seems to know how to destroy it. Each time the Magister manifests and is overcome, it is shoved into another world. But the people whose world it attacks don't know that. We wouldn't have known it either if those people hadn't come to tell us. They're jumping from world to world to find it and stop it once and for all."

The table erupted into three dozen shouted questions and multiple conversations.

"We're chronicling all this information in our archives, sharing it as we can with other places on the other side of the Veil. The more we know, maybe it can help in the future. But from what we can tell, the Magister is a being of chaos. The way it comes and goes is part of it. It's beyond our ability to understand the full scope. Old magicks like that defy explanation, so we're being clumsy but it's not on purpose."

Tosh reeled. Other worlds? Veil?

Delilah leaned close. "I'll explain later if she doesn't now."

"Why didn't you tell us?" one of the Vampires asked.

"Because right after that visit the attacks began and we've been dealing with this brink-of-war stuff. We've been trying to keep the existence of other worlds out of human knowledge. If they're this rabid knowing about us, what would happen if they knew there were countless worlds on the other side of the Veil?"

Meriel looked to Tosh. "If the military knew, what would they do?"

"I don't know." He shook his head, caught in the middle. "This is conjecture, understand, but some might see it as a threat. What's out there? Can we control it before it controls us? Are they more powerful? If so can we get their technology? Some would want diplomacy."

"Yeah, not the ones who have been trying to kill us since they found out we existed though. What would they do if they knew Simon and Faine came from a world of beasts who could take two forms? Where those beasts ruled their world in warrior castes? Hm? What if they knew about the existence of Fae? We could not take the risk." Meriel said this all in a calm, measured voice. Tosh understood it and he agreed. There was no telling just what might happen if and when this information got out.

"We've been investigating some leaks within Clan Owen, and the de La Vega Jamboree also had a leak. And this afternoon, Helena got a phone call." Meriel paused for a brief moment. "It has come to our attention that Carlo Powers, along with Marlon Hayes and the people at Humans First, has been working with the same mages who were helping the

Magister. They're trying to bring it back, thinking that they can either control it or wipe the rest of us out."

Total silence engulfed the room and nausea rose in a wave through Tosh. If what she was saying was true, Senator Hayes was taking part in a plot that could end in genocide.

Worse, he had no reason to think Helena would lie about it.

"Owen found a leak toward the time we defeated the Magister. This is how we uncovered a network of Others giving PURITY and the mages intelligence on how we operate, who our leadership is. And some of what went down with the Magister." She paused and took a deep breath. "Our people are working with the rest of the COO enforcement ranks to investigate the leaks in their groups as well. The information seems to have come from several places and we haven't uncovered anything we believe could actually bring the Magister back. But it boils down to this. We've got traitors in our midst and they're helping our enemies to attempt to bring the Magister back."

Then chaos erupted once again.

Cade stood and all the wolves instantly got quiet. Max de La Vega stood and all the cats shut up. Another man Tosh had never seen stood and the rest quieted. Then the three sat again.

Helena spoke again. "Here is what we know. The mages have been working with the anti-Other groups for some time. An outclan witch, turned witch, and her human husband were working with one of the de La Vega jamboree members. The cats took care of this issue, though the turned witch is still at large, whereabouts unknown. The mages have been working with the turned witches. Turned witches are junkies. They've used stolen magic to boost their own. Each time they do, they eat away at their connection to their natural magick. Until there's nothing left of that. Their ability to pull magick and use it in any type of spellcraft is destroyed. They have no ability to use the Font of their home clan because it won't recognize them as witches. They sort of lose who they were before. It changes them into something else. Most of the time a turned witch dies within six months or so of that complete termination with their magick. Some seem to have found a way to live sometimes three or five years after that.

"But they've been working with these mages. Just recall, mages are humans who have enough natural ability to steal magick from Others to use to work spells. They don't die like turned witches do, but they're crazy and violent . . . and addicted, just the same. So the turned witches and the mages worked together to kidnap witches and Others to steal their magick. It's how they first got the attention of the Helper, the being who procured for the Magister."

"How is it they didn't get used by the Magister then? How many of them are there that they could lose numbers like we did and still be enough to be a threat?" Gibson de La Vega, one of the cats, asked.

"Because neither the mages nor the turned witches have their own magick. We have magick, you know, with a k. Stolen? It's not natural, it's magic, no k. It's cheap and used up fast. It's not renewable. You won't recharge when you run out. The Magister only fed on Others who possess magick. It was like it didn't notice them and they were spared. I guess it didn't like or couldn't use what they had."

None of this was anything Tosh knew.

"When we overcame the Magister, we also eradicated all those who were on the scene helping. We were able to kill the Helper. But their operation was worldwide. They had a network who stalked, kidnapped and transported Others to be drained. We figured they'd fallen apart after the Magister. The disappearances had stopped and in the face of the rising attacks by humans, we had to put our efforts on keeping our members alive."

One of the people at the table shouted at Helena. "How could you let this threat go unchallenged? It was a mistake to let the witches head this up!"

Faine growled. Helena gave him a look.

Cade stood, gaze narrowed as he addressed the wolves. "We knew about this issue. The leadership of every Pack knew about this. And we all made the same decision based on the information we had. The disappearances had stopped. We had bigger threats to deal with. If you have problems with those decisions, look to me and the heads of your clans. It was the witches who saved us by getting rid of the Magister to start with. Don't forget that."

The wolf who'd been so angry was just afraid. Tosh could see it. Hell, he understood it because if these people were afraid, things were far worse than he'd ever understood.

"What's our next step then? What do we do?"

Helena took a deep breath. "Our informant tells us the mages have let Carlo Powers know about some arcane magickal texts that might help bring the Magister back. We'll let him continue to think that, but I've seen those books and they didn't have anything like that in them. However, those books contain other things we don't need PURITY or Hayes and their ilk knowing. We've worked with the leadership of the rest of the Others here and they're already investigating their own leaks. We need to plug up that information immediately."

Meriel stood, putting a hand on Helena's shoulder. "There is a reason we remained secretive for so long. The powers we have come with responsibility. We don't know what the mages know, nor do we have the total extent of the information that's been shared with Hayes. We do know it has to be addressed before any more damage can be done."

Meriel turned her gaze to Tosh. "Senator Sato, we've revealed things totally unknown to humans. Well, or so we thought. But we're heading into some more controversial territory in a moment and I need you to make a choice. You can leave now and we'll escort you back to the airport and be sure you're protected until you get home. Or you can stay and help us."

"That's not a fair choice if I don't even know what you're going to say."

"Life isn't fair, Toshio." Molly finally spoke. "Meriel's mother was murdered after she'd helped send the Magister out of our world. We all lost people close to us. We continue to because of monsters like Powers. He is hell-bent on our genocide. He is colluding with the same people who preyed on us before the Magister and who worked with it to bring our end. We are done with peaceful attempts at problem solving when it comes to these groups."

A chill worked through Tosh at that. "I understand. I do.

And in your place I might very well make the same choices. But the fact remains that I'm an elected official. I can't be here while you discuss illegal things. I'll continue to support you all through the legislative process. You know I believe in your right to exist safely. I am dedicated to helping you. But I can't break the law. Or know about it. I'm sorry."

"I'll stay." Delilah remained in her chair.

"May I speak with you before I go?" he asked Delilah.

She nodded.

Meriel turned her attention back to the group. "Let's open this to a question-and-answer session while they're talking."

"We can't just let him leave here knowing this," one of the wolves at the table spoke up.

"If Carlo Powers and Senator Hayes know this, Senator Sato can know it. He is under protection. No one is to harm him or impede him in any way." Cade Warden spoke and his tone shut all the wolves in the room up immediately.

"Thank you all for the opportunity you've extended to me. My door is always open to you and I'll keep Molly apprised on the legislative developments."

He and Delilah left the room.

Molly and Helena caught up with him just outside.

"Tosh! Before you go I wanted to say thank you. Your help has been immeasurable to us and our cause. I'm sorry it has to end this way."

Tosh took Molly's hands, squeezing them. "I'm sorry too. But I understand why you're reacting the way you are. And I respect it." He hugged her and then Helena.

"My people will get you back to the hotel or the airport. Whichever you choose." Helena kissed his cheek and she and Molly were gone, leaving him alone with Delilah, who frowned.

"I'm sorry I can't stay."

"I'm frowning because you smell like another female now."

"What?"

She leaned forward and kissed his cheek, over the spot Helena had. Then he turned his head and caught her mouth the way he'd wanted to for so long. He pulled her against his body as she wrapped her arms around him.

"Now you smell like me," Delilah spoke against his lips before stepping back. "I approve. Will you stay at the hotel? I'll come back once I'm done here. I don't know what will happen after I hear whatever I hear. But I'd like that drink and dinner you promised me."

"What if they propose violence?"

"I hope they do. Toshio, they want to eradicate my people. To think they can control something like the Magister is insane. It doesn't just endanger us. There's no way to stop a cancer like Carlo Powers, not when he's dead set on destroying us. Not with words. This is my family. These are the people who have suffered with me after the Magister killed so many of us. And Powers and Hayes, for that matter, have been working to bring that creature back? No. It ends here. It's time to make a real stand. I understand that you can't take that step. But if you would fight in a war against a nation that threatened ours, you should be able to get why my choice is different."

He blew out a breath. "Put that way . . . yeah, I understand, and yes, I'll go back to the hotel. Come to my room when you finish up."

He left with a heavy heart.

Chapter 14

HELENA had been thoroughly shaken by the phone call from the witch who'd uncovered the leak to Hayes' office. Worse, what they'd found in the man's computer had exposed a network of Others who'd been working with the anti-Other groups and the mages.

To bring the Magister back.

Why? Why? Who'd want that after what had happened?

One of the witches they'd uncovered had been a male who'd known the location of the haven in Indio. A Gennessee witch. Someone Helena knew on a casual basis had sold out innocents to the Magister.

She was sick about the entire thing.

The witch who'd been the leak in Owen—the one Lark had uncovered just before the Magister had attacked the final time—had compatriots spread across different groups of Others across the country.

Helena had seen a lot in her time. Had dealt with stupid people, selfish ones. Greedy ones. But this was something she could not comprehend at all. What Other would cooperate with beings who wanted to eradicate them from existence?

Lark was handling the questioning of the witches that'd been identified as leaks. Money seemed to be the main factor for them. But if there was more to it, Lark would find it.

Helena blew out a breath. It was over and done. All they could do was root out anyone left and tighten up their security.

Delilah Sperry came back in and Helena nodded to Meriel, who rapped her knuckles on the table to get everyone's attention.

"Clan Owen, along with Gennessee and our confederation of covens and Clans, proposes a declaration of war."

"Lycia has declared war and will sit on your council." Simon spoke, his voice rumbling through the hall.

Helena narrowed her eyes at Faine. Clearly that's what he'd gone and done while she'd flown back to Seattle. That he hadn't just told her was an issue they'd have to work through, because right then she wanted to punch him for it.

Not the going back home part. Not even the declaration of war part. But the not telling her what he was up to part. Partners her ass.

"I have been declared a Liaison between Lycia and your Council," Simon said.

"Why? What's your involvement here?" Rebecca Gennessee spoke from her place via the video screen.

"My mate has been threatened on multiple occasions. My home—my *den* was attacked while my mate, my brother and his protected were there. The male who shot Lark is dead. My honor is satisfied there. But this is not to be taken lightly. No one threatens my family this way. I can be part of your solution or not. But war has been declared and regardless of how you all choose to move, we will not stop until Carlo Powers and those he's working with are no longer a problem."

Lark's gaze shot to Helena a moment and then back to Simon. She hadn't known either. Simon was in trouble too. Ha. Helena looked to Faine, who sat, back straight, regal and strong.

Helena realized she'd forgotten that Faine was a prince. A Lycian wasn't a werewolf. He was something entirely different and she'd lost sight of that. This underlined it. His protected? What did that mean?

She didn't want to look too closely at the way it had made her feel when Simon had said it. She liked it, damn it. She shouldn't. Faine was a handful and he'd decided she was his before she'd even agreed to it. Though, frankly, she obviously had because he wasn't maimed and she'd let him sex her up. Ha, *let* him. She'd sexed him up right back and she knew before he'd touched her that he'd had some imprint thing happening. He'd been up front and she'd been playing with fire like a fool.

But it wasn't the time to obsess on that because there was more to do.

"Fair enough." Rebecca shrugged slightly. "Lycia has been a solid ally. We welcome your assistance."

Cade Warden nodded. "Earlier today the wolves also made their declaration of war."

Max de La Vega lifted a finger. "The jaguars as well. And through us, the other cats are also on board."

Franco Pendergast lifted a finger before he spoke. "As you all know, the Vampires declared war the moment a car full of Elders and our protected was blown up. We have been holding off as a courtesy as these last steps were being explored. The Magister is a threat we cannot take lightly. If they find a way, they can't be allowed to continue to draw breath."

Cade spoke up. "More than that, that they'd plan it means they are a threat we cannot continue to let go unanswered. PURITY will stop at nothing short of our total annihilation and the human government is doing little to stop it."

"If you all have questions, Helena, can you speak to the issue of our safety steps in general?" Meriel asked.

She stood. "Our people are working on the investigation of spies in our groups. I've been in touch with various enforcers, hunters and law enforcement. Our efforts will bring to ground these traitors and they will be dealt with." She knew the shifters had rough justice for this sort of treason. As did The Gennessee.

"At the same time, we need to move forward on several

fronts. The witches are urging their members to relocate to guarded enclaves. The designer of several enclave communities already in existence has volunteered to speak to you individually. We've tried to work with the situation already in place but the fact is, we cannot protect people. Not from the threat as it is now."

Many nodded heads.

"There will be no return to the way things were. There will be a new normal. I'm sorry, but we can't ignore it any longer." Meriel sighed heavily.

"At the same time, we'll need to create a militia. Our own army. We can get patrols up to protect our communities as well as enforcement groups to show up at crime scenes. The human police are not getting the job done in about fifty percent of calls now. They're not protecting us so we have to.

"We need to train our people. If we can create teams that include fighters from different backgrounds we'll be better off. Investigation, magick, defensive magick and also fighters."

"Why shouldn't we just go back and do our own thing? After all, it was one of your people who gave them the information they might be able to use to bring the Magister back," one of the Vampires said.

"This network of spies and traitors seems to span across many Other groups. Money is a powerful motivator apparently." Max de La Vega spoke. "My own brother Carlos was one of these spies. Vampires can do what they want, but the cats are happy to work together with other shifters and witches to create a militia and enforcement teams. It's the only way. If we're going to make a stand, let's make it so strong the first bloody lesson can be the last. Or at the very least, make it painful enough they'll think twice before attempting it again. They can fear us, or hate us, as long as they leave us alone."

"I can help train soldiers." Faine gave Helena a look and she nodded. His help would be important.

"The Vampires will join this militia."

Well, that would be really good. Vampires kicked ass and

they were practically indestructible. "All right then, let's break down into groups and get some work done."

SHE was very quiet on the ride back to the hotel. But he knew he'd have some answering to do when they got back. He bided his time through the checkpoints and didn't speak until he turned into the parking garage and headed to their assigned spot.

"You did a good job tonight. I know it wasn't easy."

She kept her gaze roving. Constantly assessing. "It shouldn't be easy to plot the possible assassination of someone."

Hm. Terse.

But also correct.

"Yes. It's never anything that you should do lightly. You're making the right choice though. He can't be allowed to survive. Anyone who could look at the evidence of the Magister and think to bring it on purpose isn't someone safe for the rest of the planet to be around."

She shrugged. "Killing him in a battle is one thing. This is another. I hate it. But I don't see a way around it."

"If it was easy, it would happen more often. You make tough choices to protect the people who need you to make tough choices." He pulled into the space and killed the engine.

She turned to him, her eyes narrowed. Dangerous, his woman. "Is that what you did? By sneaking off to Lycia behind my back to have your daddy declare war?"

"That's beneath you."

"Is it? You don't know me very well after all to think that's below me. You should have told me." She got out, slamming the door extra hard. He followed, pocketing the keys.

But she didn't head to the doors leading into the hotel. Instead she pulled her magick to herself. He saw the shift in her aura as she did. The surge in her scent held him fast as she began to work a spell.

There was something so fierce about her when she worked

magick. It was one thing to watch her in battle, but this was something else. Otherworldly.

She walked her way around the car as he watched, impressed. She spoke under her voice but he heard the words anyway. Felt the brush of her power as she moved. The air in the space seemed to warm all around them.

His beast wanted to eat her up.

Until she drew a pocketknife out and sliced into her skin. The scent of her blood filled the air as she drew runes on the car.

Enraged that she'd harm herself, he barely managed to hold his tongue until she stood again, her eyes clearing as she let her magick go and it misted into the air around her.

"What the fuck did you just do?" He growled instead of yelling, figuring it would be better received.

She raised her brow at his tone before she gave him her back and headed into the building.

Guess he was wrong about that.

He didn't ask in the elevator but took the keycard from her, opening the door to his room and jerking his head for her to go inside.

"You should know that's never going to work on me. Unless it's your goal to get punched in the balls." She smiled sweetly.

He growled.

She moved to grab the keycard from his hand and he grabbed her instead, carrying her inside, his mouth crushing against hers until her taste drowned him, soothed even as it excited. He tossed her to the bed and she scrambled to her knees, eyes blazing, lips swollen. She fisted her hands and it sent a thrill through him.

"You're fucking magnificent."

It was her growl this time. "You're playing with something that might end up drawing blood."

He circled her as she kept a wary eye on him. "That's okay. Sometimes Lycian love play gets a little rough."

"Don't say I didn't warn you, Faine."

He sent her a smile. "You know how hot it makes me when you're violent."

That growl turned into a snarl and he hummed his satisfaction. But he backed off. For a moment, because they were totally going to get naked in just a few minutes.

"Why did you draw blood? Tell me now." He crossed his arms and glared at her.

"Funny, I didn't hear a *please* in that sentence."

"You try a man's patience."

"I'll kick his balls into his throat if he doesn't stop this now and show some manners."

He grinned. "Damn, I am so in love with you."

She threw her hands up, scrambling from the bed. "You're certifiable."

"I am. But it's the truth. You wreck me. Savage. Fire in your eyes, fists ready to punch me in the face or worse. You're a walking, talking aphrodisiac."

"Lycians are weird."

"Please tell me why you drew your blood."

"Blood magick is older and stronger than the normal spell-work I use. I wanted to protect your car. I used my blood to bind the intent better. If anyone touches it with the intent to harm, I'll know. It'll also fry their circuits." She shrugged.

"Vicious." He stalked toward her and she held a hand out to ward him off.

"I am. And you scampered off to Lycia with your brother without telling me."

"I don't scamper."

Her look made him stop playing. "I told you I was going. Just not the why of it. I wanted to speak with my father with Simon at my side. Helena, this is a matter of honor in more ways than I can really make clear to you. Attacking while on Simon's land, in his den? He can't let that go unanswered. His *Ne'est* was placed in mortal danger. In the one place he'd made safe for her. To not declare war would be to invite shame. The bond between them is soul deep. He promised her on his own life to keep her safe."

She tossed herself in a nearby chair but her hands were no longer in fists so at least the immediate danger had passed. "And you went to support him. I understand now."

He got to his knees before her. "No, you don't. *My Ne'est* was put in mortal danger twice in one day too. I went along with Simon, but we both had to satisfy a promise."

Her eyes grew wide. "What?"

He took her hands, turning them to kiss the heart of her palms. "You are my key. We haven't performed the ceremony, but in every way but that, I am bound to you. To keep you safe. To delight you and support you. To please you and love you."

Her mouth gaped and then snapped shut. He had to control his urge to laugh.

"This is happening very fast. Too fast."

Really? She was going to try that one? "You're a witch. You just used your blood to make a spell. You call magick through a metaphysical well to use. Where your clan lives the very earth at your feet receives you. Is it so hard to believe in something like this sort of bond? That some things simply *are*?"

She was quiet a long time as she pondered until she suddenly blurted, "One of the witches who was giving PURITY information knew the location of the haven in Indio. I didn't know he was a leak. My weakness brought the deaths of twenty-two people. I am not a good risk, Faine."

He reached out, cupping the back of her neck. "When I was a little over a hundred, we went to war for the first time. My right-hand man was my cousin. He sold information about our plans to a rival Pack. By the end of our second battle over three hundred of my men died because we were ambushed."

Her mouth softened and she moved forward to press a kiss to his forehead. "I'm so sorry. Oh my goddess."

Again, she knew what he needed. Stopped her own worry to comfort him. She couldn't deny what they were to each other any longer. But first he had to finish making his point.

"No one dreamed he would do such a thing. He was my cousin. I'd grown up with him. His father is my uncle. But he wanted more, and unbeknownst to my uncle and my family, my cousin had been giving information to our enemy in exchange for the promise to be able to run Leviathan once we were defeated."

Her lip curled and he loved her more for it. Such a thing would be utterly unthinkable for her. But it wasn't for others and he said so.

"You know your path. You are righteous and would give up your very life to protect those you're sworn to. But not everyone else is. You can only do so much, remain vigilant but also understand that sometimes people do things that are heinous and senseless. I can't let you take responsibility for this situation in Indio. You made a choice. One *I* would have made, as it happens. Someone you trusted betrayed you. But the Magister? Even if those witches had been in your living room they might have disappeared. We know that. All you can do is to move on."

"I can't afford you," she whispered.

"It's too late for all that. I should also tell you that Tila is my mother, I'm half demon. They imprint on mates as well. You're it for me. I know this with all my being. Tell me you don't know the truth of what's between us. Go on. I dare you. There are things we sometimes can't explain but we know they're true anyway. You are mine. I am yours. You can't deny it. You're too honest for that."

Helena knew she should lie. Should push him back and insist he give her time and some space. He might even do it. But what she really wanted, so much it scared her, was to believe in what he said. To let herself believe that connection she did feel between them.

There was no one in the world who was anything like Faine. No one she trusted the same way. *But.*

"What about Lydia? You were married. Lark said that her life span was altered, would be far longer now that she took the bond with Simon. What happened with her?"

"I loved her. Very much. But she was not my *Ne'est*. This thing between us—the thing Seymeon and Lark have—it's forever. There are many kinds of love. Surely you know this. What I felt for her was deep. And she's someone I'm glad to have had in my life. I miss her even to this day. But you? I need you like I need to breathe. You're who I think about when I open my eyes in the morning. I not only can imagine you in my life a hundred years from now, I *want* to. I knew there was another level of love. I see it with my parents. I see it with Simon and Lark. I feel it now. I understand it now. Are you afraid you don't love me that deeply? Or are you afraid you aren't worthy of such a gift? Be honest now."

Why did he have to be so freaking in tune with her? He was so raw, so emotionally truthful with her that it made it impossible to evade his questions. "I'm freaked the fuck out that I'll let you down."

He kissed her and she wrapped herself around him, holding on tight, reveling in the feel of his body against hers.

He lifted her, taking her to the bed and putting her down carefully. "It's okay to be worried about that. I worry about that too. If we weren't worried, if we took it for granted, our bond would be meaningless, right?"

"I'm bad at this."

He shook his head. "I already told you that boy you were engaged to isn't the same. Tell me truly, Helena. Did you ever feel for him the way you feel for me now?"

"Not a fair comparison. You're a man. You're big and braw. So sexy it gives me butterflies and makes me think about sex at the most inopportune times like while I'm driving or in a meeting. You distract me and make me laugh. You fight so well I want to start a fan club and make you teach me everything you know so I can be better. Though, you also make me want to give you a chop to the throat to shut you up."

He laughed. "So much flattery."

"I did punch him. My ex, I mean. Right in his mouth when he called Lark a stupid whore. Imagine that! But while I was sad that our engagement was over, it was more that I was angry at myself for failing. And embarrassed that everyone knew it. He never gave me butterflies. I never thought, *Faine will know how to deal with this*. Well, obviously with his name instead of yours. I never counted on him. I'm older. Hell, it feels like the Magister aged us all at least ten years. But you're four hundred years old and you've been married and you have so much more experience at everything than I do and I don't know if I can be as good at this as you are."

He laid next to her, pulling her closer and she went. "I'm as new as you are at this sort of love. We'll have to make it through and trust each other. Will you then? Admit you're my *Ne'est* and go through the binding with me?"

"One step at a time. How about yes, I admit that what this is between us is deep and strong and whatever you want to call it. The binding part can come in a bit. I need to get used to it. I'm a control-freak planner. I need to know exactly what it is and what it means. I haven't even met your parents yet. My dad thinks you're too old for me."

He laughed. "I am. But too bad. He'll have to accept me. I'm nicer than Simon and he gave them his blessing on their binding."

"Fathers are not always rational when it comes to daughters."

"I suppose I'll find out one day. But for now, we should practice."

He stole her breath as he grabbed the front of her blouse and pulled it apart. Buttons went flying and she couldn't find any energy to be mad that he'd destroyed a favorite shirt.

He bent his head and pressed a kiss against the curve of her breast, over her heart. He was hot, radiating waves of warmth against her bare skin.

She managed to drag in a breath. "Is that why you're always so hot then?"

"Mmm?" He traced the edge of her bra with his tongue and she nearly forgot her question.

"Your demon half. Is that why you're so hot?"

"Ah. Yes. In part. Lycians already run a great deal warmer than humans do. When I'm . . . excited, I get even hotter."

She managed to lever her legs and get on top of him, straddling his body with hers. "I noticed you were warm. You know, when we were together yesterday." Had it only been a day? So much had changed. "Lark mentioned Simon's skin was warm, I just figured it was . . . well. Anyway."

"Are you going to share details of our sex life with your sister?" Nimble fingers parted her with her bra.

"Maybe. We're very competitive. Only the good stuff, of course."

He flipped her to her back and stripped her pants, weapons, socks and underwear from her body in record time. She lay there totally naked, nearly panting as he looked down at her with so much naked hunger in his gaze it sent a shiver through her.

"It's not all good stuff? I must be falling down on the job." He said it in a low growl of sound that crawled along her skin like a rough caress.

"So far the only bad thing is that I'm naked and you aren't."

In a flurry of movement he got rid of his clothes and dived back to the bed, making her laugh.

"How's my scorecard now?" He licked over her left nipple.

"All tens."

He laughed, kissing his way over to her right nipple. "Yes, all tens indeed."

She pushed his shoulders. "I want you on your back."

He gave her a raised brow. "Is that so?"

"I'll make it worth your while."

He rolled, bringing her with him.

"I have no doubt you'll make it worth my while. You're infuriating in your ability to get yourself into trouble in every way imaginable, but you're perfect in my bed. However you're in it."

"Man, you're good with the compliments." She bent and whipped her hair against his chest, loving the way he groaned as she dragged it across his skin. She kissed a trail over all his marks. Over his ink and his scars. Over all that muscle. He tasted so right.

She scooted back, kissing her way down his belly, pausing to really take in just how ridiculous it was. "Are you doing like eight thousand crunches a day in secret? I've exercised with you and my stomach doesn't look like this." She licked over each of those six bands of muscle.

"Your stomach isn't supposed to."

He hissed when she grabbed his cock at the root and pumped her fist a few times.

"I have some suggestions about what you could do with that. If you like."

She bent, licking over the head and around the crown. "Like this?"

"That'll do, gods yes."

Helena took her time, learning him. Getting to know the feel of him and what he liked. His thigh was hard against her palms as she kept her balance. He had great legs. Powerful thighs leading to a fabulous ass.

"Okay, enough," he said with a snarl and she landed on her back.

"Hey! I wasn't done."

She swallowed her next sentence as he kissed his way over belly, licking over each of her hip bones and the sensitive hollow there. And then he spread her thighs wide, kissing from the knee up to the seam where her leg met the rest of her body.

She slid her fingers through his hair, tugging upward. Wanting more.

He took a lick and then one more. Another. The heat of his mouth against her clit so good it was nearly too much. But he didn't stop. He stretched her with clever fingers and that mouth of his, driving her so hard she nearly sobbed. She arched, wanting more, but he drove her to the edge and backed off. Time and again, the cad!

"Please," she whispered.

He hummed his pleasure then, moving back to her clit, staying there with little licks and sucks until she flew apart so hard she was still coming as he began to slide into her body.

She would have remained boneless until he rolled. "You wanted to be on top. Show me what you've got."

Waking up as he filled her, she slid the rest of the way down, taking him fully, her nails digging into his sides. He hissed, but it wasn't a bad sound. That hiss was laden with pleasure and she ate it up.

Her magick rose, filling the space between them, and his

responded. She'd never felt anything like it. Even the first time they were together it hadn't been like this. It seemed to pour from her, twining with his until it made something altogether different. Better.

His eyes widened. *"Alamah,"* he murmured. "Beautiful. You're perfect."

She swiveled a little once she'd seated herself totally and then pulled up, starting that slow descent again.

Over and over until she forgot how to focus and there was only the two of them. The scent of his power and magick filled her senses. The forest, yes, but something else, something uniquely Faine. A musk that shot straight to her nipples and parts south. She wanted to rub herself all over him to get more.

His hands caressed her breasts, palmed her nipples before he pinched and tugged. She nearly begged, it felt so damned good. But she didn't need to beg because he sent one of them down her belly, petting over her pussy before he parted her, sliding the pad of his middle finger over her clit until she reared back, arching, taking him deeper as she came.

It wasn't more than two gasped breaths until he joined her on a growl of her name. On and on until she could do nothing but fall to the side and pillow her head on his chest as they worked to get their breath back.

"What did you say? Alma?"

He kissed the top of her head. "I called you *Alamah*. It means . . . something close to beloved."

She smiled against his skin. "Aw, that's lovely. So lovely I won't even be grumpy with you over ruining my blouse."

"You're so beautiful I couldn't wait. I tell myself I will. But then I'm reduced to a starving man and you're a buffet and all I can do is gorge and gorge."

Man, he was so good at that. A woman could get used to all those compliments. And that body, too.

Chapter 15

TOSH had tried to work. Had checked his messages and read through a ton of email. Read several bills. And all throughout, he couldn't stop thinking about the entire situation.

He'd put a call in to the president's chief of staff, requesting a meeting. Marlon Hayes was courting disaster. Not just for Others, but for everyone. If this Magister . . . thing . . . could simply evaporate Others, what if it decided to put attention on humans too?

Listening to these turned witches and mages seemed an incredibly bad idea. Junkies and criminals? People like that would only be interested in what was good for them. Hayes was banking the future of the country, of all Americans, hell, of everyone on the planet on this plan.

He picked the phone up and dialed home.

His grandmother picked up. He knew she'd still be awake. She was a night owl and caught up on all her shows on the DVR after his grandfather went to sleep.

"Hey, Grandmother."

"Toshio, I was just thinking about you. I saw you on

television yesterday after the bombing. I'm glad you're all right. Is your friend, the witch who saved all those people, okay?"

"I was scared to death when I saw how badly injured she was. But she's better today. She used a lot of magick to help the bystanders."

"She's a good friend to have. Someone with courage like that. Your grandfather and I are very proud of you for doing this."

"This?"

"All these laws to put Others in camps and take away their rights. It's not what this country is about. You need to continue to stand up and say so. We didn't raise your father to be silent in the face of injustice, and he and your mother didn't raise you that way either."

"We made mistakes sometimes."

"America? Oh yes." She laughed. "Lots of mistakes. Hurt people. But each time we learn something else. We learn to stand up and remember what we are supposed to be about. We may fall down from time to time, but it's always those voices, the ones like yours, who refuse to be silent in the face of oppression, who make the biggest difference."

He'd needed to hear it. His parents were supportive. His siblings too. They'd all been outspoken on the issues with Others and human rights in general. Over his whole life. But it was scary as hell to stand up sometimes when it felt like everyone else disagreed. When people were willing to kill Others and those who supported them simply for wanting to exist.

"You'll be home for your grandfather's birthday dinner?"

"Yes. I will. I may be bringing someone this time."

"Really? Tell me about her."

"It's Delilah Sperry."

"Oh, the pretty senator from Illinois. I like her. She's got smart eyes."

"She does. I finally made a move after sort of having a crush on her for the last year." Probably longer. He'd met her at a freshman senate mixer when she'd first been elected and had liked her instantly. But he'd been dating someone at the time.

"There'll be plenty of food and we'll be so happy to see you. It's been too long."

His family lived in Sacramento, and while he'd been in town a lot over the last months, he'd only been able to stop in for brief periods before he'd had to get back on the road again.

But family birthday parties were sacrosanct. Having so many family members in the military and now that he was in the Senate, they all tended to travel a lot. But they all made every effort to get back for birthday dinners, especially his grandparents, who knew how to throw a big party. Delilah would like it.

He heard movement in the room next door and realized she'd come back from the meeting at Cascadia.

"You're all right?"

"I'm fine. Grandpa is fine. You stay safe, do you hear me?"

"I do. And I'll see you soon. I love you."

"I love you too."

He hung up and jogged into the bathroom to brush his hair and teeth, knowing she'd be knocking on his door soon.

As he thought, she tapped on the connecting door a few minutes later and he let her in, smiling at the sight of her in jeans and a T-shirt instead of a suit.

"Come in. I have some beer in ice and I've already decided what I want from the room service menu."

She sent him a smile. "Hungry are we?"

"God yes. I cheated and ate some crackers while answering what feels like a million emails."

"I have no idea where you put it." She looked him over before she picked up the menu to scan it.

"Nervous energy, I guess. I've always had a fast metabolism."

"One of the plusses of being a shifter." She grinned and he couldn't help it, he leaned across and kissed her. Her initial surprise washed away as she opened to him, kissing him back until the taste of her dizzied him and he pulled back.

"I love your grin."

"What made you finally make a move? First, before you tell me, order food because I am also starving."

He grabbed the phone and ordered their dinner.

"Twenty minutes they say. I was just telling my grandmother that I've had a crush on you for the last year. Maybe longer. Okay, probably longer. Like since the first time I met you."

"Freshman senatorial mixer. You had on a gray pinstripe suit with a navy-blue tie. My first thought when I saw you was that you were even hotter in person than you were on television. And then that you had great hair. Then I remembered you were dating some pretty face who read the news on cable. I questioned your taste for a while."

He snorted a laugh. "Yes, at the time I was dating someone. Casually. Then I guess I let the fact that we're both in the senate keep me from making a move for a while. But I realized after Molly was nearly killed that it was stupid to hold back any longer. We don't know when our last day will be and you were a regret I didn't want to have."

"I told my sister two weeks ago that if you didn't hurry up and make a move, I was going to."

"I'm almost disappointed I didn't wait for that. Want a beer?" He indicated the ice bucket.

"Yes, god yes."

He liked the way she moved. Graceful and powerful all at the same time. She sat on the small couch, clinking her bottle to his when he came to join her.

"How did the meeting go? Or I mean, if you can tell me."

She licked her lips. "Before I tell you anything about the meeting I want to say this. There will come a time when you have to pick a side. That time for me came tonight."

"I've already chosen the side of the Others. I've spent the last months doing nothing but working on this cause."

She shook her head. "That's not what I mean. Toshio, this . . . Things aren't . . ." She sighed heavily. "This has moved past bills and speeches. We've tried that. They've responded with multiple attempts to murder anyone speaking out and by killing innocents all across the globe."

"I'm a United States senator, Delilah. I can't just carry a banner for civil war."

She rolled her eyes. "I'm a senator too. And this middle ground you're trying to hold is getting smaller every day. I'm just saying, straight up, that there will be a time when there's nowhere left to stand and you will have to step to one side or the other."

"Surely you can't endorse civil war! I choose to believe the process can work."

"That's a pretty fantasy. The process isn't working. I can't endorse a situation where a significant portion of our population is openly abused, assaulted, murdered and mistreated for something like being a witch. I wouldn't have done it no matter who the group was. The time to wring my hands and hope those in power do the right thing has passed."

"Change takes time." He didn't want to face it. Didn't want to hear it. But she was made of sterner stuff and continued.

"Time. Bah. The president is doing *nothing*. Half the *time* the local authorities do nothing to respond to the attacks on Others. How much more do you think we should take? Hm? Do you think we would go into camps? I know what your family did and I respect that, but that's not a choice I'm willing to make. I won't send my parents into a camp and see their lives upended because the government is too weak to take a stand. Or worse, too weak to stop that sort of backslide into a world where it's okay to put people into camps because they're different. It's not going to happen. These groups like PURITY are hate groups, plain and simple. It's time someone in the White House said so."

"I called President Sullivan's chief of staff to request a meeting. It's not that I disagree with you. I don't, as it happens. But I've got to try as long as I can to do things the legal way."

"I understand. I just want you to see . . . I want you to realize you're going to have to choose." She shrugged. "The Others are organizing militias and police function patrols. And special teams. Did you know many military special ops teams have Others on them?"

"I didn't, but it makes sense that Rangers, Recon and

SEALs would attract Others. Witches are the highest func-
tioning control freaks I've ever come across, and believe me,
I know control freaks. Speaking of that, are you free next
weekend? My grandfather's birthday party is coming up. I
thought you could meet the entire Sato clan."

She blinked and then smiled. "Yes, yes, I'd like that. Crafty
topic change, by the way."

"I wanted to ask while I remembered it. You're busy, I'm
busy. I just wanted to . . . and yes, change the subject."

The food came and they steered away from the subject of
Others for a while and just got to know each other as Toshio
and Delilah. But he knew she was right. He would have to
choose someday very soon.

Chapter 16

FAINE watched his woman as she ordered people around. She had no idea how hot it was when she was this way. He saw no reason to tell her so just yet. It would be his secret.

Simon came over and sat next to him. "Damn, one at a time they're bad ass. But together? Those Jaansen sisters are unstoppable."

"Let's hope so."

Helena and Lark were showing some of the other witches from various covens and other Clans how to work defensive spells. They'd all done some training with the Owen witches, who'd undertaken the skill upgrade back even before the Magister. But it was more important now.

"Our powers are increasing. We need to be aware and always working to manage them. It's great to reach out and find you can do a spell you never imagined before. But not so much fun to reach and grab something you can't control. You can get hurt. Other people can get hurt. Now more than ever you need to be aware of yourself. Take stock every day. Hone your skills. We aren't superior in numbers to those who want to throw us in camps. But they don't have magick and we do. Use that. Make it the best weapon you have."

She'd created three special operations teams and had sent them out the night before to track down the leaks and take care of them. Some of those Others were in custody. None of them would continue to be a threat.

He knew she'd had a lot of difficulty making the choices she had. But she made them anyway. Which is what made her so good at her job. Though he had a feeling she wasn't sure of that. He'd reinforce it when they were alone.

Alone. He needed that with her. She was different when she was on the job. More closed. Calculating and all business. He liked that, but he craved that Helena only those very close to her saw.

Molly's secretary, Rita, came in. "You all need to get into the conference room immediately."

Everything stopped and people turned to Helena and Lark. "Go."

They made their way across the office to the conference room where the television on the far wall was on. Carlo Powers stood with Marlon Hayes.

"Today we have passed the Domestic Safety Act through committee and it will go to a vote on the floor. Keep in mind that these monsters have had their own murdered for daring to speak out against their ways."

Faine looked over at Helena, who looked positively murderous indeed.

There was a general uproar in the press, people yelling questions.

"I know because several of these patriotic men and women have disappeared. They were helping me and our cause and they are all gone today. They admitted what sort of monsters they are, told me all sorts of things. Things I'll be exposing to you all over the course of the next few days. But suffice it to say there is a lot these monsters have not been telling us, despite their claims of honesty and openness."

"That bastard!" Molly exploded from her chair and then, unable to pace because of the cast, sat back down. "We haven't been honest? He had spies in our ranks and it's our fault? Rita, get all my contacts on the line. We need to respond. I need to get on all the networks to combat this."

"We need to be ready for them to expose the existence of the Veil. Of demons and Fae and Lycians." Meriel sipped her coffee. "But unless they have actual proof, we don't respond to anything. And what sort of proof can they have? Hearsay?" Meriel shrugged. "I don't give a damn about what someone, who conveniently isn't around, said about something he or she heard. How can we trust the word of people who won't appear on camera?"

Helena smirked.

"And we don't know a thing about any disappearing Others. Not unless there are groups of mages out there again, kidnapping them to satisfy their dangerous addictions."

People always underestimated witches, but they were just as hardcore as the rest of the Others when it was necessary. Meriel was a vicious, canny woman and he admired that a great deal. This was high-stakes politics and she was absolutely a player. Marlon Hayes thought he'd shake the Others up with this, but he had no idea what was in store for him.

"I need to get back to Los Angeles to get people trained down there and manage the movement of our people into the enclave communities." Helena stood.

"Keep us updated. I'll contact Rebecca now. I'm sure she's seen this mess already." Meriel was gone in moments.

Lark hugged her sister. "Please be safe."

"I'll do my best. You too."

Faine clasped his brother's forearm and then hugged him. "Watch over your woman."

Simon nodded. "You too. And be sure to eat plenty of protein because watching over a Jaansen takes a lot of fortitude."

"I heard that," Lark called out from where she stood with her sister.

Simon waggled his brows her way and she rolled her eyes and turned back to Helena.

"Keep checking in. I'll let you know what we get out of these prisoners."

Helena nodded. "I'll go straight to the one we've got in holding. The wolves said we could keep him at Gennessee. It's safer there anyway."

"Love you." Lark hugged Helena one last time.

"Love you too."

Faine barely restrained himself from taking her hand but did allow a brief touch of her lower back as he guided her from the room.

Their bags were already in the car and they headed off to the airport. They didn't have Mia to fly them this time, but they had engaged the services of another witch who'd handle the air travel for the time being.

They loaded in and Faine sat, patting the seat next to him. "You may as well relax for the next few hours. There's nothing you can do while we're in the air. Sleep. I have a feeling you'll need it."

"I have work to do." She pulled out one of her dusty spellbooks. "There's some old-school arcane magicks in this. We lost our ability to work this sort of magick generations ago. Like a muscle you don't use, we got flabby. But with this power boost after the Magister, I think some of us can. And we're going to need every weapon we can get."

"Why do you think there's this power boost?"

She looked up at him after she got strapped in. "I've thought on it a lot. Heard all sorts of theories. I think it's that when the Magister left, all the unused magick from the Others that disappeared bled out and we soaked it up. We lost nearly half of our population worldwide. Yes, the mages stole some and the Magister too. But we generate magick by using it. There's magick in the air and the earth. Less people to use it means more for each of us. That's my best guess anyway. Morbid though it might be."

He sighed. "A good enough guess." He leaned back and closed his eyes. He didn't need to sleep, but the quiet time to think and work things out would be welcome. There was a lot to piece through. Plus, he rarely got the chance to simply be still with her when she wasn't bleeding or being shot at.

She put her head on his shoulder and he opened his eyes,

taking in the sight. Possession roared through him. Satisfaction that she'd turned to him with a simple show of affection.

His beast pressed against the man's flesh, flexing its claws before subsiding. Just another way she was different than any other who came before. His beast approved mightily.

There were others on the plane and she'd touched him that way. He held back a smile, settling for a kiss on the top of her head, breathing her in.

"Thank you."

She sat back in her own seat so she could look up into his face.

"What for, *Alamah*?"

She smiled. "You've set aside your life to help with all this. You could live in Lycia and no one would try to kill you. No one would discriminate against you for being what you are."

He chuckled at that. "Things are not as perfect in Lycia as you might imagine. We go to war. There are dominance battles all the time. I came to you covered in battle scars, remember?"

She smiled. "Well, I guess that's true. But I . . . thank you for being there when I needed you. You've given me so much great advice. You've been someone I could turn to."

"It is my pleasure to be there when you needed me. As for setting aside my life? Pah. This is my life. Here with you."

"Lucky me," she murmured, but it wasn't sarcastic. He squeezed her hand before she went back to her book.

BY the time they'd landed Helena knew the news cycle would have begun to spin like a giant tornado. Being with Molly while they were all on the road together had taught her that much.

She turned on the news as they drove from the small airport back to the Gennessee offices. She wanted to ask Faine when they were alone why they couldn't just use trips through the Veil to cut through all this plane travel. There was a time she actually liked to fly.

But even with private planes, which she had to admit kicked ass, it was still hours she couldn't do stuff. Then again, it was hours she couldn't do stuff, and she so rarely got downtime she supposed she should appreciate it.

She didn't though. She needed to be making calls and dealing with email and all that stuff.

"Brief me," she said to her father, who'd picked them up.

"We've taken the havens and are transforming some of them into guarded enclaves for the witches and Others who live outside major cities. That was a very good idea." He winked at her and she smiled, warmed by the praise.

"I have them sometimes."

"There are four currently operating in the Los Angeles metro area. But that's not enough, obviously. We've connected with the Weres. Some of them have huge swaths of private land already. They've hooked up with some developers about turning some of that land into mini subdivisions that would include schools, retail, that sort of thing. Oh, and networking hubs so people can work remotely without having to leave to go in to offices. It's not perfect, but it's a start. It's a boom business for developers now, which is a good thing to come out of the bad, I suppose. Rebecca is looking into buying three apartment buildings on the same block in San Diego. The Vampires have offered up some property as well."

"Really? Well, that's interesting." The Vampires weren't much for playing well with anyone else.

"Franco likes Lark. I think she drew blood at their first meeting."

Helena laughed. "She did. I guess Simon nearly blew a gasket when she went into their nest and popped someone before they'd even gotten inside the front door."

Faine groaned under his breath.

"So we've got a short-term solution for most of our people. There will be those who won't want to leave their current homes."

Helena nodded. "I know. It won't be mandatory. But we can't offer protection to everyone. It's an option. People can take it or not. It's not an option or a solution for every Other." She accepted that. There was already one in Pasadena. A small subdivision had just finished the first houses. The developers were connected to the ones who created the one Faine lived in, so the new owners were all Others of one type or another. She had looked at a two-bedroom cottage-style that fit in quite nicely with the architecture in that part of the city. Maybe it was time to pull that trigger.

"Evan has been working to get a schedule up and in place to patrol each of these enclaves. The Gennessee wants you to get some law enforcement structure in place with courts and that sort of thing. If we're stepping totally out of human law enforcement it's going to be more complicated than what we've been doing so far."

She'd already drawn up a preliminary plan the night before so she'd be sure to stop in to see Rebecca first thing and drop it off.

"I don't see any way around it. I wish I did. If they're not going to help us, we have to help ourselves, and that means building our own structure. Maybe I'm wrong."

"Stop it now." Her father's voice was terse enough to snag her attention and make her turn to him, mouth open.

Faine leaned forward but she held her finger up to stay him. "Stop what?"

"Now isn't the time to second-guess yourself. You're in charge for a reason, Helena, and it's not because I'm your father. You're not wrong. You're doing what you need to to keep people safe in this new world. We can't afford to sit around and wish things were different. They aren't. You know that more than most anyone. You have seen things most of us haven't. Your decisions are good and sound and you have to stop this ridiculous guilt tripping over Indio and you have to do it right now."

Faine sat back as she thought of what to say.

"Chris Stevenson was one of their spies. He was one of my people and I had no idea he was betraying us. That's not good decision making."

"He is, yes. And he's been questioned by me. He has a gambling problem. He owes a great deal of money in Las Vegas. The mages had been watching for just such a weakness and they sought him out. Once he'd helped them the first time, they used that against him. And then when the haven in Indio was taken they had him for good. No turning back when your actions cause the death of twenty-two people. He wasn't evil. But his weakness is more than a flaw." Her father shrugged. "This is more than a mistake. This is bone-deep selfishness that brought him to his knees and still he said nothing. Still he gambled and kept himself in debt and he continued to betray our people. That hasn't got one thing to do with your decisions."

"I should have known he had a gambling problem!"

"Do you remember two years ago when you suggested to Rebecca that all Clan employees have their financials checked routinely?"

She blew out a breath. "Yes. She said it was an invasion of privacy."

"And if she'd allowed it, at least for the hunter corps and those with access to sensitive data, it would have caught all his debt. But she said no. You tried once more and she said no again. Give yourself some credit. You can't doubt yourself. Not now of all times. I believe in you. Lark believes in you. Thousands of people are relying on you because they believe in you too. You will make mistakes. Hell, I made them too. More than you. I walk with a limp because I underestimated werewolves. You're not omnipotent. But you're damned good at this. Let yourself believe it."

Chapter 17

"**ARE** you still upset that I went to Lycia to see my brother and father without telling you?"

Helena gathered her things as she planned to head home for a few hours' sleep, a hot meal and a shower. Probably not in that order.

Distracted, she looked up at Faine, who took up the entire doorway of her office. "What?"

"Are you still upset that I went to my father without telling you?" He took her weapons bag and she was tired enough to let him.

"I understand why you did it."

"That doesn't answer my question." He tried to take her keys and she shot him a look, keeping them.

"What exactly is it you want to know? You don't give a crap if I'm annoyed you went to Lycia without telling me. You would do it again in a heartbeat because you believe it was the right thing to do."

The business part of the office was normally quiet, but not so much that night. Gennessee ran an array of successful businesses, including construction, which was getting a considerable bump now that they were moving forward with several enclaves for Others statewide. People pored over plans, talking on the phone, tapping away on keyboards in order to fast-track everything.

The hunter area of the office was also humming with activity. Her people looking at maps, giving orders, coming and going for their assignments.

"Helena."

She paused at Nikola's desk. "Yes?"

The hunter handed her a file. "We've assigned three teams each to the three existing enclaves. They'll work in shifts of eight hours each."

"No one alone. Every patrol needs to work in teams of two or more. Have you spoken with the Alpha of South Bay?" The werewolves had stepped up in a way she hadn't figured they would. They were doing it, so she wasn't going to complain about how it happened, only be grateful it had. She needed to send Cade Warden a fruit basket or something to thank him for lighting a fire over there.

"I did. There'll be at least one Were on each team in the patrol. The cats are less organized out this way, but Gibson de La Vega tells me someone will be in touch to arrange to get their people trained with us."

"All right. Good work. Keep me updated."

Gennessee had a hunter squad made up of sixty-five witches in Southern California ranging from the Mexican border to Valencia. She also ran a central California squad made up of twenty-five that patrolled the central valley out to San Francisco. Owen and Gennessee ran a united squad from Weed up through Oregon.

Those squads went out every single night to patrol the land around the places Clan witches lived. Helena was changing that along with Lark. They needed to pull the patrols in, no longer so worried about rogue witches or wolves and now necessarily putting focus on protecting their people from rogue humans.

She moved toward the garage again, Faine at her side.

"I do care."

"What?"

"You're very distracted."

She turned to him at the car. "Really? Am I? Shocking when I have so little to do just now."

"Sarcasm. Unusual."

"Are you trying to poke me until we get into a fight?"

"You should let me drive."

"Why is that? You have a car here, don't you? Why are you riding with me anyway?"

One of those brows went up. "You're staying at my house."

"I am? And what makes you think that?"

"Would you like to continue this in the car? Or out here in the open?"

She jammed her key into the lock and got in, tossing her stuff into the backseat. She popped the trunk so he could stow the weapons.

"Now." He stood in the driver's side door, clearly waiting for her to move aside. She started the engine instead.

"Time's a wastin'." She put it into gear and he heaved a put-upon sigh and walked around, getting in on the other side.

"My car isn't here. I had it taken back to my house. We should stop at your place on the way so you can bring stuff to my place that would make you comfortable."

"You live across the city. I live five minutes from here."

"I live in an enclave and you're trying to convince your people it's the safest thing. Shouldn't you be a good example?"

"You don't even believe that. You're just saying it to make a point."

"I do believe you'd be safest at my home, actually. And it's not me who is trying to pick a fight."

"Puhleeze." She drove to her place, annoyed that he was right about being a good example. "I like my apartment."

"No, you don't. You have pictures on shelves, but none on the walls. The walls are all still white. You haven't painted anything. You sleep there, but you don't live there."

"Suddenly you're an expert on how I live?"

"I know you better than you want to admit."

That much was true.

"I haven't had much time."

"You've lived there for a year and a half. You're a nester, I can tell. You have not nested there. Feel free to nest in my home all you want. Since we'll be living together I want you to feel at home."

"You totally are trying to start a fight." She pulled into her spot and noted the graffiti. "Great."

He didn't say anything, but she knew he added it to the *reasons to stay with Faine* category in his head.

Her place was fine. The building was well lit and her neighbors were an assortment of artists and other types that seemed to love having endless potlucks and building-wide block parties every few weekends. After the revelation—as the media had dubbed the day when the world realized there actually were witches and Vampires—she'd been stopped and hugged more than once by her neighbors.

But Faine was right. She hadn't really settled into her place. The house she'd shared with Lark had been a home, but this apartment was a place to sleep and eat. She just kept putting finding a house to buy into the *after this settles* category. Along with getting back to dating and going to the dentist.

She would be setting a good example by moving into an enclave. She would be safer and, damn it, she would be with him and that made her happier than she ever expected to be.

She pulled out a big suitcase and he gave her a look. "What? You win. Happy?"

In two steps he was on her, pulling her close, crushing his mouth against hers. Her spine loosened as she held on. His taste thundered like her pulse. He took over, the scent of his skin, the feel of his muscles as they bunched and shifted like the predator he was, she greedily took him in. Even as she knew somewhere in the back of her head that he was being a bossypants.

When he finished and she struggled to regain her composure, he set her back. "I am happy, but this is not a game where you lose and I win. I want you with me in my den. It's my nature to want my woman in my home where I can keep her safest. I want to be with you because I like to be with you and it makes having lots of sex with you easier if you're within reach whenever the mood strikes."

She rolled her eyes.

"You're grumpy because your world is falling apart and you're doing your best to build a new future."

"I'm grumpy because you are pushy and bossy and you take over when you should back off."

He grinned for a moment. "*Alamah*, you knew I was bossy and pushy when you let me get you naked."

He was so right she should be embarrassed. "You have other attributes that seem to blind me *temporarily* to your overbearing nature."

He laughed. "Thank goodness then. Come on. Pack up. Shall I grab the books on your shelves so you can study them at my house?"

"Fine."

She moved into the bathroom to gather her toiletries. And to get some space. He clouded her judgment with his . . . well, his gorgeousness and his ability to be really good at everything and the way he just let her be bitchy and kissed it out of her when he got a mind to.

Lord, she was in such trouble.

She tried to be annoyed that she'd have to drive so far to get to the office, but when she licked her lips she tasted him again and it fled.

Her clothes went into a garment bag. She only wore a few different pairs of shoes to work, but she brought many others to his place because one never knew when she might want to wear some pretty heels after all.

If he claimed to want to be with her, he needed to understand she had a lot of clothes. And shoes. And bags. And books too.

He'd clearly run some boxes down to the car while she had pulled her stuff together in the other room because her shelves were a lot more bare when she came out.

"I took the liberty of grabbing the teas and your teapot and some of the stuff in your fridge so it won't spoil. Will you allow me to drive home? I know all the back ways and you can make calls if you need to."

"See? How hard is it to ask instead of giving an imperious *now* and frowning at me?"

"We both have to adjust, no?" He kissed her again and took her suitcase and garment bag when she was hormone addled.

"You can drive if you'll point the car through the In-N-Out drive-through on the way."

"I can do that."

He walked out, wearing a smile and when he wasn't looking, she gave one too.

"THERE are two full closets. I'll give you the one here in the master and take the one in the other bedroom." He brought her suitcases into the house.

She shoved a few more fries into her face. "I can take the other closet. There's no sense in you moving everything."

"I want you to feel at home here. A safe place."

He was so sweet she couldn't resist moving to him and kissing him. "Sorry about the salt."

He licked his lips. "Somehow you can make salt sexy."

She moved into the room she'd slept in just a week before. A week. Jeez. So much had happened in that time.

The closet was gigantic with racks for shoes and bags and lots of space to hang things. Even without the utterly beautiful male standing a few feet away looking adorably uncertain, she'd live there for this dream of a closet.

"This is a fabulous closet. I'll take it."

He smiled and it warmed her. Man, she was in big trouble.

"Why don't you look at the one in our bedroom first? Then you can decide."

"I'm going to eat this Double-Double with cheese and suck down my milkshake first. Then I'll look."

He put the box he'd been holding down on the bed and followed her out. "I'll get plates. Sit."

"Okay then. Thanks."

He brought plates and she put all the food out and they sat in companionable silence for some time as they ate.

Once they'd finished and cleaned up—he dried and she washed—they'd brought the rest of her things into the house.

She busied herself getting the layout of the closet and the built-in drawers. It was a weird thing she knew. But organizing stuff made her relax, enabled her to let go of all the insanity of the last months and focus on some problem solving. Not just where her socks would go, but how to organize the new teams going out into the field.

She turned to see him pocket a silver box. One she'd noticed on a side table earlier.

"What's that?"

"An old silver piece. It doesn't really go in here." He looked her over with that face of his and she forgot why she had that little frisson of uncertainty.

"This is your home too. I want you to . . . feel that. Put things where you like them. Tell me what color you want walls to be and I'll take care of it. Don't like the bedding? I can change that."

"You're *such* a prince." She grinned as she watched him as he stalked her way. "I have no doubt you can snap your fingers and make all sorts of things happen."

"I am what I am, *alamah*, and you'll need to get used to that too. I want you to be happy. I'll do what it takes to make that happen." He shrugged as if most people were that way when they weren't. Despite how fast things had jumped from hot chemistry to *ohmigod you're it for me*, it moved her that he was so focused on her well-being. No one had ever been that for her. It was overwhelming but in a good way.

"I'm really hard to live with." She shrugged. And then she remembered the box. Funny thing about having such a sharp memory. There was a stylized L on the lid. *Lydia* perhaps?

He barked a laugh. "You can organize your books by color and spine size. I'll make an effort to comply."

"Oh that. Well, that's why it's a good thing I can have my own closet. I like things in their place. It makes me feel better to know exactly where stuff will be. But I'm sort of temperamental."

Again he laughed. "I haven't noticed." And then he kept laughing.

"Har. Look, Mister, I'm just trying to be up front, as you seem to want to try this living together thing. I'm not all purple scarves and glitter like my sister." Or flirting behind fans and elbow-length gloves and stuff.

"You bring that up as if I don't know. You're not anyone else but you, thank gods. I crave you, not anyone else. I admit it, I'm sort of strangely turned on in anticipation of seeing what your closet will look like once you've finished."

She shook her head at him, unable to hold back a smile.

"I'm particular. I get up very early and I'm often bitchy about it. I am intolerant of generic ice cream. I only like Kraft macaroni and cheese or homemade. I am religious about my coffee. My mother will make you eat tofu and mung beans. You need to accept that. She's a total hippie. Her name is Rain after all. She will talk to you at length about how awesome veganism is and how cake with no eggs or butter is just as good as cake with, and you have to nod and pretend such a thing could ever be true. I'll need a workspace here where you will not lay your crap or borrow my pens."

"Are you trying to scare me? Because you're not. There are four bedrooms here. You can have any of the other three to use as an office. I won't borrow your pens." He snorted and she sent him a raised brow. "I promise. Or lay my crap on your work things. Though, *alamah*, I don't lay my crap anywhere. I don't even have crap. I have belongings."

"I told you I was difficult."

"But you're worth it, so stop trying to scare me off."

"I'm not nice. Or easy to be around."

He paused, leaning over to take her hand. "What's this about? Hm?"

She squirmed, uncomfortable that he knew her so well. "I don't know what you mean. I just think it should be clear what you're getting into." She wasn't a high-born fancypants Regency lady–type person. His wife probably had been gentle and had soft hands and never said boo. Helena didn't have gentle manners, though, if she did say so herself, she'd wager her fashion sense was as good as, if not better than, Lydia's had been.

He merely looked at her carefully. "Your scent changes. Just a small, nearly imperceptible bit when you're being evasive. Did you know that?"

"No. I've never dated a Lycian before."

"Of course you haven't. Also, we're not dating. You're my woman. What aren't you saying? You're standing here in our home talking about how I should know what I'm getting into. And believe me, beautiful, beautiful witch, I do. You're troublesome. You have a special talent for attracting the sort of people who seem to want to blow you up or shoot you."

He kissed each eyelid with such gentleness she found her eyes stinging with unshed tears.

"You make me vulnerable." She didn't know how to be. Not emotionally vulnerable anyway. She could deal with physical vulnerability. It came with her job. She could work on being less of that. But emotional stuff?

He tipped her chin so he could look in her eyes. Alarm raced over his features when he saw the tears. "Of course I do. If there weren't this enormity of feeling and connection between us, you'd easily evade feeling deeply for me. I would never hurt you. Not on purpose. Your heart is safe with me. Don't you know that?"

She swallowed back the panic and the sob that wanted to escape. Oh gods, she was jealous of a woman who'd died more than two centuries before. What was wrong with her?

"What is it? How can I make it better?"

"The box. The one you just put in your pocket. It was hers, wasn't it?"

She didn't need to use a name and he was too grown up to evade or deny.

"Yes. I'm sorry. It's been part of my home for so long I didn't think. Are you bothered by it? She's long gone, Helena."

"I've never really been jealous before. Especially not of a

centuries-dead woman. I'm sorry. I'm embarrassed to be so petty. I know you loved her. I don't expect you to have been a monk before I was even born. I'm just . . ."

He drew the pad of his thumb down her cheek. "Shh. It's not petty. It's all right to feel that way. I loved her. She meant something to me and she always will. I can't deny that or it would shame not only what I had with her, but myself as well. And what I have with you."

"I don't expect you to. Honestly, it's not that you loved her. I understand that. I accept that. I'm just . . ."

"Just what?"

"Not that. Not gentle born. I have weapons calluses. I say bad words and I often come home covered in bruises, cuts and sometimes in a sling. I don't know how to keep a genteel home for my husband and, well, that's not me. I can't be her. I can't be like her. I've never ridden a horse!"

He smiled and kissed her quickly. "You're you. My amazing female. Brave and strong. Smart. Angry and righteous. Full of love and passion. Protective. I love that. All of it. Lydia was part of my life then. But you're my life now and forever. The difference is vast. I'd never want you to be anyone or anything but what you are. Because that's what I love about you. And you don't need to ride horses. We don't have the time anyway."

He brushed the hair back from her face and slid his palm around to cup the back of her neck. It was dominant and tender all at once.

"From the moment I first met you I knew you'd be important to me. We have so much time to build a future. A long, beautiful future. You are brilliant. Magnificent. My match in every way. Do you know what it means to a male like me that you have weapons calluses?" His grin told her all sorts of things and made her tingly.

"I feel like a baby next to you."

"In some ways I suppose you are. I'm four centuries old. But you're no naïve baby. You've learned powerful and painful lessons. You're struggling to protect people in a time that most people, even those my age, haven't had to deal with. You have, to be clichéd for a moment, an old soul.

"It's not about high-born manners or horses or keeping a house, and I'm sorry if anything I've ever done has led you to that conclusion. You stand up for what is just and you do it at great threat and danger. But you do it because it's who you are. That's . . . it's irresistible."

"You're so sure of yourself."

"Not always. But I came up hard. Yes, I am a prince, but all my brothers and I had to serve in battles. Had to come up on our own through the ranks and find our way. Simon came here to escape that destiny. I suppose when I volunteered to come here to help Owen, it was to forge a new path for myself, and there you were. It was meant to be. You and I were meant to be. I can be absolutely sure about that, even as I am just as confused and sent reeling by many other things that happen daily in this new reality Others face."

"I hate it when things are out of my control."

"I know. We can get through it together."

"I'm still difficult and you still can't borrow my pens, even though you're exemplary in bed."

"All right. I can live with that." He kissed her long and slow until the stress melted away and she felt a lot better. He was way better than her mother's tea.

"And, by the way, I picked up DVDs of the movies you mentioned. *Thunderdome* and *Mad Max*."

"Really?"

He nodded. "Really. Want to watch them in bed?"

"I'll make popcorn."

Chapter 18

"**YOU** need to get out. It's one night. A few hours. Helena, it's been how long since you've done something that didn't involve shooting, getting shot at or blown up?" Marian, one of Helena's right-hand people and a good friend, poked at her.

Helena couldn't help smiling as she thought about some of her recent recreational activities with Faine. "I do okay."

"Okay, but you can do *that* when you get home. You'll be sweaty and relaxed. Plus, well, it's good for the Others community to see us out and about. We get to have a damned life too."

Wild Darkness was a fun club. Or it used to be. Helena hadn't gone in at least a year and a half. Part of it been that she and the ex had gone out there on a regular basis. The rest had been her life getting so busy that going out and shaking her ass had fallen to the bottom of her to-do list.

"Hell, ask Faine to come along."

"Ask me to come along where?" Faine wandered into the room looking good enough to lick. She figured having more access to him now that they lived together would ease her need of him at least a little. But that wasn't the case. The more time she spent with him, the more she wanted.

"I was just trying to talk Helena into coming out tonight with me and some of the others from the Hunter squad. There's a dance club, it's run by Others." Marian shrugged. "It would be a good sign if people saw her out."

Faine searched her face for a signal, but she could tell, given his posture change, that he thought it was a good idea. It probably was.

She smiled at him and he nodded. "I'm in. I mean, if I don't have to manage some new crisis between now and tonight."

Marian beamed his way. "I'll see you both in a few hours. Don't let her wear something frumpy. She's got great legs."

Faine raised a brow. "Oh, I'm very aware of Helena's legs."

"I don't own anything frumpy!"

"Okay, so don't wear anything elegant but so long I can't even see your knees."

"I've been dressing myself appropriately in social situations for a little while now. I think I can manage."

Marian just laughed as she left Helena's office.

Once they were alone she sighed. "Good gods. We don't have to go for a long time or anything."

He crowded her and she secretly loved it. "Oh, beautiful witch, I'm going to watch you move all night long. And then I'm going to strip you naked and show you how much it makes me want to love every inch of you."

He was so good at that. All that sexy talk that turned her knees rubbery.

"You do have really great legs. I'm undecided, though, if I want anyone else to see that. Maybe you can go dancing in a long dress instead."

She laughed. "I'd get caught up in all the material around my legs. I need to move. Plus, well, she threw down the gauntlet with that frumpy comment. I have to wear something totally fabulous." Which, knowing Marian, was what she intended from the start.

Because they were alone, he dipped down, brushing his mouth over hers. "If you dance like you fuck, I'm going to be hard all night long."

"I don't know if I do or not. You'll have to tell me afterward."

"I like this side of you."

"Which side is that?"

He tipped her chin up with his fingertip. "The playful Helena only a few people get to see. My beast presses against my skin, wanting to come out to play too."

She swallowed hard. Her magick rose and she let it for long moments before she got herself back under control.

"Stop that. I'm totally okay with playing. Later."

He smiled, kissing her again quickly before stepping back. "Count on that. Find me when you're ready to go home. I'm working in the conference room next door."

FAINE, his hand at Helena's back, passed through the front doors of Wild Darkness. He couldn't resist another look at his woman from behind in the tiny scrap of a dress she'd worn that night. She did indeed have gorgeous legs. Most of which were showcased. High heels on her feet tilted her ass just right. Her tits swayed hypnotically as she moved.

Damn. She was fucking beautiful. His own personal siren.

All in all, he had no complaints. The males could look all they wanted, but she was his. He'd been content to drink some tea and watch her get ready. She fascinated him. All hard edges and kicks to the face and then she could be found lining her eyes and putting on just the right shade of red lipstick. She smelled like heaven. Her perfume spicing the scent of her magick.

She wore tiny panties and a bra that heaped her breasts up, showcasing them perfectly in the neckline of the sparkly silver dress she wore. All her flesh tempted him. So much tawny delight.

He smiled. Later he'd slowly divest her of every last scrap of it in their bed.

They found the table her friends had grabbed for them all earlier and then he spun her, pulling her close and bending to speak in her ear. "Shall we dance?"

She nodded, a smile marking red glossy lips.

And, as it turned out, she did fuck like she danced. She moved with a great deal of passion and self-assurance. Like she fought. He hadn't seen her this carefree, not outside their bed. He was immensely glad they'd come out. People around saw her, knew who she was.

It was good for them to see her in a social setting. He really got that as he noted people's faces once they recognized her. Yes, they needed to be safe, but they needed to live too. What was the point of surviving the Magister and working so hard for their rights if they hid in their houses all the time?

Life was to be lived. She put her own on the line for them every day in ways they would most likely never truly understand. But just seeing her there, shaking her ass, smile on her face, her magick floating around her like golden dust motes, it made a difference and he approved mightily.

Hell, she needed it too. Needed something that wasn't work, or downtime related to being ready for the next bout of work. Constantly being on guard wasn't good for her. For anyone really, but she was his to protect.

And, he could admit, he liked that they had couple time. Social time when he got to know her friends better and they him. Sure he knew most of the people on the hunter team, at least by sight. But this was different. He was there not just as a guard, but as Helena's man. He knew they understood it. Liked the approval he saw in their eyes as well.

"Would you like a drink, *alamah*?"

She got close, smiling up at him. No one had ever used a pet name before. Not more than honey or babe. *Alamah* was hers alone. He gave it to her and it made her happy. It was really nice to be happy, damn it.

"That would be really good. Jack and Coke please."

One of his brows rose as he bent and kissed her quickly. "I don't think I've seen you drink more than a beer before. I can't wait to see this."

He spun her artfully and guided her back to the table, and before he could move toward the bar, a cocktail waitress made her way over.

"Hey guys!"

It was a girl Helena and Lark had gone to school with. A cousin of Helena's assistant, Sasha.

"Hey Carla. How are you? Looks jumpin' in here tonight." Marian grinned as she took the place in.

"It is. And it's good for people to see you all here. My boss is positively giddy. He wants me to tell you drinks are on the house and to thank you for helping people feel safe. It's hard to go out right now. You know? But if the Hunter is here with part of her crew, it's good."

Helena was glad they'd come. Even if she planned on getting the hell out in an hour or so because Faine looked good enough to eat and she was going to at the very least lick him—a lot—once they got home.

Carla took their orders and their thanks and headed off to get their drinks.

Helena had a great time. Drinking and laughing and dancing with her man. And it felt, somewhere in the back of her mind, like the calm before the storm.

The drink was good but she wanted to dance and he obliged, taking her back out there. Of course he was good at that too. The man was sex on legs and he moved like it.

Never in her life had she imagined being with a man like him. Men like him were fantasies. They were in books or movies, but real-life men were different.

But there he was, looking smooth and sexy, and his gaze was only for her. Well, his gaze flitted around much like hers did, but his personal gaze, the one where a man saw a woman—that was all hers.

It humbled her, even as it filled her with wonder and satisfaction, that he wanted her the way he did. Supported her. Listened to and trusted her. Even with the weight of everyone's trust and fear on her shoulders, it was easier with him there at her side.

About an hour later, he pulled her close and she tiptoed up. Of course he was still way taller but thankfully he bent down to meet her halfway. His hand slid around her, settling at her hip. The heat of him burned through her dress, against her skin. Her skin he knew so very well.

"I really think we should go home."

The awesome thing about Lycians is that they didn't really

get drunk. Not the way humans or witches did, though he did say in Lycia they brewed some type of ale stuff that actually stayed in their system in a way human alcohol didn't. That night he'd had a drink but it was through his system in less than ten minutes. He was alert and ready to drive home, though she was moderately tipsy. No need to wait any further for ravishment.

"I've just been waiting for your signal."

They quickly said their good-byes and headed out. People waved as they made their way from the club and his car was waiting in valet when they got outside.

"It's nice to feel like we're all on the same page for once. Positive instead of terrified. Though." She shrugged, settling back into the seat as he headed for the freeway. "I suppose the terror will be back by morning." Every night there was something else. Every dose of the morning news had multiple stories of some violence somewhere. Fires. Graffiti. Attacks on schools and community centers. It sucked.

"Let yourself have just one night of happiness. Yes, morning will come with sad news, the way it has for some time now. But we have each other. We had a lovely time with friends. It's all right to be young and in love. Yes?"

She took his hand. She could blame the four Jack and Cokes later. "It's all right be to be young and in love, yes. Or four hundred years old and in love. Even tomorrow when there will be bad news it'll be okay. Thanks for coming with me tonight."

"There's really no way I'd have missed you in this outfit."

She laughed. "I'm glad you enjoyed it. I haven't worn it in a long time. I was worried it wouldn't fit."

"It's just perfect." A smile ghosted his lips. "I can't wait to get you out of it when we get home."

She let go of a delighted laugh. "Well good. That's the point of living with you. Having full-time access to all the filthy sexual services you provide."

He took her hand as he drove and she allowed herself to enjoy their time together as a couple. Allowing herself to believe things could be all right when the dust settled. But at the very least, they were right then and that was enough.

* * *

DELILAH looked so lovely Tosh nearly regretted not having her all to himself. All that golden hair was pulled up and away from her face. She was old-fashioned in the best sense of the word with a brooch on her blouse and elegant, tailored pants that only emphasized her shape.

"Have I told you how beautiful you look tonight?"

"Thank you. You did, but it never hurts to hear it more than once. I promise. It's all right? My outfit I mean. I didn't want to go too casual and then I thought maybe you all keep it casual on purpose and I'll be overdressed."

"You're perfect. I promise, they're going to like you."

The nervousness on her features eased a little. "I hope so. If they made you, they have to be good people."

"You should say that to my mother. She'll love it."

Delilah laughed. "I'll try to find a way to say it without sounding like I'm sucking up. You're sure they're okay with me coming?"

"Definitely. I spoke to my grandmother about it first and then got a call from my mother and one of my brothers about it. I'm sorry to say they might be pretty excited about having you there."

"Sorry?"

He snorted. "They're going to show you pictures and ask you rude, intrusive questions about your life and your family. They mean well, but they're nosy, and since they know we're together and I like you enough to want them to meet you, my mother might make hints about marriage or kids. I'm just warning you."

"That's better than telling me I should be using birth control because of mixed babies."

He frowned as he pulled into his grandparents' driveway. "What? Someone did that?"

"Yes. It happened a while ago. Before the Magister, but if you remember, the wolves have been out for a while now. It was one of the reasons I decided to stop dating humans. Clearly I break rules for you and that heart of yours."

"My heart?"

She turned to him. "You have the heart of a lion. Full of passion and justice. It goes with your looks. All that gorgeous hair and your features, which would be perfect for an ad in *GQ*. And your brain. All in all, you're a total package. But it's your heart that proved my undoing. I can't resist."

As compliments went, that one was one of the best he'd ever received.

"I'm really glad about that. While I do admire your heart and your brain, can I tell you it's your lips that have always done me in?" And her breasts. He loved those though he hadn't seen them yet. There was something courtly about this thing between them. Though he wanted her, all of her, they'd been taking it very slow and it seemed to suit them both.

The sexual tension banked, getting hotter, and when it finally did happen, he knew it would be worth it.

He leaned in to kiss her, grabbing her bottom lip between his teeth a moment as he pulled back. In the corner of his vision he caught sight of his mother coming out onto the porch and waving.

"My mom knows we're here. Just yell for me if I'm not near and you need saving from the crazy." He squeezed her hand before he got out to take her inside.

The place was wall-to-wall Satos from his eight-month-old niece to his grandfather. And every one of them went out of their way to make Delilah feel welcome. He hadn't really worried that they wouldn't. She was pretty fabulous and they'd know he wouldn't have brought anyone to an event this important if he didn't really like her. But it was a good thing to see, as well as the way Delilah interacted with them. Open. Smiling. Joking. Asking questions and actively listening to answers.

"Stop watching her like you're worried we're going to ask her to change into a werewolf at the dinner table or something."

He turned to his sister, who grinned at him like a fool.

"Quiet you. I'm not worried like that. I just want her to feel comfortable."

His sister Suzanne laughed at that. "Wrong family event. Dad's already tipsy, Grandma's all high with babies and having a full house. Delilah's getting the full brunt of us. If she survives and takes your call tomorrow, you'll know it's meant to be. She's gorgeous, by the way. And I saw her speak a few days ago at a press conference. She's sharp. Needs to be, I wager, given the way things are right now. And really, to manage you too."

"Hey. I'm easy."

She rolled her eyes. "You are anything but easy, Toshio. I worry about you with all this insanity. Her too, now that I know her."

He shrugged. "I wish I could say you were overreacting. But what else can I do, Suz? Huh? Shut up and let all this happen without speaking out?"

She shook her head. "No. You're doing the right thing. We believe in the work you're doing. I have to admit how shocked I am by what some people are saying. I guess I thought we were past that. You know, aside from the weirdos. But this isn't just weirdos and fringe people."

"No. It's people I never thought would say such things. People who can look me in the eye and advocate for putting people in camps. Or worse. I've lost friends over this. I still do not believe it is the majority of humans, though. But for the Others, well hell, how much more should they have to lose? Delilah's sister lost her business. They ran a dry cleaning service that worked out of the hotels in downtown Chicago. One by one they told her they'd found a new dry cleaner until she had no clients left. And that's not even the people who've been physically attacked or killed. They need to be represented by their government, protected, and it's not happening. I don't think I'm doing enough. But I don't know what else I can do."

Suz took his hand and squeezed it. "You'll do all you can because that's who you are. And no one expects anything less. And now you have someone, and it's probably not the most convenient time." She snorted. "But love works that way, I guess."

"I think it's early for love. But I do like her a great deal and I have since I first met her. She makes me laugh and I can talk to her. I respect her and the job she does. It's the big bright spot in my life right now. And I'm not above grabbing it with both hands and not letting go."

"Good. Don't let go, Tosh, because that's rare enough you'd better cherish it."

Chapter 19

FAINE had been working in the conference room adjacent to Helena's office for all of twenty minutes when The Gennessee came in and turned on the large television in the room. "Hayes is doing a press conference in five minutes."

Faine sighed heavily. They knew it would be coming any day, but it had been three days of relative peace. No one they knew had been injured or killed. Helena slept at his side each night without bruises or stitches. It had been a good thing.

But that would fade, he was sure, after this statement Senator Hayes would make. So he braced himself.

The room filled quickly and Helena settled, her hip against his chair, attention on the screen.

"Meriel is watching in Seattle and we'll patch in after this is over." Rebecca was distracted and Faine understood it.

Hayes, flanked by Carlo Powers, PURITY's leader, came onto the screen. "We're here to start a dialogue on this issue. There will be no questions."

"Someone needs to buy the man a dictionary and help him look up the word *dialogue*," Helena muttered.

"Over the last months, some Others have been cooperating

with my office and with PURITY to help us uncover the true nature of the Others living in our midst. These creatures are not the kind souls they try to pretend to be. We've been given information by the Others themselves that has revealed a world you would all be sickened by."

The press in the room began to shout questions and Senator Hayes just shook his head. "No questions. This is too serious for questions."

"This human male is absurdly stupid." Rebecca sniffed, clearly indignant.

"We have learned there are demons. You can all recall they denied the existence of demons in front of my committee in the United States Senate."

Not true. Molly denied that Others called demons. Not that there were actual demons. But Hayes was on a tear, the light of a zealot in his eyes. Demons didn't give a crap about humans or this plane of existence. They had their own world and their own complicated set of rules and organization. Earth was far too loosey-goosey, as his mother would say, for most demons. They liked order.

But he knew there was an ingrained fear of demons based on totally incorrect folklore about them. He understood that ingrained fear and that's why the Others had kept the Veil and anything on the other side of it secret.

"These patriotic creatures exposed to my office a world of vice. Of evil so strong it made me sick to my stomach just to hear about it. Private armies in training to kill all humans. Bloodletting and Satanism. These creatures are not Americans. They are a threat to our very existence. And now the Others who'd been helping us have all disappeared."

Helena lifted a shoulder and a surge of desire rushed through Faine at the sight. Mmm, vicious.

"It is imperative that we pass the Domestic Safety Act and as soon as possible. We must identify and place every last one of these abominations in secure facilities they can no longer harm humans. If we can't do that safely, they need to be eradicated."

The room, instead of getting loud, went very, very quiet.

There was so much magick in the air that the hair on Faine's arms stood.

"I will personally be taking this to the floor this coming week. I urge all Americans to call their senators and representatives to tell them to vote this bill into law so that we may deal with this threat as soon as possible. We have left this long enough. The Others are a threat we cannot overlook another moment. We will also be urging an investigation into the disappearances of the Others who had been helping us."

He turned his attention to Carlo Powers. "Mr. Carlo Powers, a fine American and a guardian of our way of life, has a few words."

Powers stood forward, sending a smarmy smile out over the room. "We've tried our hardest to turn the other cheek with these monsters. If you all recall, it was PURITY who began the first steps in uncloaking the so-called Others. Though it was only from the goodness of our hearts and the purest of motives, they decided right then to try to destroy us and any who got in their way. You saw the way their minion, Molly Ryan, stood up on camera and threatened all of humanity.

"But we are righteous and none can harm us. We must unite to take care of this threat. And make no mistake, *these creatures are a threat*. They will breed into our communities until there are no pure humans left. They will eradicate our way of life, the very thing written into the soul of this country. Every last one of these abominations must be rounded up and dealt with. However that needs to happen. No American should ever have to tolerate sharing the same air with these things. Go to your phones and your computers right now and tell your elected officials what they need to do. Our very soul as a nation depends on it."

He stepped back and after the two waved one last time, they were hustled from the room as reporters shouted questions.

Molly, Meriel and the rest of the folks up in Seattle showed up on the video screen. "Why was this even allowed? That wasn't a press conference, that was a speech! They just gave those fascists free airtime for their hate message."

"Did they just say they were going to kill us?" Gage nearly growled the question.

"Yes." Rebecca took a steadying breath. "Molly, what's the plan?"

"I've got some airtime of our own in the making right now. I'm going to one of the local stations and that will feed to the national affiliates too. I'm going to do some televised remarks that will also be broadcast on the radio and Internet. I'll reiterate the talking points we've already discussed. Just remember this is exactly what we expected. We're as prepared for it as we can be."

Helena broke in. "I'm going to advise that all hunters be on heightened alert. This *will* spill over into violence against Others. Both men just called for our deaths. We'll need to step up our security and the security at all the enclaves and our offices."

"Definitely," Lark agreed.

"Make it happen." Rebecca nodded in Helena's direction and Meriel did the same up in Seattle.

Meriel spoke again. "I'm going to check in with the COO to see where they're all at and I'll update when I get that information."

Rebecca made quick notes and then looked back to the screen. "Thanks, Meriel. I'm going to issue a press release here as well, denouncing the hateful speech of Hayes and PURITY. Of course we have no idea what they're talking about regarding the disappearance of these Others who were supposedly cooperating with them. If there was such a thing, how could one trust the word of a being who'd do that anyway?"

"Exactly. I'll do the same, as will other covens and clans."

The call ended.

Helena waited for a quiet moment with Rebecca. "Sasha will coordinate with your assistant on the details of all your appearances. We can handle the pre-recorded message here, but I'm adding two more people to your personal security and more to your home."

Rebecca's mouth tightened a moment.

"I know you're an incredibly powerful witch. I'm personally totally sure you can handle pretty much whatever comes your way. But you have a family. You have a right to be safe in your home, as do they. You're our public face and you need to be as safe as possible. Don't make me frown at you, it'll give me wrinkles."

Rebecca's mouth curved into a smile, and not for the first time, Faine realized how good she was at gauging people and how to approach them.

"And what about you? Hm? Who protects you, Helena?"

"I do." Faine bowed to The Gennessee.

One regal brow rose. "Is that so, Lycian?"

"Yes, ma'am, it is my honor."

"You and I clearly need to have a long lunch and catch up, Helena. In the meantime, I will assent to more security and I appreciate your attention to detail. It's a weight off my shoulders to know how adept you are at this." Rebecca paused. "I'm going to need you to come up with some contingencies to eradicate Hayes and Powers. They've declared war and we already have. We will not allow this nonsense to continue."

From the corner of his eye, Faine watched Helena square her shoulders and stand straighter.

"Yes, ma'am."

"Keep me posted on that and everything else. This eradication is on a need-to-know basis. Keep it quiet."

Helena nodded.

The room emptied and Helena turned to Faine with a sigh. "I was going to see if you wanted to grab a coffee. I can see that is not in the cards now."

"Do your work. I'll bring you some shortly." He pulled her close and held her for long moments. She sighed, holding on, and he felt better.

"Thank you."

"Your wish is my command, so keep that in mind when you want really dirty stuff." He kissed the top of her head and stepped back, heading for the door.

She blushed and he liked it a lot.

* * *

TOSH waited to see President Sullivan. He'd met her on many occasions, and while he wouldn't say they were friends, he thought her heart was usually in the right place.

She had a big job, he knew that. But this situation was far overdue her guidance and presence.

Joe Porter, her chief of staff, stepped into the room. "I'm sorry, Toshio, but she's been called away and asked me to take the meeting on her behalf."

Tosh stood. "I'm afraid that's not going to work for me, Joe. You know why."

Porter sighed. "It's Marlon Hayes. The damn fool has just done a public statement. She's got to put out some major fires. Tens of thousands of calls have just crashed the phone lines and the servers are overwhelmed. She's got to deal with all that."

"What on earth did he say?" Tosh had turned his phone off when he'd come into the room as was polite. He had no idea what had happened.

Joe blew out a breath. "He's taking the Domestic Safety Act to the floor this week. He urged people to call in to get their senators to support it. Off the record?"

Tosh nodded.

"There were some very thinly veiled calls to execute Others. The president is concerned about violence and retaliation."

Tosh scrubbed his hands over his face. "Is she going to take a position at least?"

"She's going to call for calm and nonviolence. She wants the people to be heard on this. If she takes a position, she's cutting that off."

"Oh bull. Come on, Joe! The time for that has passed. She's the president and this is her job. This is insanity. A United States senator calls for extermination of American citizens? And she's not going to get on television right away and condemn that as un-American? He's whipping up violence. She needs to be a leader right now."

Porter's mouth flattened into a line and Tosh knew he'd overstepped, but he didn't care.

"I want a meeting with her. Please call my office when time opens up. And pray it's not too late."

"Senator Sato, you can tell me your concerns and I'll forward them to the president."

"No offense intended, Joe, but I don't want to meet with you. I want her to look me in the eye when she tells me she's got no intention of protecting the citizens of this country she was duly elected to represent. This has gone on long enough. Time is running out. I've got to go and deal with my constituents. Please do let me know when she'll be available."

He turned and left before Joe could argue, anger coursing through him as he did.

The hallways were far busier than usual. There was an undercurrent of not just gossipy *Did you hear what Hayes said*, but anger and, he was sad to hear, not all of it directed at Hayes and PURITY.

His assistant started to speak when he got back to his offices. "I know. I want to see the footage right now."

"It's queued up in your office. Go on in and I'll get you some coffee. You'll need the caffeine."

He thought what he'd heard would have prepared him for what he'd see. But nothing could have. Nothing in the world could have prepared him for seeing a United States senator not so subtly call for the extermination of a sizable minority of the American population. It was more than sickening, it was outrageous.

Worse, that the president wasn't on television immediately afterward was even more outrageous.

"Get me some time on the shows." He didn't look up from his screen as he spoke to his assistant. "We'll need to get a statement up on the website within the hour, condemning any calls to violence and encouraging a real dialogue that includes listening instead of threatening. Get me Meriel or Molly from Clan Owen."

"On it. Oh, and Senator Sperry is here."

Well that was one nice thing at least. "Send her back. Get me immediately with the rest of this."

He stood as Delilah swept in and sat in a chair across from him. "I suppose you've heard."

"I was waiting to meet with the president when it happened. Porter came out to tell me she had to cancel and why."

Delilah only barely managed to stop from rolling her eyes. Tosh could see the effort it cost her to do so. "What's her story then? Did I miss her speaking on the issue?"

"The president believes that taking a position cuts the process of input from Americans short."

"Did Joe say that to you with a straight face? Because he should be ashamed if he could."

"He's got a job to do. I understand that."

"I don't. Come on, Toshio, they called for our extermination! How is the fact that anyone can stand there with a straight face and say the president won't condemn such a thing an acceptable *job*? Huh? That's not a job. That's something to be ashamed of."

"I refused to meet with him instead of the president. I want her to look me in the eye when she says she's not going to stand up for all Americans."

"Well, good luck to you. I can't even get my calls returned."

"Are you kidding me?"

"Do I sound like I'm joking? This is how it is now, Tosh. From a lot of people. That a colleague would stand up and call for my extermination in front of cameras without any sense of shame is telling. I'm here to let you know I will be on the floor tomorrow. I may get ejected." Her smile made him a little sweaty, in good and bad ways.

"Should I set aside bail money?"

She laughed and took the teacup his assistant handed her with thanks. "No, I don't think I'll be marking that off Marlon's Christmas list. He wants us to be that. But what I will be doing is calling this what it is. I will not wear a yellow star. I will not let them send me to a camp or exterminate me if I'm difficult, and I will say out loud to the American people that if they support this bill that's what they're doing. This is not going down the way it did in the thirties in Germany. I am a motherfucking werewolf and if I'm going down, I will take as many as I can down with me. "

He nodded. "I agree. I'll be saying the same. Well, not the werewolf part."

"Yeah? You stepped out of the middle then?"

"I was never in the middle, Delilah. I have always been on your side. But I will not be silent about this. This is unconscionable."

His assistant popped a head in. "Senator Sato, I just sent the text for the press release to your email if you want to look it over. I'm also going to place a call to Molly Ryan in five minutes. She's on another call right now."

"Great. Thank you. Tell everyone we've got a long night ahead of us. Order in some dinner and let's get this show on the road." He looked to Delilah. "Want to combine efforts?"

"Yes. Let's get some others in on this too."

Chapter 20

THREE hours after the press conference, Helena found herself in front of the Defense arm of the COO, who'd called an emergency meeting after the speech. Familiar faces showed up on the screen, but she found herself shocked by what Lex Warden had just said.

"Can you repeat that?"

Lex Warden smirked but it was gone in moments. Damn he was pretty.

"I said we've elected you. You're now in charge of this body. You know, you make the decisions as to all the military and defense coordination between Others."

"Why?"

"I've watched you do your job. I've watched you do a job in what have been extraordinarily difficult times. You consistently make good decisions. Your judgment is sound. You are vicious, but not without reason and logic. You are well trained and fully capable of training others. You understand what it means to delegate and yet you do not hesitate to take responsibility when you need to. Now, more than any other time in our history, we need to work united. And to do that, we have to make use of our best. You are one of those. As Meriel will run the main body of the COO along with Cade, you will run this body."

She kept her sigh inside her head. There were no other choices to be made. She would accept, of course. But fear trickled through her veins. The stakes were so high she just decided to pretend not to think about it.

"All right. I accept."

Lex tipped his chin. "Good. Now, what do you need?"

Thank heavens she'd already thought in detail on this. "This is how it's going to be. Our current teams of three will go to teams of five. These teams will be mixed with at least two witches. I believe the mix of different skills and gifts will be best used in that combination. The magickal backup is imperative, especially on any type of sweep or investigative work. Each enclave will have constant security. At least one team at the gates and another to sweep through the neighborhoods. That's twenty-four hours a day. All leadership, wolves, witches, cats, Vampires, whatever, needs to have added protection. I can help with that should you want my assistance."

She knew how tricky that part was. Others had been on their own for so long, they really hated to take direction from anyone outside their group. Plus, there were so many alpha males that it was difficult to tell them they needed to be protected.

Still, before Lex became the Alpha of Cascadia, he'd been his brother's Enforcer for years before Cade went on to lead National, so she hoped that gave him perspective from her side of the table.

"Within three minutes of the end of that speech Hayes made, the first official death threat came in. Senate, House and White House servers went offline due to the overwhelming traffic. The phone lines were choked. Not all that was negative, I want to underline that. It is not our belief that a majority of humans feel the way Powers does. But there will be movement after this latest stuff. Our leaders need to be kept safe. Every public appearance should include a team that goes to the venue first and does a sweep and then locks it down until arrival. If they don't like it, too damned bad. We can't trust anyone else to keep us safe."

"You're right. I'm happy to start out and set that example. Tegan has been on me to up my guard anyway. I'll get the news out to the rest of the Packs."

Gibson agreed to do the same for the other shifters. She was meeting with The Gennessee right after this so she'd tell Rebecca then.

"The Vampires will do as you ask."

Okay then.

"I'm working with Owen and the other Clans to make our people available to send to Others who need them for their security teams. The new enclaves have begun to consolidate our populations, which is helpful on many levels. But for areas that may not have a lot of Others of different types, we want to be sure they're being protected. My assistant, Sasha, is keeping the list so please have your people contact her directly and we'll get on that. Lark will continue to work on cross-training programs. The wolves and cats are particularly good at tracking and we have a great deal to learn from them. Faine and Simon Leviathan have graciously volunteered to continue to help train on all things battle and combat."

She went over a few more things before everyone signed out and went their own way.

Lark stayed on the line. "Excellent job."

"Yeah, maybe. Let me know if you need anything. I'm sending some people up to Oregon later today. They're going to hook up with folks from Pacific. Are we covered in Idaho now?"

"Yes. We're good. Cascadia land includes Idaho and they're pretty organized. Most of their people already lived in close quarters and we were able to connect them with contractors and security people to get the place walled and hooked up to cameras and all that. We don't have many witches out that way, but about seventy percent of them have opted to move into the enclave with the wolves. The rest will stay where they are, but have acknowledged the dangers and volunteered to call to check in twice daily. It's the best we can do with Others in far-flung places who decide to remain out of the enclaves."

"Don't you dare feel guilty for that. People are making their own choices for all sorts of reasons. We cannot make everyone safe. We gave them options, they will take them or not, but in the end it's up to them."

Lark laughed. "Seems to me, missy, I've had this exact conversation with you."

"Yes. Well."

"I'll talk to you tomorrow to fill you in on what I learn tonight. Molly is doing a bunch of interviews. We installed some nifty new tech here so she can do sat feeds and doesn't have go to the studio every time."

"Good. I feel better knowing that. We're having dinner with Mom and Dad tonight. Faine insisted so he can announce his intentions or whatever."

"Mom's gonna love that. When are you going to Lycia?"

"He wants to go as soon as possible. But right now things are sort of crazy and I'm not ready to do the binding thing yet."

"Binding thing? You didn't even tell me!"

"I didn't? I just figured. Well, you said you knew he'd set his sights on me. How can you not know?"

"Well, the *Ne'est* thing is a whole different level! Jeez. You can take your time. He'll wait. If he's declared you're his *Ne'est,* he'd wait forever for you. It's not something more than ten percent of them do. It's rare and it's forever and it makes me so happy!"

"It's sort of weird. Two sisters. Two brothers."

"It makes sense I guess for them both to have that connection to us. Partly it's at the DNA level, or so Simon tells me. We're related."

Helena closed the door and came back to sit in front of the video conference set. "So what's it like? The binding I mean."

"I was worried. That it would be too much, or that I'd feel trapped. But really? Do you sort of feel like when you enter a room he's in, there's like a cord of energy between you?"

"It draws me to him. If he's around it's like I know it on some level. But I can't read his thoughts. He's cagey."

Lark laughed. "They all are. But the binding, it sets that connection. It amplifies it. I can think about it and know where

Simon is right now. It doesn't hurt that since all this got worse he makes an effort to be near me all the time. But still. I don't *need* to be near him. But I know where he is. I can sense great shifts of emotion. If he's angry or happy or hurt. They're rebuilding Heart of Darkness right now and he was putting up shelves in his office and suddenly I just know he's been hurt. And he's pissed off. Given our current circumstances I flipped out and rushed over there because he's not answering his phone. He had driven a nail through his hand and he'd done it stupidly and that's why he was pissed. But I don't know his thoughts. And he's a man, so. It's not like chances are it won't be about food or sex at least eighty percent of the time."

Helena laughed.

"It ties your life force to his. That's a clumsy way of explaining something that is . . . well, it changed my life. It didn't take anything away from me. I'm still quite able to be annoyed with him. I can still look at Gage's butt and recognize it for the masterpiece it totally is. I'd love Simon just as much without the binding. But Leviathan now sees me as one of their own. I made a commitment to him and his family both here and in Lycia. That meant a lot to Simon. Family and pack means a lot, you know?"

"Do you think I should do it? It seems so fast!"

"It's been months since you've known him. You have been through some hard-core stuff with him at your side. You know how he'll act in a crisis. You know he'll have your back. Do you love him?"

She thought about it carefully. This wasn't a question she should take lightly. But the answer was inescapable and she was totally, utterly sure. "Yes."

"And he loves you. More than that, by undertaking the binding he's declaring you're it. Forever. He wants to cleave himself to you. Which sounds old-fashioned, but gods, it makes me so happy. It calms me and sustains me that I have someone who commits so wholly. That's what he wants for you. You are, as long as I have known you, the kind of person who commits to something with everything she has. You are his match. He is yours. So yes, I think you should do it. I think you deserve that kind of connection to someone. You deserve that commitment and happiness."

"I'm so afraid of failing. Of failing him. Of failing everyone." She grabbed a tissue from a nearby box and tried to dab her eyes without messing up her makeup. "See, this is why I hate to cry. It's too hard to keep my liner and mascara from running."

"Shut up. You look like a freaking model even after you barf. And look, everyone is afraid of failing. What is the point of having important things in your life if you don't care enough about them to worry you could mess them up? I know we were raised to believe failure is unacceptable. But that's bullshit. Failure happens because no one is perfect. And because very few things in life are totally in your control. So all you can do is your best."

"When did you get so wise?"

"I think it might be some of Simon's wisdom I get through the binding."

Helena snorted. "That is a plus." She took a deep breath. "I guess I need to just suck it up and jump, huh?"

"Yeah. I will say up front that the first few hours after the ceremony you're sort of swimming in all sorts of Lycian pack stuff. Simon said it was like me settling into the collective space the Pack exists in. Like the heart of the Pack or something. Sort of like the Font, I guess. Will you tell me when you go? I want to be there with Simon."

"Yeah? I'd really like you to be there."

"Good, that's settled. I'll talk to you soon. And Hellie? I'm so happy for you. Faine is a lucky dude."

She was still smiling when she came out of the conference room.

Faine was across the way, leaning against a desk and speaking earnestly with her father.

"Uh oh." She gave them both a look when she got to them. "Should I be concerned?"

"I was just telling your father that you'd been named head of the Defense and Security arm of the COO and what some of your orders were. He and I agreed they were quite good orders."

"And I was telling him your mother won't break out anything with tempeh in it until he's been around a while longer. We're having chicken for dinner so don't be late."

"In all fairness, she's a really good cook. I do not agree with her stance on vegan baked goods, but her tempeh stuff is actually quite tasty. I'll bring something sweet."

"Okay." Her dad squeezed her hand and stepped back. "See you two in a bit."

"I have an other hour's worth of work and then we can head out. That work for you?"

Faine nodded. "You all right? You've been crying."

Damn that Lycian nose of his. "It's okay. I just had a nice heart-to-heart with Lark."

He followed her back to her office. "A heart-to-heart that includes crying?"

"I was going to tell you once we left the office, but since you look so concerned, I'll tell you my news now. Yes."

"I like it when you say yes, *alamah*, but to what are you agreeing? Something really dirty, I hope."

Perhaps with Faine it might be closer to 90 percent of his time thinking about sex.

"The binding I mean. You asked and I said I needed time and you've been very good about being patient. Mostly. And I know we need to go to Lycia and I was talking to Lark about it and we started talking about the binding and . . . and anyway, yes."

His smile, which had been wicked and dirty, softened into something else and it brought a sigh to her lips. One of those longing type of sighs because he was so big and badass and yet totally sweet when it came to her.

"You honor me, *alamah*."

"How can I not? Don't let it go to your head though."

He laughed and snuck a quick kiss. "Too late. I want to do this as soon as possible. When can you get away?"

"Right now? I really don't know. I . . . things are hectic and I just took on this new job. I know you want to do it and I absolutely agree. But I'm not sure when I'll have that sort of time."

"When things calm down we can go for a few weeks and stay. I want you to know Lycia." He took her hand, entwining his fingers with hers. "But I want to do the binding as soon as possible. We'll only need a few hours for it." He paused. "It will make you stronger. The link between us will enhance both our natural power and also we'll share of each other. I don't know how it will work for me. Simon tells me he's faster now. That he can shift with more ease and more often without fatigue. His senses are heightened. I imagine it will be similar for me. For you? Your life will be longer. You'll be physically stronger and have more endurance."

He smiled then and it made her tingly. The rogue. But then he quickly got serious again. "And that means you're better equipped for this damned war. I can't do what I really want. Which is to grab you and run as far away from here as I can. You have a path. I can wait however long it's necessary for the binding. But it can help you. And that would make me really happy. Along with all the rest of it. Please?"

It was the please.

Oh, who was she fooling? She wanted it too. And that he wanted it for reasons that were more about her than him touched her deeply.

"Go ahead and see what you can do. It's not like you can call home though, right?"

"No. But I can call my brother and if he's here, he can go home and have them put things in motion. Cardinian, not Simon."

"Ah, he's the one with a Fae wife and a Fae husband too, right?" She waggled her brows and he laughed.

"Yes. He and I share a mother, so he's also half demon. Mei, his wife, is Fae royalty. You'll like her. She's a warrior like you. As is Card's other spouse, Jayce. Card likes to live here and split his time in Tir nA nOg where Mei and Jayce have family."

"You and Simon are lagging behind. No princesses in this lot of sisters."

He brushed a hand over her hair a brief moment. "I'm the luckiest of all."

She smiled because he knew he got to her with all his sweet talk. But it was sweet nonetheless.

"I'm going to call him to get things moving. I'll come for you in an hour for dinner."

She wandered back into her office and got to work. She had enough to stay long past midnight, but she promised her mother they'd be at dinner and she supposed they had an announcement to make anyway.

Chapter 21

HE'D shown up at her office door and stood there glowering until she finally got herself free and came along with him to the car.

At least she'd eat well at her parents'. He'd feel better once they were clear about how seriously involved they were and they could announce the binding too. That, and he knew Rain would make sure her daughter was taking care of herself.

"Card is headed to Lycia tonight. He's going to get everything set up for the binding. He'll contact me when he gets back. He's excited to meet you and Lark both. He was in Tir nA nOg when Simon and Lark performed their binding. Might I invite your parents as well? I know it will be a quick trip there and back so there's no pressure for them to stay over or anything."

"I think they'd really like that. And so would I. You're very good to me. Thank you. I mean that. I don't say it often enough and I apologize for that. But you take care of me and I want you to know I see it and it makes me happy."

He took her hand, kissing her fingertips. She had no idea how happy she made him. And when she said things like that it only made things better. "I was made to love you. It pleases me. But thank you for saying so. We take care of each other, no?" He knew the way she'd agreed to the binding had a lot more to do with how it made him feel than the fact that she'd get stronger afterward. Knew too that the little things he found at his desk, a cinnamon roll, a cup of coffee or a sandwich, were her way of saying how she felt about him.

"We'll ask them tonight then. So I convinced you to move into an enclave. How much work do you think it would take to get your mother and father to do it?"

She scoffed. "It's never going to happen. My mother has woven her power and her magick into the ground here for nearly forty years. She won't go. This is her land. And I understand it. And my dad, well, don't tell him this, but he thinks he's strong enough to protect them here. And maybe he is. The neighborhood is one they've lived in a long time and they haven't had as many problems as others have experienced. But that also means they're known. Lark and I are worried, but there's only so much you can do when it's your parents."

Faine laughed. "Yes. I know. It finally took all of us to gang up on my father and urge him to let Pere take over. Pere is strong. He can take a beating and not even bat an eye. But my father, well, he's getting older. It's hard to deal with the constant dominance battles a Pack leader has to deal with when you're his age."

"Like how old is he? I mean, if you're four hundred and Simon is six hundred. What's the life span?"

"My father is thousands of years old. He doesn't give any exact dates, he's wily that way."

He told her about Lycia. About the places he loved and planned to show her. He thought about the house he had there and the way he wanted to make her comfortable in it. Perhaps add a nursery when she was ready.

"Oh, crap. I forgot I said I'd bring something sweet. Make a right up here. I'll run into the grocery store ahead. It's got a great bakery."

He did as she asked. "You don't have to come in," she said

as he pulled into a space. "I'm just going to run inside. It'll take me five minutes."

He frowned but got out, moving around to open her door.

"Really, Helena, I don't know why you bother to say those things. We both know I'm coming in."

She took his hand with a smile. "I know. But I don't want you to feel obligated."

He frowned at her, but it didn't have any actual menace. She knew it and grinned back.

The store was pretty empty as it was just after seven and all the folks who'd stopped in on their way home had cleared out. She led him through the aisles toward the back where the bakery was.

"We don't have anything like this in Lycia. The first time I came here, in recent time anyway, and I stepped into a grocery store, I think I stood in front of the toothpaste for about half an hour. Dazzled and a little stunned by the sheer variety."

"So what do you have then? Outdoor market stalls and stuff?"

He nodded as she gazed at the pies and realized she couldn't hear a nod. "Yes. But also stores. Usually though they're more like your bodegas. Small with a limited stock."

"I guess you probably get things fresher though. I mean if I had a boulangerie nearby I'd eat fresh bread every day. Also I'd weigh a million pounds because I am powerless against bread. Most carbs really. When I'm on vacation I make bread. And then I eat it all. I tell myself I'm going to give it away but I'm a total liar when it comes to bread."

"Shouldn't you be looking for vegan pie?"

She laughed. "Though she does love to talk up vegan baking and about half of what she makes is vegan, she's not totally there. She is very health conscious. But she loves baked goods and she will totally have some of this really yummy Dutch apple pie. And I'm bringing real whipped cream to go with. Maybe some ice cream too. I'll have to run extra tomorrow, but it'll be worth it."

"Come on then. Let's get the rest. I don't want to be late the first time I eat dinner at your parents' house. That's bad form."

She grabbed the whipped cream and some vanilla ice cream as well and they headed out.

Or they would have if they hadn't been stopped at the checkout.

The checker clearly recognized Helena, and Helena recognized her and smiled. Only the checker picked up a little plastic sign that said "Aisle Closed" and placed it on the counter in front of the food Helena had just put down.

Helena's smile faded. "Really? You must be kidding."

"We don't do business with your kind."

"I've been shopping in this grocery store my entire life. This store has stocked the pantry of my house and then even after, when I moved out on my own as well."

"Now we know what you are."

"A paying customer without which you wouldn't have a job?"

"We'd like to speak with your manager. Please." Faine added the please, but it wasn't sincere and the creature behind the register knew it.

"You need to get out of this store. Your kind isn't welcome."

A few customers had gathered, waiting to pay. All listening. Discomfort and anger radiated from Helena and he yearned to make it better. But he knew she had to deal with this in her way. He'd be there whatever the outcome.

"I need to speak with a manager. That's twice we've asked. Do be a dear and make that happen." Helena's smile was tight and sort of scary. The checker stared, but she was no match for Helena, who stared back with so much intent it sent a thrill through him.

Her magick didn't rise and he knew she made a concerted effort to keep it that way. She could have used it to make things happen her way, but then she'd be proving them right. And his female was far too stubborn to prove anyone right but herself.

"You can wait over there." The checker pointed.

"No, that's all right. I'll wait right here."

"I need to check these other people."

"You need to deal with my groceries first."

The checker glared at Helena, who appeared to not have mustered up a single fuck.

"You're inconveniencing humans. It's bad enough you have the nerve to come in here. Now go wait over there."

At this point Helena bristled and squared her shoulders and the checker finally began to understand she wasn't pushing around any old pretty, well-dressed woman who happened to be an Other.

Her eyes widened and Helena's narrowed.

The person standing behind them spoke. "Jesus Christ. Just check her damned pie out and keep your opinions to yourself."

The person behind them agreed.

But the woman with the small child in the next line piped up. "We know what they are now. You heard it yourself from Senator Hayes and Carlo Powers. They're abominations and no decent person should have to deal with them."

"Ma'am, I can help you." Another checker approached and spoke to Helena before turning his attention to the checker. "Nancy, take a break. Take your drawer with you."

The checker did her business and hustled off with muttered threats and curses.

"Helena, right?"

The new checker began to run the items through.

"Yes. I've been shopping here my whole life."

"I know. We went to school together. I graduated a few years before you did. I apologize for what just happened and I hope you'll give us another chance. Not all of us are Nancy. Fourteen sixty-five."

Helena gave him fifteen.

He leaned close and Faine wanted to growl, but didn't. "I'm a manager here. I'm going to recommend she be disciplined for that. It's clear we need some storewide meetings about this issue."

She took her change and nodded. "Thank you." And then

looked around Faine's body to the people behind him. "And thank you."

Those who'd come to her defense nodded and the guy immediately behind Faine said, "Shit got real today with that nutty asshole speaking out. I know things are scary but I hope you remember we're not all that way."

"I appreciate that. And I'd love it if you'd take a second when you got home to send your legislators a note. We need all the support we can get."

Faine grabbed the bag and the pie and they headed out.

"That totally sucked."

He tended to agree.

"It was nice that others spoke up." Always good to point out positives.

"Sure. Man, I want to eat all the pie now. In the car on the way over."

He laughed as he opened her door. "I'm sure your mother would understand if you did."

That's when they approached.

He was getting in on his side when her door flew open and her attention shifted as she was unceremoniously hauled from the car by three men.

"Stupid whore witch. Someone needs to teach you and your friend a lesson about knowing your place."

He was mid shift and up over the car before he could even think about it.

SHE'D been pushing her anger and hurt away, stunned, as always, by how good her man looked when her door opened up.

Confusion froze her in place for moments because she was looking at Faine and he was the only one who should have been opening her door but he was on the other side of the car so it couldn't be him.

Hands grabbed her by her upper arms, sending pie all over the place as it hit the dash.

Her moment of confusion was over quickly enough. Quickly enough to hook an ankle around the calf of one of her attackers and send him to the ground. She pivoted once her arm was free and elbowed another on the face, and the satisfaction of the crunch of a broken nose roared through her. He howled in pain as he stumbled back, blood flinging everywhere, and she used it, drew it around her and strengthened her power.

"You ruined my pie, asshole." She gave him a roundhouse kick, knocking him into the car the next stall over and to the ground as the alarm went off.

One of them cracked her in the back of the head with a blackjack. Which is why at first when she heard the roar she wasn't sure if it was real or something she imagined.

She nearly fell over at the wave of white-hot pain. But the blood that had been spilled kept her focus, so she reached out, spooling her power up through the concrete, the air around her crackling with it. Faine, his beast anyway, bounded over and knocked one of them down, landing on him with an *oof* of expelled breath and what she figured was also a broken rib or two given Faine's size and the way he'd jumped on the guy.

Her vision had stopped doubling enough for her to open her palm and blow a ball of energy right before she pulled her fist back and gifted him with a one-two punch of magic and fist right to his stupid pie-ruining bigot face. His eyes rolled up and he crumpled to the ground.

"Call the cops," she called out to the manager, who'd rushed to the door to see what the commotion was. "And you be sure your little pal Nancy doesn't leave."

"What?"

She turned and the nausea rose quickly. She had to breathe through her nose for a moment. She probably would have a concussion, but her mother could help with that.

"These guys knew what I was. How on earth would some random passersby know that? Someone told them. And that someone is very likely our little white-sheeted friend Nancy."

She pulled her phone out. "Never mind, I'll call."

One of the guys on the ground groaned and started to move and she kicked him—hard—before she spelled him to sleep.

The cops arrived quickly—three cars' worth—and of

course pulled weapons on Faine, who was still in his beast's skin.

She spoke calmly, but loudly enough that they could hear her over the whimpering of the guy Faine stood on. "Nope. Wrong as usual. These three pieces of filth yanked me from the car and began to attack me. One of them hit me in the back of the head with that blackjack over there near the curb."

"I'll tell you when we need your story." The cop kept his weapon trained on Faine.

She sighed heavily. "I spent the last months making excuses for you all. But I'm done with that now. You will get your damned weapon off him. I told you, *they* attacked *us*. I quit your fucking jurisdiction if you're only going to apply the law to certain people. I'm not weak and I will not allow you to play this game. So you can collect your scum but you will get your damned guns out of my face."

The group of police there seemed divided. Some lowered weapons, while others ranged between rage and confusion, but kept guns trained on her or Faine.

The officer spoke again. "Or what? Only one of us has a gun. How about we take this little convo down to the station?"

She was so totally done. If this asshole wanted to bring it, she'd give it to him. "If you think you can do it, give it a try." She flexed her power and blew just a small bit of heat his way. Enough that he should understand she wasn't defenseless.

"I think a better question to ask is whether or not you really want to push me. All I wanted was to buy a pie to take to my mom's house for dinner where I was going to announce my engagement. A normal thing. I came to the same market I've come to my entire life and had some bitch give me lip about not serving *my kind*. This after a senator called for my imprisonment and or death on the news. I come out here and three thugs come up out of the blue and assault me, and then you people show up on the scene and give me more shit? I am done. Test me, Officer, but only do it if you're sure you can handle what happens."

She saw the fear finally visit his features and she narrowed her gaze. *Yes, that's right monkey boy, I got skills and I will*

*blow your butt off this pavement. I am PMSing and annoyed
and covered in pie.*

Faine tensed and a low, really scary growl trickled from
him. She got herself back under control because the last thing
they needed was for Faine's beast to get any more pissed off.

The manager spoke up. "Um, Officer? We have video camera footage of the outside of the store. You can look at it and
verify her story. I can verify the rest about how she was treated
by one of my employees."

"We saw it all." The guy who'd been behind them in line
spoke up. "I came out right behind them. It was my call you
got first. Those three guys grabbed her, pulled her out of the
car and started beating on her. The wolf guy, he only attacked
after they jumped her."

"Stand down, Officer." One of the other cops who'd arrived
spoke up. "Our apologies," he said to Helena. "Been quite a
day. We got a bulletin from the special Federal Task Force
guys to be on alert." He holstered his weapon. "Get these
assholes cuffed and loaded up. Make sure they get looked at
so we don't get blamed for police brutality." He looked back
to Helena. "The PURITY folks' newest thing is to get into
altercations with Others, and then if we arrest them, to claim
we dinged 'em up."

"Makes you wish you'd have really done it, huh?"

His smile told her exactly that.

The manager came out with an ice pack and handed it her
way. "Here, put this on your head."

"Miss? Can you, um, get him to back off so we can take
the guy into custody?" The cop motioned toward Faine, who
continued to bristle as he growled low and scary when anyone
tried to get close.

She stepped to him, placing her face against his, breathing
in the loam and fur of him and letting him take her magick
in as well. "It's okay. I'm all right. They're going to arrest
them all. Please step back so they can do that."

He growled, but it was annoyance and not rage like he'd
done to the humans. She wrestled back a smile. "You don't
scare me, big guy."

He snorted, but stepped back, leaning against her. She needed the support, as her head felt like crap.

"He's big. Even for a werewolf."

"Yes, he's an overachiever that way." Her fingers threaded through his fur and held on; he pressed against her body and a wave of warmth hit. She knew it was his. Knew he'd take care of her no matter what. But she knew, also, that he was probably on his very last nerve with the entire situation, so she wanted to get things moving.

"Can I get my statement taken so we can leave? My parents are expecting us for dinner and they're going to be worried."

Faine transformed and stood taller, totally naked. The cops looked up and then up some more. He was just as forbidding in his skin as a man, really. "And she needs to have her head seen to."

But back to the naked thing. She stepped in front of him and he pulled her against his body. But not to shield his nakedness. He didn't care about that. And why should he when he looked so good?

He wanted to comfort her and it did calm her just to have him there.

"We can probably get a blanket for you. You know, to cover up." The cop, Officer Patterson, offered helpfully.

"I have a spare change of clothes in the trunk. If I may?"

The words were those of a question, but it really wasn't a request and they all knew it. But they allowed it anyway and he got changed rather quickly and he never got farther than a foot away from her.

She knew he was angry. The barely leashed fury from his beast throbbed from him in hot waves. She wondered if the cops could feel it, or if they only sensed it and that was why they kept a wary eye on him.

Then again it could have been because he was a massive beast under his skin, the likes of which they'd never seen.

"Can you please call my parents and let them know we're going to be held up? Don't go into too much detail, they'll only worry. But we'll be there as soon as we can."

Faine nodded, but didn't move away to make the call. Instead he moved back to his place behind her, one hand on her shoulder, and did it there.

Patterson took their statement, got all their contact information and sent them on their way after they refused to go to the hospital.

She thanked the manager and the witnesses who'd stayed to speak to the cops and then got back into the car and they headed to her parents' place.

"Your mother isn't going to be pleased. She was quite disgruntled that I wouldn't go into specifics."

"She's the wife of a hunter, it comes with the territory. Damn it. They totally messed up my pie and got it all over your upholstery. I'm sorry."

"You. Be quiet and rest. I can get my car cleaned, but you are not replaceable, so hush."

He was silent as they made their way the two short miles to the house. He tried very hard not to think about it. About the way she'd taken on those thugs and also the cops, no fewer than six holding weapons on her.

"I'm proud of you. You were a fine warrior tonight," he said as they pulled up and he turned the engine off.

"Thanks for jumping on that jerk and breaking a few of his ribs for me."

He knew he shouldn't smile. It would only encourage her. But she made him laugh. "I would have taken out the other two, but you got to them pretty fast. Though I'm sorry about your head. I should have been faster."

"I'm totally covered in goo. My head hurts like crazy and I totally threatened to throw down with a cop, so I'm quite grumpy. Far too grumpy to let you take responsibility for that dumb thing. So get out of the car and come open my door so we can go inside. Also? I love you."

He had been ready to argue, but the last thing she said froze him in place. It wasn't that he didn't know she felt deeply for him. She'd agreed to the binding already. But it meant something to him that she'd say it.

He took her hand and kissed it. "Your knuckles are raw and you taste like blood and cinnamon. I love you too. Infuriating and danger-courting woman that you are."

Before he could say anything else, her father opened the front door and her mother came out on the porch.

She waved.

"Oops, no time to scold me anymore. Rain has seen us."

"Sit still. I'll be around." He kissed her quickly and got out, waving back to her parents before he opened her door and helped her out.

Her mother got a look at the disheveled state of her usually neat-as-a-pin daughter and rushed down the front steps. Faine felt the warmth of the wards that admitted them as they moved toward her mother.

"I'm all right. I just need to get changed and fed and maybe some pain reliever. Not necessarily in that order."

Her mother tutted over her. "Hello, Faine. Come inside both of you and then someone had better be explaining why I had to hold dinner and my daughter has clearly been in a fight of some sort."

"She's been hit in the back of the head with a blackjack." Faine wanted to be sure to let Rain know up front because that sort of thing worried him. He knew Helena was tough, but she was his.

"David, please bring me an ice pack and my herbs." Rain took Helena's hand. "Come on. You know the drill."

"Dad, get Faine something to eat and drink. He'll tell you what happened."

"Faine will be right here with you and your mother, so I'll tell them both. Should I carry her, Rain?"

Rain looked a great deal like her daughters as she turned, surprised and then very amused. "Oh that would be delightful to see. But no, she's going to sit right there." She pointed and Helena sighed, sitting where her mother pointed.

Eyes closed, one hand on her lower belly, she touched the same place on Helena and frowned. Her lips moved as she slid her palm from Helena's belly to the back of her head.

Helena's eyes flew open. "No."

Rain continued to murmur, ignoring Helena. Faine looked
to David, who shook his head.

"Mom, I said no." Helena tried to move her mother's hand
and Rain's eyes snapped open and her energy built up hot
and fast. Faine stepped back and David appeared just as
surprised.

"You will hold your tongue."

Helena pushed back against her mother's command.
"You're taking this into yourself. I won't let you!"

"It's my gift and I'll do what I want with it. Stop fighting
me. It takes more of my energy and I'm going to win either
way. I'm your mother, Helena. Obey me immediately."

Helena frowned.

"Listen to your mother."

At David's terse words, Helena sighed and put her hands
back into her lap.

"Why don't you tell me what happened?" David asked
Faine.

He explained it all as Rain worked just a few feet away.
David's frown grew deeper with each word Faine spoke until
he slammed his fist into the wall next to the bathroom door.

Rain sighed and looked to them both. "You'd better not
have dented my drywall again. Go on out to the dining room.
Helena is going to shower and change. Don't go too far, Faine,
I'm going to be looking you over in a few minutes to be sure
you're all right."

Faine hated leaving Helena alone but knew he had no
choice. She was safe here in this house.

"She's more upset about the way she was treated by that
checker than the three who attacked you all."

Faine nodded his thanks when David handed him a soda
water with some lemon. He didn't know how much Helena
would feel okay with him sharing with her father. Which
seemed stupid.

"I think so. Using her fists and her magick on strangers?
That's easy for her. Having someone she trusted in some sense
betray that? It shook her."

"She likes to pretend nothing shakes her. I suppose that's

my fault. I raised them hard. Too hard, as my lovely wife likes
to say. This isn't a job or a life for fluffy bunny parenting.
Rain did that part. But both my girls have big hearts and a
seemingly infinite ability to protect people, and it gets to them
more than they want to admit when people can't see it."

Helena hated being misjudged. Faine could see that quite
plainly after all the time they'd spent together. He hated that
for her too, because she was so good and people took it for
granted sometimes.

"She'll be out shortly and I'm sure Rain will want to feed
you both. It's her way of protecting those she loves."

"You're a lucky male."

David paused as he pulled something from the oven. "Yes,
I am. And now I suppose I'm going to have to hand over my
last precious thing to another male. Yes?"

"She'll want us to be together when we tell you most of it,
but man to man, I want to tell you how much I cherish your
daughter. I will take care of her, protect her. The best I can,
that is. Your daughter is wily and seems to attract trouble as
easily as she breathes. I will spend all my days making her
happy and making sure she has everything she needs. Not
that she doesn't have the ability to do it all herself. She's self-
sufficient and eminently capable."

Her father smiled at him. "She'll beat your ass if you screw
her over. And then I will. And then Lark will. But it's really
Rain you need to worry over the most."

Faine snorted a laugh. "The Jaansen females are nothing
to sneeze at. It's no wonder that my brother and I found our
women in two of them. Intelligent. Powerful. Strong. Beautiful. She'll be right at home in Lycia among warriors."

"You could take her there now and keep her away from
whatever is to come. Keep her safe."

Faine laughed. And then he laughed some more. "Nothing
happens to your daughter that she doesn't want to happen. I
just watched her beat down two human males who topped six
feet and she barely used her magick. However much I might
wish to shield her from all this, especially after I saw her stop

a bomb, I'd never disrespect her like that. Also, she'd kill me in my sleep if I tried."

"There is that," David agreed as he put the bowls of food on the table.

"And to be truthful? I believe Helena is important to all this. She's integral in how things will play out."

"Do you say that in general or . . ."

"I have a touch of foresight. Not like my mother, who is quite powerful with it. But enough that my gut tells me she's part of this in such a way that should she not be around, things would go worse."

"**GET** out of those clothes. I'm going to burn some of these herbs in here while you shower. You'll absorb them through your skin in the steam."

Helena knew better than to argue with her mother, so she hoped Faine hadn't given her any of his love bites.

"Oh, they ruined your blouse. And it was such a pretty one." Her mother picked it up and examined it. "I might be able to fix it. The rip is at a seam." She put it aside and began to set up the brazier where she'd burn the herbs.

"Do I have to use the green soap?" She hated the green soap. It was gross and slick and she smelled like pesto when she got out of the shower. But it was healing soap and she already knew the answer.

"Don't waste my time with this nonsense, Helena. Make sure you get it on the back of your head where they hit you."

"Speaking of that." She turned the shower on and then finished undressing. The crisp scent of the herbs floated her way from where her mother had just murmured her spell and the flame sparked. "How's *your* head now?"

"I'm going to drink some healing tea, but really? I'm all right. At first when I drew it from you it was bad. I can't believe you were even able to stand in so much pain."

"I was sitting. And Faine nearly carried me to the front door. Also, I'm used to it. You aren't." She breathed in deep, knowing the herbs would work better if she just sucked it up and used the gross green soap and let the herbs her mother burned do their job.

"Sweetheart, between your father and you and your sister, I'm quite used to it. And since the Magister my abilities have grown. I'm astonished at how much in some ways."

"Mine too."

"Yes, I saw footage of my daughter on her knees, blood everywhere, stopping a bomb. Nothing I'll be forgetting any time soon. You foolish, foolish girl."

Her mother's tone was sharp, full of fear, and Helena knew it wasn't a rebuke.

"It was so brave. All that you do. Every day. It's brave and right and I'm so very proud of you."

Tears stung her eyes so she closed them and pretended it was the soap. "Thank you."

"No, thank you. Now. What on earth is this mess on your pants?"

"Pie. Those assholes not only ruined the pie I was bringing over, but they got it all over me *and* Faine's car too. It's going to be a sticky mess in there. But it'll smell good."

Her mother laughed. "I like him. Faine, I mean. I like how focused he is on you without seeming obsessive or creepy."

"I'm in love with him."

"That much is clear. He feels the same."

"Yes." She rinsed off, feeling much better.

"You have clothes here still. I'll be back in a moment with something for you to change into."

She dried off and noted the bruises beginning to appear on her legs and side where she'd hit the car door. They wouldn't be as bad because of the magick and the "green-work" as her mother called the herbal magick she used. Her head didn't hurt so much she wanted to puke anymore. But she'd definitely take some pain reliever once she got food into her body.

"Will he take care of you?" Her mother thrust some clothes into her hands. "Like you deserve to be?"

"Faine?"

She pulled on the yoga pants and an old long-sleeved shirt. "I can't believe you still have this shirt."

"You and your sister leave things here. I put them away in case you ever need them. And I like having some of your belongings in the house. It's a tie to you both."

She pulled on a pair of thick socks.

"Yes. He takes care of me like I should be. He's kind. Really bossy. But not in a gross *I'm the boss, you do that* way."

"Well, that's good, as you'd have to punch him in the sac if he acted like that."

Helena laughed as she finished braiding back her wet hair. She turned to her mother and hugged her. "I love you."

"I love you too, baby."

When they both got back out to the dining room, Helena's stomach growled rather rudely. Faine smiled as he caught sight of her. "You look better."

Her mother breezed past and took over from her dad. "She'll be better after she eats. Sit, everyone."

They filled their plates and ate for a bit, Helena answering questions from her father about the assault at the grocery store.

"I'm afraid we're going to need to add it to the list of places Others need to be wary about." They had a list, available at the website, of businesses and places throughout the country that Others had negative and positive experiences with. "I think we should give the owner a chance to issue a statement though. If they deal with this Nancy creature and they're otherwise fine to do business with, that's all we can ask really. There are bound to be problem employees all over the place. No matter how awesome the owners and management."

"You're probably right. But I want to go over there right now and hit someone. Screw being the bigger person. As they're so fond of saying, I'm not a person anyway."

Hearing her normally loving and gentle mother say something like that broke Helena's heart. She wanted to push that negativity away, even if just for a little while.

"Faine has asked me to marry him. Well, to bind with him. I've accepted."

Her mother's face lit and she was glad she'd brought it up. "A binding, like what Lark and Simon have?"

"Yes, ma'am." Faine nodded, reaching out to take Helena's hand. "There's no reason for me to pretend she's not it for me. This binding is a ceremony older than recorded history. My brother is in Lycia right now, putting all the arrangements in place."

"It'll just be a short thing this time. We'll go, do the binding and have a small family party and come right back. Things are too uncertain here for us to be gone any longer. But we'd like you to be there. Simon and Lark will be as well."

"Of course we'll be there. Normally, I'd frown and say it hasn't been long enough. But you're not one to make rash decisions. This man has been at your side for months in some rather difficult situations. And he's proven he can be counted on. It's something a mother worries over. I knew your father was the one the third day after I met him."

Helena settled in and ate, listening to her mother tell the story of their courtship. Her father leaned toward his wife, a grin on his face. Faine laughed here and there, nodded, and the sounds of it, the sheer, wonderful normalcy of it, healed her far better than a hospital could have.

Chapter 22

FAINE kissed her awake. "Hello there."

"Not that I am complaining about the kisses, but it's really early." She turned to look at the clock. "Like two in the morning early."

"Card just called. They're ready for us."

"Like binding ceremony ready?"

He nodded. "Are you ready?"

Yes, she realized, she totally was. She tangled her fingers with his. "I am. Let's call everyone. I take it you'll have to be with my parents to get us all through at once, right?"

"Card volunteered to do it. He's going to be with his wife, who is Fae, and her ability to travel between the Veils is pretty awesome."

"Let me call them to let them know what to expect." She did, and once her father knew she was calling for something good instead of another assault of some kind, he perked up and said they'd be waiting for Faine's brother when they arrived.

She went into the closet and stood. "Oh my goddess. I have no dress. I don't know what to wear."

He brought her a garment bag. "I saw this and I thought you might like it."

"You bought me a wedding dress?" She laughed. "Really?" He did have great taste so it wasn't like she was worried. "You're incredibly sweet, you know that?"

"Yes. Well. I want you to be happy. I know this is all very rush rush and not probably what you dreamed of as a girl."

She took the bag but before she unzipped it, she looked up into that gorgeous face of his. "I dreamed of weapons when I was a girl. I never dreamed of a big wedding. And I have my dream man right here."

He smiled and kissed her quickly. "Good. Then you should know your roundhouse kick needs some work. I'll help you with it later today."

She laughed, unzipping the bag. "Okay then."

Inside the bag . . . wow. A pale blue dress. Vintage styled. Chantilly lace, low in the back, draped at the front with a formfitting bodice. It was classic and simple and very elegant. And chosen by a man who clearly understood her better than she could ever deserve.

"This is . . . I honestly couldn't have picked a more beautiful dress on my own." It was perfect. "You know me well."

"I hope to love you as well as I know you." He then drew out a ring box and got to one knee.

"I'm going to cry."

"You're supposed to. Will you marry me, Helena?" He opened the box and inside was a single ring made of three interwoven bands studded with diamonds. "A band for you, a band for me and one that symbolizes us."

Crying, she took it out and he slid it on. It was perfect. Like he was perfect. "Where did you come from and whatever did I do to merit such a blessing?"

"Good answer." He stood. "Wait to get dressed until we get to Lycia. I've already called Simon and he and Lark will be there waiting. I figure you'd want to have your mom and sister help you get ready."

He drove them to the spot he said they'd use to go to Lycia. "The Fae can travel a lot easier. They sort of fold space and move through it. Like in Harry Potter. But we use thin spots. One is just here. We can hold a corridor open and go through that way."

"Can anyone do it? Is it magick? Is it guarded on the other side? What if humans came through with an army?"

He kissed the top of her head and led her to the clearing. They were about forty-five minutes east of the house.

"I've been to this park before. There are ley lines here."

"Maybe that's why we can cross in this spot. It is magick in its own way, yes. Yes, it's guarded on the other side. Though there are many spots here on this side of the Veil, they all open to the same place in Lycia. And no, humans can't cross it. Only those carrying Lycian blood can do it."

"Oh. Well that's good. Safer."

He saw her disappointment and grinned. "You'll be able to do it once we're bound. Lycia will recognize you as her own."

She perked up. "Cool!"

She wasn't sure what she was expecting, but he drew a hand through the air in front of them and they kept walking, and then they were standing in a field with a whole different sky.

The magick at her feet surged to greet her, rushing through her veins. "Holy cow. That's good."

He turned. "What?"

"The magick here. It just filled me up. The earth recognized me immediately."

He smiled. "Really? I like that."

Someone hailed them and he waved, speaking another language briefly.

"My brothers are here. Come on then. Welcome to Lycia."

She wished so much that they could stay for longer than just a few hours. It was beautiful there. The stars burned bright overhead as they headed toward a grouping of buildings ahead.

"This is Leviathan ground. All the eye can see belongs to us. The biggest building over there is a meeting hall. We'll have the binding there. That's my parents' home just ahead."

He was unbearably pleased with how much joy she wore on her features. He'd seen her in a pretty wide array of situations and moods, but this Helena was so full of wonder and happiness that he found himself unable to stop smiling. He held her close, an arm around her shoulders, and she slid hers around his waist as she peppered him with questions.

Up ahead, his parents came out of the house and waved, both wearing smiles. Lark and Simon, along with Helena's parents, approached from the gate as well. This was a good thing.

And with so many bad things occurring with alarming regularity, good things were to be treasured.

His mother approached and simply pulled Helena into a hug. "Welcome to you, daughter."

"*Mamieri*, this is Helena. My *Ne'est*. Helena, this is my mother, Tila, and my father, Cross."

And then his woman got to one knee and touched her forehead. "It is my honor to become a member of your Pack and to be the key to your son. I will guard your lands with my body and your honor with my heart and fists."

He was the one honored. He had no idea she knew to do that. But it was exactly the right thing and he could see the approval rolling from his father and the rest of his family gathered there.

Cross stood forward and touched Helena's forehead. "It is Leviathan's honor to add you to the rolls. Stand and take your place, daughter."

Faine helped her stand.

"Come on then." Tila clapped. "Helena, Lark and Rain, follow me. We've got some rooms prepared for Helena so that she can prepare for the binding."

Helena turned to Faine and he hugged her. "You do me such an honor tonight. I love you."

"I love you too. I'll see you in a bit. Don't go sniffing around any other ladies here or I'll be forced to maim you."

He laughed and hugged her again. "All right, I promise."

She was quickly swallowed up by females and swept off toward the meeting house.

His father slapped him on the back. "It's too bad there are only two of these sisters. You and Seymeon have clearly met your match. You will make fine babies to fill my home with laughter. Your mother and I are pleased with your choice."

They headed to the main house where drinks were poured and the stories began as his brother Pere performed the ritual cleanse and blessing for the binding rites.

He loved Helena Jaansen with all his being. She was his key. The one person in all the worlds who he would love forever. Vexing. Beautiful. Intelligent. Canny. Powerful. She was so much more than what she appeared at first glance. She was a worthy partner in life and they would have such a future.

This was good. And right.

"I felt the exact same when I did this with Lark." Simon stepped back after he'd finished the warrior braids at each of Faine's temples. In Lycian culture, it was the males who tended to the dressing of a warrior's hair for any important ceremony. In fact, Pere had gone to Helena just a few minutes before, to tend to her hair.

"Am I so obvious then?"

Their father raised his glass in Faine's direction. "If you are not, it's not meant to be. Doubts have no place in such a ceremony. We may take a few centuries to do it, or we may never make such a choice. But a binding is only for the certain. The magick you and Helena will create as a unit will make you both stronger and wiser. It will make Leviathan stronger and wiser. Sisters binding with brothers has its own sort of energy. It's rare and these two sisters are exceptional. Strong and gifted." He turned to David. "Your daughters are welcome here, as are you and Rain. We honor those who raise such powerful beings."

"It's all Rain. Except for the weapons work." He grinned. "That's me. And they're both pretty good at it if I do say so myself."

He had no doubts as they left the main house. A line of lit torches led the way to the meeting house. Ceremonial herbs burned in the large, open space and flowers and tributes began to fill the room.

And there she was. At the head of the room with Pere on one side and her sister on the other. Warrior braids at each temple. And yet, she still looked delicate and beautiful in the dress he'd chosen for her. She'd understood that it was more than just a gift he'd given her. The dress, the ring, the house here and the one in the enclave that he'd furnish to her liking, these things were his way of fulfilling his pledge to her.

He approached her and went to his knees. He spoke to her in their ancient tongue, pledging his fidelity, his loyalty and his honor to their union. But she had no need for an interpreter.

Getting to her knees, she handed him a bundle of flowers woven together with herbs and tied with ribbons the color of their Pack.

She spoke back in the same language. Accepting his pledge and giving one of her own. Tila and Rain came forward then and bound their hands together at the wrist. Wreaths were placed on each one of their heads and ceremonial smoke was blown over them as the oldest of them, his great, great uncle, came forward.

As the elder, he was the repository of their history. Of the Pack's magick and lore. He performed all important rites and ceremonies. One hand on each of their heads, he began to speak low, his beast very close to the skin.

Faine felt his own stir in response and scented Helena's magick as it rose and filled the air.

Pere hit the earth beneath them hard with his staff and the rush of Helena's magick filled him to bursting. His skin was tight and super-heated. She gazed at him, calm as beast rushed through him and into her. Then her head fell back as she said *oh* softly.

Her magick was cool and confident as it took up space in his gut. Where his beast usually curled up.

The elder sliced each of their hands with a ceremonial blade and their blood mixed and dripped over the cords binding their wrists and then the earth at their knees.

Her magick burst from him then, mingling with his beast

as it rushed back into his belly and filled him once more. But it was changed. *He* was changed. Her magick was part of him now and he realized his beast was part of her in much the same way.

She was satisfied. Full of joy and certainty.

"It is done." The elder spoke and removed his hands before he cut the cords at their wrists and stepped back. "You are bound."

And he was. And it was the best thing he'd ever felt.

"Now, we have but a short time before Faine and Helena have to leave, so let us celebrate this new binding!" Cross cracked open a bottle.

Faine helped her stand and pulled her close. "Hello."

"Hi there. Wow, your beast is amazing. No wonder you carry yourself like such a badass. I would too if that much power lived in my belly all the time."

He kissed her and held her for long moments. "You learned the words of the binding for me."

"Even better. Rain found a spell, sort of a universal translation spell."

"Amazing. And your magick lives in me as well. I rather like it. My beast is curled up with it as if it's his."

She laughed. "Like a chew toy? I like that."

"Me too. Now, let's drink and have food. In a few hours we have to leave here and face the day back home."

"Oh that." She winked and squeezed his hand. "I'm sorry I don't have a ring for you. But can I tell you how much I really love those braids you're rocking? I'm going to need to learn how to do them."

"I'd like that. I was thinking that we could get rings designed once this mess was taken care of. And I'll need to come back here to receive the binding marks."

"Oh like the ones Seymeon has over his heart?"

"Yes."

"Would they do it for me too?"

"It's old-school ink, Helena. Sharpened bone tapped into the flesh. It takes multiple hours over a few days."

"I understand."

"I don't know how you always manage to say the right things. But I thank you for it."

"That's why I'm your key, right?"

"Right."

They turned to their loved ones, still holding hands, and received all their love and well wishes.

TOSHIO had overheard something he was sure he shouldn't have. He hurried down the hall, heading to Delilah's office, which was closer than his own.

"Toshio!" The hail at his back sounded an awful lot like Carlo Powers. The way the man had just been saying what he had and also referred to Tosh by his first name instead of Senator Sato rubbed Tosh the wrong way.

He was a veteran. A JAG. An elected official and most definitely not a coward. He would not run from this garbage.

He slowed and turned, not bothering with a smile.

"I didn't realize you meant me at first."

"I called your name." Powers' smile was smarmy and patronizing.

"No, you called Toshio instead of Senator Sato, so I was sure you didn't mean me."

"Ah, I thought we were past such formality."

"Why would you think that? What is it you want, Mr. Powers? I'm a busy man."

"There's no need for hostility. I saw you in the hall outside Marlon's office and we hadn't yet spoken about the troubling issue of the Others."

"Like your despicable call for the death or incarceration of a significant minority of our citizenry? I should think such a conversation wouldn't be necessary. I find you and your ideas repugnant. That you have a senator in your back pocket makes it more so. My opinions regarding the civil and human rights status of Others are well documented. I'll pray for you, Mr. Powers, but there's no use in discussing your *ideas* because they're disgusting and un-American."

The smarm fell right off Powers' features then and the mean settled into his eyes. Tosh had seen that brand of meanness, usually before someone used a racial epithet on him.

"I'm sorry to hear it. I'd hoped you'd choose America over your Other-loving ways. But I guess once you get one into bed you lose your mind."

"I'm not surprised your mind is in the gutter right along with your soul."

"Save it, *Toshio*. You're nothing and neither is that werewolf whore."

Delilah materialized at his side as if he'd dreamed her up. And thank goodness she was there to grab his fist before it slammed into Carlo Powers' face.

"Careful there, Carlo. Your pornographic imaginings might get you into trouble. Run along and go find your white sheet." Delilah actually inserted herself between them, giving Powers her back in what was a supreme wolf insult.

"I was just on my way to your office." He dismissed Powers before he lost his shit and beat the crap out of him like he preferred to. "Oh, and Mr. Powers? That's still Senator Sato to you."

They continued to Delilah's office and he shut the door, leaning against it and scrubbing a hand across his face. "I apologize you had to hear such filth. I wanted to punch him. I should have punched him."

She waved it away and took his hands, bending to kiss each fist. "I appreciate the chivalry. But I can assure you, Toshio Sato, that once you do get into my bed, you won't be the same."

Her grin eased his spine a little. "Listen, I have to make a call right now. Can you be sure we're not overheard?"

"Only if you tell me what the heck is going on."

He did and her eyes got wide. "Be right back. I'll send my staff out to get me something to eat and have Allen watch the door."

He got his phone out and dialed Molly.

"Tosh, how are you?" He smiled at the sound of her voice.

"I've been better. Nearly punched Carlo Powers in the face for calling Delilah a whore five minutes ago."

"What? There's something very wrong with him. Why is he always lurking around the senate offices anyway?"

"I need to talk to you about that. You might want to have Meriel in on this too."

"That doesn't bode well. I'm not at the office right now. I'm on my way to a COO meeting."

"Okay then, you can tell them all when you get there. I overheard something today. Something I shouldn't have. Marlon and Carlo were in Hayes's outer office. They have some sort of book. Someone gave them a book and Powers says it has a spell that will open the way to bring the Magister back. One of the turned witches told him they could kidnap Rebecca Gennessee and she could perform the spell. They have her address and handed it over to the turned witches."

"Holy shit."

Given that Molly rarely ever cursed, it was an indicator of how seriously she took what he just told her.

She sighed. "Okay. I'll pass all this on. Did they know you heard? You said you had an altercation with Powers."

"He saw me in the hall, he said. But I don't think he knows I heard."

"You need to be on the alert and take extra precautions. Delilah too. Thank you for telling me."

"Of course. Let me know if I can help in any other way. I'm calling Agent Anderson at the FBI when I get off the line with you. They need to know. As for the bill, we're debating this on the floor later today and into tomorrow."

"I'll be watching. Be careful, Tosh."

"You too, Molly." He hung up and looked to Delilah, who handed him a cup of coffee. "Now to call Gil Anderson."

Chapter 23

HELENA was still riding on a lovely joy-inspired high when her phone rang. It was Molly and she smiled, answering. "Hey there, Moll."

"I wish I was only calling with congratulations."

Helena sighed. "Uh oh."

"First, congratulations. I'm so happy for you. Faine is perfect and the two of you are so wonderful together. I'm sorry I had to miss the ceremony, but Lark says your parents are planning a big party for a few months from now so Gage and I will definitely be at that one. We'll need to throw a bachelorette party. Belated of course, but still."

"Looking forward to seeing you wearing a hat with penises all over it."

Molly paused and Helena laughed, just imagining her face just then. "All righty then. On that note, and really speaking of dicks, I have some news about Hayes and Powers."

"Ugh."

Which of course was an understatement once Molly had updated her. She started her walk over to Rebecca's office. "I'm on it. Does Lark know?"

"She's next on my list. I wanted to call you first because it dealt with Rebecca."

"Have Lark call me once you're done. Do not go anywhere without Gage, do you hear me?"

"Yes, yes, of course. He was with me when I got the call. He hasn't been out of reach since."

She sighed. "All right. Thanks."

Faine appeared at her side. She didn't even need to look to know he was there. Aside from his body heat, she just knew.

"I heard part of that. I'm not going to be leaving your side either."

"It's The Gennessee we need to be worried about. Listen, I've been meaning to ask you about travel through the Veil. Why haven't we been using it? I mean it takes hours to fly to and from DC and even back and forth to Seattle. If you can leave here and exit in Lycia and then head to Seattle, can we do that and go to DC?"

"What are you thinking of?"

"Can it be done?"

"In some cases. I was able to leave here to go to Lycia and then meet you in Seattle because I came through with Simon. He'd come through in Seattle. But it's not so straightforward when it comes to originating in one place and coming out another. There are rules about Veil travel. Mainly it's about keeping numbers down, so different species can't send an army through to another place. That's why we can't send an army of Lycians here en masse all at once. It would have to be done in stages. And even then there are caps. It's the same with the Fae and anyone else on the other side of the Veil. Why do you ask? Other than making travel to see your sister quicker. Which we can do if they meet us in Lycia."

"I'd like to sneak to DC and install some spells in Hayes' and Powers' homes and offices. We need to know what the heck is happening. They're up to all this stuff, and while I don't think they can bring the Magister back, they're fooling around with dangerous stuff. We have no idea just what it could result in."

"I can't get us to DC. Not that way. There are no portals within about six hundred miles of DC. I don't know why, but that's the truth. But . . ." He paused. "Mei, Card's mate, she's Fae. They can travel that way. Let me call her and see what we can arrange."

"All right. I need to get permission first anyway. And if we're a go, I'd like to do it tonight."

"I do like it that you said *we*."

"I know you. And I need the backup. I'd ask Lark, she's great at the sneaky stuff, but she's got enough on her plate."

"Okay. I'll call when this meeting with Rebecca is over." She rapped on Rebecca's door. "I have some news."

"Come in. Hello, Faine. Congratulations are in order, I hear."

"Thank you. I'm sorry to say my visit isn't a happy one. Molly just called. Senator Sato overheard Powers and Hayes talking about a plot to kidnap you to force you to perform a spell that would open a portal to bring the Magister back."

"Well, that's bollocks. We know it's not possible. I trust our scholars over anyone they might be talking to."

"Yes, turned witches are not reliable, and none of them are ranked highly enough to have known any of the magicks to even try such a thing. But that doesn't erase the danger you're in. For the turned witches and mages, you're a king-sized snack. They could very well be manipulating the PURITY thugs into grabbing you for their own goals, but it's still a plot to kidnap you. You have five guards. There are guards stationed at your home as well. I'd like to request that you temporarily move into quarters in an enclave. There's one here in Pasadena. You and the kids can live there until this passes."

"Passes? Helena, what if it never does? Am I supposed to just yank my children from the only stability they have right now? From the home they shared with their dad?" Rebecca had lost her husband to lung cancer three years before. She had three kids ranging from nine to fourteen. They were currently being educated in the school the Clan set up two years before. Thank goodness they had, it was one less worry, a safe place free of the harassment the children of Others worldwide were facing in public schools.

"One step at a time. What would the Clan do without you? What would the kids do? We all need you. It's my job to keep you safe. I don't think they can bring the Magister back. But I do think they can use you in a horrible way. I'd prefer that not happen."

"This threat needs to be addressed in another way too." Rebecca looked straight at Helena. "Faine, I need to speak of something very sensitive."

"You can trust me. As Helena is Gennessee, I am Gennessee."

She shrugged and spoke under her breath and the privacy spell knitted around them.

"We need to think about what we're going to do if and when these bills pass through Congress."

"Yes. I've created a master plan for full military mobilization. I've coordinated with the wolves, cats and Vampires on this plan through the COO. We do not have the numbers the humans do, but we have the power they don't. Lark is working with the witches to get spells in place to shut things down. The power grid, their communications network. The Kelly sisters up in the archives at Owen think they have a spell that will create a version of an EMP, which would disable nearly all their vehicles and everything else electrical. We'd need to be sure ours are shielded and Gage has been working with Marian and reps from different Other groups to get all that in place."

Rebecca nodded, smiling. "You're very organized."

"I feel better when I make plans. If they try to advance this plan to arrest us and put us in camps . . . or worse, we have contingencies in place. I just finished it all when I returned this morning. I hard-copied everyone rather than taking the chance and emailing. It's probably in your inbox." She pointed.

Rebecca leaned forward to sift through her mail and found the envelope. "Smart to hard copy. We just don't know if they have anyone else in our ranks, or if they have ways of hacking into our email or phones."

"There's a basic evacuation plan. The kids in the school will be transported to the nearest enclave. That's where we've got the best numbers for protection. They've all been warded up tight. Once a physical evacuation has started, we'll get the spells in place. You, Meriel, the other Clan leaders, Warden, de La Vega and Franco Pendergast will issue a statement of noncompliance. I'm told you all have that in hand?"

"Yes, we agreed on wording just a few hours ago. Meriel pre-recorded it and it's set to go if and when we need it."

Helena tried hard not to think about it in a big-picture way. If she just took care of all the preparatory steps she didn't have to focus on the fact that they were actually really going to war with humans.

"I don't think the humans have a majority on these ideas. I think the fringes are driving this bus."

Helena tended to agree. "Hopefully if this ridiculous legislation passes through the both houses, the president will veto and the people will stand up and tell their elected officials to back off."

"I hope so too. But planning is important. And how are we situated here?"

"If we're stuck here, we can hold out for some time. The bottom floors are fortified. We've got food, water, generators. The armory is stocked. Several staff are trained medics."

"A year ago, if someone had told me this would happen, that I'd be sitting here in my office planning an actual war with humans, I'd have told them they were crazy." Rebecca blew out a frustrated breath. "All right, I'll move to a enclave. Today. Keep me apprised on this business."

Helena paused. "I think we need some eyes and ears on the ground in DC."

"Yes? And what do you propose?"

"I think they're watching us here as well as they can. I may have a way to travel to DC quickly and without notice. If it works out, I can go to DC, plant some spells in the homes and offices of a few people, and be back in a few hours."

"Do it then. But damn you, Helena Jaansen, do not get caught and for all that is holy do not get killed. I love you like you're one of my own and that would be something I'm not sure I could recover from."

"I'll do my best. I'll have Marian coordinate with you on getting moved into the enclave as soon as possible and report back when I hear more."

They left Rebecca's office. "Have you eaten today?" Faine asked her as they walked.

"I had wedding cake."

He smiled down at her, unable not to. "Be that as it may, other than what we ate at three in the morning, have you eaten?"

"Not in a while."

"Here's what we're going to do. We'll have lunch while I call Mei to see what we can set up for later tonight."

"All right. There's food set up in the conference room for the live feed for the floor debate in the senate. I'm expecting a call from Lark soon as well so I'll have to step out at some point."

"I'll make the call and meet you in there. Save me a seat."

She nodded. "Thank you."

Rebecca wasn't the only one who wasn't sure she'd be able to survive it if anything happened to her. He'd keep doing what he was doing, which was everything possible to keep her safe while helping her do her job.

He dropped her off at the conference room.

"I'll make you a plate too, but I can't promise I won't steal your pickle so don't be gone too long."

He shook his head. "Be back in a few."

He headed to her office and put in a call to Card's place, hoping they had stopped in San Francisco instead of heading to Tir nA nOg.

Card answered. "It's Faine, is Mei around?"

"What trouble are you going to get my lovely wife into?"

Faine snorted. "You know me well." He explained Helena's plan to them both, as Mei had picked up the other line.

"Easily enough done," Mei said. "Jayce can help. He'll bring you, since I imagine you're not going to let the two of us go alone, and Card will want Jayce with me anyway since he can't go."

"Exactly."

"We'll meet you in your living room at half past nine our time tonight."

"Thank you, Mei."

"She's something else, your Helena. I'm glad to help."

He hung up and headed over to watch the floor debate.

Chapter 24

MERIEL Owen appeared on the screen. Beautiful. Confident and calm. The perfect spokesperson on their behalf. Helena tried to relax her spine, but it was impossible.

She'd been on some of the news shows, as had Tosh and others on their side of this issue. But they also bought commercial time so she could speak directly to the American people.

"Today, the United States Senate will have a floor debate regarding the so-called Domestic Safety Act. This legislation calls for the wholesale removal of citizenship and basic civil rights for all Others, regardless of their status before the Magister appeared.

"Naturally, we are opposed to such measures and we hope that you, our neighbors and friends, our co-workers and fellow citizens of this great country, also oppose this legislation.

"That we have to beg to keep rights that are unalienable for everyone else is a humbling and disturbing moment in history. At base, this legislation is unfair. It is racist and patently hateful. Moving entire populations to camps? Chipping us so we can be tracked? I submit to you, my fellow citizens, that this is not American.

"Worry that we might interbreed and lessen the purity of humans, as expressed by Carlo Powers, smacks of the racism of the past that we have worked so hard to eradicate. Eradicating us? Well, that smacks of an entirely different type of racism, one that ended with the deaths of twelve million. How far, then, do we allow our fear and dislike to take us? This is a question you need to ask yourselves. Each and every American needs to ask it, and if your answer is that no matter our personal feelings we need to reject this sort of hateful legislation, I urge you, every last one of you, to call or contact your elected officials. This is happening right now. Today. And it's imperative that your voices are heard."

She paused and looked into the camera. "There have been accusations against us. Speeches that attempt to turn around what is truth and use it as a weapon to paint us as unnatural monsters. All I can say to that is that monsters are real. But they're not werewolves or witches. They're people who'd attempt to twist our democracy to use it as a weapon to harm those whose only crime is to be different. I reject the words of men like Senator Hayes and Carlo Powers and I hope with all my heart that you do as well. Thank you for your attention."

The room filled with applause as Faine moved to Helena. "She did good. I can only hope people listen."

"Me too, *alamah*. I spoke to Card, we're on for tonight."

She blew out a breath. "All righty then. Sit down and eat. They're about to switch over to the feed for the floor debates."

TOSH and Delilah entered the senate floor from the dais and took their seats. They had met with their caucus, made up of members from both sides of the aisle, all of whom were going to speak that afternoon in opposition to The Domestic Safety Act.

The anger he'd been holding on to all day long burned in his gut, fueling the fight. This was wrong. So very wrong.

For years he'd known the people he was going to argue with. Had respected most of them despite their political differences. But this? This was different. To stand up and support this bill made Tosh sick to his stomach. He lost respect for every colleague who would do that.

He did report to the special FBI Task Force what he'd overheard Hayes and Powers talking about. Kidnapping and that sort of coercion was obviously criminal. Plotting to bring back the thing that killed so many Others was playing with fire. Not only a threat to the Others, but to everyone.

He gathered his thoughts and his courage as the procedural stuff got done. The gallery was packed and filled with law enforcement. He hoped they could get through this without any sort of riots.

Hayes went first and Tosh tried his best to tune out all but what might be needed to be addressed in his own comments. It was more of the same. Incendiary. Hateful.

Tosh had spoken to his grandmother just an hour before. She'd told him to stand up and speak from his heart and he'd be fine. He smiled at those words and her confidence in him to do the right thing.

He looked over to Delilah, smiling at the look on her face. She wanted to punch Hayes, no doubt. But then he also remembered her words about what it would be for them after he'd gotten her in bed.

Much more pleasant to think on that than the garbage Hayes was spewing. Then again, if he kept thinking on Delilah in his bed, he might not be able to stand up when it was time.

And then it was and he hoped like hell he did his grandmother proud. He stood and moved to the podium, took a deep breath and spoke from his heart.

"Ladies and gentlemen, colleagues, there are very few times in our history that one could truly call seminal or history altering. *Brown v. Board of Education* is one. The flawed concept of Separate But Equal was done away with once and for all, and over the decades since, our children of all races have benefitted from an America free of those arbitrary restraints. The women's rights movement that resulted in the Nineteenth Amendment giving women the right to vote. The Americans with Disabilities Act. These were moments in our history when contrary to the easy thing, the courts and our elected bodies stood up and did the right thing.

"Right now we stand in one of those places. A year ago, my neighbor was a citizen. He and his family have run a bakery in my neighborhood for two generations now. And then when the Magister happened, we learned he was also a witch. One day he's the guy who makes my grandfather's favorite cinnamon bread, a third-generation American. A success story with four children and six grandchildren and a thriving business owner. His is the American Dream come true. He pays his taxes and is a model citizen.

"He is no different today than he was a year ago. Or six months ago. Or yesterday. And yet, people like Senator Hayes and his friends at PURITY want you to strip this man of his rights simply because we now know he's a witch.

"Worse, they make thinly veiled threats of killing off those we don't like. Ladies and gentlemen, this is not my America. We've seen this happen in the world more than once. How is this GPS chip they propose any more than a high-tech version of a yellow star and a tattoo? Or if we want to pretend they didn't call for extermination of Others, any different from the internment camps my family was sent to during World War II? Or the reservations we sent Native Americans to? Will we post signs at the entrance that say *Work Shall Make You Free*?

"We are better than this bill. We are better than the fear Hayes and his friends are trying to manipulate so they can in one flick of a pen eradicate the basic rights and dignity of a large minority of this country. Your friends. Your neighbors. Your mechanics. The teachers, bakers, bricklayers, senators, mayors, bank tellers, hundreds of thousands of every day Americans who have done absolutely *nothing* wrong. Different does not mean we can't live together. Different does not mean we have to fear what we don't understand. We are smarter than that. We are better than that.

"We stand here on the precipice once again. We can continue to be the better people we are capable of. We are capable of the kind of action history will remember as bold and brave. Or we can repudiate everything we stand for and embrace this murderous bill and accept that our hands will be stained with the blood of innocents. The choice is clear. I will be voting no and I urge all my colleagues to do the same."

He sat down and the smile Delilah sent him warmed him to his toes.

Delilah, who then took over at the podium.

"When I was six, my father died. Because of ridiculous medical bills, we lost everything and had to move to public housing. And from six until I was seventeen my family and I lived in a not-so-very nice part of Chicago in the projects. To many of you, Cabrini Green was a horror story you read in a newspaper. But for me? It was home. My older brother, who is now an electrician, was big for his age. He walked me and my sister everywhere. To and from school, later to my after-school job and then home again after my shift ended. We often went out together to escort my mother to one of her three jobs.

"Cabrini Green was closed by the city in 2010, but for me, the best day of my life was when we moved away from it to a small house in the suburbs. My mom still lives in that house. My sister, who is a small business owner, lives about three miles from my mother and my brother about half an hour away from them both.

"Senator Sato just spoke about the American dream? I'm living proof. I went from abject poverty and violence to college and graduate school on scholarship. And then I came back home and ran for office at the state level. Openly as a werewolf. And I was elected."

She looked around the room. "The people of my district knew what I was and they elected me. Not because I was a werewolf. But because they trusted me to represent them and their needs at the capital. I have represented the same area of Illinois now for over a decade. First at the state level and then at the federal level as a senator. As a werewolf. Openly.

"If my constituents feel like I'm not doing what's right for them, they let me know. They call and they send me letters and emails and let me tell you, my being a werewolf has never stopped any of them from letting me know exactly what they think.

"What I'm trying to say is this: We don't need camps. We don't need GPS chips. We don't need any of this xenophobic, racist hateful rhetoric that attempts to estrange us all from one another. So we didn't know this time last year that there were witches and now we do. Is this an excuse to simply lose our minds and our dignity? We are Americans. This is a time when we need to come together and be an example of how to overcome adversity, not to act shamefully and hatefully because we are afraid.

"Earlier today, Carlo Powers stood in the hall outside my office and he called me a werewolf whore."

Gasps sounded as people turned to look at Powers, who shook his head as if she were lying.

"Now, as a strong woman with her own voice, it's not the first time a man who was threatened by that called me a whore or attempted to use my gender to try to shame me. But he didn't stop there. He called me a *werewolf* whore. This, my fellow Americans, *this* is where their agenda leads us. Nothing good will come of this legislation. Nothing good ever comes from reacting with hatred to things we fear. We are Americans. We are entirely capable of taking this moment and turning it around and learning from each other. Let us join together instead of letting ourselves be torn apart. We can be stronger than the fear. Better than the haters. I'm voting no on this legislation and I urge the rest of my colleagues to do the same."

Tosh was on his feet, applauding before he realized it.

"**STOP** thinking about that right now and focus." Faine smacked her butt to get her attention.

"Hey!"

"Hey what? I'm trying to show you how your weight distribution is off with your kick and you're trying to watch television."

"There's a riot in St. Louis, for heaven's sake, Faine. I'm not watching a sitcom or anything."

"There will be riots all over the place. You know it. You can't do anything to stop it, and in an hour you'll have other things to deal with, so get your head in the game or stop wasting my time."

She sniffed, clearly annoyed, but turned the news down and gave him her full attention. Which was good. She was distracted and he realized that this thing they were about to do in DC was dangerous enough with her totally focused on it. She needed to let go of everything else for the time being.

"Your pivot is the issue here. You redistribute your weight at the pivot in a way that's predictable. Anyone who watched you fight for more than a few minutes—and they should because you're quite good—would see that flaw and they'd anticipate it. You leave too much of your body exposed for those seconds. Kick lower and snap your leg back as you pivot to cut that exposure down."

He stood. "I'll break it down here in four parts." She watched him do it twice from two different angles.

"You're doing like a hybrid of a few different styles. Instead of that lined-up karate roundhouse, you're leading with that back leg to change your weight."

"Yes. For your style, since you're scrappy, I think it'll help as you're already sending your energy into the kick."

"Scrappy?"

She tried it his way and by the third time she'd perfected it.

"Scrappy. You're all over the place. Which is unexpected. You have all your focus, of course. But you're not afraid to get in there and poke eyes or kick some balls."

She shrugged. "It's not an Olympic event. It's a fight and sometimes to the death. If I gotta poke some eyes to stay alive, I'll do so. And pull hair too."

"You'll get no argument from me." And getting her worked up in a physical way would not only keep her mind off all the stuff going on just then, but the exercise would get her focused. She was that way, he realized. The more physical she was, the better able to lock out all the other stuff and get the job done.

"I propose that since we have a little less than an hour until Mei shows up we forget this and have sex instead."

She underlined her point by pulling her shirt and bra off.

"It has been a very long time since I've had you." He circled her and she gave him one of her *I have a secret* smiles.

"Like twelve hours at least."

He laughed and gave in to the temptation of her skin. She was warm beneath his palms, pliant against his lips. The curve of her shoulder, familiar and still thrilling, the salty-sweet taste of her neck.

She pulled the shirt from his body and kissed across his chest, pausing, her ear against his skin above his heart, listening to the reassuring thud-thud-thud of his heart. "I know you're trying to distract me." She shoved his pants down and he sprang, hot and ready, into her hands.

He'd been kissing and licking up her neck but when she grabbed his cock and gave it a little squeeze, he growled and then bit, holding her in place as he took her to the rug.

Quick, clever hands got rid of her pants and underwear and they rolled, skin to skin, gasping at the heat and wonder of the feel of each other.

She ended up on top, urgency riding her. Blind need for him raced through her senses. He hissed, reaching up to cup her breasts. "Slow down."

She shook her head with a grin. "I want you now. All of you."

He cursed and she laughed, pulling up enough to grab him, guide him true and sink down, taking him deep inside her body in two moves.

She stilled. "Unless you'd rather do something else."

"Get moving. You brought this all on yourself. Now pleasure me."

Laughing, she bent to kiss him, grabbing his bottom lip between her teeth and tugging. He held her, big strong hands at each hip. He set the pace, guiding her with his hands.

She arched, taking him deeper, and he groaned. There was something so powerful about giving him pleasure this way. This big, powerful male who could easily use that strength to harm only used it to cherish and please. To adore.

She'd never been adored before. It was not overrated.

"You are the most exquisite thing I have ever seen. I can't

believe you're mine," he murmured when he stretched up to kiss her.

Sex after the binding was different. Better. The connection between them was deeper, his pleasure wrapped around hers, teased it. Took it and fed it back over and over until she nearly vibrated with it.

He let go with one of his hands and his fingers found her clit, sliding side to side until she was nearly blind with need. And then she exploded. His fingers dug into her left hip as he began to thrust back at her as she slid down on him over and over. He was deep and hard and she knew when he hit his own climax. He thrust up one last time and held her there on him as he arched his back. Her knees dug into the carpet, her nails digging into his side as he snarled her name.

Chapter 25

WHEN Tosh opened his door with a black eye, Delilah raised her brows and came inside. "Good thing I brought some dinner. What the hell happened to your gorgeous face?"

"Out front. There were protesters when I got home. One of my guards had to get three stitches because he threw himself in between me and a bottle."

She put the bag of takeout down and touched his cheek. "This makes me very angry. To mar such perfection is to spit in God's eye." She kissed the bruise gently. "And it makes me want to rip someone's throat out."

He let go of some of his tension and pulled her to his body. "My lip is a little bruised too, I think."

She kissed his mouth and he luxuriated in her taste.

"You did a great job today," he said as she pulled back a little.

"I'm told I'm an excellent kisser."

He laughed, taking her hand and leading her back through the house and into the dining room. "I meant on the floor. But you *are* an excellent kisser."

"My office got so many calls the system overloaded four

times. The server shut down more than once. My inbox exploded. I'm relieved to say it was eight in favor of me voting against to two to vote in support."

He got plates and silverware out and she began to dish the food up. "I've got about those same numbers. More like seven to three, but still, a clear indication to vote it down."

The House would hear debate on their version of the bill by the end of the week. He just hoped the people made their voices heard so this ridiculousness could be halted before it got any worse.

"Did you see the news about the riots in St. Louis?"

He nodded. "I'm concerned that it'll get worse before it gets better. The little girl who was attacked is in critical condition. One hospital refused to treat her when they found out she was a shifter. The ambulance driver was nearly arrested for assault when he attacked the hospital administrator who refused to let them bring the child in."

"That's running in Chicago. Her family is an affiliated pack to Great Lakes. The COO told me they've sent guards to her family's home and the hospital. There are already attorneys at work on the refusal-to-treat issue as well. Her mother appealed to the rioters to stop the violence. I don't know if it will help."

"How many death threats did you get today? Don't deny it, the FBI interviewed me already."

She sighed. "Six. I'm an overachiever apparently. Parrish only got one. Though once he speaks on the House floor, I'm sure he'll try to beat my record." She squeezed his hand. "It's all right. I've got two extra guards and the witches warded my house, my car and my office. They're not going to scare me into silence."

"I know." He sighed. "But it scares the hell out of me. I hate the thought of you in danger."

"Toshio, I can shift into a wolf with razor-sharp teeth and claws. I'm good."

"A silver bullet can kill you."

"Yes. But none of us is immortal. How you live is important. Your grandmother told me about how freaked out she was when she went into labor with your uncle. She nearly bled to death and there were no doctors around and people were dying in the camps from infections and complications from health conditions easily treated in the outside world. She said she was so mad at the world, but she had her kids and her parents to worry about. And your grandfather was off getting shot at and fighting the war in the Pacific. She had no choice but to live and so she did. I have no choice but to live. So my nieces and nephews can enjoy the freedoms I grew up with."

So one day, when he asked her to marry him, she could say yes and know their children would have a place in the world. He was that sure about Delilah Sperry.

"So you should put your money where your mouth is."

Surprised, she smiled. "Oh yeah? About what?"

"You promised me once I got into bed with you my life would change. I want you, Delilah. So badly it's an ache in my belly."

They'd fooled around enough that he knew she had a beautiful body and knew how to use it. He knew what she looked like when she climaxed, knew what it felt like to orgasm at her hands and her mouth. They had amazing sexual chemistry but had been taking it slow.

Suddenly it felt like slow was the last thing he wanted.

She put her fork down. "We need to talk about that."

Uh oh.

"All right. Let's talk."

She licked her lips. "I . . .This thing between us isn't just fun for me. It's far, far more."

"Well, good. Me too. Are you worried I'm going to get you into bed and walk away? Because I can tell you right now, once we get into bed I'm not going anywhere."

She blushed and he felt better.

"Werewolves mate for life. Did you know that?"

"I think I did, yes."

"Well, so how it works is when two wolves or a wolf and a suitable partner, um, have sex, the exchange of bodily fluids is part of what sets off the chain reaction that sets off the mate bond. And there are other things, complicated things, that I don't know if you're ready for. We could use condoms, but every time we're intimate sexually, the bond between us strengthens for me."

He wasn't surprised at all, now that he thought about it. He was intensely attracted to her. From what he understood about werewolves and mates, it was a for-life thing. And that didn't freak him out at all. "Are you saying I'm your mate?"

"Yes. Speaking for myself only because I can't speak for you, but yes, you're it for me. If nothing happens between us, eventually I'd find someone else. It's not a situation of one person only on earth or anything. But each time we're together sexually, it becomes clearer to me that you're my mate. And I don't think you're ready for all that will entail."

He snorted. "Delilah, I was just thinking about our children. I've been fascinated by you from the first time we met."

She smiled. "Well, that's good. Generally, nature isn't so cruel as to put a person in our lives who we could mate with but who hates us. At the same time, this is forever. Right now, we are both involved in some major stuff. Things are insane. Violent. We're on the verge of war between humans and Others. I want you to take this step with me, you have no idea how much. But I want you to do it knowingly. After you meet my family and understand my culture. A culture you'll be part of if for no other reason than your being my mate. This is so much more than sex. This will change everything, and while I am so down to having sex with you, so much you have no idea. I just . . . it's more for me and I want to take the time to be sure you know what you're getting into. Do you understand?"

He blew out a breath. "I'm not afraid to commit to you. But . . . I do understand what you're saying. Though I still want to sex you up in the worst way."

She laughed. "Meet my family first. And come to a Pack meeting in Chicago. And I'll explain all of what it means to be my mate. Once all this has calmed. Then, if you're still on board you can sex me up all you want. Wherever you want. However many times you want."

*   *   *

MEI NiaAine was astonishingly beautiful. Helena found it
hard to stop looking at her until she finally just spoke. "I
wanted to thank you for helping me with this. I know the Fae
have been trying to keep out of this issue."

Mei was even more beautiful when she smiled, and Helena
could see why human folklore referred to the Fae as the Fair
Folk.

"Thank you, Helena. Cardinian and his family have been
there for me more often than I can ever repay, so I'm always
pleased to help when I can be of service to Leviathan. What
we need to do with this travel spell is to visualize the space.
Can you do that?"

"I haven't been inside Hayes' office, but I've been in the
hall just outside. If we can get there, I can pop a lock quickly
and get in. As for PURITY, Faine has been."

Faine nodded. "I've got a mental snapshot of the layout of the
building. And of the outside of Carlo Powers' town house as
well. I've not been inside, but I've done surveillance outside."

"All right." She took Helena's hand and Jayce, her other
husband, took her free hand and Faine's as well. "Lower your
shielding and I'll look. Just visualize that hallway with as
much detail as you can."

She did and when she opened her eyes again at Mei's
squeeze of her hand, she was standing in the hall outside
Marlon Hayes' office.

It was after midnight, but a busy enough legislative time
that she knew there were others around. "You might want to
keep an eye out and also use a shielding spell if you can. If not,
I can cast one."

"I've got that handled." Jayce took care of it and with a
few murmured words, Helena got Hayes' door open and they
quickly moved inside and closed it behind them.

They stood back while she did her work, but while she was
there, Faine looked through drawers and papers while she
copied data onto a few memory sticks.

"There are some clumsy spells here. Nothing major. I've

gone around them rather than getting rid of them. That way there's no indicator anyone was here. A mage cast them so they're third-rate." She curled her lip as she gathered up the data sticks.

Faine grinned at her. "You're sexy when you're full of derision."

Jayce chuckled. "You and your brothers seem to share a love of the same type of female." He tipped his head toward Mei, who shook her head.

They then moved to PURITY's headquarters. Because they didn't know if anyone would be inside, they chose a spot down the block. Faine had them stay while he and Jayce moved closer.

They returned shortly. "Looks like the lights are off in the downstairs, but one is on upstairs."

"You all stay here. I can cast a don't-look spell and get in and out quickly."

Faine snorted. "I think not. I'm better at stealth than you are. And I've been inside to check them out once before. I know where everything is."

"Yes, but I know if any trap spells have been cast."

"Good goddess, you two are so much like Card and Mei it's sort of scary." Jayce sighed. "You're both right. Mei and I can easily hide the four of us from detection so I'm going to suggest we travel into the first floor and we'll take it from there."

Which is how Helena found herself standing in the front entry to PURITY's DC headquarters. The hatred emanated from the walls. She'd heard witches talk about such things and had been close enough to Carlo Powers and some of the others from PURITY that she'd felt their personal hatred toward her and the rest of Others, but this was as if the whole place overflowed with negative power.

Faine bristled as they moved carefully through. Someone was on a phone call but the main reception area was empty and the lights were off. There were no spells of any kind but she figured there'd be cameras. Before they'd arrived, Jayce had done something to shield them from any camera view.

Helena then sent a magickal bomb of sorts out that would

overload the closed circuit cameras and any security for about ten minutes. More than enough time. She hoped that phone call wouldn't have any trouble though.

"I'll keep an eye on the door," Mei murmured and headed out.

Helena used the data sticks and Faine searched the drawers and they repeated the process on the two other offices downstairs.

"He just got off his call. No one else is here."

Helena moved to a spot just outside the door and used a sleep spell. It would last for about ten minutes. Once he was out, she'd give him a suggestion that he had done something to mess up the security and cameras and caused a short. He'd want to cover up his stupidity so he'd keep it all to himself and no one would know there was ever an issue.

It turned out her sleeper was one of Powers' sons, his top goon.

She wished she could put him in a tree outside so when he woke up he'd fall and break something. But she reined it in. It would be better this way. No one would suspect anyone was ever there.

Helena did the spell and planted the suggestion before she also cast a surveillance spell keyed to certain phrases as she and Faine did a search and gathered data from all the computers on the second floor.

"I can get into his head." Helena looked Greg Powers over. "It's moderately dangerous. But I won't kill him."

"I don't care if you do or not." Faine shrugged as he took out Greg's phone and removed the SIM card. "This could be helpful."

She got to her knees in front of Greg's body. "If he starts to wake up, don't panic, I'll take care of him."

Using the spell she and Lark had perfected over the years, she dove into his head, riffling through his memories, not bothering to be subtle. He wouldn't know why he had a headache but she didn't care anyway.

And what she saw chilled her to the bone. So much that it was difficult to leave without doing some real damage. He didn't deserve to live.

But she didn't want to deal with the added weight on her soul of killing when she didn't have to. She had enough death in her future and some in her past. It was better to only do it when she had to.

Sometimes being the better person sucked.

She pulled free and noted they had only a minute or so until the security and cameras kicked back on.

"I was getting ready to shake you." Faine helped her stand. "Can we get out of here?"

"Yes, let's go. Back home, we don't need to go to Powers' house. It's not worth the risk and I'm pretty sure we've got more than enough information."

They ended up back in Faine's living room. "What did you see?" Faine asked.

"They have plans to attack Rebecca's house. They know where she lives. Thank goodness she went to the enclave earlier. I think we need to call the cops though and give them a heads up. Or rather, I'll call Agent Anderson at the task force because the issue of how I came by the information won't be as big a deal. PURITY is using enough explosives to injure people on the whole block. And they know where Meriel is. One of their spies from Owen got them access to a directory. That's how they knew where to find Lark and Simon's house. They have a list of all the top-ranking witches. One of the mages has told them they need one of these witches to do the spell to open a portal. What the mage told them isn't possible, so that's something at least. But they're willing to kill however many, and whoever they have to. Carlo Powers is obsessed with the Magister. He thinks he can control it."

Faine scrubbed his hands over his face. "Fuck."

"Yes. The plus is that they really have no way of bringing the Magister back. But they have no hesitation at all in killing or harming anyone to try it. I need to get all this data to our IT people. They can get in and see what we can find. And I need to get this info to Lark and the others so they can make sure all clan leadership is away from known addresses."

"We can drop it somewhere if you like," Mei offered.

Helena thanked them. She made a call, told the IT people

to be at the offices to get all the data off those sticks. She wrote a note, shoved it and the sticks in an envelope and handed it to Mei. "Thank you so much. You've saved lives by helping us tonight. Gennessee won't forget that."

"That's what family does." Mei hugged her. "Now you need to rest or get some protein in you. You used a lot of magick to get into his head back there."

Faine narrowed his eyes at her but waited until they'd left before he turned her way again. "I know you need to make calls. I'm going to make some food and you will eat it without complaint or I will call your mother."

"You fight dirty." She liked it.

"Don't forget it."

She smiled as she grabbed her phone. "I won't. Thank you." She dialed the number Anderson had instructed her to use in urgent situations.

"Anderson." He'd clearly been awake.

"I'd say I was sorry for waking you up, but I think I should be sorry you're not sleeping at nearly two your time. It's Helena Jaansen and I have bad news for you."

"Riots and bad news from my favorite witch too. Busy night in America."

Shit, she'd forgotten about the riots. She didn't know if something even worse had happened while they were gone so she turned on the TV with the sound off and plunged ahead with the reason for the call.

"I've come by some information that PURITY has plans to kidnap Rebecca Gennessee. I've heard this info twice. I know Senator Sato called you regarding the first source."

"We've got people on her location. Well, outside her location. Nothing amiss has happened."

"We moved her, as you know. But there's more. They're planning to use enough explosives to level her house and probably her side of the street for a block or so."

"What?" His tone sharpened and she knew what was coming so she headed it off.

"I can't tell you how I know. Only that I do. Greg Powers

is behind a plan to kidnap Rebecca, Meriel or possibly other powerful witches to aid his father in bringing back the Magister. They know the locations of these witches because they are in possession of a directory of sorts."

"Like my middle schooler has?"

"Probably. Look, before this mess we were just a bunch of people with magick. We had potlucks and ran businesses. None of this war or spying stuff happened. PURITY brought all this on. We just like to eat casseroles and gossip."

He snorted. "Spare me. I've seen you fight. You didn't just learn that yesterday."

"No. I've been trained my entire life to do this job and still, I've never blown up anyone's home. I've never assaulted a child or started a riot. The bald facts are that humans have pushed this situation to the brink. We've done nothing but *react* to what you've done to us."

"I apologize. I'm not trying to offend. I know. But not all of us are these PURITY assholes."

"I know that. Which is why I called the FBI instead of handling this threat on my own." She let that hang for a moment. She *would* handle it if he didn't, and she wouldn't leave a body. Just because she didn't kill Greg Powers a few minutes before didn't mean she wouldn't later on if the situation merited it.

She was giving Anderson—and humans in general—a chance to make things right.

"I've already got people on the clan leadership in the major cities. Are the explosives planted now?"

"I don't know. I just know it's part of their plan. Her house and property are warded pretty well. But if they were bringing the explosives, or if they'd planted some under the house in the sewers or next door . . ."

"I'll send teams over to check things out. So, this story about spies for Hayes disappearing."

"Dunno what you mean. I'll talk to you later. Thanks." She hung up before he could say anything else. In the kitchen Faine was making bacon and eggs. Her head hurt and she normally would have gotten a bloody nose for using that spell to get into Powers' head. But in the post-Magister world, bloody noses from overuse of magick seemed far rarer.

She watched the destruction on television as she called Lark and filled her in.

Chapter 26

HE found her dabbing her eyes and staring at the television. Her sadness hit him and he realized he'd assumed it was his own and had been ignoring it as he'd been cooking.

"Hey." He handed her a plate and let her get herself together. But he settled next to her, needing that contact.

"So happy first day bound to me. How's that working out for you?" She ate a piece of bacon. "Thanks, by the way. You're a really good cook as well as the other services you provide."

Her smile made him feel a little better. "As it happens, though the day has been challenging, being bound to you has been quite lovely. Unexpected, I suppose, because no one can really express just what it feels like to be so connected to someone you love. What about you?"

"I'm not quite sure what I've done to deserve you, to be honest. I used to be calm. Like every day. I didn't cry when I watched television unless it was *Steel Magnolias*. Being around you reminds me that I used to be that."

"You resent me for it?"

"Huh? No! Why would you think that? Can't you feel me? Or whatever?"

Her confusion was sort of adorable, but he figured telling her that would be a bad thing at that moment. "So tell me what you mean."

"No. I'm sick of thinking about it and talking about it."

"You're a difficult woman." He grinned and when she turned, annoyed, she saw it and rolled her eyes.

"I'm too tired for you to poke at."

"Eat your food and then let's sleep a while. Did you talk to Lark?"

"She's upset about the house all over again. Meriel and Dominic have moved into an enclave. Simon doesn't want to, but he wants Lark safe so they're in one for the time being. Your name may have come up in a 'Faine did it for Helena and so you should do it for Lark' way. Not by me. I think it might have been my dad."

He cringed and then laughed. "That's what it's like having a father-in-law, I guess. He wants you both safe and he has every right to expect me and Simon to make that happen. Though I do plan to ask him if he has a lawn mower and some Bermuda shorts the next time I see him."

She snickered. "You two." But then she put her head on his shoulder. "I'm so tired. I'm afraid of fucking up, but I'm so tired of being afraid to mess up that I'm sort of feeling punk rock about it. Like, bring it, I'm a cranky-ass bitch now so watch yourself."

"I have no idea what you mean by that, but it sounds defiant and good and you said it with such viciousness I'm okay with it. There's so much happening right now."

"St. Louis is on fire. A little girl was turned away at a hospital. Who does that? She may die and all the person could think of was that she was a shifter? What is wrong with the world? Who raised such a creature? I can try to report a possible bombing, but I can't stop that. It's totally out of my control."

"I know how much you hate being out of control, *alamah.*"

"I do." She frowned and he nudged her to keep eating. "Grump and eat. Now that I know you get depleted after magick and need protein, I'm going to make sure you take care of yourself. That's how I deal with my fear that something will happen to you."

She looked up as she forked eggs into her mouth.

"What? Did you think I was beyond worries? I worry about you every waking moment. It's part and parcel of loving a warrior isn't it?"

"You're very reasonable for someone who looks as good as you do."

"I do try." He paused a moment. "It's okay to be afraid. I know you were raised to feel differently. But the world now is full of things to be afraid of. You'd be a fool not to fear for the future. You'd be irresponsible not to understand the gravity of what you do and how much people rely on you and not to be worried about letting them down. Fear doesn't make you weak, Helena. It makes you strong. Because you do it anyway. You know the stakes and you get up every damned morning and you do your best."

On the screen, the cameras shifted to Birmingham. On fire.

IT was still dark when Faine woke up. About two hours before the sun would rise. He lay still because he didn't want to wake her. And because when it was quiet and she was sleeping in his arms, the world was perfect.

Things were going to happen that day. He could feel it. The buildup and anticipation in his bones. He waited until her breathing slid into the slow and deep of heavy sleep and got up.

He'd work out. Get some of the stress out of his muscles. He headed to the garage where the treadmill was. Now that she lived there with him, he'd need to clear out that part of the garage so she could park there. Since they'd both need exercise equipment, he could easily convert one of the bedrooms into a workout space.

By the first mile his muscles began to loosen up and he felt better, more alert. That day would see the House debating the Domestic Safety Act on the floor. He'd keep her busy so she wouldn't obsess.

He smiled when he remembered her preferred end to their training session the day before. If he could keep her in bed all day it would be wonderful. But he knew his female, she'd want to be out and about and it was her job, after all. He was just grateful they weren't in DC or she'd want to be at the House to watch the floor debate in person. And given how many times people seemed to want to kill her in DC, he was just fine with being across the country right then.

He'd had enough. Enough of this stupid crap with the PURITY people. More than enough of them trying to harm his woman. He had something more precious than anything he'd ever dreamed.

Being bound to her was . . . astonishing. Her strength lived in him now. He'd appreciated that before. Had watched her in action and admired her for it. But this was a different sort of experience. It wasn't like he heard her thoughts or anything like that. But it was as if he were tuned into her. Intimately so.

If he concentrated, he knew she was still sleeping. Calm and relaxed. His beast approved and he was sure that should anyone try to disturb that, he would have bared his teeth and stopped it.

He also understood how hard she was working to let him in to share her life. To make it *their* life. Never would he have thought she would doubt she was worthy of such adoration, but he got it, just little twists here and there. Surprise and wonder when he did little things for her or professed how much he loved her.

One of these days he hoped she'd simply accept all the things he did and said as her due.

He turned on NPR as he rounded into the third mile and listened to news of the country falling apart.

HELENA woke feeling physically better than she had in a while. She'd only gotten five hours of sleep, but her body felt like it had been nine.

Tila, her . . . mother-in-law? Yeah, she guessed that was it, had told Helena that with the binding she'd have some of

Faine's strengths. If she only needed three or four hours' sleep like Faine she could get so much more done.

Or at the very least, they could spend an hour or two every day in bed doing other things.

She deliberately didn't think about work as she got out of bed. She needed to do some kickboxing and do a few miles on the treadmill. After she sweated a lot and showered, then she'd switch to work mode.

Faine was in the house. She knew it, felt his presence. That piece of him that lay in her belly shifted a little, as if it knew she was thinking of him.

He came around the corner as she headed to the garage to work out. "Good morning, *alamah*." He pulled her to his body and kissed the top of her head.

"Mmm, morning." She tipped her face up and he kissed her lips, his taste settling into her senses.

"What are you up to?"

"I'm going to run a bit. Work out with the bag."

"Want a partner with the bag? I already did five miles but I'm always happy to stand around and watch you glisten with sweat as you beat the bag into submission."

"I'm pretty sure you'd be able to make any subject whatsoever sound dirty."

"I have many talents."

She laughed and he kissed her again. His joy at doing so flooded the connection between them. She threw her arms around his neck and hung on, making that quick kiss a longer one.

"You taste good." She grinned and he swatted her butt.

"Keep that up and you won't get outside for some time."

"It occurs to me that we haven't even had shower sex yet." She went out into the garage and began her stretches.

He poked his head out. "I'm going to start the coffee and then I'll be out in a bit. But don't think I'm going to forget about the shower sex comment."

She moved to the treadmill. "Counting on it."

The scent of coffee rose and woke her up nearly as well as the miles she ran, and when he came out some time later without his shirt and wearing his snug running shorts, she was plenty awake.

"Suddenly I really don't care about the bag." She stepped to him and took a lick over his right nipple. "But I'm really, really dirty. Think you can help with that?"

Laughing, he bent, caught her at the waist and heaved her up and over his shoulder and jogged to the master bath where he gave her a workout and got her all clean. Physically anyway.

FORTY-FIVE minutes later they came out to the kitchen. "You totally deserve to have me make breakfast after that performance. If I had scorecards you'd have all tens."

"You're in a mood this morning. I like it." He poured them both a cup of coffee.

"Calm before the storm, I think."

"Are we defining sleep as the calm?"

"Five hours without injury or conspiracy is a win. I'll take what I can get." She began to pull the makings for breakfast from the fridge. "And now that I'm exercised, sexed up and clean on the outside, I suppose I can no longer avoid looking at the news."

He winced and she knew it was pretty bad. "You want to get me up to speed while I cook?"

"They made four hundred arrests last night in St. Louis. At this point it's millions of dollars in property damage. The mayor declared a curfew."

"The little girl?"

"She made it through the night so they're cautiously hopeful. Her parents went on television and begged everyone to calm down. A mob showed up at their house and tried to burn it down. But the Pack had guards there and they prevented such a thing. The cops showed up and arrested everyone, even though the mob started it and the wolves were just defending themselves. Rumors are swirling around. Cats came after that and are guarding the house along with some witches and some humans too."

"Good lord. Well at least there're some small rays of hope."

"The coven offices in New Haven were trashed. Windows broken out. A security guard was beaten. He was treated at a local hospital and released. Several members of the city council showed up today to help with cleanup."

She blew out a breath. "I'm trying hard to hold on to all the positives in that news."

"Me too."

They ate breakfast and watched the national news while she scanned the local news on her notebook. She needed to get out in the field. Things at the office were being handled.

She called to check in and Marian told her Rebecca was fine and they'd moved classes to the nearest enclave and had upped the security. The kids were learning defensive magick along with geometry and poetry. That's how it had to be and no matter how sad it made her, it didn't change anything. But it would make them better able to defend themselves in a world where some people wanted to harm them simply for who they were.

"You're going to carry today?" He tipped his chin at the weapons she'd strapped on.

"Concealed mainly. But if they're assaulting children now, I'm not taking any chances out there. I need to stop over at the DMV in Montebello. They were refusing to help anyone who appeared to be an Other yesterday. Like you can tell?"

Faine gave her a long, slow perusal that had her blushing within moments. "I don't know. I can see the magick all around you. Beautiful. Makes me want to lick you."

She waved a hand to fan her face. "Stop that."

"You're breathless. I thought I'd satisfied you enough to hold you over for an hour or three. I apparently didn't do my job very well."

"You're making me all fluttery."

"I see that. It's beautiful on you. My beast loves to play with you."

"You did. *Three* times."

He laughed. "Maybe it should have been four."

"I'm going to be so relaxed the DMV people will eat me up. I need to be tough and hard-ass."

"Mmm. I'll let you play bad cop if you'll let me frisk you later."

She laughed, finishing her coffee and rinsing out her cup. "Come on. Incorrigible."

Bad things were happening all around them. But it wasn't all bad. She had this male, this being who made everything better.

"You sure about carrying? I distracted you inside before you answered."

"Yes. I've got a permit. And I've got a don't-look spell on them at the moment. No one is going to see them unless I want it."

He pulled the car out of the garage and they'd gotten about two blocks when she rolled her window down.

The sun was now up and she waited to hear the birds. But instead she heard . . . yelling and then gunshots.

"Shit. Get to the gates. Now."

She put her earbud in and called the office. "There's something going down at the enclave down here."

Which was an understatement.

Several large trucks had pulled up to the front gates, a few mounted with .50-cal guns. They sprayed the area with bullets as other humans wearing camo and masks tried to get in the gates.

She needed to pull everyone together. She spoke into her phone, "Get the rest of the guards in the area here. I don't want us to get flanked, so someone needs to get a better view of what's happening around the entire enclave. People need to stay in place, we don't want to leave any openings. Remember there are kids here, get someone to contact the school and if they're not on lockdown protocol, make that happen. Call me when you hear. Don't bother calling the local cops. Call Gil Anderson at the FBI."

Faine pulled the car around a corner and they got out, keeping low. "I need to get over there to get people together." She popped the trunk and pulled out more weapons and ammo. He took what he needed.

He understood it. He'd been in command in military

situations for much of his adult life. But if she thought he'd
stay behind while she did, she was out of her mind.

"Lead on. I've got your back."

She grabbed him, kissing him hard. "If you get hurt, even
one little scratch, I'm going to rip some people apart. Got me?
And I'll make you use my mother's green soap. So keep your
head down."

"I think I can manage that, boss."

She harrumphed and he followed her.

One of the trucks with the mounted gun had several people
in the guard shack pinned down. He knew she was drawing
magick as they moved, felt it build in the air all around them.
Their link shimmered and heated as she charged herself. But
even then he was not ready for the moment she stepped out,
shot the guy at the gun in the head with one hand and blew
back the others standing near the gates, trying to pry them
open, with a heated blast of power.

She spoke instead of yelling, but her voice was modulated
to be heard by those in the shack.

"Get out of there and behind some cover. Weapons hot.
Shifters, you're free to take either form. Witches, don't waste
whatever shot you get with anything but lethal force."

"We've got two down," one of the guards shouted.

"Leave them in the shack." It was fortified, Faine knew.
"We've got backup on the way, but let's see about clearing
out this riffraff before one of these nearby houses gets hit."

"We got them evacuated first thing. Only one house was
occupied. A lot of people had already left for work." One of
the guards, a shifter named . . . Sophie, that's right, spoke to
Helena.

She'd been training this group so they followed her orders
perfectly and fanned out, narrowly avoiding getting shot. The
problem was that one of the trucks sat at an angle behind the
wall so it was hard to get a shot at it, but they had a higher
vantage point and kept them pinned down.

"Who are they? Have they made any demands?"

Sophie shook her head. "They haven't. They just rolled up
to the gates and opened fire."

Helena made a call and ordered her people to run the plates. Faine took film of the situation and emailed it to the Gennessee office.

"I'm going to shift. Cover me." Sophie got her clothes off and in a blink she was a large, honey-colored wolf.

"Go left, along the wall. I'm going to take out this nearest truck." Helena drew more power. "They just tossed the dead guy off and there's another one now. The ones near the gates will be bleeding out the ass for a while, if they're still alive. But we need to deal with those mounted guns."

She turned to the others. "You, if you get in that tree over there, you can use magick to short out their engines. I'm going to try something with the guns. I need a distraction because I need to be closer. I'd prefer not to take a bullet the size of a small dog if I can help it."

"No jokes," Faine growled at her. "I'll shift. I can jump the fence easily."

"No. What I want to do . . . well, everyone needs to be behind me. Cover me. You're handy with a weapon."

And then she took off her shoes and began to pull magick, spooling it up at a rate he figured was pretty alarming given the way the nearby witches gaped at her.

"Go on!" He waved at them. "Get in place or this is for nothing." Once they'd all run off he got in Helena's face. "I know you're going to do something scary. And I'm not happy. I get it, I know why. But you'd better not end up dead, Helena. I mean it."

Her eyes were otherworldly now. The power arcing off her skin. The hair on his arms stood straight up.

"I got this. And stay behind me."

"Give me a forty-five-second lead. I need to lay down some fire and the rest just got into position."

She nodded and he had no choice but to put her immediate safety from his mind.

Helena's heart raced and her mind reeled. She'd never brought so much power into herself, not even when she stopped that bomb. But something about her link to Faine had grounded her. She felt the power rushing through her, knew it could burn her out and leave her brain-dead. But she held the reins.

She gave him his forty-five seconds and gunfire began to fill the air. She blocked it all out except to be sure to stay out of the line of their fire. Her focus was on the two remaining trucks and the deafening percussion of the chunk, chunk, chunk of the bullets hitting the pavement and the walls of nearby buildings.

They saw her coming and she let it go. Let them see her full of magick. Let herself be the monster they were frightened enough of that they'd attack a neighborhood filled with innocents.

They'd tried education. They'd tried diplomacy. They'd even fought back and used threats. But PURITY and their buddies kept coming. They would keep coming until all the Others were dead because that's the only thing PURITY wanted.

So she'd be sure they understood if they wanted that, it would be *their* bodies at the morgue.

She raised her hands and drew more power. The city had its own sort of energy and she pulled it from the people, from the buildings and cars, from the stored energy in the roads and sidewalks. She drew from the Font as well.

And then she spoke, and turned it on them. Focused on those guns. Made it hot. Made it so hot she knew the metal was softening. She heard a scream. Heard yells to get back. But they shot at her. Before she could shift and shield herself, three bullets tore through her thigh. Her hip was shattered with a fourth.

But she kept standing. Kept sending power at them until the screams stopped. Until the bullets stopped. Until she couldn't stand anymore and her legs buckled.

The ringing in her ears lasted a while. Faine picked her up, holding her against his body. His heart beat so fast she worried. She knew he was yelling her name, but she couldn't hear. She just put her finger on his lips and shook her head.

She said, "I'm going to live."

He frowned and she knew he growled but she couldn't hear

it. Couldn't hear the sirens. Then the police came with the FBI and they tried to arrest everyone, including the people inside the enclave.

She could sort of hear at that point as one of the enclave medics packed the wounds on her leg.

"No." She shouted this from where she lay in a pool of her own blood. "If you come in here with weapons drawn, we will defend ourselves."

"Like you did with these humans?" The cop waved at the molten metal and the mass of bodies.

"Yes. We did nothing wrong. They came here, they attacked. They shot us, they tried to harm children. We told you what would happen. And you kept it up. You kept on and on until we had no other choice. You brought this on yourself. We will not let you harm our young. We will not. So you need to figure out who the enemy is here and act accordingly."

Her lips tingled.

Gil Anderson shoved his way to the front. "Christ, Helena. Why is it that every time I see you, you're covered in blood? Stand down. Let the ambulances in. This is a crime scene, let's get on it."

"She needs a hospital." Faine wouldn't let go of her.

"Yeah, I think I do." It was harder and harder to talk.

A paramedic approached. "We're going to get you loaded up and to the hospital, ma'am." He smiled. "I'm a witch too. I promise to take good care of you. Your, um, guy can ride along."

"You should stay here and manage the scene. Let the clan know what's happening."

The heat of morphine traveled up her arm and through her body. "Oh, that's nice."

Faine frowned. "I'm not leaving you. Sophie can handle this from here. I'll make calls on the way."

They loaded her into the ambulance and she was only going to let her eyes close once, but it was very hard to get them back open.

So she gave Faine orders with her eyes closed. But it seemed like once she closed her eyes it was really a lot harder to talk.

He bent down and kissed lips that were far too pale. If he didn't have the link with her and her life force hadn't been so strong, he'd have been far more panicked than he was.

And it was already pretty bad. The smell of her blood and pain drove his beast so close to the surface he'd had to struggle harder than he had in centuries to keep it back.

He called Gennessee and told David what was going on. David assured him they'd handle everything and to just focus on Helena. He said Rain would meet them at the hospital.

He called Lark.

"Lark, it's Faine. Helena . . ."

His voice must have betrayed him worse than he'd thought because she gasped. "What? Oh my goddess, what?"

"She's been shot. Four times. She's lost a great deal of blood. Your mother will meet us at the hospital in case she needs a transfusion. There's more. The enclave was stormed. She used her magick. I'm frankly not even sure what she did, but none of them will be a threat ever again. I need to go, we're arriving at the hospital now. Your dad has more details."

"I'm coming down. Take care of her." Lark hung up and he turned back to his female, covered in blood and drugged to the gills.

Chapter 27

SHE came to several hours later.

Faine rested, his head on her bed. Her hospital bed. She remembered then what had happened.

He looked up, a weary smile on his face. "You're awake."

"I am. I guess I'm alive huh?

"You're forbidden to joke about such things."

"Is everyone all right? At the enclave?"

"One of the guards got out of surgery about twenty minutes ago. They're saying he's got a good chance of survival. Other guards surround this room and this wing of the hospital. You were shot four times. Your hip is shattered so they're going to have to replace it. You lost a great deal of blood. Your mother gave you a lot of hers."

Tears ran down his face and she got worried. "Is my mother all right?"

"Why are you worried about her? My goddess, Helena! She's fine. She's in another room, resting." He burst from his chair and started to pace.

"Why are you mad at me?"

"You. Could. Have. Died. I was pinned down and you

looked all right. You didn't even fall, hell, you didn't even register pain at first or I'd have felt it through the link. And then you were gushing blood and I couldn't get to you fast enough and *fuck fuck fuck*, Helena. I can't even think about how scared I was."

"I'm sorry." And she was. She could only imagine if it were him who'd been shot and how that would have made her feel.

"I know you are. But you'd do it again."

"Well, next time I'd shield myself better. Obviously."

He muttered something in his language and she caught a few choice words about crazy women.

Lark burst into the room at that moment and threw herself at Helena, who screamed at the feeling of her leg and hip being jostled. Faine lifted Lark up and off and there was some snarling when Simon came in and saw this happening.

Lark barked orders at them both as a nurse rushed in and, undeterred by the two giant men and the blue-haired woman, gave them all a lecture about jostling, alarming, or disturbing Helena in any way that was detrimental to her recovery.

"They attacked four enclaves. They killed kids, Hellie. Little ones."

"I thought we agreed this could wait?" Simon sighed.

"I told you not to say anything." Faine inserted himself between the sisters.

"She needs to know. She'd want to know."

"It's too late anyway. I *do* know now. Tell me the rest."

"There are riots in Seattle, Bakersfield, Miami, Cincinnati, Boston and Chicago. The Others are on the warpath and every time the humans push, we push back harder. It's a bloody damn mess. The data sticks you brought back were full of stuff. Plans to attack different cities and groups. Information about the purchase of large amounts of explosives. Biological weapons! They had this silver stuff, like from a damned movie, it exploded and sent tiny shards of silver into the air. They tried to use it on some Vampires up in Alaska. But no one ever heard from them again."

Ha. She bet. Vampires didn't mess around.

"What's going on in DC?" Her tongue was thick and felt two sizes too big for her mouth. Whatever substance they had her on really did a number on her. But the horrible pain in her leg and hip when Lark had come in had settled back on a far distant shore so she was all right with that.

"Those plates you sent? On the trucks that attacked the enclave? One was registered to a bigwig in PURITY. PURITY and Humans First have been tied to multiple attacks. Tosh is urging the president to finally make a stand. He and several others on Capitol Hill have demanded an investigation into what part Senator Hayes played in all this. His name is all over that data. Bastard. There've been some pings from the spells you laid at his office and at PURITY, but there's not a lot we can use legally. We did find the location of a few of the turned witches and a mage or two who escaped. The wolves are handling that for us." Lark's smile was vicious.

"Good. But what's wrong with the president? The country is on fire and she hasn't spoken yet?"

"Her chief of staff did about two hours ago. He announced she'd be issuing a statement later today. The governors of the states involved have spoken out, urging calm. Right now it looks like humans, most of them anyway, are coming down against PURITY for this mess."

It was hard to stay awake. Faine took her hand and squeezed gently. "Rest. You're doped up, *alamah*."

"I have stuff . . ."

He smiled and kissed her. "You will have stuff when you wake up again. Until then, your sister and her big mouth will have things handled."

TOSHIO had had enough with waiting. He'd been standing around in an anteroom of the Oval Office for the last hour. And before that, another hour earlier in the day. He'd left and given multiple press conferences demanding an investigation of Marlon Hayes.

He'd been kept apprised of Helena's condition as well as the status of the thousands of Others and humans who'd been injured in the riots. Insanity, all of it. And the president had remained silent and unreachable behind closed doors with the attorney general and White House staff for most of the day.

But he was totally and completely done with this nonsense. When the door opened and the attorney general came out, Tosh simply swept past the secretary and into the Oval Office.

"Madam President, I'd like a moment of your time."

Those sharp green eyes of hers landed on him. "Senator Sato, I'm really quite busy."

"Pardon my bluntness here, Madam President, but you've been too busy to meet with me for months as this situation has grown worse and worse." He tossed multiple newspapers and sheets of paper detailing all the riots onto her desk. "How much longer will you remain silent on this? How many more children will die because you're afraid to anger PURITY? They didn't vote for you to begin with, they'll never be all right with a female leader. But millions of Americans *did*. You won this office. The nation is starving for leadership right now. Be a leader. Do your job."

He knew he was going too far, but someone needed to say it.

"Senator Sato, I've got this." She stood. "I wanted the people of this country to work this out. I wanted them to have a national discussion on this so we could move forward without large segments of the population feeling they'd been ignored or steamrolled. I waited too long. I know that. My biggest mistake was in trusting those in the House and Senate to manage this in an appropriate way."

"Senator Hayes has betrayed his office. He's got to be dealt with."

She raised a brow his way. "You're not unbiased in this matter."

"I don't need to be. I didn't truck with terrorists and aid them in attacking American citizens. He did."

She shrugged. "You're right of course. The attorney general has sent people over to have him picked up and brought in for questioning. He'll be investigated, as will others who worked with PURITY. You know, of course, that a lot of the evidence we've been given is inadmissible."

He did. Damning though it might be, the collection of the data couldn't have been legal. But there were enough people whose lives were on the line at this point. He'd been a lawyer long enough, he knew how it worked. Someone would roll first and that would lead to more people doing the same.

"People will turn on one another. We'll get him that way."

"The attorney general agrees with that assessment." She grabbed her jacket and put it on. "I've got a statement to make to the American people. Come along if you'd like to watch."

He most certainly did.

FAINE turned the television in her room on and everyone gathered to watch.

The president walked to the podium, looked into the camera and spoke.

> *My fellow Americans. The last six months have been revolutionary for not only our nation, but for the entire world as we thought we knew it. With the revelation of the Others, we realized our world was far more complicated than we'd imagined.*
>
> *And the Others, our neighbors and friends, were reeling from the unexpected and horrible deaths of those in their communities. We struggled as a nation to understand this new reality. To find a way to balance our beliefs and social rules with what we now knew.*
>
> *I have held off speaking during this time because I wanted a national discussion to take place. An honest exchange of ideas. And I want to say how proud I've been of most Americans in that department. Most of you, no matter your personal beliefs, have been able to talk about these issues without harming anyone else.*
>
> *Minds have been changed through something as simple as a conversation. And that's why I tried to remain out of*

the fray. Real change can be complicated and emotionally painful, and you have put in the time and effort. I'm proud of that.

But the insidious facts are that some Americans were not satisfied by the free exchange of ideas. They wanted to use violence to silence those who were different. This has, I'm sad to say, been part of our history too. But we have attempted, time and again, to be better people. Better Americans. And so during the debate on the Domestic Safety Act, my office, along with offices all along the Hill, was inundated with calls and emails and letters, the overwhelming majority opposed *to this legislation.*

But some are never satisfied with the will of the people. Some, like those terrorists who have been attacking Other communities for months, will never stop. And so, while this national dialogue continues, I want something to be completely clear.

An hour ago I signed an Executive Order extending the status quo to all Others. What this means is that if you were an American citizen before the revelation, you are an American citizen now. The same rights and responsibilities you held before the revelation are yours.

There will be no more discussion as to whether or not you are Americans. You are. You were before and you are now.

There will be no concentration camps. No GPS chips. No roundup of Others. Go about your lives, ladies and gentlemen. Enjoy the bounty you have as a citizen of this great nation.

We face challenges in this new reality, yes. But they do not need to include violence. I've declared a nationwide curfew until the unrest has ended. Those not employed in jobs or mandated activities taking place after seven in the evening will keep to their homes until five the next morning. There will be an increased military presence in the cities where rioting is taking place. Looters and rioters will be arrested and prosecuted under federal law.

Lay down your arms. Go home and accept reality. You don't have to like the werewolf next door, but you are not allowed to kill him or harm his family. Be better people.

Our national dialogue on this issue will continue. I look forward to hearing from you as we move ahead into this new and fascinating future. Thank you.

The president nodded once and turned, walking away.

Epilogue

Six months later

"**THIS** is the first vacation I've had in years." Helena watched her husband swim in long, bold strokes, cutting across the lake.

"The weather here will be good for you." Lark adjusted her bathing suit top. "Mom will finally calm down a little. Maybe."

Helena had needed a hip replacement of all things. The bullets had shattered the bone to hell and so there she was, not even thirty, with a brand-new hip. But the real problem had been the secondary infection that had kept her in the hospital an additional two months.

She'd been pissy about it. Had felt like, hey, with this new strength from the binding and all her magick and being in such good shape, she should have been out and running around in days.

Then they'd found out the bullets had been treated with biological agents and a normal person could have died. One of the guards shot that day at the enclave had died from a terrible infection. The one shot with regular ammunition had been in the hospital for two weeks and was now back to work.

Tila came out and smiled when she saw them. Her mother-in-law was just as pesky as Rain when it came to making sure Helena was taking care of herself. But it pleased Faine to see it, and Helena liked Tila so it wasn't really a trial to be here in Lycia, soaking up the sun all day as she healed up.

The violence continued on and off, but after the riots had ended and the country faced a death toll that numbered in the thousands, humans and Others alike had sobered and resolved to work things out better.

The humans finally understood that the Others could and would defend themselves and quite ably. But they also seemed to realize that while the Others had a great deal of power, they hadn't used it in all the time before they were outed, and so maybe they weren't the monsters some had said they were.

Of course it wasn't all peace and love. There were several counties and towns that had declared themselves independent Other-Free zones. Others weren't in any hurry to move to any of these places and there'd been a general feeling of, *well, at least they're far away from here*, so while the states and federal government weren't pleased, they had enough on their plates to deal with.

In the meantime, she and Faine were going to spend the next two months in Lycia. He had a house there and had been making it into a home for both of them. Their days so far had been filled with lovemaking of the gentle sort. He spent endlessly creative hours on her body and she had no complaints. He helped with her physical therapy with the new hip, as did Tila.

Lark and Simon had joined them the day before and they'd stay for a few weeks as well.

"So when were you going to tell me?" She sipped her juice and looked over her sunglasses at her sister.

"Tell you what?" Lark then burst into giggles, blowing her act.

"When are you due?"

"I just got the plus on the stick yesterday. It's early days. You're the only one other than Simon who knows."

She squeezed Lark's hand. "Congratulations."

"Thanks. I'm excited and freaked the hell out."

"Gonna be an auntie. I like that. A whole new world coming up for them to be raised in."

"Scary."

She shrugged. "Exciting. This is a beautiful thing, Lark. Imagine how gorgeous this kid will be. How powerful. How loved."

"You'll have to give him or her cousins."

Helena laughed. "Not for a while. But yes. That will happen someday."

They looked out at Simon and Faine, who'd stopped swimming long enough to shove each other and enter into some sort of brotherly dunking and splashing thing. Two more Leviathan brothers jumped in and joined the fray.

"A girl could get used to watching hot dudes splash around all day. I think it's got to be part of your recovery. Good for the heart to see it." Lark nudged her with an elbow.

"Hell yes."

Glossary and Characters

WITCHES:

Clan—an official organization of witches run matrilineally

Clan Gennessee—holds territory from parts of Mexico up to Southern Oregon. United with Clan Owen. Same origins tracing back to the original Owen witches who traveled west with the gold rush.

Clan Owen—largest and most powerful clan of witches in the United States. Holds from middle of Oregon up into Canada.

The Owen—The witch in charge of the Owen Clan. Currently Meriel Owen (see also The Gennessee).

Hunters—The law enforcement arms of witch clans

Dominic Bright—married to and magically bonded to Meriel Owen. Runs the Owen Clan at her side. Co-owns an Other nightclub called Heart of Darkness.

Edwina Owen—Deceased. Meriel's mother and former head of Clan Owen. Was killed by human servants of the Magister.

Gage Garrity—Witch. Hunter for Clan Owen. Involved with Molly Ryan.

Helena Jaansen—Witch. Hunter for Gennessee Clan, mated to Faine Leviathan.

Lark Jaansen—Witch. Hunter for Clan Owen. Sister to Helena. Mated to Simon Leviathan.

Meriel Owen—The Owen, a witch living in Seattle. Married and magickally bonded to Dominic Bright.

Molly Ryan—Witch. Head of media relations for Clan Owen and the Council of Others. Involved with Gage Garrity.

Rebecca Gennessee—Witch. The Gennessee. Runs the Gennessee Clan of witches. Related to Meriel Owen.

LYCIANS:

Lycia—a world on the other side of the Veil where large packs of shifters rule

Faine Leviathan—Lycian prince. Helena's guard and mate.

Simon Leviathan—Lycian prince. Co-owner of Heart of Darkness. Mated to Lark Jaansen.

Leviathan—the name of the ruling pack in Lycia. Simon and Faine's pack ruled by their oldest brother, Pere.

OTHERS:

Cade Warden—Werewolf. National Supreme Alpha.

Carlo Powers—Human. Runs PURITY.

Delilah Sperry—Werewolf. Senator. Romantically involved with Tosh Sato.

Franco Pendergast—Vampire. Spokesperson for Vampire Nation.

Gibson de La Vega—Jaguar shifter. Bringer (chief law enforcement officer) of de La Vega Jaguar Jamboree. Mate to Mia de La Vega.

Lex Warden—Werewolf. Alpha of Cascadia Werewolf Pack. Mate to Nina Warden.

The Magister—a being of old magicks. Nearly manifested in *Chaos Burning*. Stole the magick of thousands of Others worldwide. Was defeated by Meriel and Edwina Owen.

Marlon Hayes—Human. Senator who sides with PURITY and other hate groups.

Mia de La Vega—Jaguar shifter. Pilot used by the Others as they travel the country. Mate to Gibson de La Vega.

Nina Warden—Werewolf. Alpha of Cascadia Werewolf Pack. Mate to Lex Warden.

Toshio "Tosh" Sato—Human senator. Former JAG. Advocate and supporter of Others.

TERMS:

Alamah—means *beloved* in Lycian. Faine's pet name for Helena.

The Font—the magickal bank where all the magick of a clan is held once it's used and dissipated back to the collective. Any witch who is a member of that clan has access to the magick held there.

Heart of Darkness—a nightclub in Seattle owned by and catering to Others

Ne'est—Lycian word for *key*. It's the name for a forever mate a Lycian takes.

PURITY—main anti-Other hate group. Run by Carlo Powers.

The Veil—the wall between our reality and other realities where the Fae and Lycians live.

Turn the page for a sneak peek at the first
Bound by Magick novel by Lauren Dane

Heart of Darkness

Available now from Berkley Sensation!

Chapter 1

MERIEL sat, taking notes as her mother spoke from the head of the table. The pale, late autumn light spilled through the windows of the seemingly normal conference room, casting shadows on the far wall. The tastefully expensive clock and nondescript black-and-white framed photos made the space look like a law firm instead of the headquarters of a witches' clan. A boring, non-offensive space that seemed to lack any point of view at all. This was most likely a deliberate choice, but Meriel thought pretending not to have a POV when you were someone as opinionated as Edwina Owen was absurd. But it wasn't her place to make decorating choices. Not yet anyway.

So she sat in a moderately comfortable chair around an intentionally imposing table with the same fifteen people she'd spent her days with for as long as she could remember. How sucky was it that it was days like this that made her wish for law school again? What sort of whackadoo actually *missed* law school? But in law school when she excelled, it was without the context she carried in her life here. The next in line. The princess. Magickal royalty. Blah. There, she'd just been another overachiever struggling with the realities of being in a room full of people just as smart, and in many cases, smarter, than she was. That sort of bumpy ride had been a novelty.

But this was her future and she took it seriously even if she had a stack of other things to do at the moment. Meriel really didn't have the time for this assignment, but Clan Owen's investigator, who also happened to be Meriel's best friend, Nell, was still out on her honeymoon and wouldn't be back for another few days.

Really, Gage, who was Nell's second-in-command, would be a fine substitute. But as far as Edwina Owen was concerned, as the next in line to run Clan Owen, Meriel was expected to pick up the slack when necessary. Rather like working in the mail room or running the copiers, it trained in the overall running of the clan.

Whatever, at least she'd get out of her house for the evening instead of sitting around reading legal briefs or ordering a movie on demand and eating too many spring rolls. *Mmmm, spring rolls . . .*

The lull in sound meant her mother probably expected an answer and it was time to pay attention instead of thinking about fried carby goodness.

She sat, back straight, and met her mother's eyes. "I have the file. Nell briefed me before she left. I'll head to the club tonight to see for myself what's going on." She continued to hold her mother's gaze. It wouldn't do to show Edwina Owen, the leader of Clan Owen, any weakness. Some predators ate their babies, Meriel knew. She'd actually said that to her mother once. Her mother had replied, "Then you should never give me a reason to do that." Not really warm and fuzzy, Meriel's mother.

"Take Gage with you." It wasn't a request. Very little of what Edwina said ever was. In this case, as was most often the fact, she was right. It wasn't like Meriel was unused to having guards with her. She wasn't helpless, but she had no problem having an expert on the job with her.

"I'll be picking Meriel up this evening at ten," Gage spoke from his place near the door.

Edwina looked very pleased the whole world was following her command and Meriel fought the smile edging the corners of her mouth.

"Excellent. Brief me in the morning then." Edwina dismissed her with the flick of her fingers. Meriel gladly took her up on it and got out of the room as quickly as possible.

"She scares me," Gage said as she passed him in the hall on her way to her office. She totally did not look at his butt or the way the denim was faded in all the right places. That would be wrong. Heh.

Meriel, who was *not* having nasty fantasies about a coworker, tried to emanate total professionalism for about five seconds before she simply rolled her eyes. "Whatever. She wants you to be scared, she likes it. Gets off on it even. Some men like that. My dad for instance and I don't know why I brought that up because, um, *ew*." She shook her head to dislodge that thought. Oh yeah, Gage's ass. She smiled at that much more appetizing mental image. "I'll see you tonight then? So you can protect my honor and stuff?"

He grinned. "Your stuff is awesome and I'm sure you can protect it yourself. But yes, I'll be there with bells on. Or not with bells, that would be noisy and annoying, but I'll be there." He sauntered off and she snuck one last peek at his ass. She wasn't a saint after all. It was a spectacular ass and, like any great work of art, should be admired. It was her sacred duty as an American. And stuff.

EFFICIENTLY, she made her way through the office to her side of the building. Clan Owen's headquarters took up the entire thirtieth floor of a high-rise in downtown Seattle. They were much like any other business, with a secretarial pool, legal department, accountants, sales reps even. Only their employees were all witches.

Twelve generations of Owen women had run the clan. The first Owen witches came to California in 1847. They'd come a long way from the dry-goods stores and illegal booze operations that had given them their first financial roots in the region.

Now, the clan was a multimillion-dollar business and an unquestioned powerhouse in the world of witches.

Like every firstborn daughter of the leader of Clan Owen, from birth, Meriel had been shaped to lead. Taught, formed, molded into the kind of witch, the kind of woman who could hold the clan together and keep it prosperous and powerful for the next generations.

Edwina had not been the kind of mother to kiss boo-boos and bake cookies. She'd raised Meriel to be hard and canny. Meriel liked to believe she got the canny part without the hard.

And one day she'd kiss boo-boos and bake cookies and still manage to run the clan just fine.

She stopped by her assistant's desk, picked up mail and messages and closed her door, and the rest of the office out.

The day was nice enough and she let it pull her attention from work for a moment to take in the beauty of the water glittering in the sun, of the ferries dotting the Sound.

With a happy sigh, she kicked off her shoes and opened the file folder on her desk—the dossier on the man she'd be speaking to that evening.

This man had just appeared in Seattle and had set up a nightclub in the middle of Owen territory. For months it appeared he only ran the club for humans, which is why they didn't notice him at first.

She didn't know exactly when he'd opened up the part of the club for others, but he'd been using magick from Clan Owen's font to power some wards for a few months and it had *just* been noticed two weeks before.

One, it agitated her that it took so long to be discovered.

Two, despite her annoyance, she was impressed.

Whoever he was, Meriel understood that it wouldn't do to underestimate him. She hadn't achieved bonded full-council status yet, but she wasn't stupid.

She *was* curious though.

A knock sounded on her door and before she could speak, her mother came in. Not breezed in, not strolled or barged or anything of the sort. No, Edwina came in and occupied nearly all the oxygen in the room.

"I've just received an interesting phone call."

Meriel didn't bother to ask her mother to sit. Edwina would do what she wanted to do. She pulled out a notepad and a pen and looked up, ready to take notes.

"There've been some developments in New Mexico. Three witches are missing from a local coven just outside Albuquerque."

She'd been an attorney long enough to know silence got you more information than a lot of leading questions when you were interviewing someone. So she simply waited for her mother to give her all the details.

"One of the women has been missing for eight months. They believe she is dead. Another male gone for six months and this last one went missing two weekends ago."

"Were they all active within the coven? Or loners? Drugs? Trouble at home or work?"

Her mother nodded her head once, as if reassuring herself Meriel was indeed not a total idiot.

"None of the three is very active. They don't have a font, but the parents of one of the women are leadership. Which is why it got to me at all I expect." The unspoken was that no one would have cared about the other two because no one was watching out for them.

The very idea of it burned in Meriel's belly. The very fact that her mother wasn't similarly offended also burned. This could be a totally nothing issue, or a big problem. Simply refusing to examine it very closely wasn't, to Meriel's mind, a very effective way to run things.

"Why these people? Is it connected to some of the similar stories we've heard lately?"

Her mother simply went forward as if these questions meant nothing. "I know you like open communication with other witches, even those who are clanless. I'm going to have you be the point person on this for the clan. Until Nell returns on Monday, work with Gage." She stood and then handed a file folder to Meriel. "That contains all the details." Again she paused, taking a breath. "I'm not convinced this is a problem. People disappear, Meriel. We don't know enough about any of them to get worked up."

It must have been a herculean effort to not show the sneer in her voice on her features. Meriel bit her tongue and reminded herself she'd run the show differently when her time came.

She took the file, looking over her mother's beautiful and very precise handwriting. Edwina may have thought the call was crap, but she took good notes. Meriel would head over to talk to Gage about it to get his opinion once her mother had gone.

"If they were in a clan, they'd have taken better care of their people. This may not have happened. People do themselves all sorts of damage. You know this as well as I do."

If she spoke, she'd say something bitter and she didn't want to. Didn't want to spend any more negativity on the day. Or on her mother.

One brow rose in challenge. "Go on. Say it. If you're going to take over for me, you need a spine."

It was difficult, but not impossible to rein her magick's response to her mother's taunt. There was no winning by Edwina's rules. So she refused to play by them. "I'm not playing this game with you. Also, there's no *if* and you and I both know it. Thank you for this information. I'll handle it from now on." And she was sure the witches in New Mexico would appreciate not being made to feel as if it were their own fault for getting kidnapped or killed or whatever may have happened down there.

Edwina narrowed her gaze and Meriel gave her blank face right back. She'd groomed her blank face over many, many years. Considered it perfect. It was the only way to win with her mother, who pushed to get a response. One of these days though, oh, Meriel would give it to her, all right.

"Thank you." Meriel said it again, holding her mother's gaze.

Edwina sighed and moved to the door. "Keep me apprised." And left.

Meriel read through her notes and headed to Gage.

Chapter 2

GAGE looked up as she tapped on his door. Meriel liked this part of the office. Back in a far, infrequently used corridor, Nell ran the investigative and law and order arm of the clan. They had a pinball machine. Hello.

Gage sat, boots up on his desk, a phone to his ear as he looked over whatever he had in his hands. She waved when he looked up and made to leave, but he waved her in to sit and wait.

"I have to go. *No.* Nell, if I so much as get a whiff you're back in town before Sunday, I will kick your ass. And I'll tell Meriel." He grinned up at her as he paused, clearly getting an earful. "Bye." He hung up, laughing.

"She can't possibly be coming back early. William has to be more attractive than anything she could find here. William in swim trunks. Yum!"

He rolled his eyes. "I had to call her about this New Mexico stuff. I take it your mother spoke with you?"

"Yes, that's why I'm here. It could have waited until Monday, you know. Nell's only going to obsess about it now."

"I know. But she made me promise to call if anything

unusual came up. I found a way around it for the investigation at this club. That's not new." He shrugged and Meriel laughed, delighted.

"I love the way you two are together. You keep her in line."

"William told me marrying Nell was like getting me too. But then he confessed that he was glad because it would take more than one person to keep her in line. He said as long as I had no designs on the parts he liked to keep in line we were good."

Meriel always had wondered why Gage and Nell hadn't hooked up. But she imagined it was one of those great, totally non-romantic partnerships. They teased, but there wasn't an ounce of sexual tension between them.

"He's a smart man." She held up the file. "So what do you know about New Mexico?"

"I spoke with the person who called your mother. They don't have a clan organization so no law enforcement to speak of. No investigative team. They're not going to bring in anyone else. I did offer," he added at her questioning look before continuing. "Missing witches. No real connection they know of. But there's too much they don't know for me to be really comfortable with the situation."

"We need to be sure we're keeping a good eye on everyone. Even the outclan." This would make her mother insanely angry, but just because those witches didn't want to join the clan didn't mean the clan should simply leave them without any protection. They used the Font. They obeyed the clan rules. They deserved some benefit.

"I agree. We have something in place, as you know. But I think it can be stepped up. I'm going to work with section five to see if we can't monitor through the Font. You know, see who is taking and filling. Look for gaps."

The Font was the collective energy bank for the clan. All witches within it were keyed in so that their magickal energy should be part of it, if not every day, at least several times a week. An absence could be detected; she just didn't know how hard it would be to do it.

"Good. That's a good idea. They'll tell you if it can be

done or not. Keep me apprised. I've been named the point person on this."

Gage's brows went up a bit.

"I know, I'm surprised too." She couldn't very well say she was shocked her mother had let go of the power. Her mother had a way of hearing lots of things. Most likely, her mother thought this was all bullshit so it was fine to give it to Meriel, who'd also end up with a reality check that would smack the notion of working with other witches and protecting against external threats by banding together right out of her head.

Ha. Edwina had no idea. None. Which bugged Meriel. For heaven's sake, she was Edwina's child—canny and strong willed, just like her mother. The future didn't involve this continued self-segregation and her mother could pretend Meriel didn't know any better or that she was naïve, but they both knew that wasn't true.

"Totally hypothetical question here. Do you think this might be connected to the situation in Minnesota? With the mages?"

A witch had been found nearly dead and had recounted a horrifying tale of being kidnapped by a group of mages who'd spent days siphoning her power. She had only been able to escape when she'd managed to grab back enough of her magickal power to siphon the air from the room and the mages had passed out. She'd crawled nearly a mile before someone found her and took her to the hospital. By the time the police had arrived at the house, everyone had gone.

The human authorities were looking for human monsters. Human monsters could be taken down. But mages were not human, and they had no code of ethics like witches. No, they stole power and magick to twist it and use it like a drug.

And what if they'd decided to hunt witches for that drug?

BY the time she'd made ready to leave for the day, the sun was down. She'd had plans to duck out early but of course that hadn't worked out. As it was, she still had the opportunity to stop at the little boutique just down the street from her apartment building. She wanted something new for that night. Wanted to find an outfit suitable for club wear.

Her phone was ringing when she came out from her bathroom and she ran to grab it. It had been Gage's mother, Shelley, calling from his house where he was currently suffering the throes of food poisoning. She'd assured Meriel that Gage would be fine by morning, but there was no way he'd be accompanying her that evening.

Meriel had almost felt sorry for him as he'd attempted to order her to wait until the following night and she'd refused, promising to be safe and check in the following day before telling him to get well and hanging up.

She'd made the choice to go and, she thought as she put in her earrings, that was that. It hadn't simply been a matter of their font being stolen from. It had been bigger.

No spiky-heeled sandals that night. She needed to be able to move easily and quickly. So she opted for her cowboy boots. Thankfully they went well with the outfit she'd picked up.

The skirt was a little shorter than she usually went for, but it wasn't so short she'd be in danger of showing any of her bits. And the shirt was snug and a little stretchy; the sequins accenting it here and there would catch the light. Feminine. Sexy. And it all emphasized her best parts and hid her worst.

In the garage she looked at what she'd picked up two days before. Nell's car. Nell's beautiful, cherry-red classic 1967 Camaro. All shiny and powerful.

Her own car was nice enough and all, but this, well, this was part of the whole night. Unexpected like the short skirt and this mission she went on. Silly, but it was thrilling all the same.

She traveled across the lake toward Seattle, feeling as if there was a reason she felt nearly driven to do it. Though Meriel was as rational and logical as they came, she still believed in following her gut. Her gut was where her magick lived and it wanted her at that club tonight.

There were no reasons to expect a violent response from Bright. He'd been peaceable since he'd arrived in Owen territory, though still a thief. He had to quit that, of course. And the opportunity to do something so unexpected—to act on behalf of her clan with this witch to make him stop—well, that excited her.

It could wait, of course, for the next night, or the next week for that matter. Restlessness had settled into her bones over the last year. Before that she'd been pretty much single-minded with her studies and her job.

Ambition came to her naturally. Her foremothers had created Clan Owen from nothing and built it into one of the most powerful organizations in the world. Meriel accepted that the blood of these women ran in her veins for a reason and that she was supposed to use every gift she'd been given to protect and serve her people.

From infancy there had been one path and she greeted that with joy and a sense of duty. But things were changing. The older and more experienced she got, the more the witches in Clan Owen expected her to lead and many had begun to look to her first, before Edwina, and that had created a rift. Most though weren't sure she could be as brutal and ruthless as Edwina. So she'd have to show them. But in her own way.

For the first time in her life it was hard to wait for what was next. She wanted to go out and greet it. Wanted to make things happen. Wanted to see what this heady sense of expectancy was all about.

She supposed at this point in a full-council witch's life, it was about finding her bond-mate to finally ascend to her full power. She was in limbo until that happened. Until a full-council witch performed the ascension spell with her bond-mate, she wouldn't achieve her full power and take her seat on the ruling council of the clan.

It wasn't so much that Meriel was aching to find her bond-mate. It was more than the magickal ascension, though she did want that very much, it was a lack of soul-connection. It had only gotten worse once she'd seen Nell with her new husband, had seen love in her best friend's eyes.

Things were about to change. She could feel it.

* * *

DOMINIC tucked his shirt into his jeans and gave himself one last look in the mirror on the back of his office door. He had a to-do list as long as his arm and the sense of impending *something* lay heavily in his gut.

He hated that. He didn't want this special-sense thing. He liked his gifts well enough, but it was just fine with him to be an ordinary guy with a little bit of magick. He didn't want foresight. Tom, the closest thing Dominic had to a father and the man who deserved the credit as one, got on his case for being a slacker and not living up to his full potential. That's what fathers did, Dominic knew. But he had a successful bar, didn't he? Was he not giving a place to go to both Others and humans alike? It wasn't like he was still living on the edge the way he had those years before. No probation officer. He was a businessman now. No more running from bill collectors. Hell, he even had employees. As far as Dominic was concerned, he was a useful member of society and Tom should be satisfied with that.

It wasn't so much that he never used his magick. Just that he used it the way he wanted to. This whole clan business, having to be a member and obey rules, none of that was his scene. He didn't need to be told what to do. Not by anyone.

After finally growing tired of the violence and hand-to-mouth nature of the lifestyle he'd lived for the early part of his twenties, he'd landed in New York City where he'd learned how to run a business. When he'd saved for a few years, he'd come back home to the Northwest.

He'd made something of all that energy and ambition. He took an empty space and with some magick, okay some *borrowed* energy too, had created Heart of Darkness. At first glance it was an industrial nightclub but through an arch, hidden to non-magickal eyes, it was *the* spot for Others in Seattle. Part café, part bar.

The place was packed every night and as Simon pointed out just that day over lunch, they were bound to get a visit

from some clan witches very soon. There was no way word
of the place hadn't reached them and there'd be a bill come
due from using their precious font. Even an outclan witch like
him knew he was breaking their laws by using their magick
without being keyed in. Until then though, he'd continue to
do so because he needed to and they couldn't possibly have
a use for all that spare power.

And because he still liked to play on the edge.